A Londoner, Tom Barling has worked for the national press, in advertising, as an art director and a TV producer. For many years he ran his own production company producing commercials and animated films, mostly for the American market. His previous novels include *The Olympic Sleeper*, *Goodbye Piccadilly*, *Bikini Red North* and *Terminate With Prejudice*. *Smoke Dance* is the sequel to the bestselling *The Smoke* and *Smoke Dragon*, both published in paperback by Corgi.

GW00360361

Also by Tom Barling

THE SMOKE
SMOKE DRAGON

and published by Corgi Books

SMOKE DANCE

Tom Barling

CORGI BOOKS

SMOKE DANCE
A CORGI BOOK 0 552 13583 6

First publication in Great Britain

PRINTING HISTORY
Corgi edition published 1991

This book is set in 10/12pt Bookman by
Kestrel Data, Exeter

Corgi Books are published by Transworld Publishers Ltd,
61-63 Uxbridge Road, Ealing, London W5 5SA, in Australia by
Transworld Publishers (Australia) Pty Ltd, 15-23 Helles
Avenue, Moorebank, NSW 2170, and in New Zealand by
Transworld Publishers (N.Z.) Ltd, Cnr Moselle and Waipareira
Avenues, Henderson, Auckland.

Printed and bound in Great Britain by
Cox & Wyman Ltd, Reading, Berks.

For Dieter and Cyprus

Many waters cannot quench love,
neither can the floods drown it.

Song of Solomon, 8:7

CHAPTER ONE

Malta: 1 May 1980

Charlie Dance climbed in glare and looked down into the sea. The sandstone spur shook as long breakers pounded in with implacable force, threw spray high in sizzling bouquets, and drew off sulking violet strands of undertow as the next wave rolled in to scour the broken foreshore. A stew of kelp swirled in the angry tide, and pebbles clashed in the hissing white froth. Grit and sand stung in the fresh wind, Ghargur Rock was a dull seaward loom against a low scud of cloud. Western thunderheads formed white massifs, and the coming sunset promised to be a wildness of scorched reds Charlie would toast after his swim.

He stood tall on the balls of his feet and timed his dive to hit an outgoing wave. Plunged into salty chaos, he felt himself drawn down and down and down. Touching bottom, he kicked through the eye of a curling roller. Surge took him over a sandbar, and he swam hard against the suck of undertow to reach deep water. Leaving the crosscurrents behind, he floated on his back.

Brown jellyfish floated past, and dolphin sported between him and the land. The raddled cliffs looked older than God's face, and an old watchtower on the heights was a stoic fret of military architecture. His white Rolls was a toy on a model beach, and Margot was a small orange doll beside it, as remote as a dream as she watched him through binoculars.

Charlie filled his lungs and swam for the bottom. A startled octopus made off, jetting ink, and Charlie got his fingers into a rock covered in sea urchins to hold himself down. The tidal motion was a lazy sawing at that depth, bobbing and ducking the copses of bladderwrack in idle waltz. Husbanding air amongst darting fish, Charlie counted off a slow hundred with pressure sirens singing inside his skull. Starting his second hundred, he fought the need to scurry upward for light and oxygen, released dribbles of air to aid negative buoyancy, and kept control with flames of mist gathering at the edges of his mind. Panic needles pricked his dulling senses as he finished his long count to the roar of mad orchestras. His heart thudding, Charlie floated upward, trailing the last of his air behind him.

Breaking out of his drowned submarine world was as violent as a shout in a cathedral. He gulped air sweeter than life itself. Heard himself reclaimed by sea and wind noise. Breathed ozone and the mustard scents of beached kelp, the earthen smells of farm terraces dampened by recent showers.

Striking east, Charlie swam for the flat inlet where Margot waited with a towel, and patted himself dry as she drove them home for their usual sundowners.

On the balcony Margot said, 'Still testing yourself, I see.' Her voice as flat as a boxer's face.

'Me?'

Charlie lounged to watch fishing boats chug out into the open sea to lay their night lines. As brown and lean as ever, there was a new restlessness about him that worried Margot to distraction. He looked through the world rather than at it, and his moods of introversion came more often, blinding him to

Margot, to everything. The Good Life had somehow soured, and Charlie was a somnambulist going through the motions of comfortable retirement.

'Yes, you, braveheart. Swimming out into the wildest of seas to stay under for over three minutes is a madness. Particularly for a mature male in his forty-ninth year, Charlie mine.'

'Only for one more day. Tomorrow I hit fifty. The big five-oh.'

'All the more reason—'

'To *what*? Get fat? Lose my navel in a big belly and potter about in a greenhouse of begonias?'

'Nothing could be further from my mind, you goat.'

'Glad to hear it.'

Charlie sipped Irish as the sky inked itself to indigo. Threatened rain. Finches crowded the mature imperial palm shading the balcony. Safe from the limesticks and nets of Maltese hunters, they gossiped as they settled for the night. The lights of Bugibba bled into the bay, and a jukebox crooned from the Sirens Bar beside the water polo tank. Margot sighed and sighed again.

'Spit it all out, toffee nose,' Charlie grunted.

'Are you bored with me, or just bored?'

'Can't be more than fifty million people who'd swap places with us, Margot love. We're the envied ones. The beautiful people.'

'The bored and the boring can't be beautiful, my fine fellow.'

'So we'll plan a trip. Take the Blue Train through sunny South Africa. Safari in Kenya. Buy season tickets to Disneyland. You just name it.'

'Playing tourist isn't the answer. We'd merely become more detached from reality. Can't you see that?'

'You want answers, you supply them.'

'But that's it, d'you see? I have no answers. That's what's so miserable making.'

'Now you've really lost me.'

'Yes. I have lost you.'

'When did I ever look at another woman?'

'When did you last look at *me*. Really look at me.'

'All the time.'

'And never. I sometimes wish you would look at another woman. I'd have something to fight for. Even you philandering would be preferable to this . . . indifference.'

Charlie showed mild surprise.

'That bad, huh?'

'Worse by far. You've become too complete. Too total. I can't reach you any more. I know you're in there, but you've locked me out. You go through the motions. Toss me kindnesses like Eva Peron threw cakes from a train. Tiny gestures to appease peasants with limited requirements. Well, this peasant wants more. For both of us. We have to go back to the real world, Charlie. Before we become a pair of cabbages too full of sloth to even despise ourselves with any shred of passion.'

Charlie drained his Irish and stood to stretch. The horizon was a scald of flame and peach below windblown stars, and a last finch twittered sleepily. Swimming tourists trod water in the polo tank, and a car followed skimming headlights along the coast road. Charlie lit a rare cigarette and blew smoke at sudden night, his back to Margot when he spoke.

'There is no going back, Margot. London's full of strangers who've never even heard of Charlie Dance. I'd be a nobody in a town I don't even know any more. I'd have to tour the cemeteries to talk to old friends. Lean on memorials and chat to vases of dead flowers. There's nothing out there for me any more, love. Not even indifference. You wanted this life, I gave it you. Came along for the ride. Now we're here, and you're saying the driver took a wrong turning.'

Margot's eyes misted with unwanted tears. Saw how brilliantly she had pointed up the aridity of their lives. How cleverly she had turned her Charlie into a crazy who pushed himself to the edge of drowning to put some zest into his empty existence. Her cardboard escort to dinner parties neither of them really enjoyed. Trading tired conversation with pedigreed dullards whose power bases were raw wealth and the thinnest veneer of what passed for social standing in the small island community.

Charlie had even given poker up after one of the bigger losers had accused the entire table of cheating. Charlie had just walked away and never gone back. Life's pleasures were being snipped away by the shears of time, and Margot wondered how much more Charlie would silently walk away from before the ocean bed became the final solution.

Margot came out of morose reverie to find herself being lifted bodily from her chair.

'What *are* you doing, you oaf?' she asked, losing a shoe.

'Something I should have done long ago.'

Charlie threw Margot over his shoulder and slapped her rump. Hard enough to make her squeal.

'How dare you – you animal!'

'No more talk.'

Charlie's stinging slap reared Margot's head into the door frame. Split her vision into shimmering fragments as Charlie crossed the living room with Margot trying to reach his eyes with her nails. He kicked out into the hall and took the wide marble stairs to the roof garden. Carrying Margot

11

like a sawdust doll, he banged out into spotting rain without pausing. Margot squalled. Tried to knee a kidney. To kick something that wasn't ridged muscle. Charlie's laugh rolled with seaward thunder as he paddled her rump like a soft drum. Strode her through loungers and planters to an area screened by woven rattan.

'Stop, Charlie. You have to shower. Shave. Dress. We're due at the Cunningham's . . . at eight.'

Margot sank her teeth into a shoulder tasting of salt.

'Gonna be late then.'

Charlie slammed Margot across a pneumatic mattress, winded her completely. Stripped off his robe and threw it somewhere with the vault of night snapping like electric hounds. He blocked a rake of nails with a stiff forearm. Knocked Margot prone with a hard push to trap her beneath him. Clamped his mouth to hers until her mind and the storm spun in giddy circles of crackling light.

And as the sky opened with a roar, Charlie made Margot forget about everything but their oneness, his brown back and her upturned face streaming with warm rain.

The Cunningham's villa was in darkness when Charlie turned his white Rolls into the empty drive.

'We've got the wrong night,' he said as the engine idled.

'Tush,' said Margot. 'Probably something simple like their generator went out. You know how Granny forgets basic maintenance. Come on, stud. We'll go round back and peer through the windows.'

'I'd rather go back to the roof.'

'And prove you can do everything sixty-four times when once, beautifully, is enough?'

'You're easily pleased, is all. And I've trodden in something squishy.'

'Don't be a grouch, darling. Stay on the path.'

'Bloody Granny Cunningham and his notions of self-reliance. Not as though he's short of a shilling or two. Should get himself plugged into the main supply.'

'Hush, they'll hear you.'

'If they're here.'

Margot pulled Charlie through an arch into a walled garden where tiny Chinese lanterns were strung in the orange trees. Underwater floods turned the swimming pool to liquid jade under a striped awning. A fountain tinkled off in the trees, dappled a pool of tame carp, and a generator thudded in an outbuilding.

'How lovely.'

'Oh blimey yeah.' Charlie wanted a drink and a plate of food.

Muted thunder cartwheeled south on its way to Africa.

'No other cars,' Charlie said.

'What?'

'In the drive. No other cars. Not even Granny's Volvo.'

'Perhaps he's run out for more booze, and we're the first to arrive.'

'Over an hour late? I don't think so.'

'Don't be so reasonable, darling.'

'Meaning I ain't?'

'Quite.'

With suddenness, fast trails of sparks climbed to blow vivid holes in the night. Salvo after salvo of rockets soared to pattern the darkness with brilliant whites, crimsons and golds. Fire climbed a lattice at the end of the garden to spell out HAPPY BIRTHDAY

13

CHARLIE in incandescent greens. Laughing people came out of the trees with Granny and his wife Florrie at their head, and Charlie picked out faces he had not seen for years.

'You knew,' Charlie accused.

Margot shook her head, mute with surprise. Champagne corks popped to applause as Maltese waiters came out of nowhere to fill glasses, and the toast was 'Charlie, God bless him'. Bemused, Charlie had his back slapped numb, and at the midnight hour, he was thrown into the pool fully dressed.

By then, he could not have cared less.

There was swimming in limboesque fogs.

The insinuation of questions.

'Mr Charles Dance? I am Inspector Ellul. Are you ready to help me in my enquiries?'

The patient voice came at Charlie from all points of the compass, as persistent as a full bladder in distress. A quiet scold with a copper's voice, wanting answers. As usual. But about what? About dancing in nothing but balloons and a sailor hat? Doing handstands on champagne bottles and being sprayed by beer? Betting he could stay at the bottom of the pool for three minutes at incredibly high stakes? Surfacing as a winner with money coming at him from all sides? Singing the old songs to Granny's guitar? Knowing birthday excess had made a fool of the hero of a thousand corks?

Open one eye and find out, Charlie.

Inspector Ellul was a smooth olive man in his late thirties who spoke the curiously exact English of the educated Maltese. He sat in an antiseptic white room as if he belonged there whilst a machine monitored Charlie's heartbeat and respiration. A cage kept bedclothes from touching Charlie's body as he took

14

Ellul in with distaste. A camel had kicked Charlie full in the chest and coated his dry tongue with half-digested cud.

'Who drove the car, Mr Dance?'

'Car? What car?'

'Your Rolls Royce, Mr Dance. When you left the party.'

'Last night?'

'The night before last, actually.'

'This ain't tomorrow, but the day after?'

'Yes. Tell me about leaving the party.'

Charlie frowned at a complete blank.

'Were you driving?'

'There was an accident?'

'Are you telling me there was?'

'Me? No. Was there?'

'We have to establish who was driving, Mr Dance.'

'Somebody was hurt, that it?'

Ellul would not be drawn. 'You were driving?'

'I couldn't even stand up.' Charlie spoke Margot's name. 'Who got hurt? Her?'

'I need your statement, Mr Dance.'

'And I need to know about her. About Margot.'

'Then recall who took the wheel of the car.'

'Do I need a lawyer, or what?'

Ellul looked attentive. A lurcher scenting hare.

'Legal protection against what in particular?'

'This hangover. The rest is . . . blank.'

Ellul showed official disbelief.

'I think your later actions would be fresh in your mind. Very fresh indeed.'

'I drank. I fell down. That's it with bells on.'

Ellul crossed a knee under a notebook.

'You maintain you have no recall of anything that may or may not have happened to you after you left the home of your host Mr Grenville Cunningham?'

'Not after. Before I left. Nothing.'

Ellul nibbled a full moustache. 'I see,' he said.

'Wish I bloody did. Give me something to jog what passes for brains in this blank space between my ears. You don't, we'll sit here for ever getting nowhere.'

'Very well, Mr Dance. Travelling west at speed, your Rolls Royce went off the coast road fifty metres east of the Selmun Palace at approximately 3 a.m. during the early hours of Tuesday morning. There were no brake or skid marks. The car was driven straight through the stone curtain wall on the bend. Its momentum carried it across the foreshore and into the sea where it sank immediately. Can you comment on any of that?'

Charlie touched a bandaged hand to his face. Stared at it and shook his head. 'Nothing. Bloody nothing at all.'

'Frank but unhelpful, Mr Dance.'

'Stop waltzing me around. Where's my Margot?'

'You don't know?'

'I'd be with her if I did.'

'You might find that difficult.'

'You're hinting at what?' Charlie fought a slack tongue to articulate. 'That needs explaining, Ellul.'

'Most certainly, but not by me.'

'That means what?'

'I only have questions, Mr Dance. No answers as yet.'

'Make sense, Ellul. Not noises.'

'And I ask you to pay me the same courtesy.'

'These "later actions" you threw in on the sly, what were they? What am I supposed to have done?'

Inspector Ellul looked through window blinds at a view Charlie could not see from the hospital bed. Pinched a lower lip in thought and said, 'A witness drove past in time to see your car hit the sea and turn over before it sank. He had heard the sound of impact before he rounded the bend. He saw you dive repeatedly until you brought another person up from the sunken vehicle. You dived several more times after that, came up exhausted and alone, and barely made it to the shore before collapsing. The witness had to restrain you from trying to dive again, and you were still trying to crawl back into the sea when the ambulance arrived. You had clearly suffered a mild stroke, and were unconscious when you were admitted to this hospital. Who did you save, and who were you trying to save?'

'Margot? Was it Margot?'

'You have to tell me that.'

'Who'd I save? For pity's sake, man, tell me?'

'I cannot.'

'Can't or won't?' Charlie made bandaged fists to snarl over.

'The former, I'm afraid.'

'What?'

'Our witness saw you bring someone ashore. By the time he had climbed down to the beach, you were alone.'

Charlie stared as Ellul solemnly nodded.

'Quite alone. Please try to remember, Mr Dance?' he said with quiet compassion.

Charlie awoke to find a girl in tailored black sitting on the chair Ellul had vacated hours before. She was slender at the waist and long in the leg, and her pale, oval face was intelligent and attractive without being pretty. She needed no cosmetics, and her hazel eyes glowed in the late afternoon light. Charlie expected his lawyer, and this sweet thing clearly had the wrong room.

17

'What would I do with a gallon of perfume, Avon Lady?'

'Pardon?'

'Peddle your smellies elsewhere, girly. Damn, but you people will go to any length to make a sale.'

'What?' The girl coloured up, her eyes all the more luminous.

'Sick people have no sales resistance, that it?'

'I don't follow you, Mr Dance.'

'Got my name off the records, eh?'

'Not at all. I have an appointment with you.'

'You ain't selling soap on a rope?'

'I practise law, Mr Dance.'

'Representing whom?'

'You, Mr Dance.'

'That can't be. My lawyer is a fussy old bird who lost most of his feathers; has glasses, a goatee, and a pot you could balance a seesaw on. He's also masculine, and that you ain't.'

'I am Advocate Charlotte Bujega, Mr Dance.'

'John Bujega's girl? You're still at school in England.'

'Not for some years. My father is in court this afternoon, and I rearranged my schedule on his instructions.'

'Kind of you to visit, little love. But you tell your daddy I need him faster than fast.'

Charlotte Bujega's eyes thinned with her mouth.

'Not kind. Professional. And I most definitely am not your "little love", Mr Dance. Since you are clearly unhappy about my representing you as legal counsel, I shall happily pass that piece . . .'

'Whoa,' Charlie said.

'. . . of grotesque information on to my senior partner . . .'

'Pax,' Charlie protested.

18

'. . . whom you so quaintly describe as the "fussy old bird".'

'Also to his face. That makes the difference.'

'What?'

Charlie raised a bandaged paw.

'Please sit down, Miss Bujega. I am a grouch, not a misogynist. I did not mean to insult you, and I apologize. My liver apologizes. My aching body apologizes. My good dog Toby says "sorry". Please be placated, be forgiving and understanding. I need help. Fast. Now. This very minute. As you can plainly see, this child is in no condition to go ferreting about on his own behalf.'

Charlotte Bujega had dimples in her smile.

'Daddy said you were . . . different.'

'Having two heads *is* a drawback. Much like being a gorgeous advocate, right?'

'He didn't say *how* different. No wonder he had his secret smile when he sent me over here.'

'Lawyers equivocate, they never explain.'

'Perhaps we should start again, Mr Dance.'

'Then I'm Charlie. And I call you what?'

'How do you address my senior partner?'

'I call your daddy "John". It's his name.'

'Then you may call me Charlotte.'

'Only in private. In public I'll call you Advocate Bujega.'

'I'm not sure I like how you make that sound. What happened to your hands? I was told you had a stroke after being in a car smash.'

'Popped some knuckles. Lost some dermis and ripped a couple of finger nails. Could have happened when I was getting out of the car, I don't remember. I only know what Inspector Ellul has told me. He's a CID man short on words. You know him?'

'It would be hard not to. Malta is a small island.'

'He's clever that one. You have to be smarter. You ready to go to work?'

'Yes . . . yes, I think so.'

'For starters, I want new X-rays, and urine and blood samples for private and independent analysis. My own heart specialist to run all the tests that are needed to establish my true state of health. And I want me out of this sorry excuse for a hospital as soon as you can whistle up an ambulance. Book me into the new clinic in Valletta. Can do?'

'Yes. But Charlie, why?'

'No pain or stiffness in my left arm. No heart pain in my chest. Only the hurt of cracked ribs and extensive bruising. I got drunker than I've ever been on less than I've ever drunk. I was in a smash I don't remember. In company with two people who have gone missing. One may have been my Margot. Somebody drove that Rolls into the sea, and I think deliberately. I need to know why.'

'You don't believe you suffered some kind of cardiac trauma?'

'Do I *look* like I had a heart attack?'

Charlotte took her time studying Charlie. Shook her head with, 'No. You look used and abused, just as anybody would who had been in a serious accident. I saw my mother after she had her stroke, and she had quite a different pallor.'

'I need sight of the police report on the Rolls, that's if they've craned it out of the sea yet. Then again, they may have sent divers down to check out the interior.'

'That's a little out of my line.'

'Then get help, pretty Charlotte. Money no object. The longer this drags on, the less chance there'll be of finding out what really happened. The sea could already have swept everything out of the Rolls, and that includes any bodies.' Charlie stroked tired eyelids. 'I need to know who's down there. If anybody.'

Charlotte swallowed around a ball of sudden emotion.

'You think . . . Margot could be down there?'

Charlie's eyes hardened to iced slate.

'Have you ever been close to someone, Charlotte? Really close?'

'Once. A sort of teenage thing, but it was incredibly intense for a while. We couldn't wait to be together, yet the shyness we both felt was almost crippling. Love doesn't hit you in the heart, it hits you in the stomach. I mooned around for absolute months with cramps, and he had a permanent head cold. We were not a very prepossessing couple, and it all sort of petered out when I went off to study law in England. Heavens, why am I telling you all this?'

'Because I asked under the right circumstances. Margot and I were closer than fingers in a fist. I knew where she was in the house without having to look. I could feel her. Like she sent out signals I couldn't see or hear. And it was the same for her. We'd find ourselves fixing drinks or food the other wanted without the need of words. There was a *knowing* between us.'

'How . . . wonderful for you. I think I envy you that.'

'Yeah, until we started taking it for granted. That's the sad and sorry thing about the achieving human animal. We forget to cherish those unbuyable special relationships that are forged from all those small beginnings. We're all too busy hacking out a career. Scrabbling for money, for status. Empty things that mean nothing but diplomas on walls, bigger offices, more zeroes in the old bank account. Screwing the other fellow to prove we're fitter to survive than he is. And in justification we say there's

21

always tomorrow to spend with that special him or her. Next month, next year. Some other tomorrow. But we run out of tomorrows, pretty Charlotte. And when we get around to flowers and dinners with candles, or that romantic Caribbean trip, it's over, lost. Killed by neglect. Margot and I worked at what we had without much outward show, just solid sharing and caring. She didn't even have to wake up to be there for me, we'd come together by instinct. We'd had a recent hiccup on that front, but we got it back together just before the car crash.'

'You're to be envied, Charlie. Really.'

'Not when you lose it, love.'

'But you just now said—' Charlotte broke off. Silenced by the bitterness in those sad slate eyes, the raw power emanating from the man in the hospital bed.

Charlie's voice was as remote as Alpha Centauri.

'When Ellul left, I reached out for her. A mental thing I don't have words for. She wasn't there. No signal. Just a feeling of . . . absence. Like somebody blew out a private candle in my head. Margot's gone, Charlotte.'

'You're . . . sure?'

'Yes, pretty advocate, I'm sure.'

And Charlie stared at the wall until Charlotte Bujega went away, no words left.

CHAPTER TWO

Inspector Ellul and Charlotte Bujega found Charlie tanning himself in a private suite overlooking Grand Harbour. Wearing nothing but shorts and gauze gloves, he bared his bruised hide to the sun. The stitched scar on his thigh knitted nicely, and a lot of useful muscle rippled when he waved his guests into chairs. Ellul accepted Turkish coffee and let Charlie get curious about the big yellow envelope on his knee.

The animus between Ellul and Charlotte was all too evident when he said, 'Advocate Bujega has been most strict about the parameters of this interview, and I have reluctantly agreed to them. Not that I am incurious as to your motives for seeking such protection, Mr Dance. Tell me, do you usually command such vehement devotion from your legal counsel?'

'Only always,' Charlie said. 'You've seen the medical reports, so they'll save you running down one important dead end. My heart bumps along without lesions, and my recent memory loss is accounted for by "alcoholic spasm enhanced by unwitting drug abuse". And I quote verbatim.'

Ellul's shy smile almost reached his clever brown eyes.

'I've also seen your Interpol file. Your own past may well hold the answers to why some unknown third party may have engineered that motor crash. As to opportunity, I have the guest list of your birthday celebration. Perhaps you would care to see it and comment.'

'I'll look at it, but don't expect too much,' Charlie said.

'Because you intend to take the law into your own hands?' Ellul asked with sly pointedness.

Charlie stopped Charlotte's intervention with a raised hand.

'No, because nobody on that list did anything but have a good time. Because whoever slipped me that mind-bending cocktail will have taken damned good care *not* to get themselves on any list.'

'Just as you might under similar circumstances?'

'You love knifing me with innuendo, don't you?' Charlie's grin was a biting thing. 'You'll be telling me next that I drugged myself to the eyeballs and drove into the sea for laughs. That I went through the charade of diving for someone who wasn't there just to confuse fish. Got myself admitted to hospital because I was tired of my own bed. Any more gags like that, Ellul?'

Ellul ran a nail through his moustache.

'We could always assume your drinks were doctored in misguided jest. A mindless prank that got out of hand.'

'Enough. Or have you forgotten who might be sitting in my Rolls right this minute?'

'Hardly.'

'It would be helpful to know when the car will be raised and examined,' Charlotte said softly.

'Works for me,' Charlie grunted.

'I agree,' Ellul said. 'It would also be valuable if Mr Dance's own memory of the incident improved.'

Charlie almost laughed. Managed a derisive snort.

'That's akin to asking an anaesthetized patient to comment on his surgeon's performance during the actual operation. Hell, you're the policeman, you draw us some conclusions.'

Ellul raised an eyebrow.

'More than a trifle pre-emptive at this stage of the investigation.'

'Oh, it *is* an investigation, then?'

'A very thorough one.'

'And slower than a geriatric marathon.'

'Are you being as helpful as you could be, Mr Dance?'

'Are *you*?'

Ellul controlled his rising temper, sipped coffee and nibbled a piece of halva. He opened his big yellow envelope to spread glossy photoprints for Charlie to look at.

'Shots taken at the party. Please examine them with particular attention to the waiters. Anybody you might think is out of place.'

Charlie shuffled the prints and paled visibly. Clamped his gloved hands behind his head and slumped with shadowed eyes.

'Mr Dance?' Ellul prodded.

'Waiters. I saw waiters.'

'And?'

'Nothing.'

Ellul leaned in. Said, 'You saw something in those pictures. It shows in your face.'

'You're badgering my client,' Charlotte snapped. 'Can't you see he's unwell?'

'He saw something, Advocate. And I'll know what.'

'You are in direct violation of our agreement.'

'And I am investigating a probable murder.'

'Nothing "probable" about it,' Charlie said, coming back from a long way off.

'Is this some sort of an admission?' Ellul asked.

Charlie looked at the CID man with dead eyes.

25

'You really want to know what I saw, Ellul?'

'Yes, Mr Dance, I do.'

'I saw . . . Margot, you clown. My Margot.'

Shaken, Ellul backpedalled.

'I know that must have been painful for you, but—'

'But nothing,' Charlotte said with force. 'This interview is terminated.'

'Then we'll continue at the station,' Ellul said, standing.

'Under proper medical supervision,' Charlotte stood between Ellul and Charlie. 'His present mental state can be called into doubt very readily.'

'Unfit to plead on his own behalf? Ridiculous.'

'Don't forget your pictures, Inspector.'

Ellul fed prints into his yellow envelope, walked to the door and turned with studied casualness. 'And Mr Dance is prepared to forego any further interest in the investigation due to his poor mental state, is that your contention?' he asked Charlotte.

'It is.'

'Including the occupants of his car?'

Charlie rose to sway. Made painful fists.

'What about . . . the car?'

'Only that raising it from the sea bed has proved difficult. Army divers have been waiting for the heavy seas to stop running. They managed to get a sling under the vehicle at first light this morning, and they hope to raise it at slack water.'

Charlie knuckled a temple. His 'When's that?' a raw croak.

Ellul made a show of checking his watch.

'Oh, within the hour, I'd say.'

Charlie mumbled something muddy. Listened to a voice only he could hear.

'You'd like to be there, Mr Dance?' Ellul asked.

Concerned by Charlie's appearance, Charlotte objected.

'I consider that a grossly improper suggestion, and I absolutely forbid it. My client is in no condition—'

'Forget it, Charlotte,' Charlie eased Charlotte aside. Swayed close to Ellul to make hard eye-contact, his voice ragged. 'Damned right I'll be there.'

'You have time to dress,' Ellul said.

Charlie was a silent slump during the drive to St Paul's Bay, blind to the rain-quickened wild flowers cheering the verges, the sudden greens colonizing the burned hills to bring spring to the island. The Selmun Palace offered shade for Ellul to park in, and he led off to the cordoned beach area through crashing heat. White enamel streaked the wall the Rolls had cannoned through, and a shedded white-wall tyre had a police tape to itself. A rescue team and their lifting gear were dwarfed by the slop, dimple and shimmer of the restless sea, and a diesel donkey thumped like a hangover. Ellul helped Charlotte down to the foreshore, and Charlie hobbled after them, his ribs and legs stiffened by the ride. Gulls foraged the wake of a fishing boat, and the Gozo ferry beat its solemn way to M'Garr.

The army divers had a red buoy out beside their rubber Zodiac, and Charlie visualized them working around his drowned car, perhaps already privy to the secrets it might hold. From the angle of the cable running into the sea, he could tell the Rolls must have cleared its own length of ocean before pancaking to roll and settle below the waves. He knew the bottom there sloped steeply, then fell sheer for thirty feet to sand. If the Rolls had toppled over the fall, the divers would be working at capacity depth without the need to depressurize on the way back to the surface. Feeling clammy and sordid, Charlie stood sentinel as the crane took up the slack on the cable, drawing the four tons of automobile to the surface.

Charlotte saw him shudder as she came up beside him, and wanted to take his hand. The thought was disturbing to her; puzzling. The need to comfort this strangely self-contained man with his trim body and biting smile was a madness. Not only was he old enough to be her uncle, there was a secret darkness about him, a private sanctum nobody had ever touched. Yet that was alluring rather than daunting, and Charlotte wanted to somehow be better and cleverer than she was for his sake. As if his good regard of her would be the culmination of some vague goal she had been looking for all her life. All those old scars on his body told many stories, and she wanted to touch and know the history of every one. To unlock the deep and dark place that was the core of his inner strength, to bathe it in an understanding only she possessed.

A black head broke the surface of the sea, signalled with a raised arm, and the crane clanked into a higher gear with black puffs of smoke punching from the exhaust. The sling came out of the water with a diver clinging to it, and with a long yawing sway, the roof of the Rolls rose to shed water and faint curls of petrol pattern. Water poured from the half-opened doors, and a fine-mesh net stopped any loose objects from being washed away. The boot had sprung open, and the rear window had opaqued. The Rolls swung as it cleared the sea, and slowly turned to present its smashed and impacted bonnet to the beach.

Charlie's breathing became a ragged, shallow hissing, his eyes dark hollows in a chalk face.

28

Charlotte touched his arm to feel bunched solids inside his sleeve. Her hand fell away as she followed his line of sight to the swinging car. A leg hung from the driver's door, a poor naked thing of the palest flesh, its slack toes hooked in the netting.

And before Charlotte even thought of stopping him, Charlie had walked into the sea.

Ellul stood over Charlie squatting beside the silent crane, his shirt drying beside him.

'That was remarkably foolhardy,' Ellul said.

'Had to know,' Charlie drew on a borrowed cigarette to plume smoke into his lap.

The body lay on a tarpaulin under a blanket, quietly waiting for the ambulance. The face was flattened and distorted by impact against dash and windscreen. The upper chest was crushed, the swimming shorts were pale oyster, and a yellow metal watch still ticked on the right wrist.

'Can you identify the remains, Mr Dance?'

'Nope.'

'You *are* certain?'

Charlie favoured Ellul with a hollow stare. Shook his head.

'Never saw the bastard before.'

'Ever?'

'Never.'

'So, Mr Dance, who would want you dead badly enough to hire such a man, do you suppose?'

'That's how you read it, is it?'

'A possibility, wouldn't you say?'

Charlie flicked his long stub into the Mediterranean.

'Just another maybe, friend. I've got several maybes of my own. Maybe he's in one of your snaps pouring bubbly. Maybe he planned to jump before he hit the wall. Maybe he thought to let the car sink, then swim away. Maybe he was taking us all for a midnight swim and was too damned drunk to make the corner. Maybe he was just a nice kid giving the crazy Englishman and his lady a ride home as a favour to a drunk. Pump his stomach, maybe he was as drunk as we all were.'

'We shall, at the autopsy,' Ellul held up a plastic evidence bag stuffed with deflated balloons and brightly coloured string. They were all printed with the white legend: HAPPY BIRTHDAY CHARLIE.

'You were decked out in these at the party, weren't you?'

'Don't remind me.'

'Only you?'

'Only me. There any point to you reminding me of that idiot moment in my life?'

'Yes, and I think you'll see why. This string of balloons were snagged around a hazard warning triangle in the boot. Your dress jacket was there too, weighted down by a full bottle of champagne in each pocket.'

'Where's this going?'

'I think *you* were in the boot, Mr Dance.'

Charlie found nothing to say.

'When your Rolls went into the sea, you were in the boot. I think the boot burst open on impact with the foreshore, and the sprung lock and warped frame appears to bear that out. I also think you were flung clear when the car hit the water, turned on its side and sank. That the sudden immersion brought you around long enough for you to make your dives to the Rolls. The driver's door was slightly ajar, but only the offside front passenger door was wide open when the divers went down for a preliminary investigation. The rear doors were firmly locked. I think you opened the front passenger door to bring our mysterious someone to the surface. Whoever that might have been.'

Charlie stared at Ellul and looked out across the bay as Charlotte Bujega brought cold drinks from a nearby bar.

'Wasn't my Margot, was it?' Charlie said. 'She's out there somewhere. Floating face down with nothing but all the waters in the world for company. Colder and more alone than she's ever been. Where I can't reach her to say I'm sorry for saving the wrong person. How'd you like to live with that, friend Ellul?'

'We don't really know Mrs Sadler was in the car, Mr Dance.'

'Don't we?' Charlie looked through Ellul. Through Charlotte. Through the sea itself. 'I know,' he said with low force, and went away along the sand-stone spit where fists of Madonna succulent grew in scrubby clumps, and the sea danced with flashing coins of silver light.

Ellul stopped Charlotte Bujega following Charlie with, 'Any show of kindness now would be mis-placed, Advocate.'

Charlotte held the drinks cartons tight enough to sprinkle lemonade over her shoes. 'I can't admire you for being right. We have to give him . . . something.'

'Solitude, Advocate.'

'What?'

'One does not feed honey to a wounded tiger, Advocate.'

And Ellul took a drink to slake his thirst. Thinking hard with Charlotte standing lost and undecided beside him, all her love walking with the lone man outlined by a shining and uncaring sea.

*

The light was failing when Charlie walked back to the road. The old stone buildings glowed pink as long shadows paled into the odd greyness that is the short Mediterranean dusk. There was a green flash as the sun melted away, and the seaside cafés took on night-time vibrance. Using the loom of the sea, Charlie walked past stone lions in the villa courtyard, and let himself inside to stand in the real darkness of shuttered rooms.

Smelling the ghost of Attar of Roses, he lifted the soil-tray from a planter of cactus and withdrew a heavy moneybelt of high denomination notes in ten convertible currencies. Shuffling through several passports, he selected a British one and two others, packed a suitcase with anything and locked up. On the steps above the sloping rear garden he looked at his keys, raised his arm and threw them over the wall into the sea. Hefted his case and walked away without a backward glance.

Hiring a Fiesta from the local garage, he drove to the Cunningham's villa.

CHAPTER THREE

Granny Cunningham fixed drinks for a barbeque, his comfortable belly jogging with the shaker, and Charlie could hear Florrie making clatter in the kitchen. An overweight, laughing, pink man, Granny had turned his retirement home into a permanent house party where drinks were served tall and fierce, food was basic and plentiful, and his entire living room was an exported London pub tricked out with mildly amusing pornography. Rutting pigs made bacon on the barcloths, couples coupled on the glasses and steins, and the voluptuous nude over the backbar had the recipe for a deadly cocktail tattooed on her overripe belly. Rude rugby songs muttered through coffin speakers, and the GRANNY'S BAR electric sign changed colour like a dayglo chameleon.

Charlie scratched at the window to whirl Granny to face him wearing an expression Charlie had never seen before. Granny lost his shaker and his high pink smile. Showed fear with his jowls in motion, a hand out to ward off an evil he could not face. Then he sat in a chair that wasn't there. Dumped himself painfully on his buttocks in the middle of the floor.

Charlie let himself in to watch Granny fight for breath, called Florrie out of the kitchen, and watched them both watching him for as long as it took to kill the mindless music and fix himself an Irish. To get himself a chair, turn it under him to sit, leaning his forearms on the backrest to tinkle his drink.

'You have to understand, Charlie,' Granny huffed stale drink.

'Understand what exactly?'

Florrie was close to tears, a bandaged arm hidden behind her plump posterior.

'What happened to your arm, Flo?'

'Gardening. She was gardening,' Granny said too quickly.

'Scratched by the roses was she?'

'The roses, yes.'

'Roses you don't have, that it?'

'Tell him, Granny. He's a friend.'

'No friends. None.'

Granny reached for the shaker and had no idea what to do with it. Flinched when Charlie took it away to pour a cocktail, and killed the drink in a gulp when Charlie handed it to him. Held the empty glass and managed to meet Charlie's eyes.

'Bet you could use another one.'

'I truly could, Charlie.'

'When you've told me what's going on.'

Granny said nothing with watering eyes.

'Why'd you run away, Flo?' Charlie kept his eyes on Granny.

'I . . . it wasn't like that . . .'

'You were a big lump to bring up, Flo,' Charlie lied.

'Christ, he knows,' Granny told his thick knees.

'Only my side. Get it said, old son. And Granny?'

'Yes, Charlie?'

'Get the fuck up. You look like a dropped blancmange.'

'You won't . . . won't . . .'

'Hit you? Only if you stay down there.'

'I'm . . . getting up, Charlie. See?'

34

'I see,' Charlie said, his face pleasant as he turned his glass. Granny flopped in a captain's chair, and Florrie sidled in beside him to fiddle with the drawstrings of her apron. Printed with naked breasts and a G-string, it looked incongruous on a comfortably built lady of sixty with a Mayfair accent.

'Who did it, Granny?'

'Them. The consortium. I swore I'd never talk, but they didn't believe me. Do I want to go to prison at my age? My God, look at me, could I have handled that?'

'Not much of a man are you, Granny? You could have come to me before all this happened. Doesn't it make you want to smile? I put my affairs in the hands of a straight financial adviser, and it turns out he's been playing naughties on the cash register.'

Granny shook his jowls in denial.

'That isn't it at all. I swear.'

'I'm supposed to believe that my Margot's at the bottom of the sea because this consortium threw a moody with you for being straight, is that the cock-and-bull you're selling me?'

'Yes, I suppose it is,' Granny said. 'God, what a mess.'

'But it wasn't you they came after, was it? You were here safe and soused. They came after me and mine.'

'No, Charlie . . . it was me,' Florrie wept.

'They know I'm nothing without my Flo, Charlie. Nothing.'

'They wanted Flo dead? To keep you finger tamed?'

'Yes . . .'

'Bone the carcass for me, Granny. And this better be good.'

'We changed our basic holdings last year,' Granny

sighed. 'I sent you chapter and verse on it. We had thirty million in liquid assets on short term loan, all on ninety-day notes, you remember?'

'Did well out of it too. So?'

'You never asked how it was that the capital sums accrued such incredibly high interest rates, did you?'

'With you earning your corn, why should I?'

'Because we were laundering money at usurious rates. Money that could not be traced back to source without awkward questions being asked. It was only because we worked so quickly, never kept the monies in any single country or banking group for longer than ninety days, that we successfully avoided any whiff of bother. I only became aware of what was actually happening after the first quarter of last year. By then, we were in up to our necks.'

'We were a bloody money laundry? For what?'

'*Are* a money laundry, Charlie. We financed commodity conversions at first; Nigerian oil, coffee and citrus, things of that order. Then we found a way of turning Tanzanian shillings into convertible currencies. Had a long honeymoon with some of the African states until it became wise to get a divorce. That's when the warning bells started in my mind. A good deal of short-term monies were going out through Panama, and I found myself with more numbered Swiss accounts than seemed logical or legal. It took a frantic weekend of digging in the accounts books to spot the golly in the winter wood store.'

'Get it said, Granny,' Charlie rapped. Half-knowing.

'We were laundering drugs money. Still are in principle.'

Charlie's eyes flared and hooded.

36

'Don't look at me like that, Charlie. Dear heavens
. . .'

'Why should it stop at looks, Cunningham? I
trusted you to keep our holdings clean and healthy,
and you walk me into a drugs circuit. You deserve
more than moody looks and a slapped bottom. It all
comes down to you and super-greed, right? *Right*?'

'I suppose it does.'

'And you can stop wailing, Flo. You're alive and
fifty pounds overweight. Living the good life that's
cost me my Margot. Why the hell were you in my
Rolls with some hired ape at the wheel?'

Florrie shuddered and massaged her bandaged
arm.

'You'd passed out, Charlie. You were singing, then
you suddenly went pale. Wandered off and laid
yourself in the boot of the Rolls with two bottles of
champagne. Margot had promised to lend me a
shawl and some other things for the next fancy dress
party. I said I'd help Margot get you to bed, and Mario
offered to drive. We were all a bit giggly. We had one
last drink and set off. I was quite dizzy myself, and
that's all I remember until I found myself wandering
home soaked to the skin. When I got home, Granny
was in a terrible state. They had called him, you see.
Told him he would be next if he didn't toe the line.
They'd overextended all our resourses, and without
they got Granny to float a paper issue to bridge the
interim cash-flow problems, everything would be
wiped out.'

'What's she saying here, Granny?'

'I'd got the consortium to agree to ease us out of
the package. To pay us off at a lesser rate of interest
and liquidate our association. Under those conditions I would float a paper issue to cover the three
months needed to regroup our assets into hard

37

currencies. Return to our previous operating procedures. Then the bombshell.'

'No, you can't have another drink yet. Keep talking,' Charlie lit a Sobranie and blew bitter Turkish smoke into Cunningham's face.

'Very well . . . They had liquidated eighty million dollars in the Caymans, and had no way of transferring it through the usual channels. The fools sent it out by sea with a consignment of cocaine. A US Customs gunboat sank it somewhere off the Florida keys when it refused to heave to to be boarded and searched. The moment I heard that, I refused to float the paper issue, knowing full well it could never be honoured. They made their threats, Charlie, but I stuck to my guns. I knew I could pay you your same level of interest out of my own private holdings in gilts. Leave you right out of the mess until I could get us back on an even keel. There are moves afoot to salvage the vessel on the QT, but they still need our paper issue to finance it. That's why they went to such desperate measures to put pressure on me. I did *try* to keep you out of it, Charlie.'

'And only succeeded in getting me in deeper.' Charlie fixed himself another drink at the bar and let Granny drain the cocktail shaker into his glass. Sat back in his hard chair and told Granny to start writing the names of the consortium principals. There were three. One in London, another in Los Angeles, a third man in Rome.

'And who poured those last drinks for us all, Flo?' he asked.

'Mario, I think. Yes, it must have been. Then he drove us to your place.'

'Run him down for me.'

'Mario did odd jobs around the place, and I helped him with his English. He made himself useful at

38

parties. Cleaned the pool, took the empties back. A little light gardening. He was wonderful with drunks, handled them gently but firmly. Drove them home when they were too far gone.'

'Yeah, everybody's friend. How long was he around?'

'Four, five months.'

'From about the time the consortium started pressuring Granny?'

'But I can't believe that he . . . Yes, about then.'

'Enough time for him to practise on the local drunks before he got around to the main event. All right, Flo, what was he wearing when he drove the Rolls?'

'White shirt, bow tie, black waiter's trousers. Why?'

'He was in swimming shorts when he was pulled out of the sea. The clever bastard outwitted himself though, didn't he? Hit that wall fast enough to stove his brains in. Must have strapped you and Margot in so you'd sink with the car. Margot's down there, and you're here, Flo. Not much of a swap from where I'm sitting.'

Flo looked old as Granny handed Charlie a list of names, numbered bank accounts, and addresses in Los Angeles, London and Rome. The names leapt at Charlie. Reminded him of a Maltese pimp in London he had all but forgotten. Sent him back to Hong Kong fifteen years before. To standing with two Americans on the Kowloon ferry and talking them into giving him odds of 3-1 on a wager of a quarter of a million dollars. Them covering his bet in dollars, and paying Charlie in cash when the prize fight went his way.

'Maltese George Muscat,' he said aloud. 'Doll Gardenia and Casey Pollard,' he added, tasting acrid cud.

'You know them?' Granny's eyes grew bright with hope.

'I bought two of them a drink once.'

'You could talk to them, Charlie. Be persuasive.'

'You don't *talk* to animals like this.'

Charlie bared teeth and wanted to spit in Granny's face. Sink his aching fists into the big belly until it ruptured and deflated. Kept his biting smile to make Granny and Flo cringe.

'What do we do, Charlie? Run?'

'Run? Run where?'

'They'll try again. They won't stop now.'

Charlie looked dreamily at Granny and Flo. Slowly winked.

'Now won't that be nice,' he said, hearing engine noise on the drive.

The police station was bothered by moths attracted by naphtha lamps, the chairs in the interview room were hard, and Inspector Ellul was in formal evening wear. He looked at Granny, Florrie and Charlie in turn and said, 'You three are most certainly not fair exchange for an evening of Mozart at the Grand Palace. And yet here I am, ever ready to be misled by crass mendacity. In Mr Cunningham's case, his lie was a sin of omission. He did *not* tell me he knew who was driving Mr Dance's Rolls Royce. He will deny knowing any such thing, of course, and our dear Mrs Cunningham can deny culpability as a purgerer since nobody bothered to ask her if she was a passenger in the aforesaid vehicle. And you, Mr Dance, why would you be here if not for the sole purpose of drumming up some joint story us plodding policemen will swallow?'

'Nice to know you've got an open mind, Inspector,' Charlie said. 'And probably why you've had your constable drag us down here without cautions or legal representation. What's credible and acceptable in court is what's proved by the glibbest lawyer. What would you call this but shock tactics?'

Ellul tweaked his bow tie and flicked at the frills of his dress shirt with a derisive snort.

'I'd call this aiding the police with their enquiries on your own volition. None of you demurred when you were invited here, did you? And if you need a lawyer present, I am required to give you good cause. Do you all wish to be charged formally and severally?'

'With what?'

'With conspiracy, Mr Dance, what else?'

'If that's your pleasure, do it.'

'At this point it isn't,' Ellul said. 'But you are all required to surrender your passports, and will present yourself at this police station at 9.30 every morning until further notice.'

'You've already got my passport and resident's permit,' Charlie said. 'Can I have the rest of my stuff back?'

'Don't try to leave the island. Any of you, is that clear?'

'That gets it said,' Charlie pocketed his wallet and the slip of paper Granny had written on. 'I'll be at the Britannia Hotel in Valletta if you need me, Ellul. I'll have the desk sergeant take that particular down on the way out, that's if I'm free to go?'

'As air,' Ellul said, wondering if he could make the first intermission of the concert, having put the initial frighteners on the Cunninghams. Dance was another matter, it would take a mass of softly-softly to catch that particular monkey.

Charlie found the last of Margot's Sobranies in his pile of effects on Ellul's desk. He lit it with a kitchen match and blew smoke down at the seated Cunning-hams.

'Better do as the man says, Granny. You play games with this clever copper, he'll bang you up in a cell faster than a greyhound out of trap three at Harringay.'

'That,' said Ellul, 'is very good advice.'

'Another thing,' Charlie said at the door. 'You've been worried about burglars and things that go bump in the night, Flo. Maybe being in police custody would put your mind at rest. Think about it, you and Granny both.'

Granny's eyes teared as his jowls flushed.

'But we surely have police protection, don't we, Inspector?'

Ellul's smile was no longer shy.

'Certainly, Mr Cunningham, the moment you give me just cause.'

'Just cause? My dear man,' Granny blustered.

'Yes?' Ellul said.

Granny saw the catch and gobbled into silence. Watched Charlie walk out into the night and drive the hired Fiesta away without hurry. Held his wife's hand and wondered if he would ever see Charlie Dance again. There was a new purpose about the man, the quiet menace of a stalking saurian. A fact not lost on Inspector Ellul whose two best detectives would shadow the elusive Mr Dance like the experts they were. If the late Mario Fabriano had accomplices on the island, Dance might well flush them, and that would suit Ellul's purpose perfectly. Convinced he had a case of massive extortion firmly by the tail, Ellul had a constable drive the Cunninghams home to collect their passports, and took himself off to catch the last of the concert. Humming.

Thinking the Mozart wonderful, Charlotte Bujega left the Grand Palace ahead of the crowd to meet her father for a late supper. The music had lifted her spirits, and although still haunted by the vision of Charlie Dance mourning to seaward, she determined to show her father her gayest face. He deserved that from his only daughter, and Charlotte well knew the sacrifices her parents had made to complete her formal education. Any wealth he may have accrued over the years had long gone on educational fees, and helping those poor Maltese families her father championed for the odd fat chicken or gifts of peaches and vegetables.

Charlotte left through the courtyard opposite the Libyan People's Bureau, and had her elbow taken on the narrow pavement.

'Charlie?' she said, and was sat in a small green car that took off at speed.

'Had to see you one last time.' Charlie made the St Elmo turn through the old Gut to park in the shadow of the keep housing the headquarters of the Knights of St John and Jerusalem. 'You do have time for a drink?'

'What do you mean, one more time?' Charlotte allowed herself to be led to the Britannia Hotel.

'Miles to go, promises to keep, pretty advocate.'

'I'll have to call my father. Tell him I'll be late.'

'Use the booth in the lobby. I'll be in the bar. Vodka and tonic, right?'

In the telephone booth, Charlotte wondered how Charlie knew her favourite drink. The man was all surprises. Her father said he would wait half an hour with controlled impatience, and Charlotte found Charlie in the deserted bar. He slid a chair under her with the smoothness of a head waiter, and took her hand as if it were the most natural thing in the world.

'What is all this?' Charlotte made herself ask.

'Not really sure myself. Two things I don't usually do: say goodbyes or go to funerals. This makes an exception to both rules.'

'I don't understand.'

'Yes you do. We both do. But that's something for later on, down the Road of Life.'

'I'm supposed to understand any of this?'

'Only all of it. Time has a way of passing; wasted or used sensibly, it passes all too quickly. Time can also diminish the pain of loss. It never goes away, pretty Charlotte. Just becomes bearable, a dull ache you learn to live with. Being busy helps, and that's my initial therapy.'

'Busy doing what? Ellul showed me your Interpol file. It made awful reading, and I think he did it to . . . distance me from you.'

'Did it work?'

'No, but it's made me cautious.'

'Welcome to the big kids' sandpit. The emotions are just as raw, but one knows the rules of combat.'

'Is that how you see relationships? As private wars?'

'Until we learn to declare peace, yes. You're fighting me now, even though you don't want to.'

'Now you're being clever.'

'And honest.'

'Yes, damn you, yes.'

'No victory there, love.'

'Not for either of us.'

Charlotte felt too queasy to touch her drink. Her stomach rolled just as it had when teenage kisses and fumbles had been so poignant, and there was a definite tickle in her mucous membranes. She was

44

either catching cold, or her emotions had been knocked all of a heap.

'Would you like a handkerchief?'

'Would you like me to come to your room?'

'Far too much, that's why I'm saying goodbye here.'

'Isn't that cruel and dishonest?'

'Yes, and I hate myself for it. But we'll both thank me at some later date.'

'I hate you too, Charlie Dance.'

'Thank you, but it'll pass.'

'Like time itself?' Charlotte found her cheeks damp, her eyes brimming.

'Like time itself,' Charlie agreed. And he watched her run into the night with sad satisfaction before leaving the hotel through his bedroom window.

Victor Zammit gave his stern generator just one more chance to behave. He adjusted the trembler switch a thousandth of an inch and flicked on a bulkhead light. The generator stuttered and fired, bathed the engine room of *The Lady Desperado* in sudden light, and a bank of batteries began to charge. Victor awarded himself a cold Hopleaf and went forward to enjoy the night breeze coming off a quietening sea. Wind slapped the awning, the brass brightwork borrowed glow from the lights of Marsamxett, and there was a small, oily lurch that brought Victor out of his chair, reaching for a monkey wrench.

'You need that?' the darkness off the port bow said, and a dripping figure came up over the gunwale to leave wet footprints on the scoured deck. 'I could use one of those beers.'

'That is you, friend Charlie?' Victor did not relax his muscles or his mind. He was well attuned to reacting to sudden situations, and the adrenalin still pumped. He'd once had a boat shot out from under him in Mozambique waters, and some clowns down in the Caribbean had come over the side at night to rip off his consignment of contraband. One had made it back to the shore with ought-guage shot in his buttocks, the others hadn't.

'It's me, Victor.'

'Oddball time to come calling, friend Charlie.' Victor didn't like the way Charlie stayed in shadow. How his hands were the wrong colour, had a pink latex sheen to them.

'Always the right time for a beer.'

Victor jerked his monkey wrench at the wheel-house.

'You know where is fridge.'

Charlie stayed where he was, a hole in starlight.

'How's the fuel situation?'

'Full tanks. Why you ask this thing?'

'Nice night for a cruise.'

'Maltese coastguard don't like if Victor stooge around island at night. Damned patrol boats get damned nosey.'

'Only if you hug the coast like some smuggler. Try to moor up outside the marina. We chug out to sea, they couldn't care less.'

'For why you want this thing?'

'Need a change of air. You know.'

'In shorts. No luggage. Just that belt thing that looks heavy. You making trouble for Victor?'

'I'm thirsty and running out of breath. Do we go, or do I drop back over the side?'

Victor underarmed the Hopleaf to Charlie. Saw him wince when he caught it. Fed the wrench back into its holster on his chair, curious about the heavy money belt.

'We go. Victor don't like what you do, can deep-six

46

you over the side. What wrong with hands?'

'Rubber gloves taped at the wrist. Got some cuts don't like salt water. It's a long swim from Valletta.'

Victor bared uneven white teeth and thought about that. It was a long swim around the point, and the heavy money belt would have dragged like a sea-anchor. Charlie should have been panting and winded, not sucking beer with a flat stomach. Maybe Charlie lied to Victor. Maybe he had walked around the point and then swum the width of the harbour. Or maybe Charlie was in damned good shape.

'Big trouble cost bigger money, friend Charlie.'

'And a friend buying a favour ain't a friend, that it?'

'Man gotta eat, Charlie. Fast boat cost big money to keep yar.'

'And ain't nothing but a piece of driftwood swinging round a buoy if it don't get used. We'll talk money when we get where we're going.'

'Okey-dokey. Does Charlie tell where, or Victor get to guess?'

'Catania. Where do I berth?'

'Master cabin clean. Take that.'

'Wake me when we're there.'

'Sure, you sleep.'

Victor Zammit cast off the lines and eased *The Lady Desperado* out into the deep central channel. Set a course for the east coast of Sicily, glad friend Charlie had lost that soft retired look. He turned the wheel into the wind, smelling money and the kind of fun and trouble he had begun to miss.

CHAPTER FOUR

With the big diesels throbbing under his bunk, Charlie dozed. About an hour out, he rolled off his bunk in a forward headbutt that took Victor Zammit under the floating rib, lifting him off his feet. He took a hard swing at where Victor's head had to be in the darkness, and there was a nice hard *clop* as the bunk slat went home across a hard skull. A dull *thunk* as the back of the same head came in sharp contact with the cabin wall. A meaty leg thrashed, a loose arm knocked its elbow on decking, and Charlie snapped the light on to make sure Victor wasn't shamming. He was out cold, a lumpy sprawl with too much head hair and a body as tan as a pumpkin. The monkey wrench lay in the companionway where he had dropped it.

Charlie hauled Victor up on deck and spread-eagled him. Lashed him securely between the stern stanchions and the aft deckbits, and had hunted out all of Victor's armoury before the big Gozodon came around. By then, the engines had been throttled back to tick-over, *The Lady Desperado* swung at anchor, and Charlie was shucking shells from a Kalashnikov.

'You know I had to try, friend Charlie.'

'Sure you did.'

Charlie flipped the shells over the side. Smiled at Victor and sailed the semi-automatic rifle over the rail.

'You know how much is that gun worth in Beirut?'

'Talk about Mario Fabriano, not arms deals. Give me the run around, old son, all this killing junk goes over the side.'

Victor licked a mouth bigger than his aching head.

'You just *act* being friend,' he grumbled.

'We both do. That's how people like us are,' Charlie began to strip an Uzzi machine-pistol down to its component parts. 'You'd have killed me for that money belt. Might even shed a tear or two when you'd dumped me over the side with your spare anchor for company.'

'A man's what he is, friend Charlie. Can't change that.'

'And why I chose you to get me off Malta. Had to be you who brought Mario Fabriano and maybe one other man over from Sicily. Nobody else, is there?'

'Not as good. Myself don't ask passengers names, you know this.'

'But you'd know them. About five months back. Think, Vic.'

'Victor don't have to. So what I bring these men?'

'They came after me and mine. Almost got lucky.'

'They hurt your hands?'

'Names, Victor, and who sent them.'

Victor reared his head against the rope across his throat. Cough-gagged and said, 'Was friend Charlie's white Rolls they pull from sea? Gin-swillers talk in yacht bar, but Victor don't listen to them peoples too close. Talk was man drowned in car. Woman missing. Is your lady, friend Charlie?'

'That's right.'

'This sad-bad thing. Why you don't tell this when you come aboard? Myself think they just couriers collecting dope money. You think myself wouldn't make one with friend Charlie to twist their heads around, you tell this bad thing?'

49

'You'd already seen the money belt, Victor. You wouldn't have heard a word I said. No, had to be this way, didn't it?'

Victor let his head fall back. Squinted up at powdered stars and a thin sliver of new moon.

'Is true. You gonna use anchor to deep-six Victor?'

'No choice, is there? I let you up, you just naturally have to come at me fast and ugly.'

'Is also true. Makes me feel bad. Myself liked your lady. Even like you, Charlie.'

'It's a sad old world, son.'

'There *is* choice. Listen, Victor can be real friend to friend Charlie. Is way. Will swear on holy crucifix in wheelbox. Will swear true on Eternal God and Blessed Son of Heaven to honour you as brother in Christ. Will swear too on Sacred Madonna Mother of Jesus Child. Victor is true believer. You bring crucifix, you see. Victor give you heads to twist off at shoulders.'

'Small beer.'

'You want what? I give it on sacred oath.'

'So long as I cross your palm with more than silver, eh?'

'Sure I want money. Is brother of blood.'

'Whet my appetite.'

'So I bring this Mario and his brother Carlo. Alla time Carlo tell Mario do this and that. Mario laugh and do it. Enough?'

'I want the man who sent Mario and Carlo.'

'Myself would too, Charlie. Is way of men like us.'

'So?'

'Was their uncle. From London.'

'Figures.'

'Now I swear, you forget anchor. Deal?'

Charlie rose from his easy crouch to watch for shipping in the busy sea lanes. Saw no leading lights, and nothing within ten miles of their position on the radar. Found a chunky silver crucifix by a portrait of the Madonna over the chart table, and brought it aft. Freed Victor's right hand for him to hold and kiss the crucifix, and stood away before it could be used as a bludgeon.

'You careful man, Charlie. Is good to be brother to one such as you.' Victor gabbled Latin with closed eyes and crossed himself.

'That it?'

'We brothers now. You wanna use knife to mix blood?'

'Not if we don't have to.'

'Not is OK too.'

'This uncle in London got a name?'

'Sure, brother-friend Charlie. Maltese George Muscat. Very bad person. Pay Victor good though. Is married to Sicilian woman until she die long time back. Got one daughter, but uses Sicilians to do soldier work. Has many nephews. You know this man?'

Charlie nodded. George Muscat headed Granny's list of consortium members. He worked at Victor's bonds until lights exploded inside his head. Knocked into the thwarts by the solid punch, Charlie came up with a levelled Magnum snatched from the pile of weapons to see Victor blow on his knuckles.

'Now we even, brother Charlie. We drink to that, eh?'

'Oh blimey yeah,' Charlie grumbled.

Catania was as dusty as a goat, had a lot of snarling moped traffic weaving between lorries loaded with olives or fertilizer, and the streets were loud with pealing bells. In a tourist strip traditional shops had given way to the aluminium and plastic of bland

51

Italian Modern where displays of overpriced clothes and international junk giftware were attended by vapid girls wearing garish versions of the latest local fashion. Skinny-knits and red mouths were in, civility to the customer was out. Being familiar with their stock was a stupid bore to girl assistants dreaming of disco romance and dowry houses, of rich husbands and fat legitimate babies.

Charlie padded about in flip-flops and shorts, and bought what he needed in shops passing Taiwanese copies of Yves Saint Laurent suits as originals. He shaved and dressed in an hotel stinking of sewage and broiled meat, and met Victor to eat paella in a clean kitchen on the waterfront. The Palermo agent had paid Victor his retainer for ferry services, and ordered him to forget about Carlo Fabriano until further notice. Carlo was to remain on Malta for another month, perhaps longer. The agent had been deliberately vague about any future assignments, and Victor said he knew the house near Fort St Elmo where Carlo Fabriano was in hiding. The old whore who owned the property was Victor's good friend, so he would have no trouble keeping track of the man. For a healthy consideration, of course.

Charlie paid Victor enough to keep him vigilant, and a taxi with broken springs took Charlie to the airport to board the Rome shuttle. He took a cab to an exclusive residential area off the Appian Way to check out a locked villa there. A gardener told Charlie the owner was abroad on business, and took Charlie's lire for a closer look at the grounds, convinced he wanted to shoot a shampoo commercial there. Such things had happened before Casey Pollard had bought the estate, and a written request for permission to him would be the best course of action for the man from Margot Movies. The postcards Charlie wrote to Inspector Ellul and Charlotte Bujega were posted at Leonardo Da Vinci Airport before he took a British Airways Tristar to London.

A first-floor box at the Savoy had risen to the price of a sixties suite, and the Grill Room was stiff with American publishers. The Strand brawled louder than ever, and Covent Garden was a temporary ghetto of longhair shops making trendy protest against the coming redevelopment. Moss Bros was still Moss Bros, New Row had facelifted itself from cheerless seedy to dull commercial, and Charing Cross Road was solid traffic. Estate agents' boards were nailed the length of Old Compton Street, and video porn was on sale in plain sight in Romilly Street. Black music reggaed in Greek Street, Mexican cuisine was on offer where J. C. Hatton had died sipping port from the wood, and a new building was being grafted to the corner of Soho Square.

Most of the independent film companies had left Wardour Street, and butch gays in leather and chains twittered together in two drinking clubs once used by heavy West End faces. Amateur whores were a nuisance in Meard Street, and bulldozers had flattened the south side of St Anne's Court. Chinese Cyril's restaurant had gone Italian, Maltese and Cypriots ran the Brewer Street strip clubs, and Solly Evergreen's kosher butchers was a supermarket with shouting posters. Armchair Doris' D'Arblay Street crib was an art gallery, and a porn cinema sleazed where Eyetie Antoni had schemed over supped Guinness. There were more hooked kids than alkies roaming the streets, and fast food had ousted the pasta parlours.

Charlie climbed stairs in Poland Street to have a secretary chew gum at him when he asked for Benny Shoemaker. She nodded him through a peeling door and went back to her Mills and Boon romance, letting her nails dry before she stabbed at an electric typewriter. Benny's lair was as old and as cramped as Benny, and he peered at Charlie through thick lenses, a glossy toupée on his creased and freckled head. He coughed through a chain of Woodbines, and his grin was pure porcelain when he recognized Charlie Dance.

'You here to reminisce, Chas, or you moving back in on us?'

'And give up sunshine for fog? Not likely, is it?'

'But you ain't just slumming.'

'Not when property in the Smoke is still a good investment. Has to be, or you wouldn't be acting the poor but honest broker, Benny.'

'So it's a living. And not so dusty between you, me, and granny's cat. But I'd have nailed you as Mayfair these days, not Soho. Wander around, you'll see how things have changed.'

'Already have. The clever money'll come back to Soho once they've finished tarting Covent Garden up. The right investment now means nice profits later.'

Benny pointed a nicotined finger through smoke. 'The shrewd long view, eh?'

'Why not? Diversification is the name of the game these days. So, who's holding the long leases and freeholds? Don't bother me with sub-sub-leases, they're for dummies.'

'Now would I?'

'Not now I've mentioned it.'

Benny creaked his swivel in a half-circle. Hooked a heel over the corner of his desk. Gave Charlie a long stare to see if he was serious, and decided he was.

'Some things don't change, Chas. The new company's got a fancy name with offices in the Isle of Man, has bankers in Hong Kong and the Caymans, but the face behind all those land titles is the same as it ever was.'

'That right?'

'Yeah. You'd remember Maltese George Muscat from the old days. Used to run a string of girls out of Shepherd Market before he oiled in on the club hostess business. Fake bubbly and charging the punters fifty quid to have the girls sit with them. He's still got a couple of clubs in Brewer Street, but property's where all his UK capital sits. That and what he's got going abroad, Uncle George is a stone-rich man. You must have fallen over him at some time, Chas.'

'Not that I remember.'

'What happened to that famous memory of yours?'

'Who remembers pimps?'

'So that's it. Still fussy about dealing with faces in the girly business, eh?'

'Not fussy so much as careful.'

'Same meat, different gravy. We talking discretion or big money?'

'Both. Any conflict of interest if you act for me, Benny?'

'I'm still the last of the independents, Chas. And that don't sit right with a lot of the big boys. Those big developers would just love to pick old Benny's brains, get all I know into their computers. They've offered me a desk and a fat salary, but they'd dump me the second they'd wrung me dry. My filing system's in my head. I only keep that silly cow outside as window dressing. Got the brains of a cornflake, and I like it that way.'

'Miss Personality? I wondered.'

'If that girl knew Friday followed Thursday she'd be dangerous. Some clever face could get our Marigold ginned-up and indiscreet inside five short minutes. She knows nothing, cares less, and can't be pumped about Benny Shoesmith or his clients, right? You want me to act for you, you have to tell me how.'

'Think of a box. Draw a line from Tottenham Court Road to Oxford Street, down to Piccadilly Circus, back along Shaftesbury Avenue to Charing Cross Road, and back up to Tottenham Court Road again.'

'And then what?'

'Buy it.'

'Just like that.'

'Why not?'

'You pulling old Benny's pudden, Chas? You know how many millions you're talking? You and all the Arab oil couldn't afford a square foot of Oxford Street pavement, let alone Regent Street.'

'Not the frontages. The infill.'

'The Soho back streets? That's what you're talking?'

'Looks like it.'

'You won't get the church properties. And Westminster Council will have something to say about what you're proposing.'

'Who's gonna tell them? You?'

'You want to be invisible, that it?'

'As usual, yeah.'

'You'll need a lot of paper companies to front all this.'

'Shuffling papers is what you do best, Benny.'

Benny slumped to scratch his scalp through his wig. Burned another cigarette alight and watched

56

the end glow in a shaft of light. Searched for the joke and hollow laughter in Charlie's face and saw no levity there.

'OK, Chas,' he sighed. 'I'll buy the balloon and the goldfish. Why are you doing this?'

'I'm sentimental. Let's say I don't like what's happening to Soho. Let's say I want to put the old place on its feet, better than it was before. Make it a tourist centre where people can walk at night without looking over their shoulders. Put the girls back on the streets where they belong. Where the punters can see what they're getting for their money without nasty surprises at the top of a flight of grubby stairs. Have the place run by faces who can earn good corn without robbing the punters blind. They've done it in Hamburg, so why not here?'

Benny looked miserable, the expression he wore when good business came his way.

'You'd get some argument from the locals,' he mused. 'Some families have been in the square mile for five generations.'

'Start a residents association, get the traders on your side. Make noises about cleaning up Soho. Give 'em a voice. Start a bloody magazine if you have to. They'll have no reason to bitch with me as their landlord, Benny.'

'You'll want to start by picking up leases here and there.'

'Not here and there, all of them. Starting with this Maltese Jack's.'

'It's Maltese George as you well know.'

'Do I?' Charlie looked vague.

Benny's brittle cackle set him coughing.

'Same old Charlie,' he choked as he was passed a cheque drawn on a Guernsey bank. 'Margot Holdings is you?' he asked, scratching a signature on a receipt.

'That's who you're working for.'

'Looks like they pay well.'

'You can only take out what you put in, Benny. That's sound business.'

'Tell that to the sharks I deal with.'

'You tell them, Benny.' Charlie rose to leave.

'Where do I find you, Chas?'

'You don't. I find you.'

'Just like the good old days,' Benny sighed through a sad smile of glee.

George Muscat chewed out a fey decorator for not sticking enough silver stars around his stage, hired two new Filipino girls who did startling things with live snakes, and took the time to open the morning post in his Brewer Street office. He was breathless using a letter-opener, and knew he should lose weight before his heart blew up like an unpierced baked potato. His Bianca was a fine and dutiful daughter, but she was nowhere near ready to take the business over, and a man without sons must work until the end. Muscat had nephews by the dozen, had groomed three of them to oversee some aspects of his growing empire, but he refused them any more responsibility until he was certain Bianca could not function as head of the family when he retired. They growled like empty stomachs now and again, but when their Uncle George gave them his hardest looks, they went back to sitting on their thumbs.

Muscat laid notated bills aside for his bookkeeper, and opened an envelope with Maltese stamps. Inside, was a clipping from the *Times of Malta*. A car had gone off the road near St Paul's Bay. A woman passenger was missing, and the male driver killed. No other vehicle had been involved. There was no accompanying note, and for a long moment, Muscat could not breathe. The scrap of newsprint confirmed what he already knew; the Sicilian bastards had muffed it, and that fat slug Grenville Cunningham had not been widowed. Dangerous if he talked, still useful if he co-operated. Muscat and his partners must decide how best to keep the pressure up. It was too early to call Los Angeles, and Casey Pollard had left Rome for Panama to negotiate the salvage of the *Kingston Pride* and its cargo of eighty million dollars. Muscat wished he had vetoed sending the money by sea, furious that hindsight could never make up for healthy foresight.

Distracted, Muscat answered the phone to Benny Shoemaker, and had trouble understanding what was being said. There was a song and dance about Soho leases, and sounded as if Shoemaker had found himself a live one with more money than sense. Muscat's grey cells began to work. Liquidating his London holdings had long been in his mind, yet if old Benny had a mug willing to meet Muscat's outrageous asking price, there had to be something Muscat was missing. Some clandestine development scheme he was not party to, and the bells of greed began to jangle inside his head.

Muscat danced Shoemaker around with half-promises to give himself time to make some enquiries. Profits could be doubled and trebled in the property market without laying a single brick, all it took was a strong bargaining position and a complete disregard for time. Let the other fellow sweat, time was a commodity Muscat believed he had in abundance. He was savaging a deep-dish pizza when the manager of his Poland Street sex-aid shop came to deliver the monthly trading figures. Brick Donovan wasn't the smartest face on

Muscat's firm, but he could be trusted with minor tasks.

'You won't believe who I just seen, Mr George,' Brick said.

'Won't I?'

'A real face from the past. Charlie Dance. Walked right past me like all them years never happened. Got some grey over his ears, but still looks like he could push over a bus. Gave me a turn, I can tell you.'

Muscat stopped chewing. The pizza was lead in his gut.

'You being funny, Brick?'

'No, Mr George. On my mother's grave. Comes out of some office, hails a black cab and asks for the Savoy Hotel.'

'What office?'

'One of them in Poland Street. About four doors down from the shop.'

Muscat's stomach bubbled. He snapped plump fingers.

'Benny Shoemaker's, right?'

'Dunno. You want I should find out? Old Benny's got a daft secretary who'll tell me anything without she kick-starts her brain.'

'On the quiet, Brick. What are you waiting for?'

'I've gone, Mr George.'

The pizza went cold as Muscat mused at the spot where Donovan had stood. Benny Shoemaker had to be fronting for somebody, so why not Charlie Dance? Charlie would have that kind of money lying around as small change, and maybe had the fidgets with the Mediterranean life. Wasn't a Londoner worth his salt who didn't miss the Smoke, and if Dance wanted to move back into Soho, Uncle George would make him pay through the nose for the privilege. And why stop at his own package of leases? Why not pick up options on all there were available, and ring the bastard so he couldn't move without Muscat's say so?

'Check it out, George,' Muscat told himself. 'Make sure nobody's pulling a flanker before you move, old son.'

He began dialling around, glad to have something amusing to take his mind off his larger troubles.

The architectural artist's office in Golden Square was lit by colour-corrected tubes to kill shadow and glare. Jason Mayer was young and keen, had yards of framed diplomas and frayed cuffs to his denim jacket. The fee Charlie was prepared to pay had Mayer enthusing over the Ordnance Survey maps Charlie bought in Long Acre, he promised a detailed aerial view within fourteen days; a full-colour version ten days after that. He would deliver the drawings to Benny Shoesmith's office in person, A draughtsman would be engaged to draw scale projections of the period houses Charlie planned to erect to replace the uglier modern stuff that had gone up since the war. And yes, the historical researcher Mayer would employ would be painstaking.

Charlie left Mayer making preliminary sketches, hired a local photographer to shoot every pre-1900 building in the square mile, the prints to be delivered to Mayer in batches of 100. A Beak Street printer agreed to print glossy presentation folders for a cash discount, and a Bloomsbury Square Commissioner of Oaths witnessed several documents Charlie needed sworn. Copies of these were lodged with banks in Lombard Street and St Peter Port, Guernsey. That done, Charlie took a black cab to Heathrow, leaving the pot to simmer without him.

CHAPTER FIVE

Los Angeles: 14 May 1980

A cold front from Canada had pushed the smog out over the Pacific when Charlie left his Beverly Hills suite for Hollywood and Vine. The bar was a dark barn iced by air-conditioning; was having a happy hour wake for a thin crowd with no interest in the tall blonde playing piano. She had a notable vibrato and her name on the marquee, and she threaded jazz rhythms through her early evening medley of standards, lifting them out of the musical rut with an innovative skill wasted on the clientele. The late night crowd might be more responsive, but Charlie doubted it.

He found the man he wanted in a rear booth, and ordered drinks from a waitress in skimpy lemon. An FBI field operative from San Diego, Saul Chasen moonlighted for an LA detective agency to pay alimony to his Mexican wife in Tijuana. He had a cello bass of a voice, an anonymous suit, and a nervous way of toying with a club soda. The rest of him blended with the dark woodwork, and his eyes could have been knotholes in stained oak.

'Why meet here?' Charlie said.

'I go where the business is, and tonight it's here. I don't like where this is going, I walk. Clear?'

'All I wanted was somebody checked out.'

'Not just a "somebody", pal. A certain citizen who shows in the official Washington files. That makes you a certifiable crazy, or a fellow who's more than he looks. The agency's nervous about this one, pal. And I ain't so taken with it m'self. Doll Gardenia was Detroit and New York. Now he's here on the coast playing the straight citizen, which he ain't. And here's you, straight out of left-field, checking on Gardenia like he's some auto-bandit you're skip-chasing. You I don't drink liquor with. You're a soda-pop client, pal. One I need all my marbles for.'

'That's fine with me. I don't pay dummies more than the British prime minister's salary for being stupid, Chasen. May I see some results for my money?'

'I'm talking integrity here, not bucks.'

'Can't have the one without the other.'

Saul Chasen stared with knothole eyes, turned his soda on its round paper mat and leaned in to pat Charlie down and ask if he smoked.

'Yes, but I don't carry them.'

'Fine. I've been giving up for fifteen years.'

'Nor am I wired. You?'

'Definitely a soda-pop client,' Chasen said, grudging the words.

'Who wants answers.'

'Yeah, about Gardenia, who's connected to the fifth biggest family. Detroit and New York ain't run by the Salvation Army, pal.'

'Just as the Band of Hope don't run Sicily.'

Chasen's eyes quickened and hooded as he turned his glass full circle to fill up a long silence. 'What's your real name, pal?' he asked during a lyrical introduction to 'Misty'.

'She plays well,' Charlie said.

'And you play poker with blank cards,' Chasen snapped.

'Check me out. You have the means.'

'I did already. Malcolm Philip Sadler died in a drowning accident in Rio fifteen years ago. Means you ain't him, but Interpol puts you in bed with his widow.'

'His late widow, Chasen. You do good work.'

'That would be the motive? Don't shrug, pal, I can see it in your face. And I'm damned if I'll give you anything that could screw up an ongoing investigation into our local Sicilians. Go home, put flowers on the grave. America for Americans, pal. The president declared war on these people, and I'm a loyal soldier.'

'Who moonlights for money? How would that go down in San Diego or Washington?'

'You play rough, pilgrim,' Chasen muttered.

'Is there a choice?' Charlie asked, flagging a fresh drink.

'Bourbon,' Chasen sighed, ordering Chesterfields from the waitress. 'A Mexican stand-off.'

'Like your marriage.'

'Hell no. Davy Crockett only got hung once at the Alamo. I get hung every first of the month by that bitch.' Chasen's face was lit by wry laughter before he sobered in a stream of toasted smoke. 'Never was a killer with the foxes. Not like Doll Gardenia. Man, he collects women like the poor collect food stamps. The gals he's vamped, tramped and dumped must stretch across six states of the union. None of them have ever talked though. I know operatives who've gotten real close to some of them, and come up empty. Gardenia has made fear into an artform. His psychological profile suggests he's like most rapists, he uses women badly in revenge for some childhood hang-up over his everloving momma. That comes hard to a guy like me who takes gals to dinner only to have them leave before dessert. How about y'self?'

64

Charlie looked at the waitresses and the bad decor. Thought about Charlotte Bujega and pushed the pain of Margot to the back of his mind. Guessed where Saul Chasen's thoughts were going, and decided to make him work for it.

'Why?' he asked.

'There's a gal works here used to be real friendly with Doll Gardenia way back. Knew him from New York, and could be she's followed him here. Could be coincidence she's working LA, and the right guy could maybe get close to her. Get her talking, y'know?'

'Who did you have in mind?'

'Only two of us here, and it ain't me, pal.'

'Just which cocktail waitress is it?'

'Wrong, pal. Her name's on the marquee outside. It's Della. Della O'Day, and she's doing nice things to Errol Garner right now.'

Charlie watched a spot turn the piano player pink before giving her a halo of soft white light. Her blonde-white hair was cropped close to a square face with deep sockets framing small blue eyes and sooty lashes. Her tiny mouth delivered lyrics like tender young fruits, and her black gown showed off a long leg line. She could have been any age between thirty and fifty, and Charlie wrote a request on a napkin wrapped around a banknote to get a closer look. He wove through the tables to drop it in her jar, stayed long enough to earn a meaningless professional smile without focus, and went back to the booth to find Saul Chasen had taken the cigarettes and left a folded sheet under his untouched drink. Charlie sat back to read the single page report, killing time to closing.

'What's the gag, sport?'

'Pardon me?'

Charlie looked up to find Della O'Day at his table. He stood to offer her a seat, and found she was tall enough to look him in the eye.

'I don't sit with the customers, friend. Nor do I accept thousand-dollar bills for "entertaining". You must be from Vegas, that's the freaky sort of thing the creeps down there try to pull. I should get Harry to throw you out on your dirty neck. Or do you plan to claim it was a five or ten you confused in the dark?'

'None of those things, Miss O'Day,' Charlie said.

'Listen to the agent for Brooklyn bridge.'

'You're a talented lady, Miss O'Day, but you should talk as prettily as you sing. I came to hear your music, not barroom dialogue.'

'Say *what*?'

'I bought your New York album in '72 to put in my collection. Now it goes into the garbage. May I pass?'

'You can't just walk away, you freak.'

'Why not? I'll throw myself out and save Harry the trouble. Now may I pass?'

'No, damn it.'

'You're attracting attention to yourself. And I have no stomach for scenes.'

'You don't offer ladies thousand-dollar bills, you get that?'

'Why not? This is your first gig since January. I thought it might help with the groceries. Even talent has to eat.'

'Where are you coming from?'

'Geographically? Not Vegas. London.'

Charlie turned in the narrow aisle to face a man coming fast from the lobby. Showed both palms and gave himself enough legroom to manoeuvre.

'This has to be Harry,' he said. 'Does he approve

of his staff causing uproar? Good evening, Harry, I was just leaving.'

'That you got right,' Harry said. 'You 'K, Della?'

'I spilled this gentleman's drink. I was just apologizing. Rustle him another, would you, Harry? Get the money from my jar.'

Charlie kept his face blank. The woman had thrown the dregs of his Irish across the table, and was mopping at it with a towel she'd lifted from a waitress.

'Siddown,' she hissed. 'Or we're both out of here, and I need this job.'

Charlie sat and was served with a tall and fierce Irish.

'Why the change of heart?'

Della O'Day wagged a long finger.

'If you are a freak, brother, I'll see you in traction. And a three dollar drink means I owe you nine ninety seven in change.'

'Thanks for the apology anyway.'

'Who did?'

'You told Harry you'd apologized.'

'I just said that. How'd you know about me? About my last gig in January, and all?'

'I hired a detective.'

'Sure you did. Everybody does that for Della, I don't think. The cabaret business is dead. Nobody listens any more. They just eat and run, drink and run. Period.'

'I listened. Look, I'll give it five minutes, then leave.'

'You really came from London to hear me?'

'Came on business. Saw a magazine ad about this place and you. Thought I'd drop in to listen. That's it.'

'Nope.'

'Sorry?'

67

'No ad. Harry's too cheap. The cheapest of the cheapos.'

'Then we're back with the detective.'

'Will you just stop that, it's scarey.'

Charlie tried a soft smiling shrug.

'I just walked in off the street. Didn't know it was you on the stand until you started to sing. That *is* it.'

'Nope.'

'No?'

'The January gig, remember?'

'Ah.'

'If this comes out freaky – traction.'

'You do have the right sort of friends to do that?'

'Right here in this bar, friend.'

'There's one former friend I'd like to talk about.'

'You a kiss-and-tell reporter, or what?'

'Just somebody who lost somebody. Like you did.'

'I think this ends here.'

'All right. Thanks for the drink.'

'Just like that?'

'I'm not here to lean on you, singing lady. Somebody will talk to me. It doesn't have to be you.'

'I don't want to know, but I have to. You get that?'

'You lost a nice fellow who played piano just like you. Somebody took him out to get to you, and you stayed with that somebody until you found out what happened to your pianist. Do I have to mention names?'

'No.'

'Good night, Della.'

'Wait. Where do I locate you?'

'So you can send your friends after me?'

'You're no freak, but you scare me. Just me . . . if I want to talk.'

'You know the big hotel in Beverly?'

'Only from the outside. You're travelling high, friend.'

'Come and try the pool and the cracked crab.'

'How's the room service at two in the morning? That's when I finish up here, and I'm sure tired of tuna fish sandwiches.'

'I'll phone the order through. That's if I can stay for your final set.'

Della showed long eyeteeth in a grin.

'Why not? You've got a thousand bucks worth of requests due.'

'One will do. I liked that version of "Strange Fruit" on your New York album.'

'You *did* buy it. Hold on to your hat, buster. You're gonna hear real piano.'

Della O'Day was transformed when she adjusted the microphone to reintroduce herself to no applause. The Billy Holliday song came at Charlie like waves of melancholic sea, killed the nearby conversations with its dynamic sadness, and he sat back to enjoy a rare talent, sure that Saul Chasen turned in quality research.

A swollen moon sailed beyond palms and the sleeping hills of Bel Air when Della washed the saloon out of her hair. She had inhaled the cracked crab and a magnum of Pommier, and a second bottle was in its bucket when she curled up in the darkened sunroom. Her face scrubbed, and her damp hair scraped back under a towelling turban, her small blue eyes were amethyst seeds in their large sockets, and her high cheekbones made her jaw seem undershot.

'I'm crocked,' she said, and giggled into her hand. Lost in king-sized wraps of towelling, she accepted another glass of champagne, and held it to watch bubbles rise inside the crystal. Teetering between

69

thirty and forty, Della O'Day was a vulnerable child-woman who had left her public persona under her piano lid. 'D'you hurt people, my freaky friend?' she asked suddenly and quietly.

'We all do, Della. Even you.'

'You know nothing, you know that?'

'Less and less as time goes by.'

'Doll hurts people. Doll, Jesus, some doll.'

'You were with him three years, Della. Must have been some laughs in there somewhere.'

'Sure there were laughs. He had a great laugh. Party laughs. Cocktail laughs. Laughs when he was hurting.'

'Hurting you?'

'Sure hurting me. Why not? He owned me. I didn't exist for him until I shucked my pants and he went to. Then I was special, boy. But when he was through, *this* was me, this chesterfield. Another thing in the room he had to walk round to save barking his precious shins. And you know, I went along with it like it was how it should be. Just like Glenn did when we were together. Weird.'

Della thought about weirdness as Charlie thought about the Glenn Bath in Saul Chasen's report. The jazz pianist Della had left for Doll Gardenia's up-tempo life style. Within the month, Glenn Bath had been spread over a thousand yards of railway track by a night express. A suicide, except that one shoe had been found on a tenement roof over thirty feet from the impact point. Somebody had helped him to fly into oblivion after treating him to a cocaine overdose, and there was a big question mark on the open police file gathering dust in New York.

'Who finished it, Della? You or Gardenia?'

Della tugged a lock from her turban. Teased it into a damp curl.

'Wasn't . . . like that. I was still in the house, y'know? Not that Doll didn't have others outside. Always had from day one. Used to tell me about them to turn himself on. But I was on downers prescribed by one of his tame physicians. Turned me into a grapefruit. Not all at once, but soon. Doll liked me submissive, but it got to where I was *nothing* lying there. I wasn't even there for *me*. Got my periods all bollixed up, and that got him madder than mad. I mean, how do you humiliate somebody who plain doesn't exist? I couldn't even *pretend* any more. And playing piano for his friends was oh-you-tee, out. All the melodies were a one-note thump. No more music. All gone, like me.'

Della's giggle was a chilling trill.

'And this one time? I just slid right off the stool when I ran out of black keys. Right there in front of his classy Italian friends and their fat wives, all breathing garlic and shock at me rolling about down there. I mean, I was out. And them sick to their stomachs 'cause little Della put their *business* right there in the room with them. Showed them every candy nose they made money from, right there on the Persian rug. Just *thinking* of their faces got me through detox. That and having Doll scream about how he wasted a hit on a bum musician to put a piece of crap like me in his bed. He beat me bad, but I didn't care any more. I learned to cry again instead.'

Della worked her throat convulsively.

'Still can. Wanna see?'

Charlie shook his head.

'Aw, come on, sport? Part of the act. Della *cries* the blues. Wouldn't *that* make a freaky album?'

Charlie had nothing to say. His drink growing warm, he watched Della weep and spill champagne until he took her glass. She caught his wrist to pull

71

him down beside her. Laid her head against his shirt to let the sobs come as the sky paled into pre-dawn twilight.

A distant black and white sped somewhere, and the ice turned to puddles in the champagne bucket. The electric clock swept through timeless time, and Della went quiet in Charlie's arms. When he put her to bed she curled up with a knuckle between her teeth, all the sad years gone from her face. Somehow transferred to the hard line of Charlie's mouth when he asked room service for prime steaks, an ice pick and six kebab skewers for a barbeque.

Yes, right away, please.

Out on the sidewalk, Charlie turned into the nearest canyon road. There was no traffic, and with the moon sinking, he strode through silver mono-chrome. Passed tall spindrift hedges and neat verges of Korean moss. Long gated drives curving off to unseen homes. Mansions of brick and timber and thatch, of dressed stone and wooden shingles. As the road steepened and wound, the houses grew closer together. Modern fancies of concrete and glass shaped to please outmoded modernists, modest bungalows pretending they were in Switzerland, and the odd Germanic structure being Gothic for the hell of it.

On a rise, Charlie walked a parapet between a colonnade of cypress trees, crossed a patio to a concrete sluice built to take watershed from the head of the canyon, and followed it through a deep culvert between two conjoining properties. Climbing a tiered rubble wall overgrown by sage, he found himself above an ivy-covered folly that was a ram-part guarding an acre of lawn, an avenue of tall cottonwoods, and a fine redwood house. Easing through a three-strand electrified fence, Charlie used the thick ropes of creeper to lower himself to the base of the rampart.

The sprinklers were keeping the guard dogs away, and Charlie zig-zagged through the chattering arcs to thin his scent. Soaked himself to the skin and knew it didn't matter. Skirting the redwood house, he skewered the steaks to the gravel path, lowered himself into the swimming pool, and sank without a ripple. Swimming underwater, he reached the protective grill separating the outer pool from the inner one. Kicked out the bars he had sawn through the previous night, and eeled through into the house.

Drying off with a guest towel he found in a cubicle, he went swiftly into the side lobby where an armed man dozed over a *Playboy*, his bulk lolling in a chair that could have been a movie throne. He jerked once when Charlie used steady pressure on the side of his neck, and did nothing to stop Charlie taking his Colt Python away to bury it in a potted palm. He would wake up with a headache and wonder what his name was whilst he tried to articulate his limbs and stunned brain cells.

Charlie took the stairs to the upper floor and found the bedroom he wanted. Cracked the door soundlessly, and let himself into dimly lit luxury. The bed was a huge thing of carved wood and gilt cherubs, of white cambric drapes with long English swashes. A naked Eurasian girl lay on her back, one arm flung out as though reaching for the bedside phone. Still misted by recent exertion, and smelling of lilac and musk, she slept behind a frown as though conscience plagued her dreams. Doll Gardenia lay beside her, a heavy thigh across the girl's waist, his face half-buried in a plump silk pillow. His slow cigar breath stirred the girl's coarse black hair, and the rough pelt on his back and shoulders was slicked by drying sweat.

Charlie felt stifled in the airy room. Had the crazy notion he breathed stolen air tainted by the sleeping couple's embrace. The smell of them took the strength out of his arms as it slowly mushed his brain, taking his resolve with it. Until he thought of Granny and Flo drinking their fear away. Of the emotionally crippled woman asleep in his suite. Of Margot lost in deep waters, her hair fanned out around crabs feeding on her face. Then he could move.

He applied four seconds of hard pressure to the big artery in the girl's brown neck. Her frown smoothed away as her dream was killed, and Charlie turned her head to one side to stop her swallowing her tongue. There was something important she must witness when she awoke.

Circling the bed, Charlie forced Gardenia's face into the pillow. Held him there until the man realized he was being suffocated. A massive convulsion shook Gardenia. Sweat ran out of the greying hair to oil his corded neck, and the sides of his face were a mottled purple. His thick hams heaved the girl's small breasts into soft dance, and a thrashing foot skated along Charlie's thigh. Standing away, Charlie drove a twisting punch to the base of Gardenia's spine, and the meaty back arched as the powerful legs turned to useless meat.

Gardenia swung a wild arm and got an elbow under himself. Opened his mouth wide to take air to bellow, and looked shocked when Charlie dislocated his shoulder with an easy wrench. Gardenia tried to roll away from the pain. To see who was doing this awful thing to him. Got a rubber foot to the floor and found it wouldn't support him. Scrabbled to find purchase on the silk sheets, his hands skidding about as though he finger-painted with invisible ink. A shout building in his glottis died there as a sighing whimper when Charlie drove the ice pick home from the shoulder. Pinned to the overcarved headboard, Gardenia let his eyes roll to white, and he hung off the steel spike, as uncaring as a gaffed dolphin.

Back on the canyon road in dry clothes, Charlie paused to take in the view. The canyon rim caught fire in early light, and the cypress trees formed a perfect frame to the scene. The scent of dewed pines was as clean as an honest resolution, and house lights were necklaces of glitter in the olives and tans of the canyon walls. Far candles in a roofless cathedral.

A sudden command to freeze turned Charlie's head. A patrol car had coasted down the hill to take him unawares, and Charlie blinked like a tourist as he was made to assume the position for a concealed weapons check. No money, no identification, no vehicle. His hotel room key was something, but not enough for officers Dolan and McTag who rode him down to the Beverly Hills Station for the usual formalities attached to a suspicious alien vagrant in shirtsleeves. Saul Chasen posted bail bond without revealing his official identity, and had Charlie out in time for a midday breakfast with Della.

'You're something else, you know that, pally? *Nobody*. But *nobody* walks in Bel Air at five in the a.m. You got that?' was Chasen's parting shot before he hurled his Mustang downtown.

Charlie watched the veil of exhaust fade to nothing.

And went to wake Della.

She was behind a biscuit drape when Charlie let himself into his suite. Hiding like a guilty schoolgirl.

'Where've you been, Goddamnit? I thought you'd skipped and left me with the tab.'

'Went for a walk. Ended up playing pinochle with two LAPD cops.'

'Will you quit this freaky talk?'

'Shall we breakfast here, or eat out? Pick your favourite restaurant.'

'Dressed like a Midnight Cinderella? They'll think I'm a hooker, I walk through the lobby in all this glitter.'

Charlie jerked a thumb at the door when it was knuckled by a discreet fist.

'That'll be for you. His name's Bernard. He'll fix you up with daywear whilst I shower and change. I think I got your sizes right.'

Della swallowed unnumbered negative thoughts. Said, 'Really?'

Charlie patted her cheek on his way to the bathroom. 'Really.'

As he scrubbed life back into his tired muscles he heard the effete tones of Bernard counterpointed by Della's squeals of delight over his Rodeo Drive merchandise. He was shaving when Della burst in with two outfits she could not choose between, and what did he think?

'Both. But wear the black, it's your colour.'

'You even thought of *underwear*. That faggot *knows* I'm a hooker. It's written all over his kiss curls.'

'But we know different. And that's what matters.'

'You think so?'

'I know so. I also know I'm starved.'

'Five minutes, 'K?'

'Six, I have to choose a necktie.'

Della kissed Charlie somewhere near his nose, and went away with shaving cream on her lip.

Charlie sluiced off and caught his eye in the mirror. Thought he saw Margot reflected there, her cornflower eyes mocking him. Her presence a coldness between his shoulder blades. When he made himself turn, there was just the bathroom as empty as he was, and he sagged against the handbasin, wondering if he could eat after all.

And at that moment, the Eurasian girl in Bel Air tried to scream through rising vomit . . .

CHAPTER SIX

Rome: 15 May 1980

Casey Pollard drove himself home through dusk and skimming vesper bats, too tired to think of food or women. Panama had steamed and stank, just like those damned colonels he had traded garlic breath with; and all *those* olive mothers thought about were the big numbers in their numbered Swiss accounts. Actually getting off their asses and earning the long green had them looking solemn as their lazy butts spread like ripe pears.

'All you need to earn rank in the Panamanian army is a big moustache, a bigger gut, and enough gold teeth to dazzle a firing squad,' Pollard told himself aloud, jaded by crossing three date lines in as many days.

Maybe Doll Gardenia should shuffle his tush down there, or that fat London slug Muscat. Let them try their winning ways on those South American Petes without the need to slip big denomination notes into every upturned palm. You shook hands with a Don, your hand stayed shook. A man of honour had to keep his word. But these characters you rented by the day, they just wouldn't stay bought. That was maybe OK if you bought little and often like the Jamaicans, they couldn't get ripped off for more than twenty-thirty grand at any one time. But you were talking big kilos, watch out, boy, a million could disappear up the nearest sleeve faster than a sharper's aces.

Cruising past that part of the Appian Way where early Christian dissidents were executed, Pollard used the coded bleeper on his dash to warn his staff he was coming. Those Goddamned Eyetalians could go through all their European bowing and scraping, but all Pollard wanted was straight AAA American service, a hot tub and his bed turned down for eighteen hours of goodbye world. Hold all calls unless his wife came through from New York to talk family. Let Gardenia and Muscat sweat dimes for a while longer.

Losing that last consignment of skag and money was a real stomach-heaver, but good old Casey Pollard had gotten the consortium a sweet deal with the salvage people at Oceania-Cal. A straight fee of five mill to bring the whole wreck up *sealed* whilst waiving further salvage rights. All Doll and Muscat had to do was lodge an irrevocable credit note to that amount with Oceania-Cal's bankers in the Caymans, and everybody got well again. That fey old Britisher Cunningham must have folded under Muscat's pressure by now, so what the hey? His personal guarantee would swing the deal, and by the time the note came to be honoured, the cash would be right there in the account to pay off. And the balance laundered out of Panama meant the consortium made on the deal instead of losing.

Sweeter than chicken on Sunday.

Pollard slowed to make his turn, pressed the electric gate release, and powered across the nose of a coming truck, spurting gravel as he accelerated into his drive. The gate had closed before the truck's air-brakes had stopped shrieking, and Pollard liked that. Having the fast-closer fitted meant nobody could swing in on his tail, and that was money well spent.

Pollard garaged his BMW, left Giorgio to fuss with the luggage, and told Giorgio's woman the idea of pasta and meat sauce turned his gut. So let her look sulky, the day she learned to make good coffee he'd pat her lumpy duff and give her a raise. Maybe. In his bedroom Pollard threw his clothes anywhere and wallowed in suds with a jigger of martini for company. He was plodding towards his bed when the secure phone began to bleat at him. Pollard groaned a ripe expletive and sat on his bed glaring at it. If it was Gardenia or Muscat, the hell with them. If it was Marlene in New York, there was no way he could sit through a catalogue of non-events that made up his relatives' lives in the Big Apple. Pollard cut the answerphone in and rolled over, asleep almost instantly.

Brick Donovan sauntered through the Soho dusk trying to make sense of what he'd learned using the key he'd lifted from Benny Shoemaker's secretary. That dumpling could drink, and had rumpled his bed with more enthusiasm than skill before passing out in the missionary position. Brick had banged off colour Polaroids of her gross sprawl for later use if the bitch didn't play ball, and locked them in the safe with his other pictures. If she was still out when he got back, he'd probably heave her around for his video camera. There were customers who liked the obscene and ugly to leaven their usual diet of gymnastic girls going through the motions.

Brewer Street blew with litter and the usual drift of nobodies pretending they belonged, when Brick reached the club. Two girls were doing their snake act to crackly sitar music, and a party of Dutchmen yelled suggestions that were physically impossible for reptile or woman. Brick found Uncle George snacking on salt beef in the office, and cooled his heels until he was beckoned inside.

'Good crowd tonight, Mr George,' Brick said.

'And you want what?' Muscat asked, crunching Rennies.

'I only got into Shoesmith's office, thass all.'

'So?'

'Can't make it out, really. There's all this stuff there. Drawings and things. Of Soho. Except it ain't exactly.'

'Don't drip at me, Brick. Get it said.'

'It's like Soho, but changed. Like it maybe was once, maybe. All folders of pictures and like that. Plans and things, you know. Didn't touch nothing hardly, but I took these.' Brick passed some Polaroids across for Muscat to shuffle.

'This one ain't Soho,' Muscat grunted, turning a print for Brick to see. 'Not sure it's even human.'

'Oh, yeah, well thass how I got the key. Big girl ain't she?'

'Big ain't in it,' Muscat said, trying to read the small print in the margin of an aerial view of Soho Square. 'Jason Mayer Associates in association with . . . Margot what's this? Holdings? That what it says?'

'Looks like,' Brick said, squinting. 'Yeah, that was printed in gold all over a lot of book things. Nothing inside though, all blank.'

'And who's this Mayer Associates?'

'Local ain't he? Works outta Golden Square. Does drawings and that for builders. Seen him drinking in the John Snow with all them other homos. Married too, funny, ain't it?'

'Nothing's funny in this business. Who've we got can do a job on his offices without breaking nothing, including my heart?'

'There's Blond John. Might get hold of that Fulham bloke, wass his name, Larry Lean.'

'Bigmouths both. Get Irish Denzil, he knows how to keep his clack well shut. Well, what're you waiting for?'

'Nothing.'

'And Brick, this fat girl. Keep her sweet, and you're on a nice earner of a bonus.'

Brick went out framing shots of fleshy bondage.

George Muscat nibbled a nail over the Polaroids. Charlie Dance was thinking big, and Muscat knew he shouldn't be surprised. It was the nature of the man, and Muscat only had to reach out to profit from Dance's enterprise. There was enough cash on hand to buy all the key options Dance would need to finalize the groundwork of his scheme, but this meant something drastic had to be done about Cunningham the financier. And fast.

He was pondering the double dilemma when the telephone rang, and when the connection to Los Angeles cleared enough for him to understand what was being said, he massaged the fatty tissue around his tight heart.

Listening.

Della's apartment was a box near the Hollywood freeway she shared with some lumpy furniture, an upright piano, and a goldfish she called Oscar. She was quiet in the lurching elevator, had trouble opening her door, and mumbled excuses about the state of her neat home. Charlie said coffee was fine when she clattered cups around a Cona, and turned her by her shoulders when she spilled ground beans. She shivered under his light touch to her shoulders, and looked fixedly at the centre of his chest until he put her gently aside and mopped up the spillage.

'It's . . . been . . .' Della worked her hands together.

'A long time since you entertained a man?'

'Something like that.' Della toed the fringe of a rug straight. 'You kind of . . . fill the place up, you know?'

'That's why God invented doors. Shall I walk through one?'

Della would or could not answer.

'We could ask Oscar. He has a knowing look.'

'Don't . . . laugh at me.'

'I'm not laughing, Della.'

Charlie primed the coffee maker with water and turned it on.

'You look as if you laugh at everybody the minute their backs are turned. Like a cat. You even . . . walk like one.'

'Should I apologize?'

'For being you? How?'

'Why don't you play something? I'd like that.'

'Bothers the neighbours. Mostly they're night workers.'

'Like you.'

'When I *am* working. The word goes around, and that's me out. Even here on the coast.'

'Gardenia's work?'

'I guess, but who could prove it, huh?' Della tried a smile and lost it.

Charlie hunched in a chair to give Della more space, to lessen the threat of his presence. Mildly said, 'No lawyer could, that's certain. There might be another way.'

'Take on the families? Come *off* it, freaky. Look, sorry, but you don't know how they are. Take a look at me, and I'm one of the lucky ones. I'm still walking around. Didn't end up in two barrels of cement.'

'Or under a train like Glenn Bath.'

'You know too much for both our good. I got enough guilt.'

'Another rotten gift from Gardenia. He jumped you through hoops of fire for three years. Turned your world around so *you're* guilty for what *he* did to *you*. The man's a prince.'

'I'm tired of your mouth, you know that? Words, words, words.'

Charlie manufactured a sigh and rose to his full height.

'Enjoy the coffee, Della.'

'Why not? It's my brand.'

'There were others, you know. Girls who had just as bad a time as he gave you. What about them?'

'None of my business. Or yours.'

'If you say so.'

'Where are you going?'

'Out. Away. What does it matter?'

'You're *always* walking out.'

'So are you. Without moving your pretty feet.'

'Being scared is a way of life. They'd take my face, I talk to you. To anybody. He'd have that black goon Shaggy Coltrane hold me down and take my face off layer by layer. Even had Shaggy show me the bat studded with nails they'd use . . . I so much as hinted at . . . anything.'

Charlie looked sleepy and held up a lazy palm.

'He'll do nothing of the kind. Take my word.'

'Your *word*? Stop . . . spinning my brain.'

'Have a good life, Della. I won't bother you again.'

Della dug fists at her hips to sneer.

'Another talker. Another Glenn. He *talked* the good life. But when it came right down to it, he folded easier than a tourist map. Leaned on me when the rent came due. When the bills swamped us. That *all* you do? Talk? When what's needed here is . . .'

Charlie's 'Yes?' was as soft as blown chiffon.

'Nothing. I . . . nothing.'

'That the bedroom?'

'Now he's *tired*.'

'Of talk, yes.'

'Ah, so *that's* where you're coming from. Give the sad bitch a tumble. Open up her can of worms and get her blabbing herself into a casket.'

'No, Della.'

'I'm so easy, that it? Stay the hell away from me.'

'All right.'

'The talker leaves. I knew it.'

'Yes, Della. All talk.'

'Stay away . . .'

Charlie cradled Della's face to hold her steady. Pulled her in against him. Ran a nail down her back. Arched her spine into him, and lost his tongue in her mouth as she opened up to him like a suckling infant. For Della there was vertigo and wonder and fear. Glenn Bath had been a fumbling inept, Doll Gardenia a self-absorbed mechanic who'd thought only of his own gratification, using Della as a piece of necessary equipment without needs of her own. This one was different enough to awaken feelings she had only guessed she was capable of. His mouth was a warm probe, his touch a breeze on her body, and Della felt she was being played like a celestial spinet.

The sunflowers on the drawn bedroom shade tinted Charlie and Della amber and gold and, as they sank together, Della's hair shone around her needful face like spun thread. Fear tensed her when Charlie's face moved down her body, and she swam in colours she had never seen before; every hue a chord she had played for uncaring ears in a thousand saloons. But now they were soft pastels

85

and bright primaries, singing through her in her own voice, as complete as the showcase album she should have made when it mattered. Perhaps now she would, and that strangely shocking thought stayed with her as all the colours splintered into rainbow shards with Della wanting more than there ever could be if she lived several lifetimes.

Charlie met Saul Chasen in a parking lot off Cahuenga Boulevard, and they talked without leaving their cars.

Della had shooed Charlie out to put her night face on, almost too shy to look at him directly in unsubdued light. Oscar had kept his knowing look, and Charlie had traded stares with the fish as he dressed, still coming to terms with the honest pleasure he and Della had shared.

'You've got the look of a guy's been there and back,' Chasen said around an unlit Chesterfield. 'Ain't a natural hustler, right?'

'You noticed.'

'Taking in the show tonight?'

'You're leering, Saul.' Charlie asked for a cigarette and took his time drawing it alight. Chasen was an irritant in a dull suit, as abrasive as dust under an eyelid.

'So I ain't Captain Popular with my pants outside my tights,' Chasen shrugged. 'There's only one bottom line, did you get anything I can use on your behalf?'

'On my behalf, or yours? Come off it, Saul, you wear two hats. And the one with the badge is a bigger size.'

'And you were Charlie Dance before the name transplant. Right now that stays under my badge hat, but things can change. The client turns back

86

into an alien bandit. Deportation and cuffs to LAX. Your choice.'

'And end it here? That's the last thing you want.'

'Oh, and what *do* I want, pally?'

'Doll Gardenia. Casey Pollard. And anybody else you can slam in front of a Grand Jury. If we use Miss O'Day for that, we do it my way.'

'You throw names around like confetti. Where's Pollard in this thing? That mother jumped to Italy three years ago.'

'And I've walked in his grounds outside Rome.'

'The hell you did,' Chasen's eyes narrowed, his lids fluttered. 'Not as a guest I'd say.'

'Not as a guest. You want to hear *my* proposal?'

'Of what? Marriage?'

'In a way. Interested?'

'Maybe I'm suddenly more interested in the walk you took through Bel Air.'

Charlie forced a laugh that became natural.

'And you haven't been checking on that all day?' he mocked.

'Ain't no hurry.'

'That means you people *are* surveilling Gardenia's estate. I did wonder.'

'You did, huh?' Chasen glared at himself in his rearview. 'Don't make me get crazy here, don't make me crazy!' He snapped a match at his cigarette to blend his smoke with Charlie's. 'So propose away . . .'

A sky-writing plane flew low to advertise some-body's paint, and Chasen had to listen hard through a six-cylinder drone to pick up every word Charlie threw at him. When the relative quiet came back, Chasen knew he hadn't misheard, but wished he had.

'You're *serious*?'

'As I'll ever be,' Charlie said. 'A friend of mine has

a tavern down there, and he's already contacted Della's agent. She's been offered two solid weeks in San Diego at an engagement fee Streisand wouldn't turn down. You supply the round-the-clock protection.'

'Wearing which hat?'

'Both, if the FBI stands for it.'

'She knows you for less than twenty-four hours, and now she's a target? For why suddenly? And who's coming after her?'

'Why ask me? I'm the alien, remember?'

'Wouldn't be Gardenia himself, would it?'

Charlie turned the key in the ignition. Flicked his butt away.

'Oh, I doubt that,' he said, backing out of his space with Chasen still thinking of questions. His Hertz rental took him back to Beverly Hills to check out of the hotel with three hours to kill before Della took the stage.

Chasen finished his smoke with moody bites. A black with an Orange Julius and a limping dog in tow tried to panhandle a couple of bucks, and the sky-writer came back to smother Chasen's pithy refusal. He set fire to a second Chesterfield without noticing, and used his rearview to hold a one-sided conversation with himself.

'All comes down to one thing, Saul,' he concluded. 'Dance wants that gal outta LA. All you have to do is figure out why.'

And he drove his Mustang away in search of answers.

In London, George Muscat raised Casey Pollard's answering machine for the fifth time. Swearing as he drove, he took himself home to Finchley through thin morning drizzle.

A fine instinct parked Charlie a full block down Vine, and he walked back to the club through warm night air. When he paused to admire Della's name on the marquee, he took in the street and the surrounding buildings. Checked out the patrons' parking area for cars he might have seen during the day, and went inside with that familiar feeling forming a cold spot in the centre of his back. He tried Harry's locked office on his way to the mensroom to wash his clean hands, and watched the crowd until Della came out of somewhere with swollen eyes. A waitress brought Charlie a large Irish and water, and he tipped her a five to keep her hovering.

'The piano lady doesn't look happy tonight,' he said.

'Got canned, honey. Her and three waitresses. Business is too slow for Harry. You want anything else, holler for Charlene. That's me.'

'Another in seven minutes, OK?'

'You got it, honey. Don't expect I'll lose you inna crush.'

Della sat at the piano without speaking, and went into 'A Theme For Guy' in a way that would have had Elton John reaching for a box of polka dot handkerchiefs. She followed that with some Ellington and a request for a Shorty Rogers number. Applause smattered and Della played as though alone in a night field of black volcanic rock. Harry the manager snarled at Charlene, ran figures through the cash register, and made for his office with Charlie on his heels. He had the door open before he realized Charlie was there, and was inside his office with Charlie smiling with all his teeth before he reacted. Feinting for the phone, he brought a fist up from the floor that should have sailed Charlie's head to the stars. Charlie helped the punch towards the ceiling with his rising shoulder. Dug a short left to a kidney, and emptied the bloating gut with a slamming elbow. Harry sat down as far as Charlie let him, and was dumped into his posture chair to do what he could to fill his lungs.

'You overreact, Harry.'

Charlie ripped the phone out of the wall and checked the desk drawers. Sure that the office gun was in the locked one, he didn't bother patting Harry down for his keys. He broke the house phone away from its desk mounting and dropped it into the waste basket.

Harry said 'Jesus' several times, held himself and looked up at Charlie through a collapsed black fringe. Asked what Charlie wanted with a scattering of expletives thrown in.

'Let's say I'm from the Labour Board. You laid off four people tonight. Why? And Harry, let's not discuss slow business, huh? If you were doing a favour for a friend of a friend, could be they're *both* friends of mine. Clear?'

'So I got a call. So what?'

'Any names get mentioned?'

'Are you . . . kidding? Something's busted. Can feel my ribs grate.'

'Harry, you're boring me.'

'Oh-K! I know the guy who called. He runs messages is all. Said I should let Della go. Said if I was connected I'd know better. In this town you don't question, right? You *do*. I laid off the waitresses to make it look good. And that's it boiled all the way down.'

'There a phone around here?'

'You ripped them out, for Chrissakes.'

'Tomorrow you put them back. You call the

message man. You tell him you did what was wanted, and that's all.'

'All? I don't . . .'

'Tell him more, he'll get curious. Pass it all on to that friend of a friend I mentioned. They might drop in to visit. And where would that leave you, Harry? In traction? Doing eighty down the freeway without a car? Think about it.'

'You *people*, Jesus. You wanted her fired, she's fired. What more d'you want? My fucking life?'

Charlie gave Harry a slate look that froze him.

'You sit there until closing. You lock up. You go home. Got it?'

Harry just nodded wearily, thinking of joining his brother-in-law in the dry cleaning business. Even skivvies with skidmarks had to be better than this . . .

Back in the bar, Della had finished her set, and sat with a small and excited man waving several sets of arms as he machine-gunned words at her. Harry's office stayed closed, and Charlene and the barman worked slowly, all that was required of them. Della's face questioned, disbelieved, questioned some more, then lit up as though charged with high voltage. The theatrical agent with all those arms had himself hugged, then it was Charlie's turn to face her new radiance. He would come to San Diego, wouldn't he? Sure he would. But right now she had to go home and pack. Catch the shuttle down in the morning. That didn't leave much time for, well, goodbyes, did it? Sure, we'll make hellos instead. About a week's time? Fine. See you there, and Della was gone away on a cloud of invisible happiness.

Charlie stayed for a decent interval, and was leaving when Saul Chasen sat to face him.

'Bourbon?' Charlie asked.

91

'Soda pop. I just now found out what went down in Bel Air.'

'Oh?'

'Somebody tore our friend Gardenia up. Pinned him to his bed with an ice-pick through his face. He's going through nerve micro-surgery right now in Palm Springs. He may have a permanent twitch in his left eye. He may drool out of one side of his mouth for the rest of his life. He may always have neuralgia in his lower jaw. One thing's sure, he won't be pleasuring the ladies this side of whenever. D'you wanna tell me about this?'

'How? You're telling me.'

'As if you didn't know more. But knowing you *do* ain't proving it, right? So don't answer, you limey fruitcake. Once I know where this is going, you're gonna lose that fuck of a smile.'

'Della's on her way to San Diego. Shouldn't you be?'

'Not yet awhile. Bourbon here, Charlene.'

'Irish for you?' Charlene asked Charlie.

'Why not?'

'And two packs of Chesterfields on *his* tab,' Chasen said, his knothole eyes full of Charlie's incredible calm.

'You got it, honey,' Charlene said. Sure of another fivespot.

Sitting on his rumpled bed, Casey Pollard played his message tapes until the truth of the matter sank in. Only two things mattered.

Who did that to Doll?

And why?

92

CHAPTER SEVEN

Malta: 17 May 1980

Valletta was as hot as a baked biscuit when Victor
Zammit sat over bitter coffee in Siren Street. Small
boats brought sailors ashore from an Italian water
freighter, and a luxury liner was refitting in the
Chinese-built dry dock. The old whore from the Gut
joined him to trade game humour in explicit Maltese,
and two women she knew tittered at her raw wit
before taking their Lascar clients away for a private
party. Victor stopped joking to tuck money into the
old whore's sleeve when they had the waterside café
to themselves.

'You speak now,' he said.

'There was a message for the man in my house.
They talked in Italian.'

'You speak this well, old woman. Myself knows
this is so.'

'But it is hard to remember without brandy and
more money.'

Victor showed his uneven white teeth. Tasting
something more bitter than his coffee. The ancient
bitch was trying to shake him down when there was
no need.

'You think I don't know about the money you hide
in your house? Your poor neighbours would like to
know this thing, eh? Come in the night to be rich,
and myself not there to protect your old bones.'

'You should be a son to this old one,' the old whore

93

sighed. 'I have been mother to your pleasures as all the saints know.'

'My body blesses you, mother. Now please my ears, or my tongue may slip one night, ha?'

'You will be generous? I need doctors and coins for the offertory because my time is close.'

'As always. Speak.' Victor could have snapped her scrag of a neck with one hand, and nobody would miss her but him.

'They spoke not very long. The man on the phone was the one from Catania who came here with you once. Carlo must take the English money man to a safe place. And the wife, until a paper is signed. This makes sense to you?'

'Maybe.' Victor would not be drawn further. 'When?'

'Carlo said police guarded the English people. It would not be easy alone. He would have to recruit help here. Your name was spoken then, and much money was mentioned.'

'Making you greedy, eh, mother of flesh?'

'Life is hard, though getting short, my son of appetite.'

'But your ears are long. What else was said?'

'Carlo said he would find you, but he hit his hand with his fist when he said this. Broke the pot under his bed with a kick. Then he came out to tell me to find you.'

'For which you took money, of course.'

The old whore showed bare gums and yellow molars.

'The church is an expense. I have to pay to atone. You know this.'

'And I have to pay for your ticket to paradise.' Victor passed crumpled notes across the table. 'Maybe you'll find me tomorrow. Come here then.'

'Carlo has anger and a Jewish gun.'

'So do I, mother. Go now.'

Victor watched the old whore hobble away across burning cobbles, thinking of Carlo Fabriano's Uzzi, and wondering if he should have sold it to the Sicilian in the first place. An early profit could be an expense in the long run, he told himself. Wise after the event. Needing a drink, he cycled to the yacht club on Manoel Island to wait for Charlie's call in the member's bar.

Dance would know what to do next.

An hour later, he took Charlie's instructions with roundels of sweat spreading from his armpits to soak his Rolling Stones T-Shirt. Mick Jagger's mouth had a wet look when he cycled to the house near Fort St Elmo, and helped Carlo Fabriano lay careful plans for abduction. With the right diversion, it should be easy enough.

He hoped.

Inspector Ellul marched into Charlotte Bujega's chambers without knocking to catch her reading a postcard from Italy. He took it out of her hand, read it quickly, then skimmed it back at her before she had time to protest.

'How dare I indeed,' he said, seating himself in a clients' chair. 'Your postman was pleased to show it to me before making delivery. I was merely confirming what I already knew. You got three kisses to my two. I should be jealous.'

'And thoroughly ashamed of yourself,' Charlotte said.

'Oh, but I am. Yet I claim absolution in the name of justice.'

'Not from God, and not from me.'

'Then I am found wanting in the divine court of

Advocate Bujega. My world trembles as I do.'

'I don't know where he is, you know,' Charlotte said. 'And my next appointment is in five minutes.'

'Then I'll be brief. Have dinner with me this evening, and we can exchange views on this matter. There is a place in Rabat I should like you to try, the chef does wonders with desserts, and his rabbit is a joy.'

'I don't think so.'

'But you must. Our Mr Dance said you should be nice to me, right there on that postcard. He exhorted me to do likewise in your case. I don't see we have much choice, do you?'

'And why should he push us together like this?' Charlotte said, trying to fathom the reasoning of both men.

'Matchmaking, perhaps?'

'Ridiculous,' Charlotte's face flushed apricot.

'I thought that too. Shall we say six-thirty here?'

'Shall we say seven there? I'll drive myself, thank you.'

'And can leave when you wish. You are a very singular lady, Advocate. Seven at the Bird Cage it is.'

Charlotte shuffled papers looking at the postcard, and had trouble concentrating when Mrs Corbello droned on about land leases in her village with Charlie Dance haunting the air behind her chair. Nothing but his biting smile had any substance all the rest of the afternoon.

George Muscat rubbed his heart when Casey Pollard sat in his office after catching the first available flight to London. Pollard looked sleek and rested beside the Maltese, and the Chicagoan was in no mood for further delay, his finger a gun stabbing at Muscat's chin.

'Listen up, George,' he said. 'I burned a couple thousand dollars over the wire to the US, only to come up empty. Zilch. Nothing. The family says Doll must have had some local West Coast beef. No way it connects with family business in Chi or the Apple. The figuring is this: Doll maybe hit on some broad has a guy in tow who don't care to share his bed bunny with anybody. That maybe stands up if you forget how entry to the Gardenia fortress was made. No way was that the work of some beach bum hot in the crotch over some woman. And used-car salesmen don't learn to cut through steel bars underwater without they *ain't* used-car salesmen, right?'

Muscat mumbled a tired 'Uhuh' to keep Pollard going.

'And no way was it a South American hit. Those banana heads would have turned Bel Air into a slaughter house. Chainsawed the hell outta Doll, the girl, the dogs, the help. Mushed everything to chuck. This guy has to be a pro with a personal problem to use his expertise that way.'

'Over a woman? The one Doll's running now?'

'She's clean. Came straight from the Philippines last fall. Got just enough American to order a Coke. No family there or anywhere, and had her maidenhead intact when Doll bought her.'

'He'd know if anybody would,' Muscat grunted.

'Yeah. And Shaggy Coltrane is the best soldier money can buy. I mean, how was he to know some clown would come at him outta the pool area? Cold cock him to hit Doll with the ugly stick? Doll's face is a mess, George. I mean totalled. And they thought they'd have to put Shaggy on life-support, he was such a melon case. Seeing double and gagging all the time. Trapped nerves and whatever, the medics think. And Shaggy used to spar with Foreman, for

Chrissakes. You don't take *that* mountain out with a bobby pin.'

Muscat laced moist fingers and bridged his thumbs.

Asked, 'Does this make Doll a liability?'

Pollard looked at Muscat like a man with a raised shoe stares at a roach he's about to mash.

'This ain't just *business* here. This is family, George. Doll ain't some nebish Brit you can stiff outta his store. Get your head straight on that unless you want a war.'

Muscat shrugged at Pollard's fury.

'Nevertheless,' he said evenly, 'with some lunatic after him, how can he operate for us? Sighing over a mirror in a locked room, when we need him functioning on the street where he belongs?'

'We can swing it. And Doll's pleasure hand can still hold a pen to sign the contracts. No big deal.'

'And if this pro decides to nail *us* to our beds because we're Doll's *family*, what then?'

'That's crazy and you know it.'

'Do I, Casey? Do I really?' Muscat ordered tea over the intercom and sat back with tented fingers, contemplating something more than buttered scones. 'There have been too many mistakes made already, and I'm a careful man. Remember that.'

'Careful, or running scared?'

'You don't know better, there's the door. And it wasn't me who thought up the scheme to ship the stuff and the money together, was it?'

'And you didn't say "No" either. That's one can you carry along with Doll and me. No squirming outta that.'

Muscat let that slide. Said, 'Doesn't any of this strike you as odd, Casey? The ship sinks, then Doll

98

loses half his face? How about it ties together some-how?'

'Tell me how, George, and *I'll* buy *you* the big cigar.'

Muscat tapped a moist temple.

'Something here tells me I'm right. Maybe some-body wants us at war over this.'

'Who?' Pollard half-sneered. 'And who would *that* be, George?'

Muscat shook his head with distaste. Not know-ing. No longer trusting the man from Chicago, or his friend in a Palm Springs clinic. Without knowing why, Muscat was sure the two Americans had brought trouble to his door, and it was time to plug the holes in his defences. He was too old for sudden surprises.

A stripper brought a tea tray and wiggled back into the club before Pollard said, 'Instead of seeing shadows, how about you get this business in Malta settled? Like now?'

Muscat thought of Carlo Fabriano in Valletta and smiled like a bloated corpse.

'Tonight,' he promised. 'Milk and sugar?'

'Black. With scotch,' Pollard said, and as he watched Muscat pour tea from a porcelain pot covered in delicate roses, distrust was a third presence in the room.

Victor Zammit drove the rented panel truck to Valletta through a windblown dusk, and patted the magnum taped to his ankle before drawing up outside the old whore's house near Fort St Elmo. Carlo Fabriano threw himself into the back to cover himself with sacking, but not before Zammit had seen the Uzzi. Carlo had it wrapped in towelling, but the shape was unmistakable. And damn Satan's hooves, Victor even had the serial number of that weapon memorized. The late Mario Fabriano had been a certifiable crazy, but the elder brother was as unstable as a one-legged table, with his burro bray of a laugh, and his taste for underaged girls. The old woman had gone to a lot of trouble to feed nymphets to Carlo before taking his money and running to church for absolution – information Victor had wisely chosen not to pass on to Charlie Dance.

In Floriana, Victor said, 'Myself told you no guns, friend.'

When Carlo laughed in reply, Victor bounced him through a line of potholes to silence the bastard, damning him in the names of a thousand saints as he drove to the heights above Mistra Bay.

Parking in a grove of stunted vines, Victor led Carlo down through terraces of peach and orange trees, taking the long back route to the Cunningham's villa. The dried earth kicked up like fine sugar to choke them, and Victor slowed the pace when they had to descend through a series of dry-stone walls. The clatter of a single stone might alert the men Inspector Ellul had posted to watch the house, and Victor was taking no chances with his incredibly precious hide.

In a gully choked by deadwood and prickly pear, Victor fed meat to a dog to keep it quiet, and made sign to show Carlo where to climb safely. Goats in a stone cairn watched them pass their pungent roost, and a yellow dog skirted them in the darkness, intent on his own business. Victor found the stone boundary wall by feel, and swarmed up the broken stone with Carlo panting behind him. Locked up for weeks with little girls for company was no way to keep fit, and Victor noted Carlo's ragged breathing with gratitude when he pulled on his ski mask and dropped into the garden. Telling Carlo to wait by the carp pond, Victor edged past the unlit pool and crossed the patio. Light showed through a chink in a curtain, and muted music accompanied ribald lyrics as Victor climbed to the first floor balcony. Getting inside took him no time at all, and he went down the unlit stairs to peer into the big living area.

Granny saw him first, and almost sank to the floor in fright. Then Flo saw Victor, and she swayed with closed eyes, muttering what could have been a prayer.

'You don't worry, mister, lady,' Victor said. 'Charlie say I come, bring you to him.'

The two old people stared at Victor until he had repeated his set speech three times. Then they were moving about, collecting things to take with them.

'No things. Just you, Charlie say. Myself say so too. Come.'

And they followed Victor up the garden as the watching policemen stank up the interior of their police car with cigarette smoke.

The candlelit atmosphere at the Bird Cage was far too intimate for Charlotte Bujega and Inspector Ellul, and the waiter despaired of pleasing them for his cousin the police sergeant's sake. He sulked over a cigarette in the kitchen and let the owner serve sweets and coffees. Hell, the police never paid their bills anyway, every Maltese knew that.

Charlotte was ready to develop a convenient headache, and Ellul had rubbed his moustache to a straggle when his police sergeant came bustling in to salute and whisper. Ellul's shy smile went away, and Charlotte watched the transformation without comprehension. Ellul sat bolt upright with squared shoulders, those sad and liquid eyes of his snapping light enough to guide ships into port. His sodden moustache bristled full again as sinuously as a black rodent shifting in sleep. His mouth firmed up, and his stare made Charlotte feel as guilty as a triple murderess with the dripping axe right there in her pretty hand. He drained his coffee as if giving his mouth a military salute, smacked his lips like a gunshot, and was at attention when he apologized for having to leave. Gone away before Charlotte could respond. There was the bang and choke and squeal of cars leaving in a hurry, then Rabat went back to sleep.

'And a good night to you,' Charlotte said weakly as the owner hovered with a jug of coffee and liqueurs on the house. The sergeant had had trouble articulating a long English name, breaking it down into too many syllables. *Conn-eeng-a-hammm*.

'Just the bill,' Charlotte said.

'The bill?' The owner's face was doing wild things to itself in the shifting candle light. 'The bill?'

'Tonight you get paid,' Charlotte said in Maltese, grimly wondering if the owner's heart would explode at such a wonder. And, on impulse, she passed the Cunningham's villa on her way home to find Ellul's car parked on the drive with two police vehicles. After a conflict between her legal and feminine selves, Charlotte left without entering the villa to confirm her suspicions. Intuition told her Ellul would be in her office at start of business without fail.

'But where are *you*, Charlie?' she wondered, driving slower than a Pasadena geriatric.

Granny studied the second man whilst he helped Flo into the black panel truck. His ugly laugh made him different from somebody Granny had recently

102

known. The voice was familiar too, but hearing it emerge from that known-unknown face made it strange to his ear. The voice shouldn't have a face, and that was puzzling in the extreme to a man who had lumbered vertically for a quarter-mile in house slippers and darkness.

The man in the ski mask took a circuitous route to Valletta, and the house they were bundled into smelled of whorehouse perfume and stale bedding. Forced up unlit stairs to the top floor, the mean room they were given had two steel cots and a smoking oil lamp. The windows were shuttered and barred, and a small pine table held a water jug and bowl. The towels were greyer than November, and the night pots under the cots told Granny there were no modern conveniences.

'Be a Spartan, dear,' Flo whispered. 'It can't be for long.'

Then they both saw the Uzzi and the papers Carlo Fabriano wanted signed, and Granny knew it was Mario's brother who had threatened him over the telephone. That his signature would finance a $5 million salvage operation.

'You lied,' Granny told the man in the ski mask.

'Myself do that to keep you living,' Victor Zammit said through muffling wool. 'Now you *stay alive* by writing your name. This Carlo can't shoot you for one month then, eh?'

And Granny signed to give Flo thirty days to hope in.

Charlie took Victor Zammit's call in a motel off Selma as the hot noon sun turned the parking bay blacktop to glop between the glittering cars. The bonus he promised Victor could have sailed him around the world if the big Gozitan so chose, and was almost worth chancing a bullet to keep the Cunninghams alive. Like Charlie Dance himself, Victor did things his way, and he would come up with a way to get the money without a scratch on his hide. 'My promise to you, friend-brother Charlie,' he said, clearing down under Maltese starlight, still bemused to talk to someone in a time-zone on the other side of the planet. And whilst Victor put himself to bed aboard his boat, Charlie cruised the gay bars of Selma Avenue, looking for a freckled kid whose street name was Amadeus because of his fondness for giving head jobs to the strains of Mozart.

CHAPTER EIGHT

Amadeus wore a tank top, had his hair Afroed into red frizz, and rode a powerful dirt bike adapted for purring the boulevards. When he took off his helmet his hair sprang out on all sides like a bouquet of stage flowers, and he looked like a nodding sunflower when he walked his loping walk. Charlie dozed in his rented Hertz whilst Amadeus did his afternoon thing in company with his friends, and followed him home through early evening traffic. Amadeus didn't cruise for tricks, he had a client list who contacted him by telephone, and Charlie could have led Amadeus home if he'd wanted to.

The condominium was a single storey complex around a pool, and the concrete paths were snaking curves through cactus, yucca and shrub beds that gave the illusion of seclusion to the tiny units that were designed not to overlook their neighbours' yards. Charlie parked in a vacant unit and turned on the bugging device a fellow Chasen knew had made up for him, tuning himself in on the telephone technique of Amadeus Walter Pithers III, previously of Meadowglen, Moscow, Georgia. A town that would never be ready for a nodding sunflower with capped teeth and a hipsway like ten Monroes.

The unit bleeped and Amadeus's answerphone gave him his messages. A worried business man up from Cleveland gave his name with a sweaty voice. A fried voice wanted the recipe for a taco dip and blew kisses. A whisper asked for an appointment at nine that evening, and a black voice growled for a return call. Now!

Charlie released his seat belt to work his stiff shoulders. He revolved his ankles and pinched his calves to keep himself from losing edge. The black voice was the one he was interested in, and he tapped the dash as a digital panel gave him the numbers Amadeus was punching out on his telephone.

'Come on, come on,' Amadeus said as the Bel Air number warbled at him.

'Uhuh,' the black voice said.

'Grouchy, aren't we? And I thought Palm Springs soothed the savage brow,' Amadeus said.

'Ohhh, uh, hi kid. How's it hanging?'

'You're asking me? You're the stallion here. Balls like Black Beauty.'

'Uh, who?'

'Illiterate but hunky. It's a famous horse. In a book.'

'Oh, books . . . yeah. You funning me, small stuff?'

'Of course not. Don't get ratty. You want tonight, or don't you want tonight?'

'Uh, yeah, I *need* tonight, kid. Lissen though, thass if you got Big Wilma on tap.'

'Are you *still* all nerve endings.'

'You'd better know it, kid. Wilma walks my spine, calms me alla way down to the basement.'

'I can get Wilma so long as you don't try prodding *her* with that elephant trunk you wear. That *has* to be understood.'

'And, uh, that Chinese gal. Does the needle thing.'

'Acupuncture. This does sound like a gay party you're planning.'

'I need it, kid. Them Palm Springs medics? Sheeit. Can't do nothing's worth doody on a shoe.'

106

'We'll make you well, baby. Have you back punching uglies out of the ring, no trouble at all. And I do looooove to see that.'

'Inna past, kid. Lessen you guys work miracles over there.'

'You want the whole evening, lover?'

'There any other kind?'

'You know the rate, baby.'

'I know.'

'I'll need an hour.'

'Thass, uh, fine. Can grab me a shower.'

Amadeus laughed like a sorority queen.

'Nothing like being squeaky clean, clean, clean. The gel goes on better, you know? Creams on as cool as coooool.'

The black voice thickened and cleared its throat.

'Works, uh, for me.'

'And isn't that a fact? Bye . . .'

'Uh, yeah . . .'

Amadeus punched more numbers with local codes. Spoke to a masculine woman with a foul mouth who said she'd wear her frigging golf spikes if that animal didn't treat her with more defecating respect, and was calmed down by the size of her fee. A softer Asiatic voice said she would get a sitter, and to have the couch lowered to the right height in case she was a little late. Polite but firm. Amadeus cooed at her, and then spent a further ten minutes putting other hopefuls off for *that* evening. The Cleveland salesman said tomorrow would be fine with him so long as his wife didn't arrive a day early. Amadeus told him to check with him no later than five and said, 'Another pussy-whipped *puto*,' when he put the phone down to shuffle music tapes.

Charlie massaged his limbs whilst time dragged. Lights came on around the pool and in the plant beds, tinting the spikes and leaves jade green. A Pinto parked in the road, and a big woman got out carrying a heavy sports bag. She wore nurses' whites and shoes, and her cropped hair framed a face that could have been smashed by a flying wall. She lumbered past Charlie on tiny feet that were nimble enough to block a Wimbledon power play from any part of the Centre Court.

The Chinese woman came by line cab, and her black *cheong-sam* gave her the outline of a respectable insurance secretary as she carried her small box of tricky needles to Amadeus's unit. In the green light her face was girlish, yet her eyes were older than the dinosaurs, black seeds of patient disbelief that saw perversion and love with equal dispassion. Those ancient eyes disquieted Charlie, and he almost missed the next arrival.

The Cadillac found a space in a smooth rush, killed its lights, and allowed a big Negro to unwind from behind the wheel. The slamming door rocked the car on its suspension, and the big man walked slowly through the desert vegetation with his hand to the nape of his neck, clearly outlining the shoulder holster under his coat. He glanced across at the man sleeping in the rented Hertz as he was trained to, decided Charlie was harmless, and kept going. More concerned about the pain in his shoulders and the base of his skull, Shaggy Coltrane thought about Chinese needles humming away the pain. Irma's clever feet working the knots from his spine. The mouth of Amadeus playing chords on his member, and triple-tonguing butterflies of sensation up into his crotch like the best brass man in the Basie Organization jazzing out the blues like a musical vibrator . . .

Until Charlie got in behind him. Unbelievably

lifted 287 pounds of Shaggy Coltrane off the concrete. Slammed him down on his heels like he was a human golf flag. Shaggy's spine fell apart like broken crackers, singing him off into the dark void where pain and shock destroyed his embryonic bewilderment. Then he was being dragged like a sack of bones to a car, rolled inside like he was nothing special, and a lid slammed him into a coffin of steel where spare tyres usually lived with jacks and hazard flares and warning triangles.

And Shaggy Coltrane reached for fear as if it were a flag of surrender he could wave and wave and wave to make the good times come back . . .

Shaggy came back to coconut matting biting his back. A camping lamp threw shadows away from its cold white centre, hissing like a whore when the cheque bounced. Shaggy's arms were hung with weights he could not lift, and there was a slight springiness under him when he raised his head. His torso and legs were lashed to a board running off to a railed platform, and he could smell chlorinated water. That was stranger than anything Shaggy could think of right then, and he tried harder to squint the length of his body. He was naked. There was a canvas strap across his chest that cut into his pectorals as though they were mammaries. There were cans of Coke in supermarket stacks. Some 7-Ups. Even Dr Peppers. In rows along the side of a tiled area. And Shaggy knew where he was. Tied to a diving board over a swimming pool. Doll Gardenia's swimming pool. In Bel Air, for Chrissakes. He was back home as though he hadn't been away. Irma and Amadeus and the Chinese frail would have to party without him. Shaggy was home in an empty redwood, the dogs were kennelled, and Doll was having his face rebuilt in Palm Springs with his Eurasian pussy pretending Doll wasn't hideous as she went down on his lap to keep him happy.

Shaggy saw a man off in the liquid shadows. A naked man with a bandana across his face, a hose-pipe leaking water in his right hand until he adjusted the jet to a thin stream strong enough to bounce rocks off a gravel path. The hose played up Shaggy's body. Cooled him. Then hit him full in the face. Battered his nostrils so hard he had to take air through his mouth. The hose was jammed down his throat. Filled his gut with all the water in the world. Rivers and oceans of water. Pumping him up like a human water bed. Drowning him from the *inside*.

Shaggy tried to bite on the hard plastic nozzle. To bite the water off. But it chuckled down into his stomach. Bloated him to a soggy quiver with his belly as hard and as big around as a medicine ball. He urinated in long streams but it didn't help, and he sobbed quietly when the hose withdrew. Dribbled water and thin puke over himself as the solids in his system backed up into his raw mouth. A thin gruel that tasted of every ghetto smell from across the border when he'd drunk margeritas and laughed at dumb peon kids fighting over the coins he threw.

Shaggy tried not to hypervent. Breathed as though he wore a gumshield in the ring. Fought helpless-ness as he'd fought the best before he learned the big money was outside the ropes. Leaning on frightened loan sharks and dopers instead of hungry opponents who would kill for the glory of a title shot. He could beat this naked shit at his own game if he could just keep sane and stop weeping.

The naked guy said something Shaggy didn't

110

catch. Was shaking up a can of Coke like he was mixing cocktails for a very private party. The can hissed open, the vent blocked by the guy's thumb. The guy's naked foot was on Shaggy's forehead, forcing his head back over the edge of the diving board. His neck stretched to its limit, Shaggy opened his mouth to snatch air, only to have a wad of material balled into his mouth. Soda suds shot into his nostrils. Fizzed up into his brain and exploded there. A thousand volcanoes went critical at the root of his tongue and blew up. Blew the top from several mountains Shaggy's mind could never climb. Scattered his thoughts like sprays of molten magma, and all Shaggy wanted was to confess and go home to momma.

Shaggy tried to talk against the gag. To trade anything for his sanity. It was breaking up like unstable emulsion on old film. Grain as big as dimes splitting into a mad spectrum of colours that made no sense. And the streaming soda kept coming, punching up into his skull harder than Marciano or Erskine or Ali or Foreman. Shake, fizz, BLAM. Cans bobbed in the pool, and a regiment of them waited to be fizzed up and shot into Shaggy's drowned brain. He gabbled and pleaded inside his throat because the words jammed up behind the gag. Christ and Blue Bloody Murder, he was gonna drown six feet *above* a swimming pool.

It was *insane*.

And the bubbles streamed and streamed. And stopped.

The gag went away to disgorge words. Tumbles of them.

The nice naked man listened to everything Shaggy had to say. Prompted here and guided there. Nicely, whilst he smoked one of Doll's blended cigarettes

111

right down to the black and gold tip. Smoked another whilst Shaggy confessed he'd masturbated over snitched girly magazines. About the first male butt he'd stroked. The way he liked guys as well as girls. But wholesome, sir, truly. Those appetites that came in the night and wouldn't go away. You know.

There was talking about Doll and Casey and all that Panamanian circuit of snow and skag and dough and on and on and on. How it came across the Mexican border. Right through the bandit territory between Tijuana and San Diego. Sure Doll had a bad thing about Della. That's Doll, right? He's an owner. Like other guys have racehorses or show pooches. Doll had dolls, right? But Shaggy wanted the nice naked man to *understand Shaggy*. Really *know* him. *Deep down.*

But the kind naked man went away to make phone calls, his voice echoing around the pool area with edges of flint and steel. Sounding *like* Shaggy. Calling all Shaggy's friends to a party at the redwood house. Amadeus and Wilma. The Chinese woman. Guys Shaggy knew from Long Beach who would bring beach bunnies to romp in the grounds. Butch broads and their brides from the leather circuit. A couple of gals Doll had discarded and Shaggy liked fine. A couple of torpedoes from Palm Springs who never shed their coats in the desert sunshine and were into college kids or younger. Tankers from the gym not too punchy to enjoy tankards of suds around the pool. People Shaggy had kept well apart for reasons he couldn't remember, and he wept in real gratitude as the man lit up the place from attic to cellar and opened the security gates for all Shaggy's friends to party with the new Shaggy. The *real* Shaggy Coltrane.

And he promised himself he would stop crying when they arrived, but not yet awhile. Not *just* yet . . .

Saul Chasen had his night bag half way to his Mustang when the phone rang inside the apartment. Unlisted FBI numbers don't ring unless some other seersucker needs words in your ear, and the family who detects together, stays together. Chasen was a family member of a legal cosa nostra with fat federal grants and too much paperwork. San Diego had never seemed so distant when he plodded back to lift the receiver.

'Yeah?' he said. Hating himself for answering his country's call.

'How're you getting on with your limey ding-bat, Saul?' It was that sallow roundbacked non-drinking Baptist slease H. J. Parrot who wore the night ears on the Gardenia stake-out. He and his partner Blackwell must be having a slow time watching nothing up there in the cool of Bel Air.

'You got words, string 'em,' Saul grunted.

'Being so *close* to the Mexican border makes you San *Dago* people *soooooo* touchy,' Parrot said into Chasen's annoyed ear. The fruit sounded like Amadeus talking dirty to a client.

'The night shift does something to the brain, Parrot. I hear you and Blackwell check each other out with mirrors in case you've *really* become the Undead.'

Parrot wisely changed tack. Turned flat and serious.

'We thought you might like to get up here, Saul.'

'And bring a looking glass? No thanks.' Chasen unzipped his night case for cigarettes. The cello-

113

phaned pack slid away and bounced out of reach.
'Shit.'

'What?'

'Whassat?'

'It's all going screwy up here.'

'What is?'

'Up here. Coltrane went out, Coltrane came back.
He was booked for a party with Amadeus, but he
came back. With another guy.'

'Who?'

'Unknown. He had to help Coltrane into the
house.'

'A big guy, huh?' Chasen bowed at the knees to
kick the cigarettes his way.

'Tall, yeah. But a pencil beside that mountain.'

'You get a voice print from the house bugs?'

'Not a thing. They didn't put the lights on for
almost an hour. Then the redwood lit up like Christmas *and* New Year. Half of LA turned up when
Coltrane made calls. Now the needles are off the
dials with all the *schtick* coming over the phones.
Wildest party I ever heard.'

'With Gardenia away? He'll mince Shaggy's balls.'

The Chesterfield pack skated into the skirting and
stayed there.

'You should get up here, Saul. I'm telling you.'

'Why? I'm due in San Diego tonight.' Chasen laid
on the floor. Trapped the pack between his feet and
drew his knees up, dropping it on his chest. Ripped
foil and got one in his mouth. 'Matches?' he said
patting pockets. 'Matches, matches . . .'

'You know that Calypso singer has the mansion
cross the way?'

'So?'

'Sent his security guard across to tone the noise
down. The guy went home running. Without his

114

Mace, gun and pants. Painted silver.'

Chasen changed hands to reach matches from his right hand suit pocket. 'So? So what?'

'The whole neighbourhood is calling Hollywood Station. We laid a dime there, and the Watch Commander is going apeshit. Saul, you *gotta* come. A Silver Cloud took off down the hill on its own. Took out an El Dorado, a Mercedes, and an unidentified tourer. Missed the canyon turn and's playing submarines in some millionaire's pool. Saul, I appeal to you, it smells all wrong up there. If the LAPD go in, we can sneak in on their coattails. Saul, you listening? We can get in there without breaking our cover.'

Chasen flared a match and sucked smoke deep.

'Saul?'

'I'm *here*, damn it.'

Parrot sounded to have handsful of hair in each fist. The agent was as rattled as a chauvinist's sabre.

'Saul. Shaggy wouldn't *do* this normally. It's outta *character*! He gets his jollies *away* from home. Blackwell agrees, you *see*?'

'You sound like Wilder being goosed by Pryor.'

'What?'

'I'll be there.'

'Make it soon, Saul, huh? Real soon.'

'Sure, Parrot.'

Chasen spilled ash near a bedside tray. Grinned. Sounding so very unconcerned had been worth the effort. Parrot would have bitten his nails down to the elbow by the time Chasen reached the hills. He took the Mustang north on smoking tyres, and made Beverly Hills in fourteen short minutes. The LAPD had the canyon road sealed off, and the Highway Patrol were redirecting local traffic. Flashing the tin got him past the barrier, and there were mobile units all around the estate. A lieutenant he knew was waiting for papers from the overnight court to make a bust on private property, ad the decibels coming from the redwood could have parted lacquered hair at 200 yards.

'Any reason I shouldn't wander in?'

'And screw things up?'

'I could have been invited to this thrash. Hold my coat, would you, lieutenant.'

'We come in, I don't know you from smoke, Saul.'

'Bust me too. What the hell.'

Chasen strolled up the drive past a gaggle of beach buggies that had torn up the lawn. A girl in a cottonwood dangled bare legs and watched the sky for Martians, a long roach in her slack mouth. She wasn't aware of the man beside her, or what he was doing to her unresponsive body. Some gays were off in the trees shouting poetry as they danced their spangled bodies around in sweaty abandon, and a small schnauzer had a whole cooked chicken to himself, worrying it like the rats his less pampered forebears hunted.

The outer pool was heaving with bodies and debris, and a white grand piano had been hauled out of the house for three girls to hammer with their elbows. Two men with overcoats over their swim-suits fought it out toe to toe watched by a llama who spat once in a while to keep up their spirits. Too many Coors and Olympias had turned their scrambled brains back to younger days, and the two tankers fought like Tunny and Dempsey until they fell down, out of wind. Chasen stepped over them and past a fire that had been lit to toast marsh-mallows that were being smeared rather than eaten, a body paint for the sweet of tooth. By the open front door an unconscious drunk had scaled a lattice of ivy, only to bring it down on top of him, and lay under it and the sky, blind to the world as he was given last rites by a girl in bikini bottoms.

The house was a heaving shambles of dancing people and scattered furniture, and there was food and booze on every available surface. Chasen got himself seriously kissed by a beach bunny with at least two pounds of silicone in each monumental breast, and he missed her when she found somebody taller. Nobody gave a damn who Chasen was, and he made three Sunset Strip cocaine pedlars working through intermediaries, ever cautious. In the kitchens, heavy women in severe suits held some kind of an auction for a thin girl standing naked on the table. A black woman made 'honky stew' from unopened packets of anything from Surf to Jello in a brass cauldron that had lived on the wall as decoration, and was adding cutlery to the mess to hear the silverware plop into sludge. Her laugh was as merry as her bare and jiggling buttocks.

Chasen found the inner pool area off a lobby, and shifted two overturned chairs before he could sidle through the soundproofed door. Light came from a storm lamp hung from a rail, and Chasen thought he had the place to himself until he picked up low sobs coming from a man lying supine on a diving board. Picking his way through soda cans to climb the steps, Chasen found himself looking down at Shaggy Coltrane. He was forced to swallow several times before he could utter a sound, and it wasn't much when he did. Just a soft 'hoooo' of breath that he had wanted to be so much more.

Shaggy was as big as ever, but his persona had shrunk. He was an adult brown baby with nothing in his face but age and fear.

'I'll tell you,' Shaggy said, trying to please. 'I'll tell all of it like I done with the naked guy . . . You'll see . . . you'll see . . .'

'The Mexican Bubble Up,' Chasen breathed. 'You poor bastard.'

'I'll tell . . . I'll really tell . . .'

'Go ahead, Shaggy, I'm listening . . .'

Chasen wished he'd brought his jacket to cover Coltrane as he waited with the ruined fighter for the cavalry to arrive.

I did *this*? Chasen asked himself. Silently. I handed information to that maniac Charlie Whozits, and *this* is what he did with it? *This*? From fucking pocket profiles? So, all right. He's maybe busting this consortium all the way open. But this *can't* be the way, can it?

Can it?

Think of all the innocent kids this might save, Saul. How about no more babies born with the shit in their systems from mommy's polluted bloodstream? From daddy's Saturday Night Turn-Ons? The kids who *won't* get to be the sodomized victims of mommy's and daddy's freaky customers? Kids we *won't* find dead in trashcans with asses as bloody as empty eye sockets? Think of *them*, Saul. Of *them*. Not about this adult baby and his fatcat masters who give the shit away in playgrounds to hook another generation of slaves to the habit they sell. For 50,000 per cent profit per annum, baby. And fuck the IRS. Tax free!

Shaggy was talking about the Panamanian colonels. About the badlands between Tijuana and San Diego. Deadman's Canyon where the merchandise crossed amongst migrant pollos lemming north to escape poverty.

'I'm listening, Shaggy, I'm listening . . .'

And Saul Chasen listened dry-eyed. Holding a baby man Charlie Dance had cracked open cleaner than a walnut. His portable machine whirring it all down on tape.

CHAPTER NINE

Palm Springs was having one of its windy days. Hot turbulent air came whirling out of the desert to thrash amongst the condos and sport complexes, hotels and estates, and roared around the clinic where Doll Gardenia lay anaesthetized.

Dried mesquite tumbled through the traffic in skeletal dance to cause accidents here and there, adding to the highly nervous atmosphere that kind of wind brings. It ruined picnics and barbeques, blew wave motion across swimming pools, sliced shots and ruined handicaps on the golf courses. Tennis pros mourned lost fees in empty courts, traffic cops snarled and wrote citations for anybody who wasn't the mayor, and several rocky marriages came apart at the seams as the shutters banged, screen doors slammed, and house dogs hid in their kennels. Garbage pails lost their hats, power lines came down, and as the lofty palms beat their fronds in a steady stream of grit, the sky took on a smoggy cast just to make Los Angeles tourists feel at home.

The wind turned a plumber into a homicidal maniac for the forty seconds it took him to shoot his wife in the head, miss her three poodles, and to blow off his right ear with his last round. At the police station he waited an hour for somebody to hear his confession. The cop they sent out there barfed over the plumber's wife when she sat up as he was checking for a pulse. And with the wind in his ears, he put her in the same ward as her husband, and went to a bar to blow his mind on margaritas. The 'corpse' had lost the same ear as her plumber husband, and they were reconciled in the hospital chapel where they decided guns and dogs had no place in their future. And hand in hand, plumber and wife took their sutured headaches home.

A surgical orthodontist and a plastic surgeon had finished the root canal work on Doll Gardenia's lower left jaw when the main power failed and the emergency lighting system cut in.

'Seven seconds,' said the orthodondist. 'Not bad.'

'You do nice work, Dave,' said the surgeon. 'We'll let him drain overnight. With those two molars gone, I don't want abscesses forming under the new bridge when it's fitted. The last thing I need are complications when I work on the lateral walls of his mouth.'

'This face has been elevated more times than Otis, right? You'll be seaming scar tissue to scar tissue, he decides he just *has* to look the right side of fifty again.'

'Seems the only places I haven't taken graft tissue from are the soles of his feet. He's already shaving behind the ears, and look at that exit wound. I go in now, he'll pucker up like a prune. I could try taking dermis from his shoulders. Might be enough follicles to match his facial hair. It's a rough one.'

The orthodontist stripped off his gloves and grinned.

'Lift some from his hirsute butt. Let him shave pubic hair for a change.'

'A gluteous maximus he may be, but he's *my* asshole, Dave.'

'Ours. Shared fees, remember?'

'One buttock each. Except we're working the other end.'

'How can you tell?'

121

Laughing into their masks, the two specialists had their patient wheeled to the recovery room where Doll Gardenia dreamed he shaved a face that continually tried to sit on him, and groaned nonsense to the nurse watching his vital signs on a monitor.

Saul Chasen reached San Diego at noon, and made for a cockroach hotel in San Ysidro with eyes as grainy as a pirate video. Fat Indio was behind the desk, and Thin Indio his brother was taking out the trash, a paper sack of cans from one of their regular parties. The local kids would stomp them flat and sell them for recycling, maybe earning enough pesos to put more than beans and cornbread on the family table once a week. San Ysidro was a little Mexico commune surrounded by the wealth of an American city, and dubbed Dos-Exxes-Ville by Chasen's operatives who did their tours there.

Chasen took his key and tramped up two flights to the flyblown corridor outside his suite. Once inside the door, he was back in real America where air-conditioning purled at fitted carpets and teak furniture, and the walk-in fridge contained enough food to feed half the town for a week. Chasen took a beer to the shower and padded about reading stuff that had spilled from the Fax and Telex machines. There was nothing that wouldn't hold for a while, and his bed was as inviting as a willing woman until he found Charlie lying there in a towel.

'Something else,' Chasen sighed, tweaking himself a Chesterfield from the pack on the bedside table. 'Welcome to the border, but how come I didn't see your Hertz in the street?'

'I found the toughest looking kid – paid him to garage and clean it for ten bucks a day. Plus a bag of groceries for his family.'

'You make yourself at home – in more ways than one.'

'Street kids are street kids anywhere in the world. It's the one thing that doesn't change.'

'Maybe I'll try it some time.'

'Manoel knows you, so maybe you should. Bright kid, knew exactly where I was coming. Told me I shouldn't play cards with the manager of this dump. Or his brother.'

'What're you? A tour guide?' Chasen asked. 'And get the hell off my bunk. I need to crash.'

Charlie flowed upright like a stretching cat.

'Thought you'd take the double in the next room. Sorry.'

'Singles for me since the divorce. I don't get to reaching for what ain't there.' Chasen punched the pillows his way and flopped on his back to draw smoke.

'Maybe you should go out and party more.'

'The kind you organize?'

'Me?'

'You. I was there, pally. LAPD processed forty-seven misdemeanants, seven technical vagrants, and nine possessors of illegal substances. Three drunks on burglary charges – the kind who pocket household trinkets as "keepsakes", and bagged an unpermitted hand gun. It was strapped to his chest whilst *he* was strapped to a diving board. Told us some naked man did that to him, can you believe it?'

'Should I?'

'Shaggy Coltrane was very forthcoming.'

'Is that good?'

'Better than what else went down. Like the two gooney birds high on H who tried to fly out of a cottonwood. Broke a whole raft of bones when they

123

floored the cops trying to net them. Some of them *theirs*.'

'Heroin does that to people.'

'But who did *that* to Shaggy?'

Charlie shrugged, his slate eyes cold.

'The naked man you mentioned?'

'Now who would buy that?' Chasen sneered.

'Not you, I take it?'

'A naive like good old Saul Chasen? Sure I bought it. Like I bought Amadeus and Wilma walking free. Like I bought Shaggy Coltrane's request for protective custody. Like it wasn't even *his* gun he was wearing. Like his gun is a pretty Colt Python .375 magnum registered all nice and legal with Firearms & Tobacco. Like the gun in his holster was a beaten up old Smith & Wesson he'd never even seen before. Yeah, I bought it all, and more.'

'With good reason, of course.'

'Yeah, like we all swallowed Doll Gardenia's lawyers getting power of attorney on account that their client is undergoing surgery, and is in no physical or mental state to answer charges of running a disorderly house in the exclusive residential area known as Bel Air. Don't that strum on your heart strings?'

'Not especially, no.'

'And here's me thinking you're the bleeding heart. The social conscience. The man beating the drum of freedom for the downtrodden masses. No?'

'Not this week.'

'No shit? Surprise, surprise. And you wouldn't give an infinitesimal fuck that the news boys just happened to pass by when all that excitement was going down up in Bel Air? That two big by-liners got their pieces picked up by the Eastern newspapers? That the Eyewitness News 'copter flew low to get TV pictures, further irritating the bezazz outta the local residents, huh? That it'll all be in the New York dailies tomorrow? That certain members of certain families will be pissed when they see Doll's "party" all over the fucking media, like he's suddenly a tainted social name who won't ever get invited to another polite Hollywood thrash?'

'Why should I?'

'Maybe because you figure he'll get invited to another kind of party. More select. Just him, a couple of hoods with pre-mix cement, and an oil drum teetering on the banks of the East River? That more to your taste, Mr Naked?'

'Slow down, Saul. You lose me when you talk this fast.'

'Then you must talk like Concorde. Nothing you say makes sense.'

'Must be we're both tired.'

'Sick and tired.'

'You've got this Shaggy fellow under wraps. That must be something.'

'All inadmissible, the whole crock. And you know it. Confessions exacted under stress, even by an unnamed third party, don't even get past the DA, let alone reach the court.'

'Why not act on what you've been told?' Charlie asked, leaning to yawn behind a hand.

'What?' Chasen gouted in smoke. 'On one man's uncorroborated word?'

Charlie pointed off at the southern wall of the bedroom.

'The border's a bare mile that way. Says so on my tourist map. Go make yourself a deal with the Mexican authorities. They can't all be Pancho Villas.'

'They can't, eh? A Tijuana cop's take home pay is a lousy forty five bucks a month. He has no medical

125

insurance. No union. He needs to drive his official vehicle more'n ten miles a week, *he* has to buy the gas. Even buys his own bullets. And the immigrants stream across in their thousands, wearing all they own on their backs. Maybe a few bucks in a shoe. We don't even know how many are robbed before they try crossing the border. On their own side. Not just by bandits on this side. By cops on their side. By anybody who can take one of those poor dumb *pollos*. The Beano cops figure they should take the dough before the *pollos* give it to some bandit on our side of the line. Keep it in their economy, rather than ours. I go across there, what am I, another rubber-necked tourist? You bet I am. And they get to know I'm a Fed, that's me for the Mexican Bubble Up treatment. And you know the efficacy of that, *right*? And don't snow me, Charlie.'

'I've heard of it.'

'I don't even blame those people for robbing their own. The *pollos* are so damned timid. It's a way of life over there. That's why they come here. We're rich, they ain't. We've got, they want. The *pollos* cross for the Good Life, and Border Patrol scoops all they can to send them back. Maybe ten per cent of all who cross. And knowing damned fine they'll all try again another tomorrow down the road. Christ, it's endless.' Chasen stubbed his smoke and lit another. 'Hell, we don't even *think* about the women and girls who get raped out there in the canyons. The kids who're orphaned for five or ten bucks. Make a deal with the Mexican authorities? Apeshit thinking, Dance. They *want* the exodus. The unlucky ones get dead. The lucky ones send money home, or come back rich. And that is sound economic sense to the authorities.'

'Pretty dismissive, Saul.'

126

'And who're you? My conscience?'

'Nope.'

'No, you're the clown who figures we can stop the drug shipment on the Mexican side before it gets on to American soil, right?'

'Crossed my mind.'

'Tell that to the tarantulas and scorpions. They'll maybe listen.'

'We're talking about people, Saul. Not statistics on some chart.'

'*Mexican* people. *Their* people, not *ours*.'

'Wrong. The war's on that side of the border, but the real losers are right here. The real targets of the drug barons. Your people, Saul, your young people.'

'You complete shit.'

'No contest. And everybody else loses if they don't wear a gun and a badge. They're all statistics.'

'And you'd know, huh? Another instant expert who's been here ten full seconds. Knows it all on account of he bribed a zitty car bandit *not* to steal the hubcaps off his rental. Jeez*uss*!'

'I also took out extra insurance.'

'It ain't even your car, Goddamnit.'

'But it's in my *care*.'

'Your care? Like Della O'Day? Like Shaggy's magnum?'

'Like Della, yes.'

'One without the other? Come *on*, Dance.'

'Della I need.'

'That simple, huh?'

'No, but that's how I see it. Get some sleep, Saul. I'll buy dinner.'

'You'll . . .'

'Good night, Saul.'

'Mr Popsicle. The Captain of Cool,' Chasen seethed

into his pillows when Charlie went away to occupy the double. 'The fucking guy's *unreal*.'

All the same, he wished he had a dozen Charlies on his team. Then the wheels would really hum. And Chasen carried that thought into blessed sleep like a flaming cross.

Doll Gardenia hated in luxury and discomfort.

He hated the wind beating the windows and fluttering the TV picture. Hated taking liquids through a straw, the mush of white meat and rice that was his staple diet, the maverick facial nerves that jerked his mouth out of alignment every three seconds. The taste of the draining cavities was awful, the anti-helcoid mouthwashes worse. He hated the neck brace he wore, and he loathed the armature holding his reset arm out from his body. And most of all he hated the smooth young lawyer from White, Hall & Marks telling him what he could and could not do.

'A bunch of crazies take over my house in my absence, and *I'm* responsible?'

'Yessir, legally you are. They were invited there, you see.'

'By Shaggy Coltrane. Who conveniently goes missing?'

'As we understand it, yes.'

'He invites a flock of gooney birds to my estate without my permission; takes off for parts unknown, and I'm for Chrissakes carrying the can?'

'That does appear to encapsulate the facts.'

'I'll sue the security people.'

'They have a legitimate out, sir. You ordered them to kennel the dogs and take care of the perimeter security. They were expressly forbidden to enter the house or grounds whilst you were away.'

128

'I'll sue the city for trespass.'

'You could, but it wouldn't stand up, I'm afraid. The police worked within the letter of the law. And, uh, any such action would not ingratiate you with the local residents. They have all applauded the police action. One of their security people was assaulted on your property, and there is the matter of the damaged Silver Cloud.'

'Say *what*?'

'Several are already bringing civil actions against you. The, uh, gathering was close to riotous. Our people are working on that, and we hope to settle out of court. Costs to be born by us, of course.'

'They threaten to sue *me*? And *we* settle? We don't get to fight those movie assholes?'

'Not advisedly, no.'

Gardenia stared with a twitching mouth.

'I pay city and property tax. I pay lunar orbit insurance. I pay for security. I even pay you people. And I come up empty? That's what you're telling me here?'

'I regret to say that I am.'

'*You* regret. Get the fuck outta here. Get me an adult. Better yet, get lost.'

'Uh, I will, of course, go. But you should speak with one of our senior partners before you, uh, make a decision you may regret.'

'The kid's all regrets!' Gardenia sprayed in spittle, wishing he could wipe his own drool away.

'Mr Camponello is on his way here right now, Mr Gardenia. And I'd strongly advise you listened to what he has to say—'

'Before I do something I *regret*?'

'There are complications you cannot have considered in the heat of the moment, sir.'

'Heat, you moronic puppy? Heat? Talk of heat from

129

a kid who ain't even sure what sex he is? Heat?'

'Sir . . . I, uh . . .'

'You get Joe Camponello in here right now. You hear?' Gardenia had been pressing the emergency buzzer, and two nurses came running to soothe and placate their feverish patient. 'No shots, you bitches. No shots,' he bawled, but the needle went home in his good arm, and the world receded in a rolling ball of echoes he had no way of following.

'Bitches,' he mumbled, going under.

San Diego wore her night face.

Gas flambeaus flared in front of the Wooden Palisades Restaurant, and the logged frontage looked like a stockade lit for an Indian attack. Charlie and Saul crossed a concrete moat by way of a jetty, and were bowed inside by a full-blooded Cherokee in a buttoned uniform. The foyer was a glade of palmettos and royal palms, and the carpet was lush enough to lose puppies in. Medicine masks from all over the Americas decked the walls, and the glass roof had lost its daytime tint to show starlight and night cloud. The waitresses wore short black satin sheaths with bolero tops, and wove through the tables like wraiths. Charlie ignored the line of hopeful diners waiting at the rope to catch the maître d's eye, and was bowed to a table before Chasen could worry about his unpressed suit.

'What're you, admiral of the fleet?' Chasen asked as drinks came without the need to order.

'That's the best sour mash this side of Canada, Saul. Taste it, then call me a liar.' Charlie waved the menu away.

'So it's good. You own this town, or what?'

'You're nothing without friends, Saul.'

'There's a story goes with this, right?'

'Larry Moffat is a friend of mine.'

Chasen took an ounce of liquor straight down. Felt it hit like velvet fire. Larry Moffat owned almost as much waterfront as the United States Navy, and the Mississippi sternwheeler moored across from the restaurant was his. Without Moffat, half the town's amenities would have remained paper dreams, and if there was such a thing as a noble house in San Diego, Moffat wore the crown.

'And this is where the O'Day chick gets to vamp the black notes for serious bucks?'

'Where *Della* will perform, yes.'

'Touchy, ain't we?'

'Just giving a talented lady her due.'

'And you figure she's untouchable here?'

Charlie turned his glass of Irish. Shook his head.

'No,' he said. 'They'll come.'

A tall white-haired man with the shoulders of a Sumo wrestler came out of a central forest to trade hugs with Charlie. Built like a deep-sea fisherman, he had a neck Chasen would have needed two sets of hands to circle. His frilled shirtfront was as wide as a snowbank, and his Savile Row suit had been cut by angels. When he slid into a chair, Chasen expected it to groan apart.

'Larry Moffat, Saul Chasen,' Charlie introduced.

'My compliments to the director when you next see him, Mr Chasen,' Moffat rumbled, his eyes on Charlie. 'You look good, kid.'

'So do you.'

The Director? Chasen gaped. *Of the FBI? Small beer like me*?

'How's your poker these days?'

'Haven't played a hand in three years, Larry.'

'Too busy sailing, huh?'

'Not much of that either.'

131

Moffat probed Charlie's face for clues. Found something only he could see, and jerked his head at the fourth empty chair with, 'That says it all, huh?'

'She left a lot of empty chairs, Larry.'

'Champion Jack Dupree said it right: Lose a good woman, you done lost half of your life.'

Charlie just turned his glass. Nothing in his face but shadows.

Chasen flagged himself another drink, feeling superfluous. Dance and Moffat were communing on a level he could only guess at, and it made him feel drab and isolated.

'I could set up a game. A lot of loose money in town,' Moffat offered.

'Not this trip, Larry.'

Moffat's smile was all teeth.

'Probably gut me anyway. Know how I met this character, Mr Chasen?'

'Nossir, I don't.'

'Going down for the third time, is how.'

'Ancient history,' Charlie said.

'Stow it. I was sailing a borrowed yacht from Gozo to Malta. Flat calm, and nothing to it. Then the world turned black, and one of those crazy Mediterranean storms came up out of nowhere. Chopped the sea to hell and gone. There was no way of going back, I was in a "commit" mode. I set a heading between Comino and Cominetto, two small islands that should have kept the sea out of my lap. Next thing I knew, no water under my keel. The wind scoured the channel dry, and turned my yacht to plastic toothpicks. The next scour was a wave higher than the Empire State, and I was seeing mermaids and a lot of green water when this fool came in after me. Came through on the next surge, and hooked me out of there. Lashed me to the deck with both legs broken, and nervous paralysis from a whack to the spine. Rode us home through seas I never want to see again, with me as helpless as a porpoise. Longest five hours of my life.'

'Long time ago,' Charlie grunted.

Moffat tapped his temple.

'In here, yesterday, He doesn't know me from diddly-come-squat. I'm just some boat bum ran out of luck, but I'm royalty until I'm patched up. He even flew some nerve specialist in from London. Came in every second day to play poker for matches to keep my mind off my troubles. And I never did beat the mother.'

A thin girl in tailored black whispered in Moffat's ear, apologized for the interruption, and had a phone brought to the table.

'For you, Mr Chasen,' Moffat said. 'Lift it to listen when the red light comes on. It's patched into my office, and I think the conversation will interest you. A certain party called me to utter veiled threats. I explained that I never do business over the phone, so now he's here, in person. He's all yours, Charlie.'

'I owe you one, Larry.'

Moffat smiled his brilliant smile.

'Only if your lady pianist *isn't* wondrous, Charlie.'

'I'd back her with a two high in thousands.'

'Isn't that what *I'm* doing?' Moffat walked Charlie away through palms and left Chasen with the telephone and a fresh drink.

Chasen fitted his portable tape machine to the earpiece and waited for the red light.

The FBI agent in an unmarked car outside the Palm Springs Clinic almost missed the black limousine's arrival. He had gone to find distilled water for his windshield washer, and was charging the hopper when the black limousine took the space next to his.

133

The agent blessed his luck. Joseph Camponello could have reached Doll Gardenia without being spotted. With his wipers batting desert dust into black smears, the agent cued control to activate the bugs inside the building.

CHAPTER TEN

Jack Kurtz entered the Wooden Palisades Restaurant as though he owned the place, and was asked to wait in the manager's office by a thin girl in severe black. In the good old days with an opportunity like that, Jack Kurtz would have made a killing. Fifteen minutes with the clients' register, and he could have kept his crew busy for a month. Just knowing the nights the regulars came to dine was an open invitation to plunder their homes using removal trucks and laundry vans. To hand out phoney business cards to any nosey neighbours, offering them the same advantageous valet/ restoration rates their burgled friends 'enjoyed', and boogie to the speciality Dallas warehouses where every item of linen, chinaware and furniture would have earned top dollar for cash.

Jack Kurtz began to fidget as the minutes crawled by. He smoothed his clashing tie and looked at his French fob watch for the pleasure it gave him. Patted his thinning hair and looked in vain for a mirror. Scrubbed at his dentures with a thick knuckle, and began to feel like a fake encyclopedia salesman who'd wandered into a bunco squad convention by mistake. Getting greedy for travelling expenses added to his regular monthly retainer had seemed like a good idea back in Santa Monica, but now, Jack Kurtz wasn't half so sure. He started out of his chair when a man came up behind him, and found himself shaking hands with the coldest grey eyes he'd seen since that term in Joliet he still had nightmares about.

The cold grey eyes said they were listening, and Jack Kurtz went into the speech he used with connected guys. A life contract is a life contract, right? And nobody gets to renege on them, right? And Smart Guys don't need to fuck with lawyers to square things over some dumb bimbo singer, right? A man like you knows the score here, right?

Right?

'Name me names. Starting with yours.'

Kurtz squirmed in his chair. Thought, *this ain't the way it goes down.* Said, 'No need for that, brother.'

Heard, 'There's every need, *brother.* I want that girl, I *get* that girl. I don't, somebody I respect better have good reason to "no" me. You're just a messenger boy. I'll know who sent you. And *now.*'

'I ain't at liberty to divulge—'

'Divulge? You ain't at liberty to *breathe* on my turf, you know that?'

'I don't know—'

'*Nothing,* right? First thing you got right since you greased in here. You know Doll Gardenia?'

'Huh?'

'Never mind. You're Jack Kurtz. Santa Monica. One of my people got the registration from that cheapo heap you drive. And Jack, I decide I want complaints about your driving in this town, I get them. If there's damage to any of the class wheels outside my place, that's *you* in court. I just have to say, is all.'

Jack Kurtz began to get that old feeling, and cell doors slammed in his mind.

'Wait now—' he started.

'You'd better *know* Doll Gardenia, you know that?'

'Hey, I can't—'

'I don't need a catalogue of what you *can't* do, Jack. I need what you *can* do.'

'Lissen now . . .'

'To *what*? You pumping exhaust gas in my face? You're cheaper than your wheels, Jack.'

'But . . .'

'You want I should punch up Doll's number right now? Hand *you* the phone? Have you tell him what you're trying to pull here?'

'Pulling? Me? Look—'

'*Enough.* OK, Jack, where's Doll now?'

'Uh, hey, uh . . .'

'*Yes*?'

'I came here in all good faith—'

'To put the bite on me? And you don't even know who you work for? Do *you* call Palm Springs, or do I? Listen, I call Doll, you're in the sewer, Jack.'

'Make that call we're *both* in the sewer.'

'Where's the choice, you moron? I'm through dancing with you.'

'I'm hired help, is all. You got the message. That's me coloured gone,' Kurtz blustered.

'Yeah? How?'

'What?'

'How d'you plan to *do* that? Outside that door you're on your own. Nothing I can do for you. I just sit here and listen to all those sirens as you assume the position and get to walk the white line for drunk driving. Any jay walker got hit and run tonight, guess who buys that one. You, Jack. There's also the bill here you ran up and didn't pay. The cocktail waitress who's dying to press charges for sexual assault. Maybe why you were in such a hurry in the parking lot. You really had yourself a time tonight, *Mister* Kurtz.'

'Bluff.' Kurtz felt dizzy.

Charlie's teeth bit on a hard smile.

'Try me, Jack.'

'Big mistake. I'm telling you.'

'And *you* made it, Jack.'

Kurtz stared at slate eyes. At the telephone being offered him. Felt his shorts turn clammy as gas built behind his navel. Heard metal impact outside. A deep male voice yell as brakes bound and hot tyres spun on hotter blacktop.

'Quite a time, Jack,' Charlie said mildly. 'Didn't that sound like an LTD losing its radiator to you?'

Jack Kurtz tried to swear and couldn't find the saliva. The eye of the telephone was a cannon muzzle, and its burr was the snarl of cats in jungle foliage.

'That's the number, Jack. Don't fumble the code.'

Kurtz made out big numerals on a scratch pad. Knew them to be correct. The man with slate eyes had him sweated up like a rape victim, and hadn't raised a finger or his voice. And that scared him as much as the thought of returning to Joliet.

Kurtz dialled Palm Springs.

Heart thumping.

Joseph Camponella got what he wanted from the Medical Director with little fuss, and nurses brought Doll Gardenia back from nowhere with an injection of upper-juice and an oxygen mask. When Camponella was satisfied Doll knew up from down, he told the staff to leave, and made himself comfortable in a bedside chair. Doll's face looked like a sag of play putty, but his eyes were alert, and that was all the lawyer cared about.

'Where've you been, Joe? Sending some kid, Jesus.'

'Chicago ain't ten cents of Fast Transit away, Doll. And family business comes first, you know that.'

'I'm family, Joe.'

'*Part* of the family, Doll. A member, not the mayor,' Camponella rubbed his long jaw and sucked air through ivory teeth. 'You made the New York dailies and the TV, and that's made for a lot of unhappy faces in the Big Apple. I've poured oil in Chi, but there's a price to pay.'

'Give me the bad news, why don't you?' Doll said through drool.

Camponella masked his feelings without effort. Gardenia sounded as though he talked around a waffle or pads of cotton wool, and still had the arrogance of a street fighter. The man was in deep trouble, and he wasn't remotely aware of the fact.

'You don't get it, do you, Doll?'

'Get what? That some asshole has hit on me personally? Come out of left field to do *this* to my face? You find him, Joe. Then his ass is mine.'

'Oh, we'll find him, Doll. But he's no longer your property. That's the decision, kid, so learn to live with it.'

'I don't believe this.'

'Work on it. And there's more. You want it in a carton, or one piece at a time?'

Gardenia fumbled a tissue from a box with his good hand. Got it to his mouth and dabbed at superfluous saliva.

'Well?' Camponella asked, his voice flinty on the FBI tape.

'Well, what?'

'I'm family too, Doll, and it's me who has to get your sorry ass out of a sling. Not for your sake, for the family's. There's more at stake here than some-body leaving rotten fish on your stoop – your wretched ego taking a slap. You've abused your position, Doll. Used it for petty personal reasons, and that stops here. You're on ice. Grounded. And that's for as long as it takes to buy the quiet life for everybody.'

'I'm not hearing this, not from you.'

'I'm the mouthpiece, Doll, but this is the *Law* you're hearing. As of now you sit here and heal. All your estate business goes through my office. You get to countersign the papers, but that's all. You want a daily paper, I pay out the nickels. The grass needs cutting, I hire the gardener. You don't even make outside calls. You're Howard Hughes, Doll, and my Mormons take care of business.'

'Like fuck you say,' Gardenia spat through a twitching mouth.

'Don't fight me on this, Doll. I leave, the next guy walks in here won't be changing your dressings for anything but concrete Hush Puppies. That's the word from Chi and the Apple.'

'I won't forget or forgive this, Joe. Not in this lifetime.'

Camponella nodded sagely, his eyes remote.

'That's just as well. For both of us,' he said.

The bedside phone showed a light, and Camponella had it up to his face before Gardenia could move. Said he was taking all Mr Gardenia's calls, and listened to a nervous voice from San Diego. Took a diary out of his coat and made notes with a gold pencil. Told Jack Kurtz to go back to Santa Monica when he had admitted his mistakes, and to give the man down there the number for White, Hall & Marks. Any legalities would be taken care of, and Kurtz was to present himself in chambers the following day without fail.

'And Kurtz,' Camponella said. 'Bring your desk

diary and all relevant papers with you. I want chapter and verse on this whole thing. Yeah, good night.'

Gardenia's torn muscles ached under the plaster, and his mouth tasted of defeat. He watched Camponella unplug the phone and take it to the door.

'You're a damned fool, Doll,' Camponella said. 'You use women like Kleenex, but you won't throw them away. You lose interest, but nobody else can have your leavings. That's so immature, you need paddling. This O'Day woman decides to whisper in the wrong ears after being hounded for three years, where does that leave you? Or the family? Dead in the water, is where. And Doll, hitting on you is a whole lot simpler than putting a contract on her. Even the Supreme Court has no interest in hearing bad things about a dead man. *Now* do you hear me?'

Gardenia's mouth gummed itself closed. His dulled mind was an echoing ballroom, and every elusive thought had a cutting edge that pared at his manhood.

'Don't do this to me, Joe,' he heard himself say to Camponella's back.

'You did it to yourself,' Camponella said as the door closed Gardenia away from the world.

Charlie sat across from Chasen's genuine smile.

'You know what we've got here, Charlie? Really got here? Joseph Camponella fronting for Gardenia means they're rattled to hell and wherever. They call him the Icebox, my man, and for good reason. He's colder than charity, and Doll's dogmeat he don't mind that man all the way. What's the betting he puts Kurtz out to grass in some boondocks county, and leaves the O'Day chick strictly alone?'

'No bet, Saul. Won't take them long to work out

141

Della has a friend who might be a danger to the organization. I want that girl protected around the clock, Saul.'

'You got it. What was that mayhem in the parking lot?'

'That? Kurtz must have forgotten his handbrake. His car took out some trash cans. A bent fender, but he can drive back to Santa Monica.'

'Damn, but you're good, you bastard.'

'And hungry. Let's eat.'

It was raining in London, and Irish Denzil huddled against the dawn chill until a beat copper had turned the corner into Beak Street. Denzil shinned up an ornate shopfront, and lay along a wide ledge until he got a corridor window open. Sliding inside, he padded to the rear of the deserted building where a window overlooked an enclosed courtyard. Feeding rope out in a double strand, Denzil tied it off with a deadman's hitch, and lowered himself into the flag-stoned area.

Tall office blocks took up three sides of the court-yard, and Denzil found the basement door he wanted unlocked, a small bonus for him. Steps led down to a boiler room, and beyond it was the elevator shaft and the emergency stairs. Denzil climbed to the third floor, used tools on the outer door of Jason Mayer's office suite, and was inside in seven short seconds. He drew the blinds and went to work with his Polaroid and flash unit.

Half an hour later, Denzil left a pack of prints at George Muscat's club, and cycled home to the Harrow Road through fine drizzle. Humming a tradi-tional air, he congratulated himself on the easiest thousand he'd earned in a very slow month. Irish Denzil had kept a duplicate set of Polaroids for himself, just in case Uncle George's wallet jammed. Such things happened now and again, and Irish Denzil was a very careful man indeed.

Casey Pollard was brought out of sleep by the telephone, and he fumbled it to his ear, still reaching for a blonde girl who had the longest hair he had ever seen, legs longer than a Biblical epic, and a butterfly tattoo just above her bikini line. She shredded with the rest of the dream, and Pollard grunted to let the caller know he was awake.

'Camponella,' a frozen voice said from across the Atlantic, and proceeded to give Pollard a clipped résumé of Gardenia's reduced status. 'And Coltrane's singing for the FBI. Your people have become a real embarrassment in two cities, and my office needs to give a ruling on any future action. I need your side of it to complete the initial analysis.'

Pollard's pores stung with tart sweat, and his stale cigar breath stank in his own nostrils. The last person Camponella had considered an 'embarrassment' had been neatly sealed inside two drums of industrial adhesive, a neater hole behind his left ear. If Doll Gardenia was going down the tubes, Pollard was damned if he would join him.

'We're doing good business here, Joe. Let's not forget that, and the recent problems are being ironed right now. The whole thing will turn around within thirty days, you have my personal guarantee.'

'Then that's exactly what you have, thirty days.'

'More than enough. What about Shaggy?'

'Good question. He is your problem.'

'Wrong, Joe. He was Doll's man, now he's yours. You having power of attorney and all.'

'Legally, yes. Financially, no. His termination of

143

contract comes out of your pocket, Casey. Best I can do for you.'

Pollard gripped the phone with an oily palm and hot knuckles. Swallowed a thousand things he'd like to tell that refrigerated, shafting bastard in Palm Springs. Picking over Doll's bones. Acting God Almighty and squeezing every last red cent out of the deal. His retainer had to be double Pollard's share of the consortium's gross, and without stepping outside his air-conditioned office.

'Whatever you think's fair, Joe,' Pollard said, hating the need to kiss ass. His digital travelling clock pulsed off the seconds to six in the morning, green numerals glaring with inexorable precision. The hotel room was as cold as a cadaver, and the London drizzle on the windows reminded Pollard of mucus on an idiot's chin. Doll's chin.

'Thanks for being reasonable, Casey. My appreciation will be reflected in my report.'

Yeah, Pollard thought. *Given verbatim to the family heads over a mountain of New York pasta to violins. Every silken word worth another thousand bucks, and think of the saving on notepaper and stamps, Mr Camponella.*

'Keep in touch with my office, Casey. A daily update will suffice.'

'Panama ain't Wall Street, Joe. Those waters out in the Atlantic don't have coin phones, and we'll be keeping strict radio silence.'

'You'll find a way,' Camponella said, clearing down.

'How?' Pollard asked the damp Bayswater gloom. 'Just tell me how?'

George Muscat chewed breakfast toast over the Polaroids spread across his desk, his mind churning

144

like a Kenwood mixer. It was quite incredible.

The general shots of Jason Mayer's office suite showed wall to ceiling montages of Soho streets and individual houses with special merit. A scale model was nearing completion on a specially constructed sectional table, and Irish Denzil had had the wit to get close shots of points of particular interest. Soho Square had all its good buildings intact, but the Cross & Blackwell office block had become an elegant Georgian terrace. Parking had been banned, and the area designated as a pedestrian walkway. The open air market east of Gerrard Street was now an elevated garden restaurant above a 100 vehicle basement car park linked to Leicester Square Underground Station by north-south walkovators.

Golden Square had been transformed out of all recognition. Tall Regency houses fronted new office blocks of black marble and mirrored glass, and fountains played in the island garden.

Folders of drawings of each Soho street were accompanied by detailed historical notes, and a discarded photostat of a costings analysis gave Muscat the clue to how much Charlie Dance was prepared to sink into the area over seven years. The first phase of construction alone came to an incredible £90 million, and Casey Pollard arrived in Brewer Street to find a bemused Muscat lost in cost projections, his fingers busy on a calculator.

'Remember me, George?' Pollard snapped.

'Madonna and all the saints,' Muscat said. 'How can this be?'

'George? Look at me, George.'

'I don't believe these figures. But they're there. *They're there.*'

'And I'm here, George. Will you stop beating your dummy over this crapola?'

145

Muscat curled a lip at Pollard.

'Watch the language. My Bianca could walk in any minute.'

'I walked in an hour ago, and we have to talk, George.'

'You say this "crapola", you ant. This is bigger than three years of shipping snow. And I've got it in the palm of my hand. I just have to reach out – take it away from that bastard. Me.'

'Have you been snorting, George?'

'Listen, all those years that bastard look down on George Muscat. Call me *pimp* with his eyes. Never a "good morning". Just that look. Now I got him in my fist, and I'm gonna squeeze the blood out of his stone.'

'That's personal, George. Personal bullshit getting in the way of business. Exactly how Doll Gardenia's gotten his ass in a real sling. And us with him, we don't operate smoother than silk. Get off this thing, will you? Come back to reality.'

Muscat did a breathless jig. Took Pollard by the shoulders in a surprisingly hard grip. Breathed buttered toast into the Chicagoan's face.

'You've got a score to settle here too, mister. Chappie August the fight promoter was a friend of mine. He was gutted by that bastard. Chappie told me about Hong Kong. How you and Doll lost big money to that bastard. You don't want to make ten thousand per cent profit on revenging yourself, huh?'

Pollard shrugged free. Rolled a cigar into his hard mouth and pulled up a chair. Sat slowly and waved Muscat into his office swivel.

'Talk slowly, George,' he said.

'All business gets to be personal, Casey. Just a matter of time before you're playing personalities off against profits. And don't tell me different. It's happened here, between us. You see?'

'Sure I see, but who's the bastard, George?'

Triumph wet Muscat's lips, moistened his oily eyes.

'Yes, he hurt you bad in the pocket book. You haven't forgotten his name, you just don't want to say it out loud. In case you're wrong.'

'Say it, George.'

Muscat leaned on the Polaroids to bare stained dentures.

'Charlie Dance,' he said. Then, 'Yes, Casey, *him*.'

Pollard went back to the ferry beating to Victoria from Kowloon. Dance backing his fighter for half a million dollars cash money at odds of 3-1. How he and Doll and Carmine Domino took the bet because Dance's old tanker had no chance against Sugar Boy Tatum. How Trooper Wells had taken all Tatum could throw, and demolished him like a straw dummy well inside the distance. Having to pay out a million and a half in cash plus the stake itself. Two million dollars in a suitcase, and Dance hadn't even bothered to collect it himself. Had sent some soldier to get it for him, too busy rubbing noses with the old broad he had in tow. With that kind of money Dance could have bought himself a covey of pneumatic young quail to test his mattress. But no, the man preferred a woman with a wayward nose and a voice you could file steel with.

Pollard snapped his Zippo alight to run his cigar into the yellow flame. Drew Havana smoke deep, and breathed twin dragon plumes through his nostrils. Nodded and made up his mind to listen.

'What have you got there, George?' he asked softly.

Seeing blood on the moon.

*

The daytime clatter of San Ysidro woke Saul Chasen in the early forenoon, and he found Charlie gone. Luggage, clothes, everything. Climbing into yesterday's suit without a shave, Chasen hit the streets. The rented Hertz was in the lean-to Manoel the zitty car bandit used, and the old Mexican woman there knew nothing in Spanish or English. To her, Chasen was *La Migra*, Immigration, and she wasn't ready to return to her border village without the money to change her mean life. Chasen checked her green card, and handed it back with a folded ten spot inside. Manoel's mother was thirty-five and looked seventy.

'I know this one thing, *senor*,' she told the dusty ground.

'Yeah, uh, *si*?'

'Manoel is good boy. This don't bring him trouble?'

'Not from me.'

'They go Thrift Shop. But I don't tell this, hey?'

Chasen described Dance and Manoel to the volunteer matron at the Veteran's Thrift Shop, a cheerful woman with a bust that could have suckled the Titans. Sure she remembered them. Nice guys, but they bought the oldest duds in the shop for a fancy dress party. Snakeskin shoes and a workshirt you could see daylight through. Ratty flare pants and a hat mice wouldn't have nested in. A Mexican belt no better than pressed cardboard, with a buckle of stamped brass you could buy for three bucks in Tijuana if you were crazy. He'd win the prize at that *pollo* party all right. Dressed in those rags he *looked* like an illegal immigrant. All that was missing was the smell, honey. You want the same?

Chasen drove out to the border to stare into white haze. The wire fence shimmered in the heat, and the canyon's edge was littered with garbage, thorn and scrub oak. Through binoculars Chasen could see the *pollos* gathering together to eat and sing and wait for night. A Border Patrol helicopter blatted overhead, and cicadas sawed out their mating calls.

'Had to see the tarantulas and rattlesnakes for yourself, huh, Charlie? Sand flies, fire ants, and bandits, all ready to chew on you for no good reason except you're out there. They leave you for dead, we may never find your body.'

Chasen drove away from there to find a dark and clean bar. Making bets with himself.

CHAPTER ELEVEN

Manoel Salgado sank to the ground with Charlie beside him.

They had used the late afternoon to cross Washerwoman Flats, and a puckish south-westerly carried the sound of voices, radio music, and the smell of tamales and beans mixed with woodsmoke. The sun was a fat mango in white haze to their rear, and the stunted oaks pointing their arthritic knuckles and elbows at the sky were the grey of midnight cats. East of their position was the broken slash of Deadman's Canyon, and to their right was the upper southern plateau where illegals and canyon people held endless crossing parties, waiting for night. There might have been prayers and tears of parting, but they were lost to ears lesser than the Almighty's.

At fifteen, Manoel was the man of his family, and he liked the man with slate eyes almost as much as he was curious about him. This one *saw* Manoel when they talked. Most Americanos looked at Chicanos from the corners of their eyes as if Manoel's people only existed at the edge of their world. Good for trucking garbage, mugging and raping, and keeping the basic cost of labour at rock bottom where it belonged. It was illegal to house Mexicans but not to hire them, and thousands of migrant workers slept in hedgerows under cardboard gleaned from dumps, right alongside the fields they worked for the Jolly Green Giant. Ho, ho, ho.

Manoel had stripped Charlie of anything

American, including matches and cigarettes, and forbade him to talk at anytime when other *pollos* were about. Playing dumb, he might just pass if he stayed out of firelight and kept his eyes on the ground where they belonged.

The light greyed down and down, and an early nighthawk skimmed the mottled dusk. Wind-tossed mesquite imitated rattlesnakes, and a rodent died with a long shriek of protest. The fires of the upper plateau became orange jewels, and the radio music sang of hearth and home and love in sad, sad Spanish as the canyons melted into their own shadows, and the bitter earth gave off its pungent night odours. The whole hillside seemed to scuttle with invisible life, and the mosquitoes began to swarm. Manoel dug at the ground with a knife as though troubled, and watched Charlie become a squatting fret against the darkening sky.

'You can change your mind about this,' Charlie said.

'I already *did*, man,' Manoel snarl-sighed.

'Oh?'

'Was gonna have the bloods meet up with us out here. Take you all the way out, man. For the bucks in your shoes. All that good junk in the trunk of the rental. You got clothes I'd kill for, you know that?'

'Why didn't you?'

'You're weird, you know that? Ain't pissing blood or nothing. You alive, or what?'

'Want to feel my pulse?'

'This ain't no Cook's Tour. Why you doing this?'

'To see for myself. Tourists fly from place to place. See the same hotels, the same beaches, buy the same postcards. As if the world was as safe and as bland as a one-flavour ice cream cone. Real travellers see all they can. That's the difference.'

151

'Get your rocks off seeing misery, that it?'

'As much as you do, Manoel. Answer your own question.'

'I live here, man. Think I would if I didn't have to?'

'You'll get out. But one day you'll miss it. Want to come back.'

'You're crazy.'

'Deny what you are, you deny yourself. You want to pretend you're an American, or be Manoel Salgado, his own man?'

Manoel said nothing, his blade chunking into dirt. The night was dirty velvet smelling of old blankets and ripe garbage, and the few stars were tarnished by polluted cloud.

'My father died out there, bringing us across. Had my mother run with me, and let them bash his head in with rocks. I was five, man, but I know that spot better than I know my own bed. The old lady has me take flowers out there every year. I put up a marker. You wanna see it?'

'If you'd like me to.'

'Maybe I do. Come on tourist, it's time.'

The canyon swallowed them in a rattle of stones, and they took an hour picking their way across hard clay fissured by drought. Now and again they sank on their haunches to let silent *pollos* pass in column, their guides clicking stones to keep them close; and about a mile in, they heard gunfire and screams coming out of the southern darkness. Manoel walked on as if nothing had happened, but he was cautious on the climb to the rise above Spring Canyon. Lying on the ridge, he pointed down at a cross growing from a pile of moonlit stones, whispering close to Charlie's face.

'There, that's it. We don't go down. There's five guys hunkered down in the wash.'

Charlie saw shadow upon shadow, broken ground melding with the black fuzz of thorn and brush, a monochrome jigsaw without meaning. All blindness and mystery. Manoel touched his lips to keep him silent and still, and they lay in the same position long enough for the ants to find the tender flesh of Charlie's ankles. What felt like hours passed before Manoel decided to move, and Charlie sensed bodies flanking them as they backed down the ridge. He pulled Manoel down into a shallow draw, and pointed off to where he thought the stalking men were.

'You ain't gonna like this,' Manoel hissed.

Charlie widened his eyes in question.

'They're my guys. They'll take both of us, they have to.'

'Can you get out alone?'

'What for? San Ysidro or here, they got my number, man.'

'Because of me, that it?'

'What the fuck else, man?'

'This their regular business? Talk up, boy. Is it?'

'They make a few bucks for dope this way. I *told* you how it is down here. You make what you can, any way you can.'

'They help bring shipments across?'

'What?'

'Talk to me now?'

'Maybe. Sure, why not? Makes good money. Enough to track themselves up for four-five months. Man, I was *stupid* bringing you out here inna boonies.'

'You want out of this, Manoel? I mean *out*.'

'Of here? You kidding?'

'The whole street thing. You and your ma?'

'Walk on fucking water, why don't you?'

153

'Yes or no, boy. Say it.'

'We're about to get dead, and he's talking *future*.'

'Say it. One way or the other. I didn't come out here to lose to a bunch of hopheads.'

A boot disturbed shale and crackled on dry tinder. An outline bobbed and ducked along a crest and dropped from sight. Another head with hair like an Indian showed and sank off to Charlie's right, and he could smell their ripeness closing in.

'Last chance, Manoel.'

'I'd like to believe, man . . .'

'Believe,' Charlie said. Took the boy in the side of the neck with the edge of his hand. Manoel sagged like a thin doll, and Charlie rolled him under an outcrop, covering him with loose brush. Then he drew Shaggy's Python from his waistband, and sidled into deeper shadow to watch for more out-lines.

Casey Pollard used a toothpick on a piece of beef caught in a molar. Charlotte Street was as wet as an aquarium through the restaurant window, and George Muscat had taken his bladder to the toilet. A waiter brought coffee, and Pollard stirred cream with his thoughts. Charlie Dance's Soho scheme had fired his imagination, but he had shown Muscat nothing of this. Without the consortium behind the project, even after screwing Dance out of it, Muscat couldn't hack it alone. Christ, even that icebox Joseph Camponella had to feel comfortable about diversifying into London real estate. Bricks and mortar were as solid as you could get, and paying the Mickey Mouse Channel Island taxes was cheaper than laundering drugs money by a healthy seven per cent. And totally legit business, so who could fault it?

Four days in Colon, Panama. Fifteen days tops to raise the wreck from the ocean bed. The pilot had put her down in shallow water, hadn't he? Radioed his position before the sharks got him. Or drowned. Pollard loved the idea that only he knew the truth of the matter. They had all *assumed* the consignment had gone by sea, heading for the Florida Keys. He'd even let Doll feed that to Cunningham to keep him in the dark. And when everybody just happened to hear about a smuggler being sunk by US Customs gunfire, Casey Pollard had let the fiction grow. He merely had to locate the plane, bring up the skag and the money, and run it up into Baja, California. Take it overland to San Diego where it could be banked without hassle, courtesy of Joseph Camponella's contacts there. Get that British fruit Cunningham to file certificates of transfer to the Grand Cayman banking facility, and it was over.

Naturally, Pollard had considered running with the whole package, but the family would never have let him rest. No, this way was better, New York may not let Gardenia off the hook, and too bad if they didn't. Because Pollard could waltz into the Big Apple and lay this sweet real estate deal right in the family lap. Then Joe Camponella could chew on a five cent cigar and kiss the Pollard ass, baby.

Muscat came back to sit heavily with a mild belch.

'You in on this, Casey?'

'You rushing me, George?'

'No, but you're prevaricating.'

'Long word on a full stomach, George. You get me *original* material on this project, and I'll make the presentation in New York. How's that?'

'And I lay out most of 2.5 million sterling on my own? Sewing up the available leases on *option* will take one mill. We need the freeholds, Casey. Then we've got Dance by the pubics.'

'You want I should use my credit card?'

'I want capital commitment now, not promises tomorrow. It's that, or nothing.'

'So, how much will hold you?'

'For you *and* Gardenia? Or just you?'

'In this dance it takes *three* to tango.'

'One million sterling. Each.'

'That's about all I have on my hip right now.'

'So you're poor,' Muscat sneered. 'Stay poor.'

Pollard tapped his demitasse with a spoon. He could scrape two mill together by liquidating his current portfolio of investments, and leaving his Rome estate intact. It was tough, but if Doll went out of the picture, he'd by God have controlling interest in the whole schmeer.

Pollard thrust his hand at Muscat.

'Shake, partner,' he said.

Crossing fingers.

Charlie could feel the night like a second skin.

He crossed the stench of a sewage outlet, his cheap shoes turning spongy in the lagoon of faeces below the outfall. The canyon bottom was marshy there, and he stepped out on to hard clay with relief. He could hear two men following the trail from the west, and knew another man must be coming through from the east. The others were up in the heights somewhere, and he waited for them to come sliding down at him. He tossed a rock back into the mire. Followed up with a handful of pebbles, and hugged the steep incline with his back. A shape loomed to his right, and he caught the slick of a rifle growing out of a black poncho. The face was a blob under a bandana, and the moccasins were noiseless on the hard crust. Charlie let the man pass, and fell in behind, closing cautiously.

Stones clicked from somewhere up ahead, and the rifleman in the poncho glided forward, rapping his rifle with a pebble. There was a click in answer. Two more from the southern heights. Another from the north. They had formed a rough circle around the unconscious Manoel's position, sure now they had he and Charlie trapped.

Charlie stepped in behind the poncho. Jammed his hat over the man's face and brought his knee up into an unsuspecting crotch. Lifted the man off his feet with the power of the move, and helped him drive his knees at the ground. Slammed the Cobra against the skull with the slap of a chopped cabbage. The rifle skittered away, and the darkness up ahead asked startled questions.

Charlie loped forward for about fifteen feet, and squatted against the canyon wall like a diffident *pollo.* Judging himself to be about eighty yards from the spot he had left Manoel, he was worrying about stray shots when an outline came at him like a rolling barrel. A youth with muscles and a sweatband came in at Charlie behind a yard of kife, and Charlie kicked him full in the chest. The cheap shoe burst on impact and lost itself in the darkness. The youth barely staggered. Bored in spitting saliva, the knife carving the air ahead of him. Charlie fired once. The broad face blew inward in a white sear of muzzle gas, long hair spreading out from the huge exit wound. The body flailed, took a step away, and went down like a sack of offal.

Momentarily blinded, Charlie fired west with closed eyes, scrabbling backwards up the scrubbed slope. Thorn snagged his clothes. Tore at his buttocks and his shoeless foot. He ignored the pain

157

and kept kicking himself upward. A big and stinking body smothered him. A hard forearm trapped his throat, and he looked up into eyes as black as marbles. Dead eyes without humanity. Pitiless beads fronting a mind nobody would want to read. Charlie spat up into those eyes to make the head jerk away. Put the magnum against the thick throat and pulled the trigger. Lead shavings spattered his cheeks as the Cobra kicked and smoked. Hot filth and tissue burst from the hollow neck, and the huge head opened a black mouth to disgorge blacker blood.

Charlie shouted through sudden drench and bulled the body away.

It wouldn't die. It crawled away with beating fists and drumming feet. Crabbed around looking for something to pummel. Shook the earth with its waning power, the dying head hanging from the shoulders like a pouch of stones. The body shook itself, a big dog shedding water from its pelt. Sagged and fell to puddle the clay with arterial blood thicker than soup. Lay still with twitching fingers.

Charlie's lungs had solidified around an agony yet to come. He surged upright to draw breath, then crouched through instinct. A wild shot cut through the scrub, knocking the bark of an oak at waist height. There were shouts of discovery in foul Spanish. A short fusillade and the thump of running feet.

Charlie wiped off his fouled face with a stiffening arm. Blinked gummed eyelids. Stood to see two dark shapes running away down the canyon. Took aim with shaking hands. Spat air and another man's blood out of his mouth and fired a cluster of two. Snapped off his last round. One of the figures fell flat. The other spun gracefully, hit high in the shoulder. Opened his face against the rock wall, and slid all the way to the canyon bottom trailing a ragged arm behind him. The prone figure sprang up, jumped a snarl of fallen oak, and disappeared into the darkness as if he had never been.

Charlie found himself on all fours. Puking into thorn that had scratched him up without pain. Bright blue light had him pinned down, and dust blew up all around in a sudden whirlwind. Charlie's hat blew away, and he let it go without regret. He had lost the Cobra somewhere, and thought he might have thrown it away. If only the screaming wind would blow itself out. Blow out the harsh blue light and leave him to heal or die in the darkness. His limbs shook inside his clothes. He was colder than he had ever been, and a white cross of metal burned in his upper chest. He looked at it without comprehension, trying not to go into shock.

He fell on his back and lay there. The white bone-handled knife a singing crucifix close to his face in the wild blue light that threw up the stinging clouds of debris. Wondering how the blue light could do that, Charlie told the night to leave him alone. Leave him be . . .

There were dark blue shapes then. Tan shapes. Uniforms. A stretcher and a man with Saul's face yelling at him through rotor wash. Leaning close to hear about Manoel, those big brown knothole eyes showing care and fury.

'You crazy, crazy, wonderful asshole.'

Charlie smiled, and took that with him as he was airlifted through stars as clear and as bright as Margot's earrings.

Benny Shoesmith was shaking his umbrella dry when he heard weeping from inside his office.

159

Puzzled, he listened to racks of sobs, snotty blasts into tissues, long sniffs, and a low keening that started the whole cycle all over again.

Benny cracked the door to peer inside.

Marigold sat at a desk heaped with soggy Kleenex, her fat face even more swollen by grief. Her fall of chins rioted as hard as her full and flaccid bosom, and he saw all of her rear fillings when she opened up to give vent to her feelings. That reminded Benny she had taken the morning off to see her dentist, and he wished she'd at least *cry* in her own time.

'The injection wore off too quickly?' he said.

Marigold just sniffed.

'He hit a nerve, maybe?'

Marigold whimpered.

'You need root canal work? What?'

Marigold started to wail.

'A nice cuppa tea, eh? You can take hot liquids?'

Marigold showed Benny fillings and tonsils, wailing harder than ever, and Benny wondered if a slap would stop the flood.

'An aspirin,' he yelled. 'It's a tooth, not a pregnancy.'

Marigold went rigid. Showed rings of white fear around her muddy pupils, and sagged to bleat into her hands.

'You? *Pregnant*?' Benny couldn't believe it. 'Some schmuck could fancy *you*?'

Contrite at once, Benny found the medicinal brandy and poured two measures. Got an arm across a plump shoulder, and patted Marigold's frizzy hair with rough compassion. A bachelor for seventy years, Benny knew nothing about women outside the magazines he sneaked home in his old briefcase. He had once fallen against a woman on a

160

braking bus, but she had been all bone. This one was softer than his eiderdown.

'You're sure now?' he asked, putting brandy to the wet mouth.

'Yesssss . . .'

'There's no mistake?'

'Frogs are infallible.'

Benny thought about frog princes, completely lost.

'There's a man?'

'Of course there's a maaaannnnnnn . . .'

'Who'll stand by you? Marry even?'

'Noooooooooo . . . Mmmaaaarried . . .'

What had the schmuck at home if he came after Marigold? Benny wondered. *A gargoyle?* 'He'll make provision? Mantain you?'

'He said abooooortion.'

'For that he'll pay?'

'I said nooo . . . Mmurder.'

'You'll keep it?'

'It's mine.'

'You? *A mother?*'

'And it's yourrrr ffffault.'

Benny Shoesmith drained his glass. Drained Marigold's. Sat on the arm of the chair grinding his dentures. His mind screaming *Me?* Finally, he asked how he was to blame, and pieced together what Brick Donovan had done to make Marigold betray his office secrets.

'I saw the photos,' Marigold blubbed. 'Dirty pictures of me. And I didn't even know. Now he says I have to do videos and films. And go with men he says I should. Men I don't even know. It's dirty. Filthy. Wrong. And I loved him, Mr Shoesmith. Really loved him.'

Benny had a hand on softness he had never known before, and it both thrilled and frightened

161

him. With his eyes closed, he could bring all his photographs alive. Marigold had his hand deep in her warm, damp cleavage, asking for help. Anything to kill the shame. If she rolled on him, she'd smother him in pneumatic bliss.

Benny got his hand back. Choked a Woodbine alight. Stood away from the lump of a girl and made his mind go to work. Brick Donovan worked for George Muscat, and Muscat hated Charlie Dance. It all fitted neatly into place. OK, so they wouldn't have stopped at searching his office. They'd probably screwed Jason Mayer's place too. They wanted a fight, they'd get a fight. Benny Shoesmith knew property better than any pimp. It was time to play a few jokers. Make Muscat think the scheme was bigger than it was. Bloody gigantic.

'Marigold,' Benny said. 'Here's what you do . . .'

And he dictated letters she was to steal for Brick Donovan.

With a very long night fading into day, Saul Chasen summed up what he had. Since nobody was much interested in what happened to illegals in the canyons; by airlifting corpses, wounded and unconscious to an Oceanside hospital, he had avoided any possibility of news coverage. The two dead men had police blotters that read like *Black Mask* fiction. The shoulder-shot bandit was known as Snow Ramirez on the streets. Rapist, pusher and user. Known member of the Raiders street gang. If he survived surgery, he would live with a permanent stoop, and a claw for a hand. Punching through the deltoid to shatter the clavicle, the magnum round had exited through the armpit. Torn the elbow joint apart, ripped the length of the forearm, and blown out through the palm of Ramirez' right hand. Mr Ramirez would need help tying his shoes, let alone holding *pollo* women down for his nocturnal pleasure.

The rifleman in the poncho had track marks in his neck, and a curious nurse counted more than two hundred more all over his body. A San Ysidro deputy sheriff made him as a gang enforcer known as Negro Nogales, and Negro was happy to talk to *anybody* about *anything* once he had seen his dead friends in the mortuary. With his head shaved and sutured, he talked for Chasen's recorder in bad English and border Spanish, and *loved* the ducky little cell they finally gave him.

Manoel Delgado had double-vision for a while, but he willingly corroborated all that Negro Nogales told the tape machine. The man who got away had to be Big Ugly Sanchez, and he owned an M-16. Sure, a real one. The white bone-handled knife that came out of Charlie's chest had belonged to Honcho who lay on a slab with most of his throat missing, and Manoel would not rest until he knew Charlie was alive. Saw for himself that was true, and blessed the air above Charlie's hospital bed before being taken into protective custody.

Saul Chasen was at Charlie's bedside when he came to, and shared a Chesterfield with him despite the big red and white sign banning such foul personal habits.

'You have a way of stirring up the silt, pally,' he said.

'How bad am I?' Charlie mumbled.

'Clean in and out. The blade must have hit a rib and skated off. You've got two sexy holes in you. Went in above the right nipple, came out below the pectoral. You won't be pumping iron for a while.'

'Fine. Sleepy anyway . . .'

'You just had to go in there, huh?'

'Only way. Saul . . . Felt more alive out there . . . than for a lot of years . . . Almost better than . . . good poker hand . . .'

'As good as a woman?'

'Don't . . . be silly,' Charlie said, slipping into sleep.

CHAPTER TWELVE

Victor Zammit bought clothes and groceries on Republic Street and took them to the house near Fort St Elmo. The old whore let him in on her way out to mass, and Victor climbed to the top floor where Carlo Fabriano sat with his Uzzi. Banned from using the phone because of the danger of a police wire tap, Carlo was as much a prisoner as the Cunninghams. He had become moody and introvert over the last several days, and he resented Zammit as much as he relied on him.

'There is news from Catania?' he asked. His usual question.

'The family wants your brother's body released for burial. They have sent a lawyer with money and papers. Myself didn't understand all the legal things, but this man must do.'

'I am the brother. I should do this thing out of respect.'

'They say "no" to this. Leave it to the lawyer.'

'I am the brother,' Carlo hissed to himself. 'The eldest.'

'And must honour your father's decision. They are awake?'

'When do they sleep? The Englishman cannot without a drink. The old woman weeps for him. I hit him, he just stares at me with his hand out for a glass. He has no shame, no manhood. When the time comes, I will throw him out of the window and save a bullet.'

165

'They die, we all die. Your father will bury two sons.'

'Did you bring beer?'

'So you can taunt the old Englishman with it? Drink it slowly as he watches? No beer.'

'I will kill *you*, I think,' Carlo said.

'Myself knows you cannot. How would you get back to Calabria? Swim?'

'There will come a time, Gozitan,' Carlo promised.

Victor took comfort from the gun taped to his ankle, and took the food and clothes to the Cunningham's. The room smelled stale, and the chamber pot had not been emptied. Granny was thinner, and Flo's hair showed grey at the undyed roots. She forced a smile when she saw the new clothes, and was grateful when Victor took the pot away and brought fresh water for washing.

'Leave them with their filth,' Carlo jeered. 'Let them think of dying in dirt. Maybe I bury them alive. Shovel dirt on them and leave their faces to last. You would want a drink then, old man.'

'If dresses too big, lady, I bring needle and thread, eh?' Victor offered.

'You're very kind,' Flo said. 'Thank you.'

'Is nothing, lady. You get husband to eat.'

'Let them starve. Let them die,' Carlo called.

'Charlie come soon,' Victor promised. 'I come again tomorrow.'

'Always whispering,' Carlo grumbled. 'Tomorrow you bring beer, or I take woman's ear with my knife.'

'Charlie will come,' Victor said, locking himself out of the Cunningham's room. Hiding his worry, Victor cycled back to his boat. He had not heard from Charlie for over a week, but he would go to the yacht club as usual and wait.

*

Inspector Ellul disliked the Sicilian lawyer from the first handshake. The meaty fingers seemed to writhe against his palm all through the interview, and he congratulated himself for not scrubbing his hands clean there and then. Instead, he had coffee brought, and politely listened to the legal arguments for the release of Mario Fabriano's corpse. Took his time leafing through the triplicated documents slapped before him, and invented loopholes he could employ should the man irritate him further.

Ellul should have handed the whole thing over to the legal section. Left them to play their bureaucratic games of shuffle and stamp. Sign and countersign. Duplicate and triplicate. This section is closed, come back next week, next month, when you receive notification to do so. The Maltese had learned well from the British Colonial Office, and could spin the game out for as long as they wished, but Ellul decided to *appear* helpful.

'To lose a son in his prime is a tragic thing,' he said. 'The family you represent will not find rest until the body is interred in his native soil. We Maltese understand these things, we are of the same church, after all. Until the body finds rest, the soul cannot rise to Glory.'

'Yes,' said the Sicilian. 'Quite.'

'For their sake you should take steps to avoid delay. If you permit, I suggest you engage a local legal representative to act for you. Such a move would save you weeks of waiting.'

'And result in further expense, I've no doubt.'

'Which the grieving relatives would consider worthwhile. It is their sensibilities we must consider.'

The Sicilian grunted. 'And you, of course, have someone in mind.'

Ellul passed one of Charlotte Bujega's cards across.

'A woman? Impossible.'

'How so, in this day and age? She has the ear of the Minister of the Interior. But I'm sure you're more than capable. And patient.'

The Sicilian hated the wall behind Ellul's desk.

'Give me back the card, it was a foolish suggestion.'

'I'll keep it. Consult my clients.'

'As you wish.'

Ellul let the Sicilian out with a bow, blind to the proffered hand. Sure he now had everything under his personal control.

George Muscat studied the blue onionskin copies, and glared up at Brick Donovan.

'How long have you been sitting on these?'

'No choice. She only fed 'em to me a couple at a time. Said they wasn't no good apart. Blimey, with her bawling all the time, I've had a hell of a week. Her talking marriage and other nonsense.'

'You got that lump up the dove?'

'Well up,' Brick admitted gloomily. 'Told her I was a married Catholic, didn't I? Said she oughtta go to a clinic and have herself done. She said I'd burn in hell for it.'

'Maybe you should. For being careless.'

'There's more she says. More letters to City banks. Now she wants money, can you believe it? For her bloody baby.'

'She's putting the bite on *you*?'

'Seems like it, don't it?'

Muscat's smile was unpleasant enough to tighten Donovan's scrotum.

'You'll have to pay then, won't you?'

'That's a bit harsh, guv. One minute she's a soft dollop of mush, next she's the queen of extortion. What about my image?'

'Pay her off. And keep this stuff coming, you hear?'

'Where have I got two hundred pounds to tuck in her knickers?'

'For that you get what?'

'The rest of the letters. All of it. But guv, two-bleeding-hundred?'

Muscat peeled tenners from a roll and scribbled a receipt.

'Sign that. You get those letters, I'll tear it up.'

'That's dead white of you, Mr Muscat.'

'And get Irish Denzil. And a good camera. You two are going back to Jason Mayer's office. This time I want professional pictures of all there is. And find out where he gets his pictures taken. Might be we can get the original negatives. Print them ourselves.'

'You're serious?'

'And find me a model maker. I want a duplicate scheme made up in three-dimensions.'

Shaking his head, Brick Donovan went out into overcast, and left George Muscat with letters of confirmation to three chartered City banks, two offshore finance houses, and a Scottish linen bank, for bridging loans totalling £100 million subject to a starting date in early October. There were photostat telexes of several like offers to Margot Holdings at the Channel Islands address, and a list of sites Muscat had not seen before. With a thumping heart he realized what the proposals meant: the scheme had spread north of Oxford Street, and west of Regent Street. Charlie Dance was rebuilding the entire West End of London. And it was all dependent on his securing the Soho area for phase one of construction.

'Got the bastard,' Muscat crowed. 'Got him.'

The *Oceania-Cal Princess 2* was almost as broad as she was long. With her box stern, hollow centre and blunt prow, side banks of hydraulic lifting gear, a four-storey bridge and crew module rearing from her after deck, and huge sectionalized air tanks that could raise or lower her freeboard from eighty feet to four feet, she was nothing more than a highly-powered working platform. She had a forward speed of twenty knots when she aquaplaned on her twin skis, and she could lift five times her own weight from the ocean bed with the use of her hawsers, grabs, and flotation bags.

Her captain had fifteen deck crew, seven engineers, a midget submarine pilot who doubled as navigator, a chef and four cooks under his command. A Force Six gave his ship two degrees of roll in a beam-on sea. It would take a Force 12 *and rising*, to give her a deck-tilt of ten degrees, and his crew could work under those conditions so long as they obeyed the strict safety regulations he rigidly enforced. Nobody ever made *two* mistakes under William J. Caunter's command; and that also applied to clients who came aboard at their own risk, like Pollard and the stinking green cigars he could only smoke in his box of a cabin.

Lying off the Caribbean coast of Panama, the lights of Colon off her port quarter, the *Oceania-Cal Princess 2* looked very like the gas and oil rigs moored all around her. There were American warships anchored due north of her, and liberty boats were creaming in and out of the jetty at Fort Randolph. Pollard had been aboard an hour, and Captain Caunter told a deck officer to bring him up to the bridge. Immediately. And to notify the navigator he was also required to report. It was time to find out what this fixed fee contract was all about, and the owners had better beware for sending *his* ship out blind. Caunter knew the outer reefs of the Florida Keys were as treacherous as the two-dollar whores sporting phoney health certificates down in Rio, a cause of some regret to his navigator who abstained from alcohol for the fourteen weeks it took for expensive medication to heal his stricken genitals. Perhaps naive ashore, the navigator was a pro at sea, and kept an updated log on all wrecks in all waters. He had found the *Salem Lady* listed as sunk by US Coast Guard fire a bare four months before, had wasted no time informing his captain of the fact, and Caunter's reaction was typical of the man.

'We go in, do our job, count our bounty, Mr Denning. Salvage is salvage, and all owners are bastards. We're only raising the cargo, not landing it. We'll be a good many sea-miles away before Pollard makes landfall. Give me the right heading, Mr Denning, and remember the twelve-mile limit.'

Caunter was at the chart table when Pollard and Denning reported to the bridge, and was anxious to get under way.

'Can we go through the canal at night?' Pollard asked.

'Have you no sense of direction, man?' Caunter snapped.

'They're the co-ordinates,' Pollard laid a piece of paper on the chart of the North Atlantic. 'You tell me.'

'In the Pacific?' Denning asked.

'That's right.'

'You told the owners this?' Caunter was furious.

'I told 'em I'd save fuel. It seemed to be enough.'

'It bloody would be,' Caunter snarled.

Denning was making calculations in his head. 'We save at least five days steaming, captain.'

'There you go,' Pollard drawled. Grinning.

'Raise Colon Control,' Caunter ordered. 'We might jump the queue at first light. You know the form.' He turned on his heel and went below to fume over a rum toddy before retiring.

'Got a short fuse, huh?' Pollard said.

Denning gave him a bleak look.

'Take my advice. Keep well out of his way, mister. There's no sense of humour in his duffle, and you're a loose cannon on his deck.'

Pollard's shrug was unconcerned. A contract was a contract.

A viral infection flared and died in Charlie's chest wound, and his powers of healing had surprised the medical staff. Saul Chasen took him fishing on a charter boat, and they talked over their rods on an easy swell.

'Pollard's in Panama,' Chasen said. 'Got an old army buddy down there, and everything's for sale in that neck of the woods. Including information.'

Charlie thought about the CIA as he baited his hook.

'And?' he said.

'He's gone aboard a salvage ship. And right now, it's headed down the canal to the Pacific side. Beats the shit outta the stuff going down in the Florida Keys.'

'But makes sense. I never did figure out why they planned to bring the stuff up through Tijuana, when it had gone down off the east coast.'

'Using blinders, is why. And Pollard's stacked up a whole rack of messages for Joe Camponella's office. Bribed a guy in the post office to send one a day for most of two weeks. You think Pollard's gone into business for himself?'

'Do you?'

'Rat on the five families? They'd dig to Australia with their bare hands to find him. No, I guess I don't.'

'Then he's not letting Camponella know what he's really up to. The consortium has its own secret drugs trail, and they're keeping it that way.'

'There are no wrecks reported along that coast.'

'That your people know about.'

'That radar network can spot a solo Canadian goose.'

'Or a wave-hugging light aircraft?'

Chasen scratched his thumb on a hook barb.

'Shoot. That's *it*.'

'And outside US territorial waters. You still can't touch them.'

'And you figure you can?'

'Did you find the fifth man?'

'Big Ugly Sanchez? He's under surveillance in San Ysidro. That don't answer my question.'

'He's the key to this,' Charlie said, making a strike. 'Damn. Lost him.' He reeled in fast enough to make his Penn snarl.

'He'll have to recruit fresh help.'

'Won't he though?' Charlie said, feeding sand eel on to his hook.

Saul Chasen thought about the border canyons and shivered.

'Let's catch fish,' he said.

Benny Shoesmith visited five City offices to discuss business in principle, and got back to Poland Street with blank headed notepaper and crested envelopes from all of them. Borrowing a golfball typewriter with several different typefaces, he forged five letters of intent, and sent them to himself by express mail from the correct postal addresses. Marigold made sure she was waylaid by Brick Donovan the following morning, and in exchange for an envelope stuffed with fivers, allowed the day's post to be photocopied for George Muscat. Returned to Benny's desk by the time he arrived, he had Marigold file them before she shopped for baby clothes with Muscat's money.

The phoney scheme now encompassed Trafalgar Square, and made heavy reference to the controversial redevelopment of Piccadilly Circus. An alternative was under review by a finance house Muscat drooled to do business with, and he spent all day negotiating freeholds on the strength of it.

Benny awarded himself a stout and oyster luncheon, ordered three Savile Row suits, and had himself measured for six pairs of handlasted shoes from a bootmaker with the Royal Arms in his window. When the craftsman told Benny he would have to live until he was 120 to wear them out, Benny thought that was a splendid idea. He would work on it, and watch Marigold's baby grow to adulthood.

Two men he knew by reputation rousted him out of bed in early grey light and took him for a ride downtown. They had nothing to say, and ordered him about with head jerks. Jack Kurtz came fully awake on the drive, and was glad to see the Plymouth headed away from the Angeles Forest where many of his acquaintances had shallow, unmarked graves. Elevated to an office suite in a refurbished building, Kurtz was left to stew in a waiting room as the law firm came to life around him. A severe woman in hornrim glasses took him along corridors to the suite occupied by Joseph Camponella.

Ignored until Camponella had made neat notations in the margins of a file and sent it away with his secretary, Kurtz did some more worrying. Then those yellow-green eyes took Kurtz in as if he had a pin through his thorax like a display moth from the Amazonian basin, and a long hand flicked him into a chair. Kurtz wanted to gibber as his empty stomach rolled, and his shorts bound him like tight diapers.

'Running never solved anything, Kurtz.'

'Nossir.'

'It took exactly one half-day to discover where you'd skipped to. Think how easy it would be if we were really interested in you.'

Kurtz nodded. Anything to please. They must have traced him through the car. He should have dumped it, gone to another state.

'You keep sloppy records, Kurtz.'

'Just me inna office, Mr Camponella. Mostly I'm onna road.'

'And your "client" Mr Gardenia wasn't overly concerned so long as you got results, that your contention?'

'Right onna money there, Mr Camponella.'

'But your memory is good enough to recall times and dates, should I need them?'

Kurtz squirmed. His thighs hot inside damp trousers.

'Three years I been doing this for Doll. Can't lie to you, Mr Camponella. Ain't no way I got any real recall of any of it.'

'So, forgetting totally would not be impossible?'

Kurtz gripped hot knees with hotter hands.

'Easier, tell the truth. All them dives and saloons looked the same after a while. "Just don't let the bitch settle" is all I got from Doll when he slipped me some bills.'

175

'Referring to the O'Day woman, of course.'

'Who else? Sure.'

'And does that "bitch" know you by sight? By name?'

'Never did get invited to the house when she was living in. Never saw her in more than a coupla dives the whole three years. I'd just find the owner or manager, lay the news on him, and gone. She was never to know why she got canned, just have that certain feeling, y'know?'

'How many times were you refused over the three years?'

'From club owners? The odd redneck here and there, then Doll would send soldiers to make the point. To keep her in eating money, Doll'd give the nod to connected guys inna restaurant business. Like she'd get union basic, and Doll got the real payoff. He gotta real kick outta that.'

'But nothing like that in San Diego?'

'You want the unvarnished here, Mr Camponella?'

'Unless you want to kiss integral parts of your anatomy farewell.'

Kurtz smelled his own fear. Hoped it didn't cross the shiny desk to annoy Camponella's nostrils. Quickly said, 'That San Diego guy was real different. Thinking back, the whole set-up was unkosher. He talked real American, but it came out screwy. Like he was Australian. Boston-Canadian, y'know? But I got this tin ear, Mr Camponella.'

'British, perhaps?'

'Not old movies British like Niven or Colman. But near, y'know?'

'Describe him.'

'Tall. Like you. Late forties, maybe, but real trim. Some grey around the ears. Coldest grey eyes I seen outside of—' Kurtz did not say *this office*. 'Joliet.

That's it,. the joint. Cold, real cold. You take that guy's head off with a cannon, he'd come at you with his toenails. You get to know the type when you've done hard time. Jeeze, that I do know.'

Camponella steepled his fingers and laid the manicured tips to his mouth. Stared across at the sweltering Kurtz. Smelled the man's funk despite the air-conditioning. Saw hubcaps of sweat spread from the armpits. Stark despair in the pink eyeballs. Kurtz was a lemming who could flee across the Gulf of Mexico without leaving a footprint in the waves.

'What good are you, Kurtz?' he asked. 'What earthly good?'

Kurtz heard cement slop into the oildrum of his mind. Felt his naked feet plunged into gravel mix as he pleaded through a gag. Then the mourn of a garbage scow as the river came up to swallow him whole. Thought: *What have you got to lose, Jack? Tell the man.* Said, 'I done my very best for Mr Gardenia. He called it, he got it. I could do the same for you here. I did my job, and I'm up to my tush in I don't know what. Lemmee work for you, Mr Campo- nella? I'm *asking* here.'

Camponella gave himself an icy silence to think in. Kurtz' description of the Briton in San Diego matched the one extracted from the manager of the bar on Vine where the O'Day woman had last worked. A Captain of Detectives from Hollywood Station had paid his dues by running a computer check on the night Doll Gardenia had been as- saulted in his own bed. A stray British tourist had been picked up in Bel Air around that time, and Officer McTag's report gave the man a name, a height and build, and a last known address in Beverly Hills. A brief Immigration sweep had the man travelling on a passport issued in London to a dead man. It was enough to act on.

Camponella gave Kurtz precise instructions, and sent him away to collect travel expenses from the secretary in hornrim glasses. Just for once, Camponella planned to combine business with pleasure. He hadn't been to an opening night for months.

Delivered back to his apartment, Kurtz took a very necessary shower, and checked himself out physically to see if he really was in one piece. Dressed in his newest old suit, he drove to San Diego.

Whistling *Dixie*.

CHAPTER THIRTEEN

Larry Moffat found Charlie in San Ysidro, and they drank Dos Exxes outside a cockroach saloon, a *muriachi* band blowing its brains out inside. Ragged cloud blew into Mexico, and the humidity was low.

'I should stock this at the Palisades, it's as good as imported German beer.'

'What's really on your mind, Larry?'

'Don't play poker with my face, you limey ding-dong.'

'Ante up, Larry. You're only insulting when you're worried.'

Moffat glared at early hookers drumming up noon-tide trade. At macho kids in gang colours smoking inside their fists, looking for easy marks amongst the *pollos*. At Charlie's impassive face and the new scars knitting under his thin cotton top. A girl with old track marks and a face to stop traffic leered as she passed on six-inch heels, and a couple of American drunks were loud at a table under a tree dying of thirst.

'Kid,' Moffat said. 'You don't know how deep you're getting.'

'No such thing as a short tunnel to a claustro-phobic, Larry.'

'I'm just scared for you. Margot was a very special lady, but dying for her memory is dumber than dumb.'

'And eighty million dollars,' Charlie said.

'Revenge *and* a profit? Is this you talking like a refugee from Captain Kangaroo?'

'There has to be another motive, is that it? A greater truth?'

'Well, is there?'

'Not that I can explain easily. If at all.'

'Try, you mother.'

Charlie looked off at dying strands of ivy in unwatered tubs.

'I've been a walking dead man for a lot of years, Larry. God help me, but I lost the last five years without noticing. Margot's dying brought me back to life. I hated so hard I stood upright again. I tingled with it, Larry. Shed my empty existence like an old skin. And down in those canyons I was back amongst the living. Truly alive, all the moving parts oiled, tuned and ready to go. It was a good feeling. A wholeness. And I swear I'll never lose that feeling of *edge* ever again.'

Moffat shifted uneasily, seeing his friend anew. An awareness that both chilled and fascinated. He could have been staring into the lidless eyes of a cottonmouth.

'You'd rather die alive? That's crazy enough to be laughable.'

'To you, perhaps. Not to me. It had all become a dull game in which I *owned* all the royal cards. All the jokers. The entire deck. And where's the joy of winning if you can't lose? All the hands had been played a thousand times before. A tired ritual worth nothing.'

'Jesus, kid,' Moffat said. 'I owe you my life, I have to see you keep yours. That's a trade-off I can live with.'

'Not if *I* can't, Larry.'

'He wants the whole turkey. With onions.'

180

'And another beer.' Charlie tossed warm dregs into the ivy. Raised two fingers for refills.

'We all kiss ass, Charlie. Even me, Goddamnit. Comes down to how high or low we stoop or stretch to do it. Some sugar-asses are on higher pedestals.'

'Buy elevated shoes. Me, I'd kick the pedestal away.'

'I'd just bet you'd *try*.'

'You can't shoot a horse for trying.'

'*They* can. *They* do.'

'Who are *they*, Larry?'

Charlie's biting smile mocked Moffat as drinks came on a tray. He gave the Mexican moppet a five for wiping and polishing the table, ruffled his glossy hair and called him Chiquito.

'Still making friends,' Moffat hedged.

'Get it said, Larry.'

'Jack Kurtz came back hat in hand. Wanted you, got me.'

'And?'

'Jerked himself around with apologies. Said Miss O'Day was home free. The previous management had torn up her "contract". Hustled me for a table to entertain some high-rolling clients he wants to bring to Della's opening tomorrow night. Clients from White, Hall & Marks.'

'Joe Camponella and company. Sincere suits. Magnums under the lapels.'

'You could catch the show another night.'

'Stay out of the canyons? Stop *trading*, Larry.'

'Friends trade.'

'Not on friendship, they don't.'

'Bull. Every *one* – every *thing* has a price tag. Not just dollar signs, big numbers and zeroes. Secret handshakes and kissy-ass. Whatever it takes to deal.'

'So what's your price tag?'

181

'You don't get dead.'

'You won't shoot this horse for not—'

'*Trying* won't cut it, Charlie. Only losers *try*.'

'You play the cards you're dealt, Larry.'

'Twos against royalty? *They* own the deck this time, Charlie.'

'And being underestimated is an edge.'

'You're impossible. A total fruitcake.'

'I drew a joker. Saul Chasen.'

'What can he do? Hide you in a mineshaft under the Sierras? They'll hunt you for as long as it takes. The minute they identify you, you're theirs.'

'More than one way of dying, Larry. Running and hiding is the slowest form of suicide. Forget it.'

'So you face them off, you macho moron? A blindfold and a last cigarette ain't what they'll hand you. Honourable men are anything but. I'll understand you the day snakes grow antlers.'

'Try scratching an amoeba behind the ears. That *is* impossible. And a whole lot more sensible than thinking you can kiss Camponella's arse on my behalf. Unpucker, Larry. Stick to what you're good at, running saloons and this city.'

'You miserable hardhead. I wasn't . . .'

'Weren't you?'

'Yes, damn it. Camponella has to have a price tag.'

'He has. Fitting me with a noose.'

'Too clean, Charlie. You know what those people did to Action Jackson the loan shark? They had him pegged as a federal informer, and they shot him for openers. Took him bleeding to a meat plant. Hung him on a meat hook naked. Used ice picks and baseball bats on him. Wore out a cattle prod on his anus. Took him two days to die, and the families still crow about it. You, they won't be so nice to.'

'I know it. Changes nothing.'

'Talk to me, Charlie.'

'It's all been said, Larry.'

'We've exchanged *words*, that's all. We have to *talk*.'

'Tomorrow night.'

'If you're still alive by then.'

'No time to waste then, is there?'

And Charlie walked away to his hired car. Drove to the airport, and joined Saul Chasen on the flight to Palm Springs.

MAYDAY, MAYDAY, MAYDAY . . .

The voice edged with hysteria came at them in crackling mono.

Gave its last known position through static.

GOING DOWN, GOING DOWN . . .

Denning the navigator doodled on the plastic overlay of his electronic chart table, and Captain Caunter stared off at the receding smudge of Panama losing itself in Pacific blues. Pollard chewed on an unlit green cigar as the *Oceania-Cal Princess 2* aquaplaned past Punta Mariato on the long curve north, untouched by the taped drama he played.

A LIGHT, I SEE A LIGHT . . . I SAY AGAIN . . .

Vicious interference garbled the voice and the faltering aero engine.

A CRESCENT . . . SAND . . . GOING FOR IT . . . I REPEAT . . .

A loud crack and snarl ended the transmission, and Pollard rewound the tape. 'Heard enough?' he grunted.

Denning shook his head at the seascape glowing in magnification on his screen.

'Makes no sense,' he said. 'There are six thousand metres of water in that area. Look for yourself, d'you see any islands or sandbars marked? Crescent-shaped or otherwise?'

'He saw something,' Pollard said.

'Yes, the goblins of fear,' Caunter told the Clear-View port in his bridge windscreen.

'I knew the guy, Cap.' Pollard ejected and pocketed the tape. 'He hadn't the imagination of a horsefly. Whatever he saw is *there*.'

'And the walrus is a mermaid,' Caunter snapped. 'Why was there no air-sea search by the authorities?'

'Nobody monitors that frequency, is why. Was picked up in Mexico by some ham who happened to be listening.'

'A bald-faced lie, Mr Pollard,' Caunter said. 'That signal was picked up by one of your people, whoever they are. I don't know what you're up to – and don't want to. And any guess hazarded on my part would be counter-productive. We'll find your sand crescent and the plane if it's there. And that's where it ends.'

Pollard's grin was as false as a silicone breast.

'Makes you smart, Cap. And me smarter for picking you.'

'Keep to your heading, Mr Denning. Mr Pollard will leave the bridge at once. You'll be advised when you can return, Pollard.'

'Suits me.' Pollard went below to smoke. Being disliked bothered him not a jot. So long as those mothers found that plane, who gave a good God-damn? Eighty million bucks could wipe out all the dislike in the world.

Camponella's instructions were brutally precise, and the two men moved at once. Taking the Santa Ana south from Los Angeles, they drove to Long Beach and parked their anonymous car in a shopping mall. Crossed a walkway to a public park, and strolled through a condo complex like local residents. A federal agent came out of the house they watched, and was stuffing a garbage sack into the communal disposal unit when they reached him. His unconscious body went in with the garbage, and using his keys, the two men walked into the house to surprise an agent reading a newspaper over a Coors. Shaggy Coltrane was asleep in an upper room, and died without waking, shot through the mouth like the informer he was. The men were back on the freeway before a third agent arrived and raised the alarm.

Charlie was toying with a Waldorf salad when Saul Chasen came back from the restaurant phone, knothole eyes sombre in a pale face. He gulped cold coffee without tasting it, and lit a Chesterfield in the No Smoking section where they sat. Charlie took it from him before the management could bleat protest and crushed it underfoot. Daylight faded outside, and Chasen saw nothing outside himself.

'Which hat are you wearing now, Saul?'

Chasen could have been carved from soap.

'Washington rejected your monthly expenses?'

No response.

'They put salt in your coffee?'

Chasen's rapid eye movements were the only sign of life until he reached for another cigarette with an unsteady hand. Charlie's fist closed over hand and cigarette and crushed them to bring Chasen back.

'How did they find out?' Chasen asked. 'How?'

'About what?'

'Huh? Oh, yeah. They found the safe house. Took out two agents with some kind of gas. Blew Shaggy Coltrane away like a swatted fly. Get the check, we're going.'

185

In the rental they had picked up at the airport, Chasen regained colour as he chainsmoked.

'Can't *talk* to animals like that,' he muttered. 'Kill a Fed, and they've broken all the unwritten rules. They're finished. But no, they use gas for Chrissakes. Leave two cabbages inna garbage. Technically alive. You know what nerve gas does to the brain buds? Those guys will be lucky if they can spoon their own soup. Collect their retirement checks. Count their fucking fingers without help.'

Charlie drove into Palm Springs in silence as Chasen raved.

'Surveille and keep files. Shave and wear neckties. That's what being a Fed has come down to. Scared of being accused of entrapment, of violating some shithead's civil rights. What the fuck are we but empty suits, we don't scoop them up like doody? Put the motherheads where they belong? Inna toilet with the other crud. Throw away the keys and let 'em rot down into compost. No, we don't do that. We're cyphers going through the motions, is what.'

Charlie lost the mainstream traffic on a turnoff. Drove past hotels and found the road to the section they wanted. Overshot on his next right turn and doubled back on a parallel road.

'Building files and *talking* law enforcement ain't the road to go. Nossir, nossir, NOSSIR. A dead man's testimony ain't worth the death certificate it's printed on. We're wasting time – they're wasting *people*. The scales of justice? Jesus, about as much use as a flaking sunburn to a fashion model.'

Charlie eased the rental under gum trees on an unlit lot. Killed the heads and sidelights, and sat behind the wheel in the glow of the dashboard dials. Opened his window to release smoke and give him a clearer view of a building beyond immature trees and a storm fence.

'How did they know about the safe house? They got an ear inside the bureau? Or are they better than we are at surveillance? My brain spins, my ulcer bites, and they sit back laughing. I'd rather swallow dog spit than choke on that peachy thought.'

Charlie unscrewed the bulb from the interior light. Opened his door in darkness. Turned off the ignition and waited for Chasen to wind down.

'You've got a whole lot of nothing to say for yourself,' Chasen sneered. Looking for somebody to focus anger on. Anybody.

'You're the one with all the words. The talk.' Charlie sounded deceptively mild in the hum of far traffic. The muted roar of a descending aircraft.

'And all I've got, that it?'

'You tell me, Saul.'

'Whaddya want? My vision of flag and country? From sea to shining sea? It's a toilet linked together by shit and more shit.'

'Then talk *yourself* to death.'

'And you think that interviewing Gardenia is a waste of time.'

'That depends on how he gets talked to.'

Chasen unlocked his seat belt. Rocked in his seat.

'You're a fascist, you know that?'

Charlie gave that remark the silence it deserved. Names and labels meant nothing to him. Only results mattered now. He toyed with car keys without humming.

'Break the unworkable rules,' Chasen said. 'Why not? They have.'

'At last,' Charlie said.

'And you've got a game plan I shouldn't wonder.'

'Only if you've got the bottle for it.'

'You mean balls? Elephants blanch when they see me strip my shorts, my man.'

'I'll take your word for it without a demonstration.'

'So move it, smart ass. Before I have a rush of rationality to the head.'

'Don't worry. Wouldn't find you home any way.'

'What?' Chasen hissed, trailing Charlie across the dirt lot to the storm fence. *'What?'*

Amadeus and Big Wilma had a live one.

They hooded the Cleveland salesman and strapped him to the pink couch. The salesman's belly heaved in anticipation as he was coated in gel, and Wilma selected the whip she would use in perverted foreplay. The weals from his previous visit were fading on his fleshy pectorals, and he was already whining inside the hood when Amadeus leaned close to promise exquisite agonies. A Luftwaffe march pounded from the coffin speakers, and the salesman screamed like a diving Stuka as the first lash striped his rubbery chest. Amadeus teased the flaccid penis with soft downward strokes and talked of emasculation with sharp razors.

The two men sent by Camponella were inside unheard, and the first bullet hit Amadeus in the lower neck. Knocked from his crouch, he yawned blood until the second silenced round punched a hole in his thin brown chest. He spread his afro across the salesman's chest as Wilma turned towards the odd popping noises, her whip snapping like her furious eyes. A soft-nosed slug hit her huge left breast above the nipple. She looked bewildered and put a hand to her chest. Hit twice in the stomach, she staggered to sit on the salesman's face. Sat upright, and let her mouth sag open as another bullet hit her in the heart. She fell on her side with a thump, and there was just the martial music and the moans from the salesman.

The two men left him there and drove away without a word.

Doll Gardenia dreamed uneasily when he was lifted on to a gurney. Camponella was telling him things in a language he knew he should know, but it came out all wrong in the drugged stupor. In an elevator that tried to drop away and leave him suspended in the shaft, he opened a dreary eye and tried for focus. Wild perspective made spirals, and he stopped trying to see until he was wheeled across tarmac with night smells confusing him. The blackness revolved when he raised his head, and all the stars streaked his eyes with rocket trails. If the men pushing him away from hospital odours had faces they were blobs of jiggle he couldn't hold still.

Gardenia wanted his dream back. However crazy, it was more reasonable than all this motion. A wire gate opened against rust, and the gurney wobbled him over rutted ground to a shadow car under dark trees. His face would hurt if he thought too hard, so he left clever cerebration to the dream Camponella who still talked on in an elusive language he could not translate. Legal mumble from the bastard Icebox. The hell with him.

Laid across the back seat of the shadow car, Gardenia wished his plastered arm would stop scraping the rear window. A nail on glass that ground his soft teeth together. Made splinters in his mind. Hurt him with doubts he hadn't the will to consider. Street lights whipped their poles past the windows, and Gardenia smelled Chesterfield smoke. Time tilted on an axis, and the tyres drummed on highway surface. Night was leaking into a new day,

and the taste in his throbbing mouth was bitter
aloes. Burned oak chips.

Freeway signs he knew to be familiar passed
overhead, their greens and whites and numbered
shields telling him he was on the Interstate
approaching Los Angeles. Jarred into murmuring
aloud to himself, he heard a man remark on it in a
spurt of fresh smoke. Wanting a cigar, Gardenia
tried to ask for one. The dream Camponella refused
in strange tongues, and doctors shook their heads,
concerned to keep his torn mouth aseptic.
Gardenia's mind tripped, and a wallow of sick lassitude claimed him.

Lifted into daylight proper, Gardenia was man-
handled into the rear of an apartment block and up
cement stairs. Taken past a fish in a tank, his nose
almost scraping carpet, he was dumped on a yellow
counterpane in a bedroom with a sunflower blind.
The ceiling glowed chrome before he was rolled on
his face to smell perfume he thought he knew
from somewhere. The scent teased him, and he was
trying to make all the blurs into wholes when a
blindfold blocked everything out. He was too weary
for panic, too confused to know who had brought
him from Palm Springs. He found a simple mind
game to occupy him. Scrabbled through the litter of
memory to find a loved-hated face dabbing that
smell behind small ears. Zeroed in on shocked
knowing.

Della the toy. The drunk. The musical bitch who
hated him.

Gardenia fell into the vagueness that passed for
sleep, and was dragged back from nowhere to sip
juice through a straw held for him by the Chesterfield man. Was helped to urinate in a bucket and
laid back on what felt like a rubber sheet. Wanted

to plead or deal, and was cut off by a prod to the chest from a metal eye with a front sight.

'Your ass is mine,' the Chesterfield man said. 'Just you and me left inna whole world. I own you, Gardenia.'

'Whatever she paid you, I'll double it.'

'You're dreaming, bucko. Ain't no she.'

Gardenia whimpered drool.'You got tears there, Gardenia? Shed 'em for Shaggy Coltrane. Your buddy Camponella made him dead. You're meat in our sandwich. He's the rock, and I'm the hard place. You're in the crusher, Doll.'

'And *she's* paying you.'

'Ain't no *she* but the cat's mother. Just the Icebox, Pollard and Muscat. And me. Your friends ain't your friends no more.'

'None of them would do this . . . to me.'

'Only all of them, you clutz. Think about it.'

'There's no good reason . . .'

'I count eighty million reasons.'

Shock cleared the mist from Gardenia's well of self-pity.

'You can't know about . . . that.'

'No? So how come I do?'

Gardenia wept into his blindfold.

Sorry for nobody but himself until the drugged orange juice put him back into blank oblivion.

It was 8 a.m. Eastern Standard Time when Charlie called the Manoel Island Yacht Club from a drugstore payphone two blocks down from Della's apartment. Victor Zammit came on the line, a finger in his ear to block out the jolly fuzz from the bar. The gin-and-tonic sailors were at a birthday thrash for a fair-weather admiral; and from the noise, Charlie knew the sun was well over the yardarm. He listened

191

to Zammit's report, told him to act immediately, and the bonus he promised sweated up the Gozitan's money finger.

Charlie strolled back to the apartment to find Saul Chasen feeding Oscar with shaking hands.

'Mr Gardenia will sleep twenty-four hours around now, Charlie. But it by God comes to something when you have to act badder than the bad guys.'

'Some sleep and some breakfast will put the sunshine back in your soul.'

'What d'you know about it?'

Charlie lounged in a chair with a small bourbon, offered a larger measure to Chasen. 'Get that behind your belt. Just the one, you need to be sharp tonight.'

Chasen drained the drink with a toss.

'I don't need to be patronized by a cold fish, pally.'

'You've crossed the line. No going back now.'

'Enough already. *Enough.* Don't hand me all that "fold or play" bull. My eyes are all the way open, my navel is fluff-free, and my anus is tighter than Fort Knox. Not *liking* being an animal don't mean I can't handle it. You hear me here?'

'I hear you. Point taken. No problem.'

'Gimmee another shot. And no "buts".'

Charlie poured a healthy slop in the glass thrust at him.

'Cheers,' he smiled.

The drink disappeared between Chasen's teeth in a hard bite that thinned to a tight grin. He sluiced both glasses in the sink and wiped them dry. Leaned against the pine unit with folded arms.

'Two of my guys will be here after dark. Best time to move Gardenia out, seeing as Della's neighbours are all night workers. My guys'll have Doll tucked up in his Bel Air bed before you can say "J. Edgar

Hoover". The last place Camponella's hoods will look. Neat, huh?'

'As embroidery. If you can trust your people.'

'Those two? Parrot and Blackwell think it was *me* brought Moses and all them Commandments down from the mountain. And the eleventh one reads: Thou Shalt Obey The Prophet Chasen, Or Be Castigated Unto Death.'

Charlie listened for sound in the passage and stairwell.

'Ready for breakfast and the Icebox?' he asked, cracking the door.

'Born ready,' Chasen said, his fists as hard as his grin.

When the night nurse found Gardenia gone, she called Schofield the Medical Director, and he contacted Camponella's office to leave a coded message on the answerphone. Camponella got back to Schofield the moment he arrived Downtown; cancelled his morning appointments, and got to the Palm Springs Clinic a minute past noon. Taken to the locked room, he was shown the bed and the ice pick pinning an invitation card to the pillow. An engraved Della O'Day smiled above cursive script printed on gold Astrolux card.

'Has anybody else seen this? Apart from you and your nurse, Schofield?'

'Absolutely not. My nurses are trained to discretion. If this were to become public, the clinic's image would suffer untold—'

'So would your budget. What does our endowment run at?'

'I . . . take your point, Mr Camponella. May I offer you—'

'Nothing but silence. This goes no further. Clear?'

193

'Very,' Schofield squeaked, seeing more than a million a year gone out of the window if the Chicago foundation withdrew its funds.

Camponella used the phone before leaving. There was a lot of ground to cover before he attended the opening night in San Diego. The 'dead man' from London was more than an intriguing nuisance now. He was a menace who must be neutralized at speed.

Victor Zammit marshalled and polished his lies aboard *The Lady Desperado* as he doctored an expensive Sicilian wine with a hypo of powerful liquid sedative. The Mosta chemist knew Victor bought the potent draughts as a treat for the old whore when visions of hellfire killed her rest, and had taken his money without a second thought. Breaking into the Cunninghams' villa to bring away a suitcase of assorted clothes had presented no difficulty, nor had borrowing a cassock and a goblet from St John's Cathedral in Valletta; *The Lady Desperado* was fuelled and provisioned, and the only problem now was how Carlo Fabriano reacted to Victor's simple fabrications. Good lies should be so close to the truth that the listener cannot spot the weave between fantasy and fact, and every Gozitan with Phoenician blood in his veins knew the art of the clever canard long before his first pubertal shave.

Victor taped the magnum to his ankle and packed his satchel. Drove his panel truck to Valletta through a night as hot and as black as boiled molasses.

CHAPTER FOURTEEN

The old whore opened the door with her face averted, and Victor took her by the chin to turn her towards the street light. One gaunt cheek had ballooned under a closed eye, and a fat blood grape grew from her lower lip. For the first time, she smelled as old as she looked.

'You fell?'

'*Him!*' The old whore jerked her head at the stairs. 'With his fist, the hero. There was no money for drink, so he gave me this for my apology. I got credit in Siren Street when I said you would pay.'

'Myself will pay, as he will pay me.'

The old whore clawed Victor's wrist. Strong with fear, the yellow nails bit deep, and her working eye was a pale spitball in a shadowed socket. The beating had shaken her closer to the spiritual world she longed to inhabit once her purification was complete, and she was afraid she would die before she was in a state of grace.

'Take care, son of lust. He has the madness *and* the drink. I think he hit the old English ones. I heard, but I did not look.'

'Myself will do this thing. Go to the church and stay there.'

The old whore hobbled into the night, and Victor plodded upstairs with the slow deliberation of a weary man. Carlo Fabriano had the Uzzi and the bottle before him, and he made no move when Victor laid his satchel on the table. His dull eyes took

Victor in like a thing of no interest.

'There is news from Catania?' he asked.

'A long day, friend Carlo. But yes, there is news.' That much was true, anyway. 'Fraternal greetings from home. There is more, but you must be sober to hear it.'

'On seawater rum? Ten bottles would give me one belch.'

'True. I will see to the old ones.'

'Later. I come first here.'

'Friend Carlo, I can smell their waste from here.'

'I breathe their stink all day, all night. You have the nostrils of a woman.'

Victor held his temper. Showed Fabriano a look of disgust.

'One does not drink good wine in stench.'

'You have a bottle?'

'After I freshen the air, eh?'

'A man should not do such things. The old whore should do that. She does nothing.'

'And why you had to chastise her, eh?'

'She asked for it. They all ask for it.' Fabriano slopped rum into his mouth, spotting his dirty shirt with it.

Victor went into the Cunninghams, and Granny lay facing the wall, trembling with defeat. Flo looked like a bloated hind with a knife at her throat, a blue bruise on her plump upper bosom. Victor raised a finger to his lips and shook his head at her. Said:

'You are foolish to disobey our friend. Sit still and quiet, eh? I will clean, then you must both sleep. I must take our friend to his brother to pay his last respects. When you wake up tomorrow, it will all be over.' Then he mouthed, 'Charlie will come.'

Fabriano blocked the doorway when Victor turned

196

with the chamber pot. 'What about my brother, Gozitan? Speak.'

'Where is your respect, Sicilian? Wash. Change your clothes for clean. Find a razor. Then I will take you to your brother's casket.'

'Tonight? Now?'

'It is arranged.'

'And leave these two alone?'

'They will sleep,' Victor said. 'Myself has arranged this.'

'I will tie them to their stinking mattresses.'

'They will drink and sleep. There is a bottle in the satchel with the wine. Bring two glasses. And wash your body, Carlo, there is little time.'

Fabriano pulled at his shirtfront. Rasped a hand against his unshaven jaw. 'Si, si,' he muttered, his wild eyes as unstable as droplets of brown mercury. 'I must light candles. Say the words.' He crossed himself rapidly three times.

'There are candles, friend Carlo.'

Victor went down three flights to empty the pot. Heard Carlo splash water into a basin and sluice himself. Went back up to find him lathering his beard with laundry soap, his olive back rippling with hard strings of muscle. Found two glasses himself, and poured mild sedative from a small bottle. Took them to Flo and Granny and made them drink. The measures were small enough to relax them, no more, and Victor comforted them both with a wink before locking the door. He sat at the table and took the Sicilian wine from the satchel, set it down with a thump for Fabriano to see.

'Your family told myself this must be drunk as the blood of Christ. The blood of your brother. It was bottled the year Mario was born, as is fitting, yes?'

'This is a good thing.' Fabriano grudged the words

197

of faint praise. Hated being beholden to this outsider over the strict form of family mourning. 'There must be a cloth. A silver goblet.'

'I have a white cloth of silk. The cup is pewter. Myself could do no more without robbing a church.'

'It must do, I suppose.'

'True piety is more to the Almighty than silver. Burned meat on gold plate is still burned.'

'Keep your riddles.' Fabriano's sneer was dismissive. He trimmed a sideburn and threw the razor down. 'They are meaningless.'

'To one confused by loss, perhaps,' Victor sighed. 'You do not need the gun for this. We go to a hallowed place.'

'It goes where I go, Gozitan.'

'As you wish.'

Victor repacked the satchel. Coldly resolved.

Carmel Commaros the mortician knew the dream for what it was. Nailed inside one of his own coffins as his wife slept beside him, he could hear his fists beat on the lid as a bell tolled too fast to make sombre runs like a true carillon. More vivid than ever before, it repelled him from sleep. He fought upward through clinging winding sheets to pick up his bedside clock. Saw the time, and went downstairs untangling the arm of his dressing gown. Threw open his front door to look out at a priest he didn't know.

'Father?'

'Commaros, my son, forgive me for disturbing you, but there is the urgency of grief to consider.'

Commaros picked up the Gozitan accent. The reason this priest was a stranger to him. The crucifix he wore was as big as the bishop's, which meant he came from a rich diocese. Maybe the cathedral itself.

'I am Father Avellino. This unfortunate young man is of the family Fabriano. He works on the rigs in the Gulf, and came here to see his brother, only to find he has died. He came to me for help, and I bring him to you.'

'But this is a police matter, Father Avellino.'

'Their jurisdiction halts at the gates of paradise. This man is bereaved, not a felon. He asks only to pay his last respects. A man of the true faith would understand that. Are you not such a man, my son?'

'I . . . yes . . .'

The priest bulked close to the frail mortician. Smelled of mothballs and incense. His rumble of a voice close to Commaros' ear.

'He wishes to dedicate a window. That is the measure of his grief. And Arab monies coming to the church through this unfortunate man shows our faith to be the stronger, you see this great truth, Commaros?'

Confused, Commaros nodded.

'You, of course, would handle the transaction. He will be generous. Venetian glass and English leading will last a thousand years. And for what? The opportunity to stand vigil until dawn. It is so little to ask.'

Commaros saw the temporal profit. His nod more emphatic.

'The body is to be flown to Sicily tomorrow, Father. Why cannot this man go there for the memorial service?'

'He must return to the Gulf. A contract is a contract. And the damned Arab cares nothing for the Christian Church. You see?'

'I'll get my keys. But forgive me, he must be gone before the hearse arrives at eight tomorrow.'

'At cock's crow, the very time Our Lord was denied the third time.'

'You want me to stay nearby, Father?'

'Not unless you wish to join our small ceremony. I will lock the mortuary. Return the keys. Post them through your letter box, eh?'

'Satisfactory, I think. Come.'

'Mother Church blesses you, Commaros, my son.'

The *Oceania-Cal Princess 2* had cleared the South-East Monsoon Drift and left Guatamalan waters for Mexico when Denning the navigator asked to hear the pilot's tape again. He played it through at variable speeds, came to a conclusion, and took his thoughts to Captain Caunter. It all boiled down to a single error being compounded, and Denning made a fair plot of the plane's probable course.

'Puts him down in the sea just off the Revilla Gigedo Islands. Probably west of the main group. There *are* some submarine peaks there. Not true islands as such, but in the right light, and seen from a low-flying plane, they might seem to be atolls. There was intermittent cloud that day. One good shaft of sunlight picking out an underwater feature with unusual clarity might be the answer.'

'He was night-flying, Mr Denning.'

'And the same goes for brilliant moonlight. It was full moon.'

Caunter grunted.

'I'm at a loss to come up with any other conclusion without we make an extensive grid-search, and that could take weeks, Captain.'

'Months, Mr Denning. We're clear of the shipping lanes. Plot a course that brings us in on that group from the east. That puts the light at our stern, and we might just see for ourselves what that fly-boy nosed into.'

'Do we tell the client, Captain?'

'Pollard? No. Let him stew in cigar smoke.'

After the heat of the night, the refrigerated mortuary and its chemical smells stole their breath.

Mario Fabriano lay in an ebony coffin on a draped trestle, a rosary in his clasped hands, his broken face rebuilt into a parody of itself. His impacted forehead was covered by a padded bandana sewn with a black cross, and the metal face-former inside his mouth gave him a beatific smile he had never worn in life. Overstated cosmetics gave him the look of a wanton chorus boy.

Carlo looked even less alive as he stood there shivering, trying to remember the Latin he had not been fluent in since boyhood. He laid the Uzzi aside and needed two hands for the goblet Victor filled for him, gulping at it as if the elusive words were drowned in wine. He stumbled from station to station with Victor prompting him through the many half-remembered complications. Kneeled when he was told to, and counting off the prayers with the rosary beads. The bottle was finished when Carlo had steeled himself for the final kiss of farewell. He made the sign of the cross over Mario's face, drained the goblet, and pressed his mouth to the cold cheek.

Carlo had collapsed before Victor could reach him, and his head struck the coffin before he hit the floor. The empty goblet rolled away, and Victor checked his watch to find that time was still on his side. It was a few minutes before 6 p.m. in California, 2 a.m. in Malta. He had two clear hours to finish what he had begun.

Victor worked without hurry. Or relish for what was to come.

What was necessary was not always pleasant.

*

The agent in Catania ripped the phone from its hook and snarled his name into the mouthpiece, his head pounding from last night's grappa. The woman lay across his legs with her mouth open, and he tried to remember her name.

'Frazetti. What?'

'Is myself,' Victor said. 'There is big trouble here.'

Frazetti got his watch close to his face.

'At four in the morning?'

'I've looked all over. The maniac has disappeared.'

'Who, who?'

'Carlo.'

'Carlo?'

'The old woman called. I went there. She had been beaten badly, very badly. This is not a good thing.'

'This matters?'

'Carlo got.rum from somewhere. Beat the old woman and left the house with a priest. He had been bad with the English ones too.'

'What priest?'

'Myself does not know this. He took the priest with him. To see Mario's body, I think.'

Frazetti was awake now. He filled a water glass and moistened his mouth. Brought the harsh taste of grappa back with a mild sense of nausea. The woman had matched him drink for drink until after midnight. Grabbed his genitals the moment he got her back to the house. Tore the buttons from his shirt. God's scrotum, but she was a magnificent animal. As blonde as Frazetti was dark, she had wrestled him to the bed and worked on him like ten experienced whores.

'Frazetti?'

'Yes, yes, I'm here.'

'I went to the place where the body is being kept. It was in darkness, so I broke in. There was wine spilled there. Candle wax on the casket. I cleaned it up and came back to the house. The old one could speak then. She said Carlo had talked of death when he drank. Of joining his brother. You understand?'

'That is just wildness. The talk of too much drink.'

'There is something wrong here, Frazetti. Who was this priest? Carlo knew no priests.'

'Go to bed, Zammit. This will all look better in the morning.'

'Carlo took the Uzzi. The old woman wants us out of her house. How can I sleep?'

'Pay her more money.'

'He broke her jaw and some teeth, I think. I must get her a doctor. Say she fell on the stairs. Money will not be enough.'

'Money is always the answer.'

'No, Frazetti. Supposing she talks when they sedate her, eh? No, I must move the English ones. There is already too much gossip. Myself will move them out of there.'

'What will happen when Carlo comes back to an empty house?'

'I will wait there for him. Take him away with me. He is a danger to us. A madman. An Uzzi is not an umbrella you can walk around Valletta in daylight with. There is barely an hour to dawn.'

Frazetti saw the logic in Zammit's proposals. Carlo had always been a wild dog. Fearless, but no true sense of caution. It was just like him to act without thinking. If he was cornered with a gun, he would use it.

'Find him, Zammit. Then move the English people.'

'I have one hour of darkness left. I must move them now. The Maltese police are not stupid, and they have issued pictures of the English ones. Carlo is on his own. And Frazetti? He took the old woman's sedatives with him.'

Frazetti frowned at the woman and tried to think about rum and sedatives and the priest. About Carlo loose with an Uzzi, but it all seemed so distant. Her name was Karen something, a divorcee off a tour ship from Stockholm. A lazy hand stroked his thigh in foreplay, and without opening her eyes, she tongued his calves and used her teeth on the inside of his knees. Tiny sensual nibbles that aroused him so completely, he had trouble breathing.

'Do what you think best, Zammit,' he said. Got the phone back in its cradle and reached for the full breasts with both hands. Now it was his turn to show this woman what kind of a man she had found.

Victor grinned in the phone booth on Republic Square. The old whore would corroborate his story if asked. She even believed Victor had acted on her behalf like a true son would. He climbed into his panel truck and winked at the Cunninghams.

'Myself will make one call to Charlie. Then we go from here. You like Italy?'

Tinted searchlights cut swathes in the night sky above the Wooden Palisades in playful homage to the 20th Century Fox opening title, and DELLA O'DAY TONITE glowed neon in a revolving ring of pink stars. Fountains played through the spectrum in the concrete moat, and the gas flambeaus jetted dramatically at full pressure. The whole forecourt had been carpeted in red, and Larry Moffat greeted his guests at the door, gladhanding like a politician. A photographer recorded every smiling handshake, and the framed pictures were presented to the guests at their tables. Della's New York album played softly in the lobby, and her face was on every gala menu. Deputy sheriffs controlled traffic, FBI agents supervised valet parking and perimeter security, and a woman agent checked fun furs by the yard.

Jack Kurtz yearned for the old days when he saw the jewellery on the women, the stickpins and rings on the men, and almost yelped when Moffat's paw swallowed his hand in the glare of a sungun. His personal Polaroid of the event gave him the look of a startled pickpocket, and he was crowded into the lobby before he could effect the introductions he had practised on the drive down from Los Angeles.

'Glad you could make it, Mr Camponella,' Moffat said smoothly. 'Your host for the evening will join you at table. Smile for the camera. Fine. You'll find the vintage wine to your taste, I think. Gentlemen,' he said to the two men at Camponella's back. 'Enjoy the evening, won't you?'

Camponella blinked afterburn away in the lobby as Della did pretty things to the middle eight bars of 'A Train'. A security man ran a metal detector over his party without pressing the panic button, and a leggy girl in black led them to their table, seating them according to the named place settings. There was an empty chair between Kurtz and Camponella, and Kurtz read off the name on the card.

'You know a Mr C. Dance, Mr Camponella?'

'Champagne, sir?' the leggy girl asked.

Camponella peeled the napkin back from the label.

'Bollinger '72,' he read. 'Whoever he is, he's done his research on my palate. Serve it.'

The cork popped with a discreet curl of vapour, and sparkling wine creamed into hollow-stemmed tulips.

'You want I should taste it first? They got my right

name printed here,' said the man who had liquidated Big Wilma and Shaggy Coltrane.

'Mine too,' grunted his partner. 'This smells, Joe.'

'I said nothing,' Kurtz said quickly. 'Nothing.'

'You wouldn't have to, Jack,' Camponella said. 'Don't gulp it, you nebish. Costs out at two hundred a bottle. Wholesale.'

Kurtz drank carefully. Wanting a beer. Wanting out.

Everybody seemed discomfited but Camponella. He was as relaxed as a lottery-winning five-Librium inept with a year's dishes in the sink, and her kids in care. Going with the flow like an acid-house surfer. Admiring the decor and spotting celebrities; trading nods with half the Californian legislature, a couple of senators and their ward-heeling PR people. Faces he had done business with in the recent past. Kurtz was out of his league, but Camponella knew a perfect set-up when he was the target. He couldn't even wear the wrong expression in this company without earning unwelcome locker-room talk in several exclusive country clubs. He must wear his urbane public face as if he hadn't been shafted with a cyanide pessary. He was too close to the top now to make mistakes like Doll Gardenia. Like Sam Giancana had when he sued the Government for harassment, and was shot in the head from behind whilst warming over an evening snack of Italian sausage. Sam had *owned* Chicago, and blew it by becoming as public a figure as any Las Vegas entertainer, his sex life in motels painstakingly taped by the ubiquitous FBI. Camponella poured himself more Bollinger, and waited for the empty chair to be occupied. As patiently poised as a hungry mantis.

His dream world of limber girls in white cloud and

sunshine was jangled apart by vicious nails of warble. He rose through the leaden wool of sleep to lift the phone to his face. He was Inspector Ellul again, and it was a few seconds after 5 a.m. He listened to the sergeant on the graveyard shift drone facts at him, the phone hooked into his neck as he searched for clothes.

Ellul chided himself. He should have pushed harder for a search of the old whore's house. Ellul was bitterly ashamed of his complacent superiors too. Manning the summer fireworks festivals had been thought more important than his investigation, and even surveillance of the house had been watered down to the sketchiest minimum. And this latest twist of events was infuriating.

'Seal the entire area off,' he ordered. 'Nothing is to be touched. Nothing.'

Ellul horned himself into his shoes with savage twists.

One way or another, it promised to be a very long day indeed.

A tall Irish was served before the empty chair as Jack Kurtz wolfed prime steak and Iowa corn. He twisted in his seat to look up at the man with Joliet eyes. Glanced across the table at Camponella to see him staring at Dance, the tension between them almost tactile. Two predators with narrowed eyes locking mental horns. Carnivorous Titans turning Kurtz into a pygmy, and he had the crazy idea they would turn on him if he didn't roll under the table or run for the mensroom.

Then Dance sat easily, and the atmosphere hummed rather than crackled.

'Well,' Camponella said. 'The dead man has a face.'

'And a name, Camponella. Try using it.' Charlie

looked around the table at closed faces as if they all held low cards. 'There's ten minutes to showtime. Let's not waste it snarling.'

Camponella bared long, ivory teeth.

'All right, Mr Dance. Return Gardenia to me right now, and the lady lives to play. My first and final offer.'

'Forget it. I don't give a damn about Doll's ex-live-in-lady. She was, and is, a convenience. Another pawn in the game. Just like Kurtz here, they brought you to this table.'

'To what end, Dance?'

'To stop a war. Trade more than bodies.'

Camponella's mouth tightened.

'All I see is a single opportunist making noises.'

'And I'm looking at a careful man who disappoints me. Those two clowns of yours are carrying magnums. Englese packs a Dan Wesson. Rizzo a Colt Cobra. The late Shaggy Coltrane had one of those before it was taken away from him. Get the point?'

'Which is?'

'I could have had them nailed to the wall of the lobby. A gun's only as good as the man behind it. And right now, Englese and Rizzo are as worthless as they're undecorative. I could pull their noses, and they'd have to sit and take it.'

'Call them insurance, Dance. I'm in a high-risk business.'

'Then have them walk Kurtz around the block. Leave the adults to talk. What I have to discuss is for your ears only.'

Camponella dabbed a napkin at his mouth and leaned back.

'You'd have to prove that. Give me a general rundown. Then I'll decide whether to take you seriously, or stamp on you like a bug.'

Charlie winked at the sweating Kurtz.

'Hear that, Jack? He plans to make me history like Shaggy and his perverted playmates. He starts burying business associates, you just have to be next. Then Englese. Then Rizzo. Where does it end, Camponella? When there's only you left?'

'Where's he coming from, Joe?' Englese asked Camponella.

'The man's talking hits here,' Rizzo said.

'Jesus,' Kurtz wet-mouthed. 'Jesus . . .'

'Calm down, people,' Camponella soothed.

Charlie's laugh was as dry as desert sand.

'Can you take your own advice? There are several sudden deaths you know nothing about. A small matter of the abduction of a financier and his wife. The loss of eighty million dollars. Half of which belongs to me. Try laughing that off, Camponella.'

'You're fishing, Dance.'

'Like Casey Pollard is, somewhere off the coast of Mexico? When you think he's salvaging a wreck in the North Atlantic? You've got problems you plain can't handle without we deal.'

Camponella tried to keep the surprise out of his face.

'How's he know about all this, Joe?' Rizzo asked.

'Good question,' Camponella said.

'How?' Charlie pointed a finger around his Irish. 'Read the small print, my friend. We've been partners for going on two years. *I'm* your money laundry, not that poor bastard Granny Cunningham. That's right, Camponella, he works for me. You should have kept a tighter rein on Gardenia, Pollard and Muscat. They should have looked past Cunningham, and found me buried in all those paper deals. They're your morons, Joe. Yours, not mine. And because of them, the toll to you so far is nine dead. I've lost one

209

on the sidelines. If that isn't a shooting war, what the hell is?'

'Talk to the man, Joe,' Englese said. 'He's making all kinds of sense here, and the families ain't gonna like all this coming at them sudden. Doll and his druggies have smeared shoot on our shoes, that makes them extra to requirements. Right?'

'Gets my vote,' Rizzo grunted. 'Let's do business here.'

'And what's this garbage about Pollard fishing on the wrong side of Miami? Those are serious bucks he's fooling with,' Englese said. 'Seems he slipped your net, Joe. You wanna tell us about that?'

Camponella hated everybody with his eyes. Sipped champagne and watched bubbles rise in the hollow stem. Underestimating Dance had been a grave error, and he had compounded the mistake by not facing him in private. He had to save face in the here and now. Make the situation work for him in the long term.

Charlie watched Camponella's shift of attitude, and played on it with, 'You're the coming man, Joe. Let's keep it that way. That eighty mill doesn't reach San Diego, you'll smell worse than the manure they grow violets in. You guarantee me my thirty-eight mill, I'll cover the immediate future with an irrevocable letter of credit.'

'For which you want Cunningham back, that it?'

'I already took care of that,' Charlie shrugged.

'You get around,' Englese said. 'Who the fuck is this guy, Joe?'

'I'm beginning to find out,' Camponella said. 'And Gardenia?'

'He's fast asleep in Bel Air. He's yours so long as he never gets to play macho man again. I owe Della that much, and so do you people.'

'So long as she only sings for the paying public.'

'She knows nothing anyway, Joe. I thought different, she wouldn't be here tonight.'

'This just has to be the guy who folded Shaggy up like a fucking tent,' Rizzo said. 'I just wanna know why.'

'How's your Latin, Joe?' Charlie said. '*Bis peccare in bello non licet*, gets it said.'

'In war,' Camponella translated, 'one may not blunder twice.'

'And the consortium have,' Charlie said. 'Eighty mill under the ocean, all their working capital. And instead of using their combined grey matter, they lean on the nearest soft target. Cunningham. Big people get big and stay big by taking care of the small people. Not by making them scapegoats for their own mistakes. None of us can afford to do business with such dangerous fools. So, either you take care of them, or I do. Your choice.'

'Don't give us what's already ours, Dance.' Camponella needed a lever to crack Charlie open, but he was as seamless as a platinum ovoid. 'Offer us something we can live with.'

Charlie laid papers on the table. Turned them for Camponella to read the standard clauses of irrevocable letters of credit. Said, 'Dated and submitted to my Guernsey bank, they'll clear the moment my thirty-eight mill reaches me. Means I'm out on a limb for your forty-two million until Pollard brings the entire eighty mill across the border. Pollard doesn't make it, or doesn't *choose* to make it, we all lose money. So, who is trusting whom the most here?'

'You want thirty-eight clicks transferred to the Grand Caymans?'

'By noon tomorrow.'

211

'I get to keep these, it's a deal,' Camponella said.

Charlie offered his hand, and had it taken.

'Makes us partners by design, rather than by default, Joe.'

'And me personally liable.'

'The way I like things. Personal.'

They shook hands in dimming light and rising applause as Della O'Day appeared in a pink spot.

Collected from Luqa Airport as they completed the final releases for Mario Fabriano's remains, Charlotte Bujega and the Sicilian lawyer were sped to St Paul's Bay in a fast police mobile. Led down to the foreshore between yellow tapes, they found Inspector Ellul standing where Charlie Dance had walked into the water all those weeks before.

'You've found the body?' Charlotte asked.

'Body?' Ellul seemed distracted.

'Of Mrs Sadler?'

'Ah, Miss Bujega. They brought you too, did they?'

'Your men were insistent. Well, have they?'

'There is a body. I needed our Sicilian friend to attempt a positive identification.'

Charlotte was irritated and puzzled.

'Signor Accardo never knew Mrs Sadler.'

'That has no relevance, does it?'

'I would say it has.'

Ellul stroked the hard little arrow of concentration between his eyebrows. Looked out to sea and back to the fussy Sicilian lawyer. 'They told you what is expected of you?' he asked.

'I've been told nothing,' Accardo snapped. 'We were abducted and brought here without a word of explanation.'

'My apologies. My men are . . . excitable some times. I ask you to forgive me on their behalf.'

'That isn't even proper English,' Charlotte said. Cross.

'Isn't it? Shall I speak Maltese?'

'To a Sicilian? Are you quite well, Inspector?'

'Will you make the identification before we remove the body, Signor Accardo? We think you may know him.'

'Him?' Accardo said. 'Who?'

'This man,' Ellul flipped a tarpaulin aside.

Carlo Fabriano lay on his back with upturned palms. A huge bruise blued his right temple, and his face was as slack as a becalmed sail.

'Do you know him, Signor Accardo?'

'It's . . . the brother of the deceased. It's . . . Carlo.'

'You identify him as Carlo Fabriano?'

'Si . . . yes. It is he. How . . . ?'

'We found a wine bottle beside him. A goblet stained with wine lees. The face wound is consistent with a fall, or a blow to the head by an unknown third party. He was face down in the water, and could well have drowned. Nothing can be ascertained until an autopsy has been conducted by the coroner.' Ellul talked like a somnambulist, his eyes full of unspoken thoughts. 'There was a fully-loaded Uzzi machine-pistol beside him. Also, a priest's cassock.'

'I don't understand,' Accardo said, glad when the tarpaulin recovered the dead face.

'Nor,' said Ellul, 'do any of us. Only the priest who swam out to sea.'

'Inspector?' Charlotte was concerned about Ellul's drained look. 'Are you all right?'

'Where is Charlie Dance, Miss Bujega?' Ellul asked, staring seaward.

'Not here,' Charlotte said firmly.

'Who?' asked the Sicilian lawyer.

'A private matter, Signor Accardo, I assure you.'

'I must telephone,' Accardo said, more than ozone turning his stomach. 'The family . . .'

'Every son has a mother,' Ellul told the sea. 'Even priests who aren't priests.'

Unnerved by Ellul's odd manner, Charlotte followed the Sicilian lawyer away.

Swept back to her dressing room by applause, Della shut herself away with her success. Grinned at her moist reflection in the mirror with its surround of naked bulbs, her mind still throbbing with chord sequences nobody had put together before. Not the Duke, Garner or Tatum himself. All the bad years had flowed from her fingers to lift her repertoire of evergreens from the rut of the overly familiar into the freshly sublime. She and the songs had come back from the dead together. All those sleazy saloons and crummy hotels were there in the music, in the poignant union of delicate improvisation backed by her driving left hand. Doll Gardenia's fists had become thumping fifths, and wet highways unwinding for a dirty Greyhound bus the lyrical use of sad counterpoint. Her voice had scatted barefoot through dewed grass, and soared clear to spiral in birdsong above cornfields. Had painted bloody light above steel towns; the isolation of being stranded in a winter motel, the fearful wonder of giving herself to a stranger with a tender mouth and a whipcord body.

The dressing room was a private garden of bouquets giving fragrance to success. A single black orchid was taped to a bottle of pink champagne, and the card read:

Congratulations
Freaky XXX

214

Della stared at it without emotion. She had given all she had to give to her audience, and there was nothing left but the need to recharge for her next performance. Personal involvement was out. There was only the music and her need to succeed. She had found a new inner strength, and no longer needed to lean on another human being. Larry Moffat had offered her a resident spot for as long as she wanted, and he had contacts in the business she had only heard of.

'You're all set, kid,' he said when she came offstage to meet two talent scouts he had in tow. 'Leave the biz to Uncle Larry.'

'You'll explain how things are to Freaky?' she had asked.

'He knows, Della.' Moffat had nudged her back into the spot for a third standing ovation. 'My office, gentlemen?'

Della stroked the orchid. Smelled distant jungles on her fingers. The farewell smile she'd beamed at Charlie's table had been wasted on ice melting in an abandoned drink.

Chasen sulked on the drive back to San Ysidro, and his apartment was a bachelor slum after the opulence of the Wooden Palisades. He filled a glass stein with beer. Dumped corn chips into a bowl. Slumped to play the taped conversation between Dance and Camponella's party as if he were alone in a Death Row cell.

Charlie watched Chasen brood until the tape wound into silence. Then said, 'Spit or swallow, Saul.'

'With a mouthful of crow? I *know* those bastards took my agents down. But knowing ain't proving. I wanna pull Camponella off his throne like it's a low-suite toilet. All I can do is maybe slam him with a Grand Jury subpoena. Have him claim the fifth, and climb back on with a few ruffled feathers. I need to catch the mother with both hands inna cookie jar. But you won't see Camponella in Deadman's Canyon. No way is he gonna be his own bagman bringing that consignment across the border. He'll be drinking ten dollar cocktails in front of a hundred witnesses when that sweetheart deal goes down. *If* it goes down.'

'No "ifs" about it, Saul.'

'You know zilch about it, pally.'

'You talking to me, or to Washington?'

'They got their thumbs in my neck. What can I tell you?'

'You bucked them once.'

'Wake up, will you? As far as they let me, I did. You just have to eat the whole barrel of worms, don't you? It's over, Charlie. Done. Finished. You get escorted outta the US as an undesirable alien, or you stay to testify against Camponella. That's it, friend.'

Charlie confirmed something to himself with a nod.

'You rabbit,' he said. 'You've switched hats on me.'

'Take your thirty-eight mill and run for home. I would. How much further did you think you could take this thing? Even your borrowed time is borrowed. Cut and run. Leave the rest to Washington.'

'Nice to have worked with you, Saul. I'll send the agency a cheque.'

Chasen swayed to his feet. His necktie in his beer as he made a gun of his index finger.

'Switch me off, sure. But you can't terminate the *federal* agency, Dance.'

'And Camponella won't live to take the stand. They'll pop him in the eye quicker than you can spit. Your pathetic security isn't even *worth* that much sputum.'

'Listen to the ultimate mental spaghetti junction, will you?' Chasen asked the floor. 'You obdurate goat. You're about as cuddly as a cement dildo. I should throw down on you with my issue weapon. Cuff you, and throw away the keys.'

Charlie looked at his hands. Laced the fingers to stop them balling into fists. Said, 'Your choice, Saul,' coldly enough to pierce Chasen's alcoholic haze.

Chasen swayed. Wrung beer from his tie and spotted the silver carpet with suds. Slapped his head and capered in a circle. Ground his teeth in cartoon rage like Alice's Red Queen. Huffed a few times and flopped on a black leather couch.

'Sit the fuck down,' he said.

Charlie sank into a fat armchair.

'I hated letting that bastard Camponella walk,' Chasen told the wall. 'Him and Rizzo and Englese.'

Charlie nibbled a corn chip.

'I feel like yesterday's garbage,' Chasen moaned.

'Appearances aren't always deceiving, then.'

Chasen could only hear his own voice.

'They're out there now, figuring ways of putting your ass inna ground, Charlie. That sonbitch Pollard's trawling the waters west of Guadalajara for drugs and big bucks. Somewhere near the Clarion Fracture Zone, whatever *that* is, and I can't lay finger one on him until he hits American soil. Maybe not even then, he moves fast enough. Then they'll all be coming after you.'

'But not yet awhile, Saul. Good old Joe'll wrap me in cotton wool until this deal is concluded. Dead men can't honour personal financial guarantees, right?

217

That gives us all the time we need.'

'Us? There ain't no "us" any more. They're sending people down from Seattle to take this operation over. I'll just be a gopher, and you they'll wanna jerk around for their own ends. I was supposed to make nice with you until they get here some time tomorrow. Let them scoop you up without a "sorry 'bout that".'

'Why didn't you?'

'Because I've got gravel for brains.'

'And?'

'Big Ugly Sanchez crossed the border with his M-16 and five of his sweetheart bandits. They're maybe just out to rob a few *pollos*, ball any women they come across. But then, they're maybe doing that to kill time until they hear from Pollard. One thing's for sure, Big Ugly had a call from Camponella's office this a.m. That makes him Joe's man, and I get the feeling Camponella will send Rizzo and Englese to back Sanchez if Pollard pulls a doubleplay. Rizzo and Englese met with Sanchez out inna boondocks before they went to the Wooden Palisades. Means nobody trusts Pollard with that kind of heavy merchandise. If you've achieved anything, Charlie, you've got them all looking sideways at each other.'

Charlie thought back to the canyons. Saw that lone survivor sprinting away from him and his empty revolver. Young Manoel lying unconscious in thorn, and the searing blue light as bright as the pain in his chest when rotor wash blew him on to his back. Standing on the foreshore of St Paul's Bay with Margot lost in glittering seas. The sadness in Charlotte's face when he let her walk away from him, and the expressionless Joe Camponella a short hook away across a crisp white tablecloth.

218

Softly said, 'Endings are just disguised beginnings, Saul.'

'And I figure you've got eight short hours to make
your break.'

'It's enough. If I get Manoel.'

'A fifteen-year-old car bandit? You offered him out
and relocation with his ma. Why should he buy your
crock of shit?'

'We can only ask him. I need him out there.'

Chasen sighed and belched. Bloated by beer and
tension. Wrote on a scratch pad and flipped an
address into Charlie's lap.

'Go to that house when you hit Tijuana. You'll get
all you need to operate that side of the border. And
forget you ever knew me. What I don't know, those
Seattle seersuckers can't pump me about, right?
Now get the hell out of here.'

Charlie took his overnight bag out into a soft warm
night, and drove towards the border. Found a motel
on the outskirts of Tijuana, and slept dreamlessly
for the first time in several weeks.

Leaving Kurtz and the limousine in San Diego,
Camponella, Rizzo and Englese flew back to Bur-
bank Airport in a chartered Cherokee. They drove a
rental to Bel Air where Agents Blackwell and Parrot
got clear pictures of their arrival at Doll Gardenia's
redwood mansion.

CHAPTER FIFTEEN

The *Oceania-Cal Princess 2* was a raft of light in dark Pacific waters two hundred miles due south of the Revilla Gigego Islands. Hissing like acid on glass, cold upfalls of water rose from the depths to form boiling rosettes on the idle swell all around her, a sure sign she was closing in on submarine cliffs. Running slicks of white-green phosphorescence snaked with her prop wake as she manoeuvred for position, dying in slow ripples as her filling bilge tanks settled her above the shifting blip on the forward side-scan sonar screen.

Crouched over his consoles, Denning the navigator compared the print-outs from his scanners before selecting the best three for joint computer enhancement. Rows of digits bred in high-speed profusion on a monitor before translating themselves into a visual display of thin grey overlays that built a monochrome composite Denning enlarged to fill the screen. The final result was a fuzzy cross of Lorraine with a stub where the second cross-stroke should be. The damage could have been caused by impact, or layers of differing water temperature warping the signals. A scatter of smaller blips might be read as debris of predatory fish drawn to a source of food.

Denning decided not to think about the grey rot that might be in the cockpit. He had enough data to justify a dive, and he woke Captain Caunter for clearance to prepare the submersible for a descent.

There were three hours to dawn. The weather was set fair apart from a small storm rising in the south east, and the sea was moderate despite some local turbulence.

Caunter was on the bridge in seven short minutes, and looked to have enjoyed eight straight hours of dreamless oblivion instead of a snatched half-hour. He had Denning punch up colour on the image, and they studied a yellow wreck lying in blue fissures amongst a litter of orange blips.

'Flesh, fowl, or good fresh fish,' Caunter muttered. 'That's no lost paravane, or a forty-foot fairground cigar. I'd say she's lying at an angle to the surface. That stub is a torn-off wing folded back under her. And this whole frontal mass is the fuselage in three-quarter elevation, with the intact wing running down away from us. Comments, Mr Denning?'

'Good analysis, Skip. Could be she raked in with her port wing. Flipped when it tore away. Pancaked, and went down trimmed square until she settled on that incline. Slid in the rest of the way.'

'Time we made sure, Mr Denning. Have the *Nemo* ready to dive in thirty minutes.'

'Aye, aye, Skip.'

Caunter summoned the deck crew to take up their forward positions. Woke himself all the way up with good black coffee before having Pollard brought to the bridge. Denning's intuition may have boosted the crew's bounty to a full quarter million. And those kind of serious clams were not turtle eggs. Caunter congratulated himself, buying the best was no false economy in the salvage business.

Doll Gardenia came back from nowhere to explain something to somebody. The Chesterfield Man's threats of exposure were gone in dream smoke, and

221

other faces Gardenia hoped he knew hovered on the edge of focus. Everlasting night had swallowed all the days, Bel Air had replaced the sleazy room where orange juice had furred up his tongue and blurred his mind with thoughts of betrayal. Was it all to end in sure retribution after the kiss of *omerta*? Oblivion after the garlic bullet in the neck?

Gardenia formed logical arguments in his mind whilst his tongue babbled about missing millions and misunderstandings. Not his fault at all, none of it was his fault, was it? They had to see that he was the victim, not the perpetrator. The Chesterfield Man had lied about everything.

'He's flipped all the way out,' Englese said. Bored.

'Who did this to you, Doll?' Rizzo sounded disinterested.

'He did. The Chesterfield Man. He said Joe sent him.'

Camponella stayed silent, his lip curled a millimetre out of alignment with his trim moustache.

'Joe who?' Englese prompted.

'Joe trusts me. Why would he do that?' Gardenia mumbled.

'Joe who, Doll?'

'Camponella. We go back too far for . . . *this*.'

'Not Charlie Dance?' Rizzo asked.

'Who?' Gardenia rolled his face on his pillow. 'Get Joe here. Get Joe, he'll know.'

'Maybe we will,' Englese said, looking at Camponella with hard calculation in his eyes. 'Maybe we'll do just that.'

'Yeah,' Rizzo agreed, smoothing the lapel over the magnum. 'Mr Camponella knows more about all this than any of us, right?'

'Don't jump to the wrong conclusions,' Camponella warned.

'Joe, is that you?' Gardenia tried to see more than blobs of tinted mist. 'Somebody hit on Shaggy, Joe? That right? The same guy who hit on me?'

Camponella picked up a plump satin pillow. Weighed it looking down at Gardenia's ruined face. About ready to smother the weak fool.

'Who can tell, Doll?' he said.

'This guy Dance. What about him, Doll?' Rizzo asked.

'You said that. He the guy?'

'You don't know?' Englese said.

Gardenia's loose mouth drooled and over-salivated.

'Are you telling me? He do this to me over that whore Della?'

'Tell him, Joe,' Englese said.

'Can't get your mind out of your pants, can you, Doll?'

'Wouldn't have nothing to do with eighty mill of family money, huh, Doll?' Rizzo said. Disgusted.

'Or you getting us into a shooting war?' Englese grunted, taking the cue. 'Snatching some financier to get your ass out of a sling?'

'I left that, uh, to George. To, uh, Casey.'

'You're the only one who sees it that way, Doll,' Rizzo said.

'Ask them, Joe. This ain't what you think.'

'Really?' Camponella sneered. 'Just some personal thing over a forty-year-old fox with a trim body and a fistful of chords, huh? Nothing to do with business.'

'I'll tell you who did this to you, Doll,' Englese said, taking the pillow.

'I knew you'd see it my way,' Gardenia said.

'You did, Doll,' Englese said.

'What?'

223

'To yourself,' Rizzo dropped the pillow on the drooling face. Pressed down with all his body-weight until the body stopped jerking around. 'Cat got your tongue, Doll?' he asked the unconscious man.

'Guess he fell asleep,' Camponella said.

'You want me to wake him?' Rizzo said, dragging Gardenia to the bathroom to fill his lungs with water.

'No. There's always tomorrow.' Camponella lit a cigar. 'Check the security out before you leave. I'll be in the car.'

'Sure, Joe,' Rizzo said for the FBI bugs.

Slim brown legs in froths of petticoat were always around the next corner as a naked and invisible Pollard plodded through festive Mexican streets. A mere appendage to his own erectile need, he was drawn on through damp tangles of sheets with fireworks and dogs snapping at his heels. Laughing eyes promised easement. Tempted him on as he panted through twists and turns and cloying damp. *Rurales* came at him from behind, and one got a hand to his wet shoulder. Shook him hard. Bounced him off a wall as spongy as a mattress. Rolled his face into a soaked pillow. Reared him off the bed thinking of Doll with an ice pick through his face. Had him eye to eye with a crewman who should not have been in La Purisma for the Day of the Dead. Used bluster to intimidate, but the insolent crew-man's grin stayed where it was as Pollard covered himself.

'It's the middle of the Goddamned night.'

The crewman agreed. 'Sure is. God wants you onna bridge. Seems we're making a dive.'

Pollard dressed in Khaki fatigues. Threw water in his face and towelled off vigorously. Got his portable transmitter from his travel bag and sent his call sign to a point on the mainland he located with the inbuilt self-seeking compass. A single red blip confirmed 'message received', and Pollard followed up with a morse H which put the plane on alert to fly at his command.

On the bridge he had a clear view of the docking arm swinging the *Nemo* out over the central pool. Denning's system check came through wall speakers, and Nemo's TV cameras threw pictures on to three screens. The submersible was an elongated egg of steel and plexiglass with two forward arms fitted with sophisticated grabs, a folding dorsal arm with a magnetized foot, and she was attached to the mother ship by three thousand metres of umbilical cable supplying secondary power, air and the communications systems.

Pollard felt his neck and scrotum tighten as he studied the image on the monitor. If he wasn't looking at the mother lode, he was a laughing jackass hatching mule's eggs in a chafing dish. For a brief lunatic moment he entertained the notion of keeping it all for himself. Sanely tempered overwhelming greed with the knowledge he wouldn't live long enough to spend dollar one. Ducking out on the five families was as impractical as racing supercharged bananas at Indianapolis, and Pollard forced himself to consider his moves once these arrogant salvage experts were through with their part of the operation.

The *Nemo* sank from sight when the support cables released the magnetic hull clamps. For a wallowing moment the plexiglass housing was a wet yellow eye staring skyward, then Denning put the nose down, and it dipped from sight with the docking arm paying out cable above the calm water blanket.

Caunter's TV screens showed blue-black waters alive with minute marine life, and electric numerals pulsed off the depth of the dive in fathoms and metres.

'We have a positive A-OK on all systems here. Mr Denning.'

'Affirmative, Skip.'

Caunter watched a small swirl of bad weather move across his radar screen some fifty miles off his port bow. So long as it kept to its present course there was no danger to Denning or the submersible. The last thing Caunter wanted to cope with were 100 mph winds churning the bottom into a blinding stew of mud, sand and kelp.

Long minutes dragged as the stately descent continued, and Pollard's mouth dried as Denning activated his forward spotlights. The converging beams showed a towering black massif where fish darted in shoals of silver chaff. The cameras skim-panned at a steep angle as Denning sideslipped across an overhang into a greater darkness that remained lifeless for a drop of a hundred fathoms. Then there were spiny starfish walk-swimming above a fissured belly of downslope, the wriggle of an immature moray eel, and the alien geometric shapes of machined metals.

Denning trimmed the *Nemo* into a hovering mode; used reverse power to drift backwards along the fuselage of the twin-prop aircraft. One wing had torn away, and the engine nacelle was gone completely, but apart from the missing pod of the cockpit housing, the rest of the airframe was intact.

'She'll raise clean, skip,' Denning said.

'Positive ident if you please, Mr Pollard?' Caunter asked, without turning from his screens.

Wanting an analgesic for a pressure headache,

Pollard cleared his throat. Said, 'That's her.' Feeling strangled.

'Proceed to secure for lift, Mr Denning,' Caunter ordered.

Charlie drove into Tijuana through a wasteland of used car lots, half-smothered by the diesel exhaust of ancient buses burning Mexican crude. Parking near Hussong's famous bar, he skirted a business section, crossed a low-cost housing project, and found the old house at the end of a blind alley. A doorphone rapped in fast Spanish when he used the bell pull beside a nailed door, and a large-sounding dog growled at him through three inches of hard timber. His, 'Saul Chasen sent me,' earned a long silence punctuated by spits of static. Bolts were drawn, and the door opened just wide enough for Charlie to slip into a walled garden where alligator-pear trees formed shade for a wolfhound and a woman with a sawn-off shotgun.

'A lot of armour for one tourist,' Charlie said, showing his palms.

'Chasen doesn't send tourists. Only strays and trouble. Which are you?'

'It's a simple world with only two options.'

'I like it that way. Pays dividends dealing with Chasen.'

'Means he didn't call ahead about me.'

'Means just that.'

Charlie let the wolfhound lick his hand. Found a rough ear to scratch without looking away from the woman. An ace over five feet tall, she had a lot of black hair caught back in a loose tail by an orange bandana. High Indian cheekbones gave her olive face a slightly hawkish look. Her sharp brown eyes were heavily lidded under thin arcs of eyebrow, and

227

her grin of a mouth had a generous lower lip. She wore a loose brown shirt over tan pants, and her tiny feet were bare on the stone path. She held the sawn-off Ithaca with the quiet confidence of the weapon-trained, and the pulse in her throat was slow and steady.

'I expected a man,' Charlie said.

'Did you now?' The woman's look put Charlie on a slab with a tagged toe. 'Did you really?'

'Really. Makes me stupid, I guess.'

'The damned dog seems to like you.'

'Has he a name?'

'*She* has a name. What about you, buster?'

'Charlie.'

'She's Rosie.'

'And you?'

'Did you eat breakfast?'

'Coffee stewed by a foodomat machine didn't tempt me.'

'Throw those bolts. Mine's fresh ground.'

Charlie followed the small woman into a high-ceilinged room that served as a kitchen-diner. An archaic black stove gave off baking smells, a scrubbed pine table took up floor space, and the plain white-limed walls had been decorated with stylized Mayan warriors. A barred window over-looked the walled garden, and Rosie the wolfhound looked in at Charlie through ironworked leaves and green light as he was served hot crusty rolls and wild honey.

'You married?'

'No. You?'

'Once. Didn't take.'

'I'd marry you for your baking.'

'I might take you up on that.'

'Only if you have a name I can use.'

'Don't need one. This is Anarchyville. Anything goes down here so long as you don't hack off the law. You stay out of the crazier cantinas, out of jail, and don't have an auto accident involving a local citizen. Otherwise, you don't walk on the grass, you smoke it. You get the last swig of mescal, you eat the worm. And you never touch tequila without salt and lemon. You do not do heavy drugs, and fooling with the local women earns you your nuts in the ringer. Carry a knife, you have to use it. Pack a gun, the cops'll make you eat it before they throw away the key. Mexican jails are garbage food, chiggers big enough to chomp off your toes, bad water and amoebic dysentery. Die inside the joint, they bury you in quicklime for free. That's if you don't get shot in the back trying to escape, and that can happen in your sleep. A bad gringo is a waste of a good blanket, *comprende, amigo*?'

'Do I really look as though I need that kind of advice?'

'Chasen sent you, didn't he?'

'And that makes you one angry lady. Why?'

'Ask him.'

'I'd rather you told me.'

'So would he, the coward.'

'Whatever the problem is, I think you should take it up with Chasen himself.' Charlie pushed his coffee away, ready to leave.

'Maybe I will. The next time he's late with the alimony check.'

'You're the wife who keeps him poor?'

'Is that what he told you?'

'Not in so many words. He still hurts over you.'

'Terrific. I should have a conscience?'

'How can I answer that?'

'Hannah.'

229

'What?'

'My name. Hannah.'

'Hello, Hannah. Why are we yelling?'

'How do I know? Yelling at Saul was a way of life until I split. He tell you anything about us?'

'Only that somebody at this address could help me down here.'

'And only if I choose to.'

'That's understood.'

'He told you nothing?'

'Nothing.'

'Figures. Christ, he's such a coward in so many ways. If I'd stayed, he'd have folded all the way up. Gone completely to pieces. That kid was everything to him.'

'What . . . kid?'

Hannah's eyes showed moons of white around the chocolate pupils.

'Our son. He'd have been seventeen now, if he'd lived. Four years now. Life's a bummer, huh?'

'What happened?'

'A pusher happened. My son overdosed his first time out. The other kids said he'd never handled a needle before. He'd pill-popped, they said. Speed, they guessed. Then somebody pushed him cocaine. He was unconscious for three days before he finally slipped away. Had a heart spasm and died. Our marriage died with him. Nothing left but two empty people unable to handle the guilt. One needle, three dead. Nifty, huh?'

'Hardly that,' Charlie said.

Hannah's grief was as searing as a naked blade trapping sunlight. Charlie went to the window to scratch Rosie's muzzle through the bars. An avocado fell with a soft thump, and rolled away with Rosie in sniffing pursuit.

'Happened on my birthday,' Hannah said. 'Happy thirty-fourth, Hannah. Saul tracked that pusher down, but there was no trial. The sonbitch ran off to Canada, and got his in the head with a Saturday night special. You know what Saul and I felt, Charlie?'

'No.'

'Cheated. Can you buy that?'

'All the way,' Charlie said.

Rosie had the avocado in her soft mouth as she padded about the yard looking for somewhere to hide it. Hannah came to stand beside Charlie, and her snort was amused.

'She does that all the time. She'll eat them if she thinks she's stolen them. If I fed her one, she'd turn her nose up. Just like a woman, eh?'

'Only the foolish ones, Hannah.'

'Yeah? Tell that to Chasen when you see him. He thinks we're all clockwork and rioting hormones. The yummy bits are there to trap a guy's paycheck.'

'And scar tissue doesn't heal if you pick at it.'

'And you can shove your correspondence course psychology.'

'All right.'

'Lose a kid and see how *you* feel.'

'Congratulations. You outrank me in the loss Olympics. You went for gold, Saul gets the bronze, and I rate nowhere. His loss cannot compare with yours because you were the mother. He was only the husband, and I only lost a woman I liked a good deal. I'm not even an "also ran".'

Hannah dug a small fist at her hip. Tilted her head to look Charlie in the eye. A miniature with flawless, fine-grained skin, she was ready to tear down the walls of any argument he presented.

'Shoot your mouth straight from the hip, don't

231

you?' she said, her cheeks flushed. Eyes dark with fury.

'No other way in my book.'

'Wrong book, *amigo*. The one most people read is called subject avoidance. You cage all the forbidden things in your mind. Tiptoe away, and let the sad-bad things fester in the dark. Filthy maggoty things that never, never go away.'

Charlie wanted to slap Hannah. Hold her close.

'Stop it, woman. Forgive Saul, then you can forgive yourself.'

'That was uncalled for, you savage bastard.'

'Oh? Just listen to yourself. You're schizoid about your ex-husband. When you describe jointly ex-perienced hurt, he's Saul. You talk money, he's Chasen. And the one time he talked about you, you had no name at all. Either walk all the way away from each other, or try being kind. Give yourselves some measure of peace. Right now, you've got the worst of both worlds. Like Rosie out there with her alligator apple. She doesn't really want the damned thing, but she'll eat it all the same. A prize she doesn't want, and won't give up. Isn't that a little like you and Saul, Hannah?'

'It's nothing like us. Nothing.'

'You can't own the hurt, Hannah. You can't own it in order to deny it to Saul. Or Chasen.'

'The cockroach told you nothing. It's always me who has to string the words, Charlie.'

'Your words for you, Hannah. Not for him. He's still going after the bastards who kill kids for profit. And that gets it said in my book.'

'Cute. Good for good old Agent Chasen. He still buried our marriage without a marker. D'you under-stand that?'

'Yes.'

'And still he sends you to me for help. How tall are you?'

'Six-two.'

'You bend in the middle somewhere, don't you?'

'Yes.'

'Then bend. Get your face down here. My feet have been tingling ever since you walked in here, and I need kissing very seriously.'

'You do?'

'And I'm not doing this to get back at Chasen. You'll be the first man in must be three years.'

'A long time between cocktails.'

Charlie bowed into a moist and eager mouth, and the room took a couple of turns before he broke away, his hands firm on Hannah's shoulders.

'Thanks,' he said. 'But no thanks.'

'You're turning me down?' Hannah's eyes were misty with mischief.

'Knowing my low boiling point, only temporarily. Persist, and I'll topple. Is that what you truly want?'

Hannah's crisp chuckle almost surprised him.

'OK, *amigo*. You pass, but it was close there for a moment.'

'For whom?'

'For me, Charlie. Chasen was right, you're really something.'

Charlie's face closed in on itself.

'Don't ever do that again unless you mean it, Hannah.'

'My God, you're serious. You want what? An apology?'

'And do what with it? Hang it on my belt like a scalp?'

'So it was a lousy thing to do. But I found out what kind of a fellow you are, right?'

Charlie's eyes softened briefly.

'And maybe why I'm so angry.'

'Huh?'

'It *was* close. Too damned close.'

'You phoney, you're really genuine,' Hannah squeaked. Pleased.

'Keep *that* to yourself.'

They were laughing arm in arm when they left the house, and Jack Kurtz trailed them to a large walled *hacienda* before calling Rizzo and Englese in Los Angeles.

The glass fell at 9.07 a.m. Pacific Standard Time, almost two hours into Denning's second dive.

High winds tore a perfect mackerel sky apart, heavy rain pounded the sea into dance, and visibility dissolved in blinding banks of shifting murk. The *Oceania-Cal Princess 2* lay in a dark womb of foul weather, and Caunter conned his ship in silence, calculating the odds between success and failure; the hard core of his concentration on the *Nemo* some eighty fathoms below the surface.

'The *Nemo*'s torch had cut the damaged wing from the fuselage, and Denning had slung cables the length of the airframe. Flotation bags were rigged, ready to be filled with compressed air for the lift, and Denning had the *Nemo* in a hover mode – waiting to bring the wreck to the surface, or abort until the weather changed. There was already a slop of motion stirring the weed on the rockface, and the severed wing was lifting on the erratic currents. Denning panned and zoomed to fill one of Caunter's screens with the moving aileron, the exterior microphone at full volume to feed the grate of metal against rock into the bridge speakers.

'Cap?' Denning softly goaded.

'Stand by,' Caunter said, turning to face Pollard.

'Your decision, I think, Mr Pollard. Lift now, and risk some damage when we get the thing to the surface. Or wait, and maybe lose the whole wreck in deeper water. Perhaps have her break up completely. That chasm goes down to China as far as I can read, and this storm could last two hours or two weeks. Once we get the plane raised into the central pool and close the sea-doors, she can be lashed. Then the deck crew can offload in the dry. Well?'

Pollard stared at the screens. The severed wing was rising with the slow majesty of a manta ray's cloak. It was almost upright when it found the edge of the overhang. With a suddenness that stole Pollard's breath, it arrowed from sight into the lower depths, leaving background buzz and silence.

'Go for it,' he said.

'Time that at 9.11 a.m. PST, Mr Denning. Blow up your balloons, it's party time,' Caunter said.

'Aye, aye, Cap,' Denning said.

'Just tell me what you think?' Pollard asked Caunter.

'Me? What difference would that make? You made the decision, and win, lose or draw, we have to live with it, don't we?'

Pollard could see Caunter's skull through his leer of humour.

'How long before you send the divers down to secure her?'

'An hour.'

'Gives me time to drink my breakfast then,' Pollard bit on a green cigar on his way to the rear companion.

'So it does.' Caunter thought Pollard a first class prick, and was pleased he had lied about the duration of the storm. It would have blown itself south before noon, not that that fact changed the equation in any way. Lifting the wreck immediately was the right action to take. The undertow was already running down the cliff face at ten knots, and getting the *Nemo* and the wreck out of that race soonest made all kinds of sense.

'Three minutes to full inflation and flotation, Cap,' Denning said.

'Affirmative,' Caunter said. 'Ease her due south when she comes off that ledge, Mr Denning. Get your nose out of that wash before the cables take unequal strain.'

'Aye, aye, bridge,' Denning said, thinking something more pithy about grannies sucking eggs. If he pulled *Nemo* out with simple reverse thrust, he'd lose all control in the biggest submarine backflip of all time, and Denning planned to live for several decades more before dying in bed with the woman of his choice. Using finger-tip pressure on his power-assisted controls, he eased *Nemo* close to the cliff face with her nose down, waiting for the flotation bags to fill to eighty per cent of maximum. The first ten fathoms of ascent would be the optimum roller coaster if he wasn't a very careful submariner indeed.

'This is what keeps Chasen poor,' Hannah said in a sunny yard noisy with playing children.

'A school?' Charlie felt outsized and clumsy, as if any sudden move on his part would crush something small and precious.

'In part. It started out as a refuge for addicted mothers and their babies, and sorta grew like Topsy. Our annual budget would run a small banana republic. If I was a priest the locals would kiss my feet and ask for a blessing. Me they shrug at. The crazy *gringo* woman and her sickos, and I'm as

236

Hispanic as any of them. At least the old women don't spit any more.'

'That's something.' A small warm hand had crept into Charlie's, and he found himself looking down at huge eyes in a pinched olive face.

'You've made a conquest,' Hannah said.

'Me? I know nothing about children.'

'What's to know? She smiles, you smile. That's it.'

'She's not smiling.'

'My God, man, is that a blush? You're actually blushing?'

'She's got a hell of a grip.'

'Because she likes you.'

'Me? Why?'

'All little girls love their daddy, you oaf.'

'What?'

'She doesn't have one. So, she's picked you.'

'Me?'

'Why not you? You're a man, aren't you?'

'Hannah, this is ridiculous.'

'Not to me. Not to her. Pick her up, she'd like that.'

'I doubt that.'

'Charlie, you coward. She won't break, and she won't disgrace herself. Her name's Angelica, and she's four years old.'

'Uh, like this?'

'Just like that.'

'She's warm.'

'What did you expect?'

'I don't know. She weighs so little.'

'Born prematurely to a teenage mother with a serious cocaine habit is the reason for that. Angelica was so pitiful, we didn't know if she'd make it past her first birthday. Well, she did. And you, my fine fellow, are the first male she's taken a shine to.'

'Come off it, Hannah.'

'Off what? Listen to the ninth wonder of the world. A grown man who's never held a child before. And you're a natural. She's gone to sleep on your shoulder. And that, my friend, is trust of a high order. Maybe I should offer you a job here. Non-salaried, of course.'

'Heaven forbid. Take her, please?'

'You know we were followed here?'

'Yes, a butterball called Jack Kurtz. Works for a man called Camponella. Very observant. The child?'

'Six years working gang-related crime sharpens your street sense, my man. I made sergeant.'

'You're a wonder. Can we terminate the child-minding now?'

'Why? You said she wasn't heavy. This is drug-related, right?'

'Yes. Any single shipment could run this place for a thousand years.'

'Big numbers. And you plan to dump all over it?'

'If I can, Hannah.'

'And you don't have a shield to slow you down?'

'That's right. The kid?'

'Don't be such a grouse. She's only just found you.'

'The *child*, Hannah.'

'The *canyons*, Charlie. You already have a serious souvenir.'

'For two people who don't communicate, you and Saul do damned well so long as the subject isn't yourselves.'

'A blade in the chest *needs* talking about.'

'We're shouting again.'

'You'd make a saint scream blue murder.'

Hannah glared at Charlie as Angelica's hair blew across his mouth in fine black strands. Recognized more than acute discomfort in the grey eyes. Saw naked loss for the briefest of moments. The flick of a minnow in dark waters, gone too quickly. Holding the child had played flame on a raw nerve. She took Angelica away and passed her to a volunteer helper, linked arms with Charlie and walked him out into the streets of Tijuana. Found a bar in the tourist area and ordered drinks.

'A little early, isn't it?' Charlie said.

'We both need a shot or two. Unfeigned innocence has a way of opening wounds, and I shouldn't have done that to you.'

'Who made you the conscience of the world?'

'Are we gonna squabble again.'

'Only if we work at it.'

Charlie threw his tequila back, licked salt and bit on a wedge of lemon. Felt the alcohol hit hard and liked it enough to order again. Three rounds later, Hannah wore her mischievous face, and the walk home was heavy with unspoken promises.

Ignored by Caunter and Denning who exchanged esoteric data over the phones like lovers under a blanket, Casey Pollard split his attention between the changing weather and the shifting depths. The sky had cleared itself with tropical suddenness in a great shout of wind that had punched the sea into rolling peaks. The rain pall and its cloak of torn cloud had rushed towards the Galapagos Islands in a whirling tantrum, to leave the sea round the *Oceania-Cal Princess 2* heaving sullen flanks in the glittering light of a rainwashed noon. There was good weather all the way to the mainland, and if it held, Pollard knew he must time his next moves perfectly.

Framed by its own remote camera, the *Nemo* hung in transparent limbo above the cradled wreck and its grape-cluster of flotation balloons. Denning had reversed the submersible out of the treacherous downrace slicker than an oiled dildo, and was guiding the salvage prize to the surface with the slow majesty of a royal procession. Trimming for the final ascent with an escort of divers, the *Nemo* hovered at thirty fathoms. It seemed that Caunter and Denning planned a single elevator ride up into the central water blanket, to pop both the *Nemo* and her salvage through the upper turbulence like a couple of steel corks.

Pollard gnawed his lip, his empty stomach growling at his breakfast of Jim Beam mash. If he started the seaplane now she would arrive just as the wreck was being unloaded. If the weather changed she could abort midflight and arrange another rendezvous in more clement weather, and what was lost but a few gallons of aero fuel? Pollard left the bridge by the rear companion, and hurried to his cabin to send his call sign and a morse A. On acknowledgment, he took another snort of bourbon and assembled his spurt gun, loading it with a magazine of soft-nosed slugs. Whatever he hit would lose interest in further resistance, and that suited Pollard down to the deck. Grinning at his nautical turn of thought, Pollard went back to the bridge with the weapon zipped inside his bush jacket.

Hannah was a shapely bronze languish in the shuttered gloom, afternoon sunlight striping the wall above her carved bed. She drew Charlie in the dark with the seeing fingers of a sculptress, curious about the scars she traced. She kissed the healing puckers on his right pectoral, just the weight of her lips themselves making contact.

'Are you the kind who mumbles excuses and scuttles away?' she asked. 'All guilt, regret and shirttails.'

'Nope. You?'

'Me? Heck, I want to do it several more times. Each time very differently, until I know you. Then I want to purr in my sleep like a contented cat.'

'One of the up-front honest and shameless ones, huh?'

'You weren't exactly a puritan back there, brother.'

'Glad you noticed. I thought I was just hanging on to the tail of a comet on its way out of the solar system.'

'You're the one with the solar engines, tiger.'

'Are all your allusions feline?'

'Maybe. Great fireballs, how did you get that?' Hannah's fingers had found the dragon coils of ridged tissue on Charlie's shoulder.

'Hatchet. Long time ago. Forget when or how or why.'

'Sure you do, you liar. Just as the canyons won't even be a memory this time next year.'

'What canyons?'

'You *see*, you . . .'

'Leopard, jaguar, civet?'

'Tom cat is all *you* deserve.'

'Thanks.'

Hannah propped her chin on a fist, a warm breast nosing Charlie's neck. Asked, 'She was something special, hmmm?'

'Who was?'

'The lady I saw in your eyes when you held Angelica?'

The sigh in the dark was a ghostly hem brushing ancient flags.

'I can't talk about her.'

'Can't? Or won't?'

'Can't, Hannah. She's too alive to be neatly laid to rest in the museum of memory. She was you for

241

an instant back there. Something you did . . .'

Hannah shuddered. 'Jesus, I asked for that.'

'I'm afraid you . . . yes.'

'Damn, now I'm sober. And miserable.' Hannah wriggled in against Charlie for comfort.

'Mourning isn't a flag of convenience you can raise or lower at will, love. It isn't even an honest black. It bites you in the heart when you least expect it. The times you can't be on guard. When you wake up with your hand on a cold pillow. When it rains, and the earth smells of her. When her song plays on the radio, or gets murdered in an elevator.'

'For somebody who can't talk about her, you're doing fine.'

'I'm talking about me, Hannah.'

'But she's why you're here.'

'Is she?'

'Well, isn't she?'

'Maybe at first. Now I don't know.'

'Captain Absolute shows doubt? Am I hearing this?'

'You want your dragons killed, buy Saul a tin suit and a horse.'

'No need to get snitty because I hit a nerve.'

'You're right, woman. I apologize.'

'Me too. Was a time I'd have had Chasen kill giants for me. But that was me in the romantic way-back-when.'

'He still would, you know.'

'That's just talk. Never doubt feminine intuition.'

'Or a gentleman's motives?'

'Yours, you mean?' Hannah's laugh was as warm as her breasts. 'You can seriously say that to me in your condition?'

'A man *does* need to be fully clothed to feign injured dignity, my lovely Mexican-American.'

242

'And you're living proof that a man can be supine *and* erect.'

'You're very astute, madam.'

'And appreciative.'

'I don't think I want to talk any more.'

'Just as well,' Hannah said, slowly lowering herself.

The *Nemo* had clamped herself to the docking arm to be swung clear of the central pool. Captain Caunter had closed the sea doors, started the pumps, and the water blanket had dropped low enough to reveal the tip of the wrecked aircraft's tailplane. Tasting salt from his bitten tongue, Casey Pollard watched Denning spring the pneumatic seals to release himself from the *Nemo*. His watch was frozen in some local time warp, the sweep hand as sluggish as a snail in rain. Pollard's pilot was already airborne, his estimated ETA a mere seventeen minutes away, and Pollard felt himself age with each passing moment.

Let this be over soon, he prayed to any listening deity.

CHAPTER SIXTEEN

Hannah left Charlie dozing when she answered the kitchen phone, her body adrift in buttery clouds of pleasure when she panted her number.

'Hi, honey,' Saul Chasen said. 'Been jogging?'

'Stone floors need scrubbing, Chasen,' she said.

'Uhuh. Did my guy turn up down there?'

'He showed.'

'And stayed to give you an asthma attack.'

'Badmouth me, and I'm gone, Chasen.' Hannah quelled unbidden guilt. How dare her very ex-husband turn a rediscovered joy into a sordid encounter by sly innuendo. Her inner world still looped the loop whilst her heart was a gate banged by high winds, and Chasen's flat voice was popping her clouds like party balloons. 'Are you crocked?' she asked with sudden insight.

'Mildly, honey. The main event comes after I breathe in my guy's ear. 'S'important.'

'So long as you remember we're yesterday's news when you do. I don't want him snagged in one of your jealous fantasies, you hear?'

'Divorced is divorced, business is business,' Chasen slurred.

Hannah felt Charlie at her shoulder. Leaned back against him, the phone held away from her face.

'Your word, Chasen,' she said. 'No nonsense.'

'With my hand on my heart and all other organs, I do so solemnly swear.'

'OK. Hang on.'

Hannah put a hand over the receiver. Turned and lifted her face to be kissed, tasting her musk on his lips. Wanting to be wanted again. Right there with cool tiles under her feet, the clock ticking over unwashed dishes. The scrubbed pine table a shadow play of sunsplash and nodding leaves.

'He's coming,' she said, sharing the phone with Charlie.

'Again?' Chasen asked himself wryly. 'Best pretend you didn't say that, Saul my man.'

'I thought we were divorced too,' Charlie said into the mouthpiece.

'I'm in a payphone, so this ain't happening, right?'

'Fine by me.'

'I'm drunk enough to talk. Not enough to sleep. Been up through all last night, and the hangover comes later for me. Yours comes now.'

'Oh?'

'You can scratch your old buddy Doll Gardenia from your next Christmas list, Charlie. He had three visitors last night. They left two hours before he became clinically dead. Got high-fidelity FBI tapes to prove it. Got high-resolution photographs of the three of them drinking martinis and boilermakers when he finally got to be deceased. Right there in front of authorized FBI witnesses, Charlie. Know how they did it? They rigged him up in his shower stall. Made it look like he fell and got jammed head down, his rigid arm-brace pushing his face down over the soakaway. The faucet was just dribbling, right? The poor bastard must've swallowed five or six gallons of water before he plain couldn't drink any more, and the water came right up over his mouth and nose. Drowned him dead. Course, he wouldn't have been sane by then, would he? Would have thought he really was a salmon swimming home with a walrus on his tail. And just to make certain, they had him leave a note in his own handwriting. Scrawly like it would be, him using the wrong hand and all. So good in fact, our experts say there's no point them gainsaying it in court. They've done it again, Charlie. They've walked. Walked clean away, leaving this dumb sonbitch with the same bad-tasting mouth, the hangover yet to come. You getting this, pally?'

'I'm listening, Saul.'

'You get my Hannah on your side. All the way on your side, you'll maybe get to kick ass like a champion mule.'

'So far, I'm a mascot at a children's school.'

'Yeah?' Chasen's coughing laugh was wind in winter leaves. 'There's more to Hannah than kids. Do it right, you'll find that out for yourself. Just don't go hurting her, you—'

The disconnected tone burred.

'He cleared down,' Charlie said.

'No, I did.' Hannah's face was pale and tight; as shivering, naked and shy, she rehung the phone. 'I won't have him patronizing me like he owns me. Christ, it's humiliating.' She eeled past Charlie, padded into the bathroom ahead of him to start the shower, her back rigid.

'I'll be going.' Charlie reached for his shirt. 'You're a lady who needs some time and space to herself.'

'Very wrong, my friend. You're about to find out the truth about this lady and her refuge for the used and abused. It's the perfect mask. Trouble is, I've worn it for so long I chose to forget that tomorrow does come. It's here. It's now. And what I really want has to be admitted loud and clear.'

'And that is?'

Hannah's eyes were bruises in gypsum.

'Simple, awful, basic revenge, Charlie. Them hurting. Them dying. As Biblical as burning for burning, God forgive me. For all the children. For all the mothers. For me. We're going out there, Charlie, you and I. To finish them any way we can. And if you've got something to say about that, use your hands, damn you.'

Wordlessly, Charlie walked Hannah under the jets, and they came together as easily as lacing fingers. Hannah's pleasure clouds grew in the steam, and she expurgated all bitter guilt by losing herself in a womb of pearl blindness where she and Charlie were the only reality.

Captain Caunter cut the communications link with the *Nemo* when Denning arrived on the bridge to write up his dive log. He ordered his service engineers aboard the submersible for a standard systems check; noted his deck crew were stowing the deflated flotation bags prior to entering the salvaged plane through a midsection door, and turned away from his consoles to find himself covered by Casey Pollard's lethal spurt gun. Showing no surprise, Caunter sat back in his command swivel, a knee crossed over a thigh, one eyebrow raised.

'I suppose one *must* ask why you've armed yourself, Pollard?' he said.

Denning looked up from his log to blink, and Caunter patted the air to calm him.

Pollard forearmed his streaming forehead and said, 'I like people to listen up with both ears, Cap. Including you.'

Caunter considered that civilian impertinence for a moment. Raised both eyebrows in question. 'And that requires a weapon? How insecure you must be.'

'I would be crazy to go out on deck without one?'

'Any why should that be necessary?'

'Because that crashed bird is wired for more than sound. Your people try and open her up without me along, say bye-bye to them and half your ship.'

'The plane is booby-trapped?'

'Bingo. Standard procedure, Cap.'

'Amongst your circle, perhaps.'

Pollard shook a sweatball from his chin.

'Go ahead, Cap. Play the sarcastic mother superior. This gun will stop any of your crew thinking to bean me while I'm busy playing tunes on that door. Electronics and plastic make a hell of a sweet combination, don't they? And listen, Cap. Old Casey don't plan to get himself jumped singing "open sesame" to twenty kilos of plastique "goodbye baby".'

'Take my word, none of my crew will touch you.'

'Hell, take my word,' Pollard slapped his gun. 'They won't with this mother along.'

'We're technicians, not policemen, Pollard. All of us want you off my ship yesterday. It is in our very best interests to see that you do just that soonest. So, when do you plan to leave us? And more practically, how?'

Pollard pointed to a shape growing out of the eastern sky.

'There's your answer, Cap. The hot second me and my merchandise are aboard her, colour us gone.'

Caunter's snort was glottal.

'If that's your plan,' he said. 'We're all going to be very disappointed indeed.'

'Don't snow me or yourself, Caunter. Just tell your deck crew to stay out of my face when I get out there.'

'No seaplane can live in those waves. Take a look out there, man. She'll flip and sink the moment she ploughs into that swell. Warn her off. All my frequencies are at your disposal.'

'The hell you say!' Pollard slammed his cap to the deck.

'Think, man,' Caunter snapped.

'You're looking at the shortest fuse in history, Cap. I don't come up with something, you plain better had.'

The speakers behind Caunter crackled static and a call sign Pollard recognized. His grin was wide and ugly when the aircraft made a low pass over the *Oceania-Cal Princess 2*, its configuration very different from the expected Catalina.

'Damned if that thing don't come as a surprise to both of us, eh, Caunter?' Pollard's soaked face lost some of its tension as he attempted a swagger.

Caunter said nothing, hearing turbofans and rotors instead of propellers.

'It's a 'copter fitted with floats.'

Denning looked as bemused as he sounded.

'She sure is. See where my mind's running now?' Pollard asked.

When she had made several local calls Hannah had Charlie drive her to a phoney Spanish mission that sold pottery and ironwork to tourists. An old woman whispered when she brought iced well water in handblown glasses. She gave Charlie a venomous look when she kissed Hannah's hand, and favoured him with dark backward glances when she waddled off to lose herself in the fluttering darkness of a firing room of lit kilns. Time wandered by in low gear, there were no tourists on the highway, and the roaring kilns serenaded the ranks of pots around the courtyard. A barefoot boy brought a note that needed no reply, and a thin girl with glossy plaits talked to

Hannah in a musical murmur before leaving on her bicycle. Two mothers in a battered Chevrolet used their hands when Hannah talked to them in undertones, and left the acrid smell of burned oil behind them.

Charlie felt jaded by the waiting and the ease with which he and Hannah had seduced each other. Wondered if liking and wanting somebody at first sight was enough reason to scratch the oldest itch in the world after the most fleeting of second thoughts. And there was no real balm or salvation in knowing Hannah really had become Margot for a long moment during that commingling of lust and easement. Had taken on her physical form; her nervous, sinuous way of working hip and thigh and knee on that long liquid climb to a summit beyond all other summits. That warm float of hanging above the ultimate zenith before the heady plunge away from the climactic into that loose, damp tangle of limbs and heartthump and shared musk that came after. That time when shyness can intrude like the strangers he and Hannah really were. That time of oddness and withdrawal and moving apart to reach for covers or discarded clothes that did not come. Only more need, a more leisurely wanting perhaps, but as unavoidable as death or taxes. A second conjunction that blew fuses at the molten core of the sun, brightened the rings of Saturn, and turned two solitudes to a sticky, grinning, clinging wonderment of sharing.

Charlie's sigh did not carry to Hannah who watched the highway from a gateway that missed being pleasingly proportioned by millimetres. Modern man aping his forebears' style of architecture always gets it incredibly wrong. As wrong as Charlie finding Margot in the small, hard vitality that was Hannah Chasen. As miserable an act as locating and pressing all Della O'Day's emotional buttons. Opening up the Piano Lady like a free magazine, idly flipping through her pages in search of something useful. As wrong as talking eye-to-eye with the vulnerable and wonderful warmth that was the deliciously young Charlotte Bujega. Gaffing her in the shallows where she had been lured by the grizzled and knowing hunter. Using a bludgeon to make sure, when a warning pebble should have sent her back to the cool depths of the nursery to mature.

Charlie knew himself for a pathetically ageing stud plunged into the black abyss of post-coital depression. Knew that *knowing* as much did not help one jot or smidgeon. He was overcompensating for Margot's loss with a blatantly crass celebration of sex that was as arid as it was grotesque. It could not matter that the women seemed willing, able and pleased by his performances, could it? A man took his revenge with any weapon or subterfuge to hand, right? With a gun, a knife; with bedroom technique? What possible difference could the method make to the successful outcome of the exercise?

None, right?

'Wrong,' Charlie said aloud.

'No,' Hannah said without turning. 'It's him.'

'What?'

Charlie arose from the pit. Felt adrenalin spark his mind into external awareness. Hannah was back beside him, an arm hugging his. A muddy car turned off the highway with the caution of a ratting dog. Under the dried red spatters was the faded livery of the Mexican police force.

'A cop?' Charlie didn't know why he was surprised.

'And I'll do the talking, OK?'

251

'Two fingers gets me a beer. That's the sum total of my Spanish.'

The patrol car put its nose across the rental and stopped. A crumpled cop in faded tan unwound from behind the wheel and hitched his gunbelt square. He walked across the gravel with inturned toes as if his boots pinched him. His hat was the only new thing about him. He had a long olive face with a mouth that had tasted too much life, all of it bad. The square moustache flourished on a long upper lip, the nose was flat and Indian, and the eyes were just brown beads that could have belonged to a malevolent doll. He took Charlie in feature by feature as he came, a chunky gold ring on the pinky he scratched his moustache with. When the old lady asked if he wanted water, he waved her away with contempt as he looked down at Hannah without warmth.

'Sergeant Ramirez,' Hannah greeted.

Ramirez looked over her head. Directly at Charlie.

'This *gringo* is gonna be trouble for me?'

'No. He could help you.'

'Him?' The lip curled, the moustache bristled. 'You used bad words to me on the telephone.'

'Must be they were the right bad words. They got you here.'

'There are others you used bad words to. They have told me.'

'It was time to,' Hannah said, drawing the dead eyes back to herself. 'Too little has been done for too long. Now that must change.'

'The others said you told them that. I must know what bad words you used on them some time.'

'The minute you prove your worth to us, Ramirez.'

'You make my name a curse, woman. This *gringo* knows the bad words you used to me?'

252

'He knows nothing,' Hannah said with quiet force. 'Just as the others who complained to you know nothing about each other. But that can change if the clever underpaid sergeant wishes it. He could get to write his own ticket in the police department.'

'Using blackmail?' Ramirez hated Hannah with his eyes. 'And by turning myself into a baby man who listens to the madness from your belly of a mind?'

Hannah's nails bit Charlie's bicep, yet her voice remained even and mesmeric. 'Only ignorant Indians believe the lights in the night are the eyes of gods. Those lights are made by men, as we all well know. As the fat American will have confirmed if you picked him up as I suggested.'

'Kurtz? I had only to show him a soda and he talked. He is in much fear of the man with you, woman. He also said this Englese and this Rizzo crossed the border today with guns. I will know where they are before dark.'

Hannah's laugh was short. Brisk. A vixen's bark.

'Let me tell you now,' she said. 'The Hot Melon Motel. Cabin five. They drive a pickup with sand wheels. There are many women who tell me things, Ramirez.'

'Women,' Ramirez said in disgust. 'Blackmail. Have you no shame, woman? Or you, *señor*, for allowing this in your name?'

'You can always walk away,' Charlie shrugged.

'Ha! That proves you don't know what this one said to me,' Ramirez looked up at the white afternoon glare for divine help. Found none, and seemed unsurprised. 'What can a man do?' he asked nobody in particular. 'I must place my trust in a woman and a *gringo*. Where is the justice in that for an honest man?'

'Just as we have to trust you, Ramirez,' Hannah

253

reminded him. 'All liars must one day face the truth. Let it be today.'

'Prove you have the mayor in your pocket, and I will take this whole thing seriously,' Ramirez said. Fishing with a naked hook.

'His honour has a young wife who has told him to stop accepting gifts from a Mexican who makes a living off the backs of the *pollos* in the border canyons. She has lost relatives herself in this way. It was poverty and not love that put her in her husband's bed, and he will sleep alone for a very long time to come if he does not heed his beautiful bride.'

Ramirez almost grinned, turned it into a sneer.

'The old goat still has his mistress.'

'Another tragedy,' Hannah's sigh was manufactured. 'That lady has been reminded of her past by a woman who worked by her side in a certain house when they were younger. There are photographs. She has left Tijuana far behind.'

'You have not wasted your time among us,' Ramirez said.

'There is more. Documentation of land deals that could put his honour in jail for the rest of this century. Those papers will be yours if you prove worthy of our trust. There is also a house in El Centro. The females who work there cannot *all* be his honour's nieces.'

Ramirez was no longer a cynical cop in faded browns. His dead eyes had brightness now, and his mouth twitched when he blinked.

'By the saints, woman,' he said. 'You have killed yourself.'

'With you to protect me? Nonsense.'

'Then we are both dead.'

'Not if you are quick and clever, Ramirez. Without

254

the mayor's protection, Big Ugly Sanchez has to become visible. Even you could find him and his sweetheart friends.'

Ramirez became wooden. A carved man with glass eyes.

'Just like that,' he said.

'Just like that,' Hannah agreed.

'And if I find this man?'

'*When* you find him, you give him to us.'

'In exchange for gossip and a few papers? Nobody comes that cheap, woman. What can a poor man do against the monied? Nothing. Even Kurtz offered a thousand dollars not to breathe through soda. You think I am yours to command for a few *centavos*?'

'One million US dollars,' Charlie said. 'Cash.'

Ramirez's mouth tasted itself.

'For that you want all these men?'

'All of them. And the shipment.'

'To trade with?'

'To destroy.'

Ramirez looked at Charlie for a long minute. Scratched his moustache with his little finger, and toed the gravel with a scuffed boot. Said, 'You will kill these men, I think.'

'If I can.'

'Go to the eastern highway in one hour. Wait by the big green sign. I will come to you there.' Ramirez sauntered back to his patrol car. Gunned it into life with unnecessary violence, and chewed gravel into dance on his way back to the highway.

'Just what *did* you say to him?' Charlie asked.

'I told him I knew he was Angelica's natural father, that he was the reason the mother turned to drugs and prostitution. She was fourteen when he forced her, and to take an underaged girl child's virginity down here in old Mexico earns emasculation with a

255

dull knife, and it doesn't matter who the hell you are.'

'*That* I'll bear in mind,' Charlie grinned.

Casey Pollard clamped his magnetized circuit breaker to the side of the fuselage door. Arming it, he set it to the 'seek' mode, and watched the rainbow flutter of an unstable spectrum until it formed a glowing orange trident in the liquid quartz display. Working quickly, Pollard attached two terminals to the stiff outer lock mechanism, sent a 12-volt pulse down the line, and heard the interlocking tines open in rapid sequence. The door swung upon with a light creak, decanted a slop of water over his thighs, and he looked into the interior, his heart thudding.

The grey plastique explosive was a thick collar around the door frame. Still hanging in their netting cradles above the water line were the heat-sealed plastic packages of cocaine and mint treasury bills. Pollard wanted a cigar to celebrate with, but there was no time for such indulgences. He told the deck crew to start offloading with care. Once the wrecked plane was stripped, Caunter could open the sea doors and return it to the depths. The central pool could be flooded, and the circling helicopter could set down for loading and refuelling. Things were bumping along nicely, and Pollard planned to keep that fine equilibrium going all the way back to home base.

On the bridge, Denning had armed the heavy-calibre machine-gun mounted on a concealed swivel and positioned to sweep the forward deck area. A security precaution the owners had taken when their expensive salvage vessel operated in the pirate waters of the South China Seas.

'Got him in my crosshairs, Captain,' Denning said.

'One short burst, and Pollard's nothing but an unpleasant memory.'

'Just cover his departure, Mr Denning,' Caunter drawled. 'It may just have escaped your notice, but that Sikorski is an S-72 armed with side-mounted Gatlings. We are somewhat outgunned should the pilot decide he dislikes us enough to open fire at two thousand rounds per minute.'

'Sugar,' Denning swore.

'Exactly,' Caunter agreed.

Jack Kurtz got as far away from Sergeant Ramirez as he could. The gold pinky ring had chipped a front denture, and Kurtz tasted fizzy caramel with every sip of terrorized breath. The policeman had been coaching him, and when he dialled Englese at the motel he was word perfect.

'It's coming in tonight,' he said. 'I just got the word.'

'You got the word?' Englese was furious. Suspicious. 'Why you?'

'Sanchez told me. Had me picked up by the local cops. Man, he owns this fucking town.'

'Pollard's tame Mex? A dumb border Beano? What are you handing me here?'

'That's how it is, Mr Englese. And Pollard wouldn't use no Mex who wasn't halfway smarter than he need be,' Kurtz said, his stomach rolling as Ramirez stroked his moustache and the hated pinky ring caught the light. 'Sanchez knows all about us. You. Me. Rizzo. Maybe even about Mr Joe, know what I mean?'

'So Pollard has a fat mouth. Gets his jollies sounding off about his heavy connections. He wants to talk himself six feet under, whadda you care? What's the dope on this guy Dance? He still sniffing around?'

Kurtz heard his voice get ragged. The mere

mention of Charlie Dance had made Ramirez thin his mouth.

'Uh, yessir. He's got some local chick in tow. Sanchez says she runs some chicken shit outfit for unmarried mothers down here. Sanchez has the cops watching them. Dance jaywalks he's jail-bait.'

'This Sanchez has the Beano cops that far in his pocket?'

'All the way, Mr Englese. This town's tighter-lidded than a moneylender's vigorish jar. You guys wanna play poker in this burg, best you wait until they hand you their deck of marked bicycles.'

'Where the hell are you now, Jack?'

'At the police station.'

'Where?'

'I'm telling you, Sanchez runs this town. They even gave me a cop as a driver. Can you believe it, a sergeant yet.'

'Not funny, Kurtz.'

'But true, Mr Englese. Whadda you people wanna do here? Me, I'd just as soon head for home, but you're calling it, right? Uh, there's a highway runs east outta town. I can meet you right there at the junction. That, or give you directions out into the boondocks where this is all going down. Whadda you want here?'

'Wait,' Englese ordered. Muttered at Rizzo across the room with the phone away from his face. Sergeant Ramirez smiled his mean and meaningless smile, and Kurtz swallowed to keep from gagging. A flyspecked wallclock had stopped at some forgotten midnight, and the calendar beside it was five years out of date. Englese came back to say he and Rizzo would meet Kurtz at the highway in one hour.

'You got it,' Kurtz said when Ramirez agreed.

'There's a big green sign shot full of holes, you can't miss it.'

'Just see *you* don't, mouse,' Englese said.

Kurtz passed the phone to Ramirez and waited to collaborate with anybody who would let him. Anything to avoid another beating, another taste of Bubble Up. Dance, Englese and Rizzo scared Kurtz, but Ramirez filled him with real dread. He was the kind of crazy who'd shoot the office chairs if they squeaked too often, would use a blowtorch on a man or a peeling door with the same dispassion.

Ramirez sat at his desk, his back to the dead clock and his eyes closed. As if a sweep hand in his mind would tell him the exact moment to move. Kurtz wondered about the lies he had told Englese for Ramirez. The sergeant had not contacted this elusive Big Ugly Sanchez, and Kurtz wasn't even sure if Ramirez knew the man from a pine dime in a handful of change. Kurtz didn't even know if the merchandise really was coming in when Ramirez said it would.

Nothing made any kind of sense. Yet.

'Did you buy any of that, Rizzo?' Englese recradled the phone as the motel sign began to blink VACANCIES at the dusk.

Rizzo shrugged as he worked the oiled action of his automatic rifle. 'We were supposed to?' he asked.

'Kurtz sounded a true believer, like he'd vote this Sanchez in as chief of police.'

'That's his problem, wouldn't you say?' Rizzo snapped a full clip of high-velocity shells home. 'It's simple. We go in now. Let Kurtz and his tame Beano cop sit on their thumbs all night. Let's just keep the surprises coming outta our hat.'

Englese stamped into a combat boot and started lacing.

'That's bad-assed country out there, partner. They'll need more'n a team of mules to truck that shipment stateside.'

'What d'you care so long as we get to be the only gatecrashers at the party?'

'How come I don't swallow that?' Englese muttered.

Polluted smutch drowned the sun in dark feathers of cloud when Charlie parked under the green sign, a Dan Wesson from Hannah's small armoury snug in his waistband. She had a nine-shot Heckler & Koch holstered under her bodywarmer, and the sawn-off was locked in the trunk with the spare ammunition. Sergeant Ramirez was nine minutes late when he pulled off the highway with Kurtz beside him, and aligned his driving window with Charlie's to talk around a thin black cigarillo.

'Englese and Rizzo will be here in about forty minutes,' he said. 'The rendezvous point is an alkaloid lake maybe four miles down this road. Nobody goes there because of the loco weed and the bad water. A bad place for bad people.'

'I know it,' Hannah murmured.

'What about Sanchez?' Charlie asked.

Ramirez leaked sulphurous smoke through bared teeth.

'He has gone from the house your woman spoke of, very early this morning, I was told. He has maybe four with him. The woman there only saw them one at a time when she cleaned. Never saw them all together. Sanchez will be at the lake.'

'You're very sure of that,' Charlie said.

'Sure I'm sure.'

'How far is this lake from the border?'

'For the crow and the buzzard, twelve miles. For you and your woman, three days march. Maybe. There are no roads.'

'But an aircraft landing near the lake would show up on the American radar?'

'How would I know this, *señor*? We are a poor race without such expensive toys.'

'But you're sure about Sanchez being there.'

'At the lake? Sure.'

Charlie nodded at nothing.

'How?'

'The tanker for the aero fuel. It delivered a full load to Sanchez a week ago. One more the week before. That is much gas, *señor*, and the broker tells me such things to keep his government licence clean.'

'For which he pays handsomely,' Hannah said.

'Your woman knows many things, *señor*,' Ramirez said flatly.

'She does, but she ain't my woman.'

'No?' Ramirez showed sharp interest. 'Then she is nobody's woman, *señor*, and that is bad for her.'

Charlie gripped Hannah's wrist to keep her silent.

'Then she is my woman, Ramirez. As you are my man once my money lines your pockets. And honour dictates you protect her for me.'

Ramirez thought that over.

'You too have learned quickly,' he said.

'Now we come to Englese and Rizzo.'

'They will meet me here. I will send them to the lake. Nothing could be simpler.'

Charlie looked across at Kurtz.

'What about him?'

'How is he your concern, *señor*?'

'He isn't. I'm just curious.'

Ramirez flicked dark ash into the night.

261

'It is simple. He will sign a most beautiful confession. Then there is a cell, or he swims away with
the fishes too small to eat.'

'Which, Ramirez?'

'Let us say a little of each, eh?'

Charlie found no depth to the eyes a foot from his.

Said, 'Let's hope you don't get to thinking about
us in the same way.'

'How could that be? You are about to make me
rich and grateful. Such bad thoughts make me sigh
for your suspicious nature, *señor.*'

'Keeps me awake nights,' Charlie said.

'No,' Ramirez said. 'I don't think so.'

'Nor do I.'

'Good fortune to you and your woman.'

'That's you and not the money talking, is it?'

'Money is always a consideration,' Ramirez said.

'I love an honest man,' Charlie laughed. Found a
forward gear and bit dirt with spinning wheels as he
jumped the rental toward the hills hiding the lake.

'He's lying about Sanchez,' Hannah yelled above
highway noise. 'The cleaning woman hasn't been out
to the house for three days. Her husband has
pushed a broom out there so she can be with her
sick kids. Means Ramirez hasn't been near the
place. Why, damn it?'

Charlie watched the rearview as he drove through
potholes.

'Means he's playing his own game.'

'Damned right. Ramirez doesn't move without he's
got twenty angles of his own to boomerang into the
arena.'

'Like the tanker? Fact or fiction, Hannah?'

'I know that lake area. You could hide fifty tankers
there. I've quartered that entire area over four years.
Know it better than a thirsty quail. The lake isn't just

262

a solid body of water. It snakes in and out of sandbanks, sinkholes and buttes. You don't know what you're doing out there, you'd walk in circles until your legs gave out. Wouldn't cover five straight miles before your tongue had swollen to the size of a football, and that's if you didn't drown or get sucked into a mudhole.'

'Ramirez could have himself a turkey shoot out there, if he wanted. It's remote enough.'

'With us in the crossfire,' Hannah said.

'You can always go back,' Charlie said without inflection.

'Sure, if you'll go with me,' Hannah grinned. 'You out there without me is a risible notion, Mr Dance.'

'So I shouldn't have said that.'

'Is that sorry excuse an apology?'

'Probably. I open doors for ladies, and stand when they come into the room. It's called basic manners. Trying to keep one feisty lady from harm comes under the same category, doesn't it?'

'Way back when, maybe. Now? Not.'

'Then I mourn those bygone days of chivalry.'

'Stop laughing at me behind that deadpan, you rat.'

'Would smiling be OK?'

'At a pinch.'

Charlie swung to the hard shoulder to avoid a crater in the road surface. Bumped the rental over shale and gravel, and came to a halt in a depression that hid the vehicle from the road.

'One thing Ramirez doesn't know,' he said. 'Englese and Rizzo drove past whilst we were talking. Means they're ahead of us. Means he gets to wait for as long as it takes to decide they won't be coming, or they went ahead. Suppose we drive all the way past the lake? Come in at it from the far shore? That leaves Sanchez holding centre ground, and if Englese, Rizzo and Ramirez don't follow our route, they'll be on the eastern side of the lake.'

'You think good strategy, Mr Dance. But you're still laughing behind that deadpan of yours.'

'There's a cure for that. I lower my head, you raise yours.'

'Like this?'

'Uhuh.'

'Hmmmmmm,' Hannah ended the kiss with a big wet sound. 'Now can we go hunting, poppa?'

'If you drive.'

'Me? Why?'

'Because my pants are two sizes too small.'

Hannah's laugh chased its own echoes down an arroyo.

'You sure know how to boost a gal's morale, mister,' she said.

CHAPTER SEVENTEEN

With the rental hidden in a box canyon east of the lake area, Charlie and Hannah moved through a silver and charcoal wasteland under a rising moon. The huge night sky had dusted itself with rashes of starlight, and the soda lake shimmered black on black. An upper flatland broke into fissured slopes and high buttes the wind of ages had carved into fanciful shapes. Where earth tremors had toppled the cliff-sided heights into rubble, great sinkholes had opened up and flooded with alkaline water. Picking their way down a stepped ravine, Charlie and Hannah reached a curving strand of sugary sand and shale lapped by the restless waters of the lake, and crouched down to rest and listen.

'Nothing but dead air,' Charlie said. 'This place smells like burned ironing.'

'You want smells, toss a rock into one of those sinkholes,' Hannah watched the northern fore-shore through binoculars. 'You'll need a new set of lungs.'

'Anything?'

'Nope. But that doesn't mean they ain't out there somewhere. I vote we keep going north-west. Makes sense if they operate as far from the road as possible, doesn't it?'

Charlie agreed with a nod. Thought he caught something in his peripheral vision, and stared at the spot about a mile to the north. 'What's the terrain like over there?' he asked, pointing.

'Sheer cliffs and caves around a sort of cove. Like an inlet, you know?'

'Can we get there using this beach?'

'Most of the way, yes. But it breaks up real bad this side of the inlet. You can turn an ankle just *looking* at those boulders. There's no way through unless you turn inland and come back to it from the top of the cliffs. To get down there we'd need ropes.'

'Which we don't have.'

'Same for everybody, Charlie. We can't get in there, how can anybody else?'

'With a boat, pretty one.'

'Damn,' Hannah swore, and strode off along the beach without waiting for Charlie.

The sand ran flat for five hundred yards, then began to rise in a series of sandstone terraces. The heights above were sculpted into ridges and horizontal ribs that were made all the more stark by hard mooncast shadows. A dry wind mourned in the crevices and funnels, and the lights of Tijuana formed a small mustard smudge to the south-east.

Working their way down a rubble path between two buttes, Hannah and Charlie reached the shoulder of a sinkhole that stank of sulphur fumes, and skirted it as quickly as they could with handkerchiefs to their faces. Tumbled overhangs of rock turned them away from the lake, and they worked their way through a bewildering maze of fissures to return to the foreshore. Emerging from the sighing darkness on to a short run of beach was as pleasing as it was sudden. The inlet was barred by towering cliffs with sheer faces, and the path to the uplands was a treacherous goat track.

Calling a halt, Charlie unlaced his boots to cool his feet in the lake. Hannah wet her lips from a canteen and stared moodily out across the black water until she picked up the flutter of rotors somewhere in the southern darkness.

'Charlie?' she whispered.

'I hear it.' Charlie watched for movement from the inlet.

Something as grey and as slick as a whale nosed out into the lake. A thin bow wave creamed, and growling outboards powered the craft forward in overlaps of echo. Overhead, port and starboard lights showed red and green against the stars as the Sikorski S-72 dropped flares.

'What is that thing?' Hannah asked, binoculars on the steel whale.

'A fuel bowser mounted on a raft,' Charlie said, stripping to the waist. 'Enough fuel there to fly that 'copter any-damned-where she wants to go.'

'They're gonna fly the cocaine out?'

'Right under the radar at zero feet. If that thing's fitted with a contour beam she'll skim across the border six feet above the deck.' Charlie threw the useless revolver down. Dropped his shirt over it. Bitter bile in his mouth as Margot sank in dark waters inside his mind.

Hannah's throat contracted. Whatever Charlie was seeing was a private vision not to be shared. His body had tensed into an anatomy lesson. His pectorals were hard ridges of muscle, his long laterals stood out from his back, and his stomach sucked in to form a shadowed hollow. Hannah read his intent, and had to spit to talk.

'Forget it, Charlie. The lake is alkaloid. You'll burn your eyes out if you swim under water. You'll blind yourself, you ox.'

'Yes, Margot,' Charlie said, swaying.

And his face was dead in the acid light of the flares when he walked out into the shallows.

When the water closed over Charlie's shoulders he fell forward into an easy breast stroke, and swam after the raft without hurry. The Sikorski had set down on the lake, its feathering rotors bobbing the float-flares in a spreading iris of ripples. The moon had reached its zenith and sailed in reflected majesty just beyond Charlie's forward strokes. He kept the steady rhythm going, his empty heart swimming away from a lady lost in other depths as he swam for a target whose cynical greed had squandered her without knowing or caring she had existed.

The wake of the raft reached Charlie as an undulant chop, and he turned into it to make sure it didn't break over his head.

Hanging there in the water, he watched the raft begin a series of sluggish manoeuvres to bring the bowser in alongside the Sikorski. Heavy machine-guns were mounted fore and aft, a high-speed diesel pump would feed filtered aero fuel to the Sikorski's tanks, and five of the men aboard wore dark coveralls and holstered sidearms. The sixth man wore crumpled browns and a new hat, smoothed his moustache and looked bored. Sergeant Ramirez, blatantly making himself the missing link in the local puzzle. Making public show of his dismissal of Charlie and Hannah as unimportant bunglers who could do no harm to him or the organization.

Charlie trod water until the raft crew made her fast to the helicopter. Then, keeping well away from the ring of flares, and circling until he was on the Sikorski's blind quarter which in turn hid Charlie from the raft; he swam in, any sound he made swamped by idling rotors and the steady chug of the diesel pump.

Coming in on the stern, Charlie made for the port float. Hauled himself from the water and lay prone in shadow to watch the activity aboard the raft. Two men watched the fuel lines and gauges, two others manned the machine-guns, a fifth man talked to the helicopter crew through a headset plugged into the fuselage, and Ramirez was shouting up at somebody standing at the open midships door, his voice all but lost in engine noise.

Charlie decided to move. Used the float strut to pull himself upright and peer through the open port door at the cocaine and money neatly stacked along the central aisle of the loading bay. The man exchanging shouts with Ramirez had his back to Charlie, and waved an unlit green cigar in one meaty paw. Charlie rolled on to perforated metal decking. Crouched up on his toes and got out of sight behind the plasticated packs of money. Nobody shouted, no torches glared, no guns kicked smoke at him.

Keeping low, Charlie searched the port side of the central loading bay for what he would need, and was not disappointed. The Sikorski was equipped for every eventuality including ditching at sea, and he made a mental shopping list before checking on the gunship's armaments. The arming lights of the side-mounted Gatlings were on, and Charlie guessed the man talking to Ramirez would fire them manually if the need arose. Hooked up to the cockpit, they could also be fired from the pilot's seat.

A door slammed closed against its seals, and Charlie lay flat. Listened to a man complain about being choked by fumes from the pumping fuel, and knew the starboard door had been locked. Knew this had to be the time to act, and arose with suddenness. Stared into the shocked face of a man he had not seen since Hong Kong thirteen years before. The

269

face was fleshier, the skin coarser grained, the eyes baggier and more jaundiced. But it was him, and Charlie Dance reached for Casey Pollard with both hands. Got a firm grip on the twill shirt and butted Pollard in the face. Kneed him in the genitals, and butted him again to make sure. Let the eyes roll to white before lowering the slack body to the deck. Stood over him with bared teeth until the need to hurt him dissipated in a shudder. Patted the burp gun Pollard had tried to reach with mock affection, and used heavy-duty insulation tape from a tool locker to bind and gag the unconscious man. Rolled Pollard under a steel bulkhead bench, and collected all the equipment he needed as quickly as he could without being careless.

Outside, the fuel was still being pumped aboard, the machine-guns panned for targets beyond the circle of dwindling flares, and Ramirez breathed through a neckerchief. The air was heavy with aero fuel, and the machinery thumped noisily.

Moving carefully, Charlie lowered two Zodiac life rafts into the water and inflated them. Tied them off to the float struts, and loaded the twenty money packs into the second inflatable. Put Pollard, the burp gun, ammunition clips, emergency packs of food and medicine into the first one. Went back aboard the helicopter to use a bolt cutter on the Gatlings' gas feed, to drive steel pins into the ammo feeder belts to jam them solid, and remove the diaphragms from the bulkhead phones. Then he lashed the two Zodiacs together, cast off, and paddled for the southern shore, his naked spine expecting a burst of automatic fire any second.

OK so far, Margot? he thought.

Hoping Hannah would follow his reasoning.

*

Lying on the scrap of a beach, Hannah found her eyes being painfully drawn by the powerful but slightly misaligned lenses. Fifty minutes had passed since Charlie swam out into the lake and, apart from a glimpse of him swimming to the rear of the Sikorski, nothing more for almost twenty minutes. His shirt was a pathetic white puddle of linen on the sand, his neatly aligned boots pointed their toes out into the lake, and Hannah began to believe she should have followed Charlie out there.

She had a clear view of helicopter and raft, and would know every man out there any time she set eyes on them again. Seeing Ramirez had been a shock until logic took over. Who else but Ramirez could the corrupt local officials use to deal with Sanchez and his American paymasters? And Ramirez hadn't needed to check on Sanchez's whereabouts since he knew them better than anybody else. And showing himself like this meant he knew himself to be invulnerable. Above exposure or reprisal, as if Hannah and Charlie were ants under his heel.

'Where the hell are you, Charlie?' Hannah's palm came away wet when she rubbed the base of her skull where migraines were born. Realized the women she had befriended at the refuge had told her only what they thought it was safe for her to know. Knew that none of them had volunteered a single fact on their own volition, had only confirmed what she had found out for herself by other means. They may have admired her for her fierce independence, but when it came to the bottom line, Hannah Chasen was a woman alone in a society with no sympathy for her ideas of feminine suffrage. For a long moment, Hannah felt as isolated and as unpopular as a *Drum* reporter at a Klan convention in Whiteyville, Boondock County.

Then she saw the rubber boats being paddled towards the far southern shore. Charlie's back muscles working hard and hidden from the fuel bowser raft by the bulk of the Sikorski. Knew he was richer by eighty million dollars if he reached the shore alive. If he could escape from Tijuana and Sergeant Ramirez. If he could cross the border badlands and reach the relative safety of San Diego. Shake Englese and Rizzo. Avoid the long arm of Joe Camponella and the Five Families.

All those ifs dried Hannah's mouth. She let the night glasses hang from her neck as she kicked sand out into the lake in a fear tantrum. If Charlie needed a diversion, Hannah meant to be on the spot to provide one. Tying his shirt around her waist, the magnum tucked into her belt, she carried Charlie's boots back the way they had come as fast as she dared.

Charlie was pulling through the shallows below a bullhead bluff when a flare burned a green hole in the night, showing him the saw-backed rocks just below the surface. Backpaddling wearily, Charlie worked the Zodiacs out and around the bluff into a lazy shimmer of moon pattern above an expanse of shelving sand. Saw the nearest place he could make landfall, and drove the inflatables over a sandstone ledge between high walls, beaching himself in squeak of hard rubber. A searchlight sizzled on as men shouted questions and countermands, and a machine-gun test-fired tracer at nothing.

Charlie fought lassitude. Hauled the Zodiacs clear of the water before deflating them, then carried the still unconscious Pollard up a narrow corridor into a high-sided arena of living rock and sand. Dumping Pollard on his back, Charlie carried the money packs, emergency supplies, tools and weapons into the natural amphitheatre, located a folding shovel, and set about digging a hole under a rock overhang that would hide it from airborne surveillance. Marking out an area six feet square, and planning his hole should be as deep, Charlie worked the shovel hard enough to keep his sore muscles from seizing up. He dug like an unthinking automaton, refusing to contemplate the furious panic there must be aboard the raft now they knew Pollard and the money were missing. That was their problem, not Charlie's.

The powdery top crust gave way to a strata of loose shale and prehistoric shell fragments in porous travertine deposits the colour and consistency of brown sugar. Then there was a layer of hard sandstone biscuit. Charlie was just over five feet below the surface when the bottom began to snatch at the shovel with gross sucking sounds. He unwrapped a couple of Coolite sticks, activated the chemical lights by bending them in the middle, and jammed them in the ground to light the hole. There was a steady seepage of dark and brackish water, and Charlie decided he had dug deep enough.

He took a short breather, then dragged the deflated Zodiacs up to line the bottom of his neat excavation. Stacked the money packs in a neat square on the rubber, and when he had taken time out to make up a backpack of food and medicine anyone travelling through the badlands would need to survive, he dropped what was left into the hole and began filling it in again. He was very tired now, and the idea of sleep was as tempting as the apple of Eden. By the time he had levelled the surface and blew on his palms where the blisters were already forming, his hands shook, and he wanted a quiet cigarette knowing there was no time for one even if he had any.

His limbs trembling, Charlie crouched over Pollard to search his pockets. He left him his passport, zippo and cigar case, the heavy crocodile wallet with its credit cards and family pictures, the Polaroid of a brown girl with bordello eyes and bare breasts, his ten mint one-hundred-dollar bills. All Charlie took was an open-ended return ticket from San Diego to Chicago, and a typed list of telephone numbers with Illinois and New York State area codes Saul Chasen might find interesting.

Then he untaped Pollard's mouth, hands and feet. Felt for a pulse that wasn't there, and realized Pollard had choked on his own vomit. Lifted the body by the armpits and let it flop face down over the freshly filled hole. Dropped the shovel near the outflung right hand, and carefully brushed his own footprints away from around the body before climbing to the upper lip of the arena where a huddle of boulders had lain since the time of Montezuma.

His first effort to move them cost him a scrape of skin from his right shoulder. The second angrier heave produced a rockslide that partially covered Pollard's body, leaving his legs visible in the light of the Coolite sticks. Charlie rested then, his temples pounding, his muscles jerking involuntarily. If nobody found Pollard and the money before the Coolites burned out, they didn't deserve to, he thought. Hoped Ramirez would read the signs aright: that Pollard had gone into business for himself and run out of luck when his digging had brought a rockfall down on his head.

Dreaming of his motel bed, Charlie watched the Sikorski lift off to fly a circuit of the lake, its searchlight slashing the shadows like a questing silver sword. The raft held station in the water waiting to be told which shore to head for in pursuit, and the moon was running down the sky on its way to setting. Almost too tired to care whether his subterfuge succeeded or not, Charlie went down the side of the bluff and away towards the highway where he hoped to meet up with whoever he had come with all those centuries before. Something hacked the air close to his face, slapping him hard in the temple, and he fell all the way there was to fall.

Hannah was fifty feet from Charlie's rental when the Sikorski came in so low it blew her over and away in a stinging wind of sand and silica grit. The whole canyon floor lifted in whirling dance to bowl Hannah into a dip gouged out by the twisting downdraughts. She went into a foetal curl with Charlie's shirt over her head until the hovering giant gained height and took itself off to the south. The howling turbofans died away to a dopplering mutter, and left a sighing silence for sand to cascade and dribble in. Hannah kicked herself from her dusty nest and waded through freshly formed drifts to the mouth of the box canyon where she had left the car. What had been a hard-packed and level terrain was now a static sea of troughs and hummocks, and the rental was half-buried by a sandslide brought down by rotor wash.

Swearing long and low, Hannah spent precious time digging a path to the driver's door, opened it wide enough to wriggle inside, and got the engine started after several tries. Putting the rental into reverse gear, she let the clutch out slowly, backing the car out of the slide. The rear wheels spun a little, and the back of the vehicle began to slew. Braking,

Hannah put the car into first gear and turned the driving wheel into a hard lock. The rental shed sand and shale as it ground left in a shuddering arc, the tyres spinning up clouds of dust. Then, with Hannah trying to understand what was happening, the hood tilted slowly forward with the ground opening up like a great stone maw all around.

Metal screamed louder than a screen heroine. The chassis dropped against rock as the front wheels turned on air. Panelling crumpled on sandstone as the rental slid forward into the opening sinkhole, and Hannah found herself being slid under the dash. She got a hand to the door, but the car had subsided to the right, trapping the door closed. She threw herself out of the driving seat, used the dash to kick herself over her headrest to scrabble for the left rear door. Got it open and fell out into a long slide of sand and shale. The rental hit the far wall of the dry sinkhole. Jammed itself there with its rear wheels off the ground.

Hannah apologized for losing Charlie's boots. Stretched as tall as she could to open the trunk and retrieve her sawnoff and cartridges. The lid sprang up, and she actually touched the walnut grip of the shotgun before the car dropped away from her in a graceless nosedive. Thrown backwards, Hannah fell into a treacherous landslip and kneed herself in the nose. Felt herself being carried after the rental, and twisted about to catch at a rockspur standing out from the riptide of debris. Dug her other hand into a fissure. Held on with aching arms as the dirt of centuries waterfalled over her head and shoulders.

The rental was grinding apart under layer after layer of sand and rock, and Hannah found she had the will to move no more than her eyelids until she heard the Sikorski sweep in for a second pass over the canyon.

Then there was no choice.

Hannah was up and running anywhere without time to think of negatives. She pressed herself into a shallow cave just as the thing howled in to batter her senses with a wall of sound. The turbofans squalled like a million furies. The huge rotors churned her brains to mush, doubling and redoubling their bellowing volume in the confined space of the canyon. The air itself vibrated like juddered rock, and the stone shell Hannah clung to shook itself with renewed vigour when the Sikorski lifted away in a banking turn to cross the lake.

Hannah broke cover and ran with subterranean rumbles reaching up through the ground for her. Ran for the entrance to the box canyon with dark mouths and pits opening up behind her. Clawed her way out of that mad and shifting place as two stone pillars leaned together overhead in a lethal spatter of chippings. Rolled away down a long slope of sand to a long bed of static sandstone beyond the area of unstable faults, and lay on her back to flutter her eyelashes at the unchanging stars.

The underground grumbles faded and petered out. There was nothing but the faint whisp of dustfall, the tink and plink of pebbles finding a place to rest; the very distant sound of the helicopter hovering above a bullnosed bluff on the southern shore.

Her fingers and toes mere tingles, Hannah's body seemed to be a disorder of oiled and knotted snakes, all of them trying to unravel her entirely, and she seriously considered bursting into tears. She was frightened, tired, bruised and filthy. There were pounds of grit inside her bra and panties, and enough Mexican real estate in her boots to fill a bucket. God alone knew how long it would take to ever get her hair clean again, and she dared not think about her ruined complexion.

Fighting the terminal sniffles, Hannah found her feet and brushed herself off. Found the binoculars still hanging around her neck, and held them like a far-sighted talisman as she climbed out of the stone depression she had lain in for that timeless time of silly self-pity. Emerging on to a flat upland of crazed sandstone that rose sheer from the lake, she could see the Sikorski hovering above the bullnosed bluff. The bowser raft had made landfall below it, and men in coveralls were climbing the bluff to see what the helicopter had trapped in its beam.

Visualizing Charlie surrounded and unarmed, Hannah broke into a trot. Pacing herself for the long run around the lake, she refused to wonder what one woman armed with a nine-shot pistol could achieve against bandits with automatic weapons.

We live in hope, she told the setting moon.

Jogging on.

Sense of self was confusion and dreamy concern.

Charlie lay at the foot of a sloping crumble of lime marl. The ground glittered like powdered glass in the setting moonlight, and just thinking about feeling himself down with careful hands hurt. He dimly remembered toppling outward, his optic nerves blinded by a shouting violet flash as he hit a down-slope with his mind going dark. His hand crabbed along the ground to the pulpy place above his right ear. The weeping graze along the crown of a massive weal the size of his face. Touching it made the mirrored shards of a dual universe spin apart and reform as a sickening whole. He hicked bile into the dirt and made noises he wasn't happy about. Then lay still, waiting for the world to explain itself in its own time.

A boot toed him in the side. Hooked him over on to his back. There were two of them above him, the closest they had been to Charlie since Joe Camponella drank Bollinger over dinner at the Wooden Palisades. Englese was tricked out like a photogenic hunter promoting good bourbon in a magazine layout, and Rizzo just looked capable.

'Can you talk, Limey?' Rizzo's boot found a grazed thigh to toe.

Charlie said, 'Essh,' surprising himself. 'Essh eye cann.'

The heights behind the two men hid the hovering Sikorski, and the rotors were no louder than a moth drumming on a lampshade.

'Where's your girlfriend? The one Kurtz mentioned?'

'Other shide offa lake. Shummwhere.'

'That where you lost your shirt? Your shoes?'

'Essh. Shwamm, you shee,' Charlie said. Reminding himself.

'That right? For why?'

'Shmelled wrong. All wrong.'

'Oh?'

'Essh. Hadda shee, you see. Shaw Pollard.'

'Doing what, exactly?'

'Loading money onna rubber boat. Took it ashore. Left the cocaine.'

'Casey Pollard did that? Shit you say. You were where?'

'Shwimming to the raft. Had to rest when I got there. Cramp. Too late then. They went in after him. Aye got dragged ashore. Then swam away. Made forra highway. Then . . . you.'

279

'Guess you hit the mother too hard, Englese,' Rizzo sounded sad. 'Scrambled his thinking buds. The moron's saying Pollard stole his own dough from his own people. Why, when all he had to do was fly the whole fucking package across the border?'

'Essh,' Charlie agreed. 'Shtinksss.'

Rizzo showed his teeth to the stars.

'Enough. This Limey mother has a score to settle with Pollard. He'll do and say anything to dump over the consortium, we both know that.'

'Shtinks,' Charlie said amiably.

'Shut it.' Rizzo used his boot to confuse Charlie's stomach.

'Forty two mill *belongs* to this mother,' Englese told Rizzo. 'If Pollard walks with the full eighty, only Joe and Dance are outta pocket for big bucks. They own this consignment of dough between them. The snow is all Casey has a piece of. And his slice of that don't pan out to no eighty clicks, partner.'

'Essh,' Charlie said. 'Double-triple cross.'

Both men looked down at him.

'What?' Englese said.

'Sanchez and Ramirez could buy Mexico for eighty mill. Shee how things are here? Only Pollard between them and every single thing they ever wanted. Was *them* Pollard was running from. He had a good start on them, maybe he made it into the badlands.'

'We saw enough back there to know otherwise,' Englese said.

'Essh?' Charlie touched his pounding temple. Felt the pulpy place under his hair. 'I'm out of pocket, but it's Camponella who's the big loser here. I can live with my losses, but good old Joe won't allow himself to be taken for a buffalo nickel by a couple of Beano border bandits. Scuse mee, gonna bee glooo . . .' Charlie vomited without the need to act. The universe wheeled with his stomach, a disaster he wanted to disown, and raising his head from the ground was a madness. Lying down was a temptation he fought with foolish doggedness, and only to impress some woman whose face he had filed somewhere else.

Englese slapped his rifle.

'Slingshots against artillery if we go back up that hill,' he said. 'But we *don't* find out what's really going down, it's our everloving asses, partner.'

'Go up against Gatlings and Brownings with these?' Rizzo was too angry to shout, and he hissed spittle with his words. 'Fuck Camponella. He wants to know what's going down here? Have him call Information.'

'We have to go back up there, and you know it.'

'You're as flaky as this bird.' Rizzo toed Charlie again.

Charlie smiled somehow. Wished he could tell them about the spiked Gatlings.

'You stay with him, then,' Englese shrugged. 'I'll go.'

'He needs no minding. And you're going nowhere without me.'

'That settles it, then,' Englese said.

Rizzo shook his head. Spat at the dark hill. 'You did it to me again,' he said. 'What about flaky here?'

'He'll keep. And he'll maybe come in useful when we have to tell Joe the whole thing, right?'

'If we ever get to tell Joe anything ever again. Just don't get brave up there, Englese.'

Rizzo would have kicked Charlie again, but the Englishman was holding his skull together with both hands and puking hard.

'He doesn't look so much now, does he?' Englese asked.

'Why don't that make me sad?'

Rizzo followed his partner up the hill, and Charlie lost all sense of time. There were hot squiggles of hurting colour inside his eyelids, and the ground he lay on turned to liquid when he tried to stand on it. Lying down was a misery, and rocking on his haunches with his knees under his chin was the only way to stop his stomach from rioting. He took shallow sips of air through his mouth, crooning as he rocked. He was beyond anger or self-disgust. All he wanted was a new head to rest on his motel pillow, legs that articulated, and a way out of there that wasn't an uphill maze of water beds. The night spoke to him in Hannah's voice, but he wasn't fooled. Rifle butts in the head caused hallucinations, and if he could have figured out where the voice came from he would have told it to go away.

A hard shoulder wormed into his right armpit and got him unwound with a heave. His head would not hang right, but making his legs move in the right sequence took all his concentration as he leaned on somebody smaller than he was. The top of the head near his lolling chin smelled of dust and sulphur and hot woman. A baked bread smell that made him think of breakfast muffins. The idea of food was fine so long as he didn't think of eating the stuff. That might come later when he was out of the arroyos and had his new head screwed into place. Then he would find Hannah and buy her all the crispy bacon, waffles and syrup she could gulp down. He could smell the coffee, really smell it, and he was so thirsty he would have killed for a cup if he remembered how to do such violent things.

There was a slithering descent into a shallow

282

draw, and he was leaned against a flat surface cold enough to cool his face. He kept his legs from buckling, and wondered why the woman-smelling person was walking around two vehicles with caution. One was a muddy police car that belonged to somebody Charlie didn't like, and he sneered at it for a while. The other machine was a Japanese jeep with outsized desert tyres, and he knew he disliked the men who drove that. One of them had hurt and confused his head, and Charlie thought he must do something about that when he was well enough to buy Hannah breakfast.

The woman swung something against a side window and glass flew, the driver's door of the jeep opened outward, and a small fat man rolled out on to the ground, looking very dead indeed. That worried Charlie into a higher plane of awareness, so he tried talking to the woman person. His tongue hinged all wrong. Was a furry sliding thing that got between his teeth.

'Hannah,' he said. 'That Kurtz?'

Hannah brushed hair from her streaked forehead. Glanced at Charlie as she felt for a non-existent pulse.

'You're back with us, huh? Yep, it's him. A single shot through the heart. Sergeant Ramirez's work, I'd say. Guess he plans to fly out with the helicopter and be a rich man somewhere else.'

'Leaving Englese and Rizzo with a body to explain or bury.'

Charlie pushed himself away from the slab he'd been leaned against. Swayed and stayed upright. The hard spit of a rifle was answered by a stutter of machine-gun fire, and Charlie held his gut as if he had been punched low. Something huge had brawled in from over the ridge, a great bass thing that shook the earth itself. Hannah felt it too, and her eyes were wide when the northern horizon seared blue-white with a monumental whack of sound. Hannah's hair was blown free of her ribbon as she covered her face. A fine and stinging rain of dust swept through the wash with the pressure wave. The night rolled back on itself with a secondary clap of sound, and a reddish brown fireball rolled skyward as a fiery fist trailing tentacles of incandescence like a burning octopus. A warm rain fell as a brief drench, and Charlie could hear the lake smashing at its shoreline.

Hannah clutched at Charlie, yelling something only she understood. The Sikorski sailed over the ridge with its nose down, its rear rotors blown away. The exploding fuel bowser had blackened its silver belly, and it shook itself like a wet dog as it tried to trim its flight. Fire spurted along its fuselage, and with a majestic disregard for time, it blew itself apart. Erratic sprays of tracer made spiteful patterns, and the whole blazing mass boiled out of the sky as a tumbling stew that lost cohesion as it fell. Trails of smoke and flame thudded into the canyons, riddled the lake and arroyos with hot shrapnel, and broadcast its echoes as an overlap of heavy artillery. The fireball burned to nothing, the hot napalm stink of burned fuel spread on the light pre-dawn wind, and the stars came back to a silence as hard as they were bright.

Charlie could only shake his head when Hannah wondered if anybody could have lived through the conflagration. He didn't even want to take a cursory look for survivors. His exhaustion was a numbing thing that robbed him of curiosity, and he sat beside Hannah as she drove the jeep to Tijuana, his eyes as empty as his mind.

'Ouch.'

'Hold still.' Hannah dabbed glycerine on Charlie's headwound. 'You're a long day's march from death's door, so be a brave soldier.'

'Yes, mother.'

'Don't "mother" me, you mother.'

'You took me by surprise.'

'Men are all small boys when it comes right down to it.'

'I'm hungry.'

'There are cold cuts in the fridge.'

'Scrambled eggs,' Charlie yawned. 'Fluffy scrambled eggs. Toast oozing with butter. Coffee as black as an African princess. Streaky bacon as crisp as new banknotes.'

'Stop it, you sadist. You're making me want to pig out.'

'Why not? We earned it.'

'I'd get as big as a house.'

'More to love. I'll cook it.'

'You?'

Charlie rummaged through the refrigerator.

'Why not? All men aren't helpless, you know.'

'Or modest, eh?'

Charlie smeared a skillet with butter and added a couple of beads of oil. Broke eggs into a bowl and began to whisk them.

'I can't get warm, Charlie.'

'Reaction. Quite natural, sweetheart. Not every day you witness a murder and a disaster, do you?'

'It was all so *big*, you know? Almost too big to take in.'

Wrapped in an oversized towelling robe, Hannah looked so young she made Charlie's throat ache. He sliced a packet of bacon open and laid rashers in his warmed pan. Ground coffee beans and charged the percolator with water.

'Now I'm really hungry,' Hannah complained. 'And . . . sad.'

'You'll probably have a couple of weepy days. Let it happen, and don't worry about it.'

'Thanks, coach. I'll need to be held very close tonight.'

'My pleasure, although it'll be light soon.'

'We'll pull the drapes. It'll be dark enough to sleep.'

'We should cross into the United States as soon as we can, you know.'

'You mean in case some of . . . them survived?'

'Exactly that.'

'But that isn't possible, is it, Charlie?' Hannah asked as a man stepped into the room behind her. Sergeant Ramirez was a comically blackened and tattered scarecrow, but his expression and the way he held his revolver were anything but risible.

'I'm afraid it is very possible,' Charlie said calmly.

CHAPTER EIGHTEEN

Charlie stood straight and still as Hannah became aware of somebody behind her. Without moving, she read the situation from Charlie's face, and remained seated at the scrubbed pine table. Sergeant Ramirez had lost his hat, half his hair had been singed to a frizzle, and he stank of braised flesh. His blackened face was pocked by stone splinters, his right eye was swollen closed, and there were burn blisters on his forehead. His uniform shirt hung in tatters, and his burned legs showed through scorch burns in his trousers. He caught Hannah by the hair, dug his revolver into her neck and hated Charlie with his one good eye.

'You make trouble,' Ramirez said. 'This one dies slow.'

Charlie kept his voice level as he turned off the gas jets under his pans. 'No trouble, Ramirez. But you must let me call a doctor for you.'

'No doctors. You will drive. She sits in the back with me.'

'Drive? Drive where?'

'Across the border.'

'Not with you looking like that, Ramirez. The customs boys would be all over you like a cheap deodorant.'

'You don't worry about that. You want I should shoot you? Just take the woman?'

'I'm listening.'

'Yeah, that figures. The woman will fix my burns.

You will go outside. Unload my car into the jeep. You will do this now.'

'Unload what?'

'You will see.'

'Dressed in a towel? That should excite comment amongst the locals, wouldn't you say? I lost everything in the canyons, including my shoes. Let me go to the motel and collect clothes for both of us.'

Remirez blinked his good eye. Licked his cracked lips and winced. 'I'll give you eight minutes to get there and back. Any longer, I open this one's face. Maybe take an eye.'

'Be reasonable, Ramirez. That's a twenty-minute round trip. I lost my cabin key too. I'll have to get the manager to open up, and that could take some time.'

Ramirez's smile was a venal leer.

'You made the trouble for me, Gringo. Now it comes back in spades. You want to hear this one scream?'

'Do it, Charlie,' Hannah said in a small stiff voice. 'Do it now.'

Charlie's stomach growled and turned acid. He went out of the kitchen wanting his thumbs in Ramirez's throat, passed the sleeping wolfhound, and climbed into the jeep. Grey light had seeped out of the darkness, and Charlie had no memory of the drive out of town. He was screeching to a halt outside the motel, there was a confused shouting match with the manager who lost all his English when Charlie threatened to feed him his own head. He was in the cabin scooping up papers and money and clothes. Then running to dump it all in the jeep before driving in a dust cloud with vehicles of all shapes and sizes getting out of his way. In his hurry he drove on the wrong side of the road, and didn't realize he'd done so until he braked outside Hannah's house.

Panting hard, his eyes spangled by liver spots, Charlie was back in the kitchen, spilling clothes all over the table. Ramirez sat in a chair, his gun between Hannah's breasts as she dressed his facial burns. A fresh bruise was turning livid on her throat, and Charlie saw perverted pleasure in the single brown eye Ramirez watched him with. Forcing all expression out his face and voice, Charlie showed Ramirez every item in his travel bag, allowed him to choose what he wanted to wear, calm in the knowledge that he would kill the Mexican the moment he could. Dressed in slacks, casuals and a woollen polo shirt, Charlie was sent outside again, and discovered what Ramirez had in his police car.

Ramirez had dug up four of Pollard's money packs, and Charlie laid them under a tarp in the back of the jeep. At the nearest gas station he filled the main tank and two jerry cans, had the oil and water checked. Made certain the tryes were pumped to the correct pressure, and bought himself a steel tyre lever that sat snug in his sock. When he had abandoned Ramirez's police car on a waste lot flanked by windowless adobe walls, he went back to Hannah's house on foot.

Ramirez wore one of Charlie's lightweight suits as he waited in the walled yard, and he had Hannah's Heckler & Koch as well as his .38. He sat in the rear seat with Hannah at his side, and he directed Charlie up the northern highway for about a mile until he turned him down a rutted track to a lone *hacienda*. Ramirez took Hannah inside with him, and dozing at the wheel, Charlie was prodded awake to find the sun high in the sky. Ramirez had been atttended by a physician, and the smell of the aseptic cream larding his face and hands stank of hospitals.

They ate tortillas at a roadside hovel, drank Dos Exxes rather than trust the water, and Ramirez directed Charlie down remote trails that seemed to take him in great interlocking loops without getting any closer to the border. The whole route seemed designed to confuse, and Charlie's head pounded with exhaustion. Ramirez finally called a halt. He ordered Charlie to park in the shadow of a butte, handcuffed him to the steering wheel, chained and padlocked Hannah to the rear bumper, and went to sleep on the tarp covering the money. Charlie closed his eyes against the glare and wouldn't respond when Hannah tried to start a whispered conversation. Whatever Ramirez's plans were, Charlie and Hannah had to figure prominently in them at some future time, and Charlie meant to be as rested and as mentally agile as possible when that time came.

Night came on with its usual suddenness, and Ramirez was in a foul mood when he awoke. He chewed on painkillers, and Charlie noticed he held his head at a stiff angle as though it pained him to straighten his neck. At moonrise, Ramirez headed Charlie due north through featureless scrubby flats. Two hours later, the terrain had not changed, and Charlie was directed towards a range of low hills off to the east. A chain link fence came out of the night to mark the border, and Ramirez had Charlie drive along it until the wire ran out, and there was nothing between the jeep and the United States but a few canyons and a lot of darkness.

Ramirez was muttering to himself in an odd mix of English and Spanish, and his directions to Charlie became harder to understand. He used his revolver to prod Charlie like a steel finger, and Charlie expected a bullet every time he was jabbed. A mud-brick wall showed in the headlights, and driving through a doorless opening, Charlie found himself in a cemetery. The markers were rough wooden boards jammed in the earth. Some were painted white to show up the names painted there, others were raw wood bearing a pencilled name. Charlie knew where he was suddenly, a make-shift burial ground for illegals who had died in no man's land.

Ramirez pushed Charlie out of the jeep and stood him in the glare of the headlights. Hustled Hannah out and stood her at Charlie's side. Laughed a laugh that would have curdled milk, and told himself something funny in Spanish. A private thing of hidden meaning only he understood and would not share.

'He's totally apeshit,' Hannah whispered.

Charlie agreed with a grunt, shielding his eyes. Ramirez was invisible behind the jeep's lights although Charlie could hear him rooting about back there. There was a grunt of effort and one of the money packs curved out of the night to thud at Charlie's feet. The others followed in quick succession, and Ramirez chuckled to himself like a rooting she-bear.

'First you dig, Gringo. We bury this money.'

Charlie folded his arms. Said, 'Then you bury us, that it? Use us as markers in case somebody decides to investigate? Nothing like nicely rotting corpses to deter curiosity, is there?'

'You're pretty smart, but that don't stop you getting dead. You dig now, or I shoot the woman low in the belly so she takes a long time to die.'

'Dig with what?'

'Use a marker, use your hands, I don't give a damn for your manicure. You want something to look at

291

as you dig? Ramirez gives you a last pleasure from the goodness of his heart. You, woman. Strip. Strip and stand where we can both see you.'

Charlie took a step towards the jeep. 'In the belly, I swear,' stopped him dead. The snap of a cocking pistol made him reach for a wooden marker. 'Such a smart man,' sneered at him goaded him into digging at the loamy soil to give his body something to do. Hannah had stepped out of her trouser suit, and made a pretty sculpture of light and shade as she shed her underwear.

'She has a good body, eh, Gringo? Maybe I pleasure myself with her before she goes in the ground. But you will be dead by then, so it will not cause you pain.'

'No,' Hannah said in hot denial. 'You won't lay your filthy paws on me, you animal. Not unless you shoot me first. And that just about sums you up, doesn't it, you necrophile.'

Charlie drove the marker in a chopping rhythm. Kept his eyes down so he wasn't blinded by the glare. Threw dirt to the side as far as he could.

'You say I sleep with the dead?' Ramirez's voice was thick with venom.

'Dead children. If you can get them,' Hannah taunted him. 'Shoot me in the eyes. Then I won't have to look at you.'

'Such a body. Such an ugly mouth,' Ramirez crooned.

Charlie tried to lose himself in the digging. To become an automaton without feelings, with no fear for Hannah as she pushed Ramirez over the edge.

'Dig here, Charlie,' Hannah said. 'This is a child's grave, I think. A souvenir for the brave sergeant. Sergeant Ramirez, the fucker of flies.'

A shadow came out of the headlights, became

Ramirez reaching for Hannah. The slap was as loud as a snapping breadstick, and Hannah went down on her knees with Ramirez holding her by the arm, his fist and gun raised to strike her again. Charlie hit Ramirez in the face with a stream of dirt. Swung the marker against his neck and felt something give. Ramirez released Hannah. Turned the revolver on Charlie and fired point-blank. Muzzle flash exchanged Charlie's night vision for fanciful patterns of light. Charlie's fist hammered Ramirez's mouth open and askew. Smashed the hook of a nose. The revolver had spun off somewhere, and the Heckler & Koch was snagged in the lightweight jacket. Charlie was roaring as his fists swung and connected with jaw and rib and eye. What had been firm muscle softened to sand and broken brittle. Ramirez was a loosely stuffed mannequin. A man-doll made to be punished and punished and punished.

Beyond exhaustion, Charlie lifted Ramirez by the neck. Drove the lolling head aside with a last smashing punch. Threw the body away from him to see if it dared to come back for more. Hated the sprawl it made, the lifeless twisted way it lay there on the trampled dirt. The way it made union with the earth, more than ready to become one with it.

Charlie wanted to stamp it out of existence. He went forward to lift an arm and feel for a pulse. Felt the light knocking in the wrist and made sure by feeling for heartbeat. Hauled the man up and laid him in the back of the jeep with the money. Took great gulps of night air as the world whirled back to up, down and sideways.

Hannah was in Charlie's arms then. Her voice soothing him as he sobbed-breathed and came all the way back from that dark place where he had been pushed by necessity. Off in the blackness beyond starlight where nothing but the need to destroy with extreme prejudice has any currency with the Lords of Murderous Intent who rule that dark kingdom with deadly force.

Cicadas strummed in sawing song, Hannah was girl-soft in the night, and just holding her to him was not enough for either of them. And right there amongst the dead in that lost place, Charlie and Hannah came together to celebrate life and the living in the only sure way there is to make the heart thud true, the body soar in red mists, and the mind and soul spit in the eye of mortality.

The bedside light came on automatically when Joe Camponella answered his night line with an anonymous grunt. His scrambler system was the most sophisticated available, and all calls were processed through an exchange of over two hundred numbers, any one of which would terminate itself if bugged. All the numbers were unlisted, and were changed in batches of ten at random intervals. His voice was electronically resculptured to deny the possibility of accurate voice prints should the system fail to detect a bug and neutralize it with a solid signal of white sound. The service was wildly expensive, but the true value of Camponella's privacy far outweighed any financial consideration.

A simple digital code identified the caller as a member of the San Diego border patrol, a man who had been recruited very recently by Casey Pollard. The officer made his report without preamble, and when he had cleared down, the system unscrambled what it had cocooned in a web of broken pulses, restored the sequence and played it to Camponella in plain language only he could hear.

US radar had tracked a low-flying signal up the

western seaboard of Baja, California. It had dropped off the screens in an area east of Tijuana where there were no landing areas able to cope with a blip of that magnitude unless it were a helicopter, probably a Sikorsky with rotors and turbofans if sound analysis proved correct. The Sikorski reappeared within the hour, circled a soda lake and disappeared whilst in a hovering mode. Ground sensors had recorded an explosion and shock wave in that same general area at the same time. A domestic flight approaching San Diego from the midwest reported a visual sighting of the flash and fall of debris.

The report ended, and Camponella gave the 'erase' command when he replaced the receiver. The bed-side light dimmed and went out, leaving Camponella with dark thoughts in a darker darkness. There had been no word from Englese or Rizzo since they followed Jack Kurtz down to Baja, and Camponella knew he had no choice but to investigate what must have happened south of the border. If the entire shipment had been destroyed in some freak acci-dent, he must cover his tracks before wind of his deal with Charlie Dance came to light. Resolving to wait for twenty-four hours, Camponella lay on his side with closed eyes, willing sleep to take him.

Saul Chasen was barely awake when his San Ysidro apartment was invaded. A bitch wolfhound gave his face a serious licking before loping off to explore, his ex-wife gave him two heavy suitcases to carry inside, and Charlie Dance had what appeared to be a male corpse over his right shoulder.

'It'll take more than sweet words from the prophet to explain this, people,' Chasen protested, crowded back into his own lobby.

'Chasen,' Hannah scolded. 'You're God's biggest

fool. We are tired, testy and tarnished. There'd better be hot coffee and hotter suds in this firetrap, or you don't earn word one.'

A damp nose came up inside Chasen's robe to prod his bedwarm backside.

'Back off, Rosie, you illegal rabid immigrant,' he yelped.

'Nonsense. Rosie's had more shots than the moon shuttle.'

'Quarantine regulations. You heard of them, lady?'

Hannah looked ready to slap Chasen hard.

'There was no time for formalities, you deadhead. Which room and bath do I take?'

'Whaddaya think this is, Hannah? A government Hilton for ex-dependents with menageries?'

'Good comeback,' Charlie said, dead on his feet.

Chasen turned on him. Livid.

'And just what the thump is that you're carrying? A shooting range dummy you got too fond of?'

Hannah whirled Chasen to face her.

'You want us to go to some cheap motel, is that it?'

'Listen—'

'To an ingrate?' Hannah interrupted. 'And after what we've done for you and your people? No thank *you*.'

'Do I read minds?' Chasen said. 'How the hell do I know what you've done for anybody?'

'You ask. Humbly. After you've made us welcome. Made us comfortable. Show gratitude for us saving your FBI buns. Then, and only then, will we impart our great doings.'

'Thank you, God,' Chasen said fervently. 'I think I'm cured.'

'Of what?' Hannah snarled.

'Marriage,' Chasen said faintly.

Charlie pushed between the squabbling couple and laid Ramirez on the black living-room couch. Sat in a chair and fell asleep waiting for Saul and Hannah to run out of hurtful things to spit at each other.

The dark thing clawed him from sleep, and Camponella realized he had dozed off again. The curtains were drawn back from a yellow morning, his breakfast tray lay across his lap, and he had a crick in his neck. He put the secure phone to his face, and the digital display showed the call originated in Mexico. The voice was faint, the words as disjointed as if the system scrambled them against eavesdroppers. Camponella screwed the receiver to his ear and swore at the blue jay imitating a lawnmower outside his window.

'Rizzo? That you?'

The voice was familiar yet changed. Stressed with pain.

'Englese?'

The voice stumbled on without responding to verbal cues. Too intent on getting it all said before he ran out of words or life itself. Camponella caught odd words here and there before the connection melted into a crossed-line gibberish of Spanish and English. He had to wait for the system to enhance what there was and play it back to him with the interference filtered to a low background hush. A transcript of what he heard would have read:

. . . SHITTING MEX PHONES . . . ABOUT TIME . . . LISTEN UP (oblit.) THEY HAD IT FIGURED AS . . . TRIPLE PLAY. (oblit.) TOLD HIM . . . WOULDN'T HEAR A THING ABOUT IT. POLLARD TOOK FOR THE HILLS WITH PART SHIPMENT. (oblit.). N'T TRUST HIS OWN . . . GUESS. HAD HIM BOXED

WHEN WE WENT IN TO GIVE HIM COVERING FIRE. FIGURED TO KEEP THE MOTHERS' HEADS ALLA WAY DOWN. (oblit.) LEFT THAT BRIT DANCE ONNA BACKTRAIL BY OUR JEEP WITH A KNOT IN HIS HEAD. MOTHER WAS TOO BUSY EMPTYING HIS STOMACH TO SASS . . . (obliterated.) . . . POLLARD HAD TO HAVE GONE DIRTY ONNA SYNDICATE . . . I GAVE A BIG NO TO THAT . . . (expletives.) . . . HE JUST WENT APE ON ME . . . OPENED UP ONNA RAFT WITH TRACER . . . NEXT THING . . . WHOLE FUCKING THING CLIMBED FOR THE SKY . . . I MEAN GONE . . . (oblit.) . . . LOST A YARD OF HIDE OFF MY TAILPIPE . . . LOOKED FOR . . . (oblit.) . . . FOUND WHAT HADDA BE HIM . . . BOULDER BIG AS A LINCOLN CONTINENTAL HAD SMEARED HIM ANN HIS FUCKING TRACER ROUNDS ALL TO FUCK . . . MOTHER NEVER LISTENED, JOE . . . (oblit.) . . . GOT MY ASS OUTTA THERE . . . JEEP GONE . . . DANCE GONE . . . SOMEBODY HAD WASTED JACK KURTZ . . . LEFT HIM FOR THE BUZZARDS . . . NOT DANCE. NO GUN . . . NOT EVEN SHOES . . . HEH HEH . . . HADDA BE A MEX COP NAMED RAMIR(oblit.) . . . NO ACCOUNT MOTHER . . . WALKED ALL NIGHT TO THIS CHICKEN SHACK TOWN . . . NO NAME OR NOTHING . . . LOOK FOR ME, JOE . . . I'M . . . (message fades and ends.)

Camponella's lungs had solidified inside a cement corset. He asked the system for a Voice Print Ident, but it glowed negative. He had to breathe real air, not the ersatz stuff his conditioner wafted at him. His breakfast tray hit the floor as he kicked himself free of bedclothes. On the stairs his upstairs maid stared in frank fascination. Nobody saw the great *señor* Camponella in his nightwear. Not ever. Nothing on his bony white feet either. Camponella ripped the pool door open and sank into a sun lounger to gulp air, to take in the view he had paid millions for. The box canyon was lost in tendrils of fog, and the air tasted bitter. Los Angeles and the San Fernando Valley had disappeared in yellow nothing, and the only clear sky was behind him to the north.

Camponella stared into the deep end of his kidney-shaped pool. Saw his future twist and warp with the reflected image of his cypress trees and his own worried face. It would have been better if neither Rizzo nor Englese had survived. They had caused the disaster with indiscriminate gunplay, but that would mean little when the council of families met at the end of the month. Clever old Joe Camponella had sent the two men down there, hadn't he? So, who else could be blamed for the most expensive disaster in the organization's recent history? Not the family heads. No, the man with the watching brief. The man who must carry the can of worms all the way to the fishing party on the banks of the Hudson. Let's hear it for the late, great Joseph Camponella. The man who was so smart he outwitted himself.

There would be wreaths by the thousand. Fine words from the elders of the clans. Tributes by the hundred for good old Joe Camponella who would not be there to recognize how much he had been appreciated in life.

Think, Joe, he told himself. *Think or perish.*

Now there was coolness where there had been unpleasant heat.

Ramirez opened his one good eye as he tried to draw his legs up into the foetal position. Metal rings tagged his ankles and restrained his outstretched arms. Cuffed to a stripped bed, the boxframed springs hummed under him when he moved. Somebody had given him rough and ready first aid, and hope flickered in his dulled mind. Nobody helped to heal one they planned to kill, did they? Or were the *gringos* that different to his own people? Was pretended humanitarianism part of the punishment? Was the British *gringo* making Ramirez strong merely to extend the term of his resistance to the pain of torture? Ramirez did not know.

The cell was windowless, and the door must be in the wall he could not see. The ceiling was high, the light was a naked bulb protected by a heavy wire cage. There was no washbasin and no toilet, only a basic soakaway, and that told Ramirez something he did not wish to know. He was to be treated like any ordinary Mexican offender who fell foul of the serious crime squad, and that involved electric cattle prods and the Bubble Up treatment.

Ramirez hoped he could stop his heart before they stole the last of his manhood.

Agents Parrot and Blackwell watched Saul Chasen blow Chesterfield smoke at Ramirez beyond the one-way mirror. They had been called upon to do some pretty strange things in the past, but this set-up was one they could only think of as highly novel, and not a smart career move for any of them if the higher echelons of the FBI got wind of it.

'Nervous, boys?' Chasen did not look around.

'Frankly?' Parrot said. 'Yes.'

'Guess so,' Blackwell added.

'You want Joe Camponella's tush, don't you, boys?'

'I also want to die in bed with two ingénues when I'm ninety,' Blackwell joked, 'with you holding my coat for me, Saul. That don't make dog doody sweet potato though, does it?'

Chasen laughed without lightness.

'And practising self-abuse in mensrooms won't make you the perfect jerk-off, either. But don't let me knock your hobbies. Answer the question.'

'Sure, but at what cost?'

'Whatever it takes, what else?' Chasen said dismissively.

'This Beano is the answer?' Parrot asked.

'Part of it.'

'And the rest?'

'What the hell we can make of ourselves and the situation,' Chasen said.

'As usual,' Blackwell sighed.

'As usual,' Chasen agreed. 'Well? You in or out?'

'In,' Blackwell said.

'Where d'we start?' Parrot asked.

'Right here. Make that Beano think he's in his own police cell. Send him to the moon, boys.'

'And you'll be where?'

'Me?' Chasen stood and stretched. Thought of Charlie sleeping beside Hannah and surprised himself by feeling nothing. 'Why, I've an appointment to see the great man himself.'

Parrot grinned with tension, joking to ease his stiffening neck.

'Best of three means it ain't Walt Disney or J. Edgar Hoover. That means good old Joe himself, am I right?'

Chasen trod on his cigarette butt. 'Uhuh.'

'Take care, Saul,' Blackwell cautioned. 'That old boy wants your ass badder than a Sunset queen pants to tune Liberace's piano.'

'Nice talk,' Chasen grinned. Leaving San Ysidro for Los Angeles.

Camponella had regained most of his composure when his butler brought him a portable phone. He cancelled his day's appointments with appropriate regrets, and added flowers for two of his wealthier women clients. He then called a number he had memorized against the day it would be useful, and talked to a man about hiring a day boat from his fish bait store on Santa Monica pier. The boat discussed was the red one with the flying top, and the man would call another public phone later in the day to receive his final instructions.

Camponella dressed and drove himself to the central public library to use the payphones there, and to test the efficacy of the FBI's surveillance. An hour later, he knew he had nothing to fear from the agency. He was free to concentrate on his survival whilst making himself all the more indispensable to the five families. The man from the fish bait shop collected an envelope containing used high denomination bills, clear photographs of Rizzo and Englese, and orders to kill on sight. Were it possible to make sudden death appear to be accidental, a substantial bonus would be earned. Strictly cash, the client totally unknown to him.

Camponella's sure touch improved as the day wore on. By late afternoon a team of 'university geologists' had crossed the border at El Centro to make a grid search of the soda lake area, and would report exclusively to Camponella. If bodies were found they were to be positively identified before burial in unmarked graves. And unwelcome interest shown by local or federal Mexican agencies was to be handled with speed and discretion. Physical proof of what had been carried aboard the crashed helicopter to be gathered and brought back for laboratory analysis and identification; the comprehensive report to be finally edited by Camponella before being passed on to New York and Chicago.

His appetite and good spirits revived, Camponella dined alone at an exclusive seafood restaurant in Malibu, and had himself chauffeured home by limousine. Before retiring for the night he instructed his security staff to offer Rizzo or Englese every comfort his mansion could offer should they arrive. But on no account was he to be disturbed before his usual breakfast call at 6.30 a.m.

Joe Camponella was in control once more, and the only version of the truth to be published would be his own.

Naturally.

Charlie found the cellar under the apartment block by following Saul's instructions, and walked in on Parrot and Blackwell during a smoking break. Ramirez had lost all his previous arrogance, and looked like a man who would welcome death if it brought release.

'You want the novel or the obvious stuff?' Parrot asked, not the least surprised by Charlie's sudden appearance.

'Are there any surprises?' Charlie helped himself to one of Blackwell's Kools.

'Sure. This character never even heard of Joe Camponella. He knew Casey Pollard by another name. Ramirez claims he found the *late* Mr Pollard under a fall of rock, and I believe him. He says that being in that hollow bluff was the only thing that saved him when the bowser raft blew up. You wouldn't know anything about four money packs Ramirez dug out of that pit and kept as souvenirs, would you?'

'All there is to know,' Charlie admitted.

'Ramirez only remembers getting to the *pollo* graveyard. That leaves a gap only you and Mrs

Chasen can fill,' Blackwell said.

'Really?' Charlie looked sleepy.

Sudden insight made Parrot click his fingers.

'You and La Chasen went back to the lake. You brought the money out. All of it. Sure. Fits snugger than the fat lady's briefs.'

'It's upstairs in two suitcases, and you guys get to keep it as evidence. I get a receipt for it, though.'

'And the rest of it? The other thirty-six mill?'

'Must have slipped through my fingers.'

'Chasen said you were slippier than a wax ball,' Parrot sighed.

'Where is Saul?'

'Gone to brace Camponella.'

'With what? Eagle Scout bullshit?'

'With the fact that we've got Ramirez. That we've got access to Camponella's self-protective telephone exchange. That we have proof that Camponella sent Rizzo and Englese down to Mexico to queer Pollard's play any way they could, and bring the bacon home to poppa.'

Charlie's eyes frosted. 'Did I get a mention in the foreplay leading up to the big shaft?'

'Surely did, and I quote: He gets in the way, he gets to stand in the middle of the lake in cement hush puppies.'

'Camponella likes things simple,' Blackwell said dryly. 'Dead is best. No witnesses, no trials. No transcripts, no evidence. No shit on the shyster's shiny shoes.'

'Saul should have remembered that,' Charlie said. 'You should have stopped him running off half-cocked.'

'Nobody tells Chasen nothing,' Parrot said. 'He's wanted to hand Joe Camponella the long finger for too long. Now he figures he can.'

'Then he's a dead man,' Charlie said. 'Just as dead as Rizzo or Englese if they go back to play patty-cake with the Icebox. Don't you see, all has to be silence for Camponella. His own, or your people won't matter to him now. This is plain survival, and he won't let one bullheaded federal agent stand in his way.'

'You could be wrong, you know,' Parrot shrugged.

Charlie flicked his butt at the wall. It skidded off in a shower of sparks before hissing to death in a puddle.

'Yes I can,' he snarled. 'But it's Saul's neck on the line, and I don't feel so complacent about that. Ramirez won't do either of you white hats any good at all as a hole card if Saul Chasen goes down and dirty. Now, when did he leave for LA?'

'Who, Chasen?'

'No, Baby Weems,' Charlie said.

'This morning sometime. Five or six hours ago.'

'Damn,' Charlie felt cold all over.

'But he won't get within a mile of Camponella until tomorrow,' Parrot said. 'Camponella cancelled all his appointments and went riding around the city. Even read a couple of books in the library. Spent some time on the phone, had dinner in Malibu. Saul wouldn't know where to look for him without he phoned in to check with us or central exchange. He hasn't, so he's safe.'

'Who did Camponella phone?'

'Who knows? His bookie maybe.'

'Or his private enforcers.' Charlie pushed out of the cellar with a lengthening stride.

'That guy really looks on the bright side,' Parrot said in dismissal.

Blackwell looked worried when he turned the phone to face him.

'You're not buying this faggoty vapouring?' Parrot asked.

'When we've lost every time?' Blackwell said, punching out a code. 'All the way. And then some.'

Charlie's scalp crawled as he walked to the jeep. His hands were numb and he could not get warm trying to think like Saul Chasen psyching himself up to broach Joe Camponella. The intrepid government agent bearding the Icebox single-handed. No niceties. A nose-to-nose drag-out knock-down no-prisoners brawl. If Chasen got his way, which Charlie doubted. He was an ape with dragging knuckles closing in on a master swordsman. A Model T Ford racing a state of the art Ferrari, outclassed in the ultimate game of chicken.

Trembling, Charlie reached the jeep. Climbed behind the wheel to be licked by Rosie as Hannah laughed at his surprise.

'Save your chauvinist protests, Charlie. I know Saul's being stupid. He left me a note.'

'He does not fill me with confidence,' Charlie told her, the heater full on as he drove for the Santa Ana freeway.

'With me he never did,' Hannah sighed.

CHAPTER NINETEEN

Los Angeles sulked in smog when Saul Chasen turned his Mustang into a new downtown underground car park and paid an exorbitant rate for an all-day ticket. Parking between a silver pick-up and a green tourer with out-of-town plates, he wondered if he could sell his phoney scenario to Joe Camponella after a night of hard driving and insomniac planning. He had eaten nothing but dry toast washed down with indifferent coffee, and lost that before leaving the motel. His shield was cancelled if Washington got wind of his recent unauthorized activities, and he knew that was immaterial if Camponella decided to spend thousands having somebody lodge a cheap bullet in his tiresome head. He smoked a listless Camel at the wheel in contravention of the zoning laws and whistled one of Hannah's old favourites, trying to recall the words. With the first line forming in his mind, he watched a man weave through the parked cars on his way to a restroom in one of the bays. The song died on his dry lips, and he eased his issue weapon in its holster. Checked the load and spun the chamber as procedure demanded, knowing he should make no further moves without back-up and clearance to proceed from the local Agency command officer.

Leaving the car was hard. Remembering to lock the doors was a reason for lingering there in safety. It was one of those days when zippers jammed, doors opened the wrong way, and his own keys fitted no known locks. Bread fell buttered side down, shirts lost their buttons, and all his socks grew holes. There were always muddy puddles to step in, cigarettes lit themselves at the filter end, and all the Mustang's forward gears worked in reverse. All dogs wanted to bite him, and pigeon guano splatted with unerring accuracy.

Chasen's hands shook as he listened to the restroom door open and close. He stood straight without realizing he had been crouching behind his car, and was slammed in the back by an opening car door. He banged his nose on the roof of the Mustang and tried to see his assailant through teared eyes.

'You,' he said. Sounding as foolish as he felt.

'Me,' Hannah said through a salt blur. 'You park next to me without knowing it, and you say "you" like I was a puff of yesterday's smoke.'

'I got things on my mind. I was, er, startled, is all.'

'Yeah, enough to make you whistle at both ends.'

'I need the john.'

'Who was that you were watching?'

'Nobody. Go home.' Chasen touched his nose and found a graze. 'I never should have stopped your monthly beatings,' he sighed.

'You're the one who needs his rump paddled.'

'Where's Charlie?'

'Charlie?' Hannah looked and sounded vague. 'Out there somewhere.'

'Leaving you to sniff my exhaust. Great.'

'He's doing his best to look out for you, Chasen. Facing Joe Camponella off alone is hardly sane.'

'Who asked you? Who needs him?'

'You do, Katzenjammer.'

'All I need is the john.'

'Sure, you facing the porcelain with your hands full has to be an irresistible target. Just make sure

308

nobody's in back of you when you shake the dew from the lily.'

'Come down off the chandelier, woman. Leave me to do my job.'

'Go relieve yourself, then. Get it shot off.'

'No need. You took care of that small chore years ago.'

Hannah drew back a clenched fist, ready to strike. Stood there completely disarmed by the raw anguish in Chasen's ugly loving face. His hurt was so deep it was almost a solid thing in the air between them, and she saw Charlie and herself naked together in his sad knothole eyes.

'Don't hang your scalp on my door,' she said. 'We both lost it, Saul. It wasn't just me.'

'Knowing that doesn't help either one of us, does it?'

'Not a damn,' Hannah said sadly.

Chasen almost smiled. Almost touched her pale olive face. Thrust his hands in his pockets and felt the linings give. All they had as a bond was past regret and loss, and the woman he wanted back no longer existed in the here and now. Hannah just looked like somebody he once knew better than himself, and he had been widowed when their son died with a dirty needle in his arm.

'A divorced man's gotta do what a divorced man's gotta do,' he said, making a poor joke of it. Hannah could have been close to weeping, but he couldn't be sure in the poor light. He made himself walk away from her and pushed the restroom door open with a shoulder. Self-flushers hissed, and the glaring white tiles smelled of chemical pine forests. He used a stall without checking under the other doors. Sluiced his face and hands in a basin, and was drying his hands under a blower when a Colt Cobra touched the back of his neck. Chasen found his reflection in the wall mirror, the face beside his as familiar as it was gaunt and unfriendly.

'You're calling it,' he said. Moving wet hands in hot air.

Barney Rizzo had the look of a sunburned tourist. One eye was lost in swelling, his lips were split in several places, and his cheeks were flaking and sore. He wore a billed cap over his singed hair, and his clothes had come off the peg without much regard for style. He put Chasen's nose to the tiles and patted him down. Took his issue weapon and found the holdout Airweight in its ankle holster. Holstered his Cobra and turned Chasen to stare at his own guns.

'I get to suicide from ten feet away, that it?' Chasen asked.

'Make the right noises, you could live to eat dinner tonight.'

'That earns my full attention.'

'You planning to face Camponella alone?'

Chasen hesitated before nodding.

'That makes you one of the unneeded. A brave dumbass putting the shaft to a man who don't forgive or forget.'

'And puts us in the same league of losers, eh, Rizzo?'

'He'll have you smeared, nobody the wiser, Chasen. Like me and Englese carry the can for the Mexico fiasco, and good old Joe Camponella plays Mr Clean. Except Englese's under twenty tons of Beano real estate on account he tried to go the full distance for that mother. And I'm here trying to get out from under. I laid a dime on a Fed I know, and I'm a candidate for an urn.'

Chasen's shock showed in his face, and Rizzo winced-grinned.

'Money buys loyalty. Everybody has a price, just the numbers change. Even in the FBI. What's the matter, Chasen? You don't think your guys are dirty?'

Chasen refused to digress down that bleak road. Praying that Parrot and Blackwell weren't in somebody's pocket he said, 'You'll have to prove that to me.'

Rizzo dangled his game bait with a painful leer.

'Deal with me, I'll give you that fink. Gift-wrapped in American cement. And I'll take the four mill you lifted from Ramirez as a deposit.'

Sure now that Rizzo had impeccable inside information, Chasen stalled with, 'I don't talk those kind of Vegas numbers with my back to a toilet wall.'

Rizzo showed anything but defeat. His one good eye shone with confidence.

'Hey, Chasen, we're both in the toilet here. Camponella has a contract out on me. You go up against him with nothing but your mouth you're deader than me. And that Ramirez sonbitch is nothing but a memory the minute Joe knows you monkeys have him jumping on your stick.'

'So, put all your crumbs onna bird table.'

'Camponella goes before we do. I get a new face and a raft of devoted broads who love me for my fat monthly government cheques.'

'That's a Hollywood budget. Not a federal one.'

'To burn Camponella all the way down to barbeque ashes? We serve Joe up as shark food, who's to say good old Barney Rizzo didn't run outta luck alongside Bobby Englese? Nobody looks for dead men, Chasen. It's perfect.'

'Except that the guy who sold you the dope on Ramirez knows all the moves I've made. Knows damned well you didn't die down in Baja. If you

311

bought him, Joe Camponella can buy him twice.'

Rizzo blink-frowned, his mouth twitching as he thought about that. 'My Fed's in communications. A desk jockey. He leaves messages at a dead drop. The guy's no field operative, so relax.'

Chasen disbelieved Rizzo with no outward show. The big lie was buried deep, but he meant to quarry it out.

A small fist hammered the door and a woman called, 'Front and centre, Chasen.'

Rizzo raised Chasen's guns fluidly.

'That's who?'

'My ex-wife Hannah.'

'The chick Dance fooled with down in Tijuana?'

Chasen could only nod with knives in his heart. If Rizzo had leered or made an obscene gesture, Chasen would have walked through a wall of lead to bite through his jugular vein.

'That so?' Rizzo said. Uninterested.

'Where's this going?' Chasen asked as knuckles rapped the door again.

Rizzo jerked the Airweight at the wall.

'There are garlic bullets out there for both of us. Knowing Camponella, he'll have hired Morrie the Fish from Santa Monica. He's the best, apart from me and Bobby. We nail Camponella now, the contract dies with him.'

'If Morrie knows who his client is.'

'Who hits on a wise guy except another wise guy? Morrie is anything but dumb, he'll figure it right and nail Joe as his fairy godfather. You think he won't have laid a dime on Chicago to check? And that's another thing: there was no problems before that Dance character dropped out of the sky. You smell a weird connection here?'

'No,' Chasen lied.

'You seen Dance since I put a knot in his head in Baja?'

'No.'

'I'd sure like to. Ain't nothing I can finger, but that mother has somehow turned everything around. Don't you get that feeling?'

Chasen saw Hannah with Charlie, choreographing balletic sexuality in his celibate mind. Said, 'Do we have time for this?'

Rizzo leaned in over the guns.

'Do we have a deal?'

His emotions reeling, Chasen measured personal need against professional gain, and his shield won by a shaved margin.

'I want Camponella upright and breathing.'

'For a trial none of us will live to see, you asshole?' Rizzo looked as if he needed to squeeze off shots or slap his forehead. 'Joe's gotta be dead meat before he's arraigned by judge one.'

'Doing it your way means there's no difference between us.'

'Screw your shiny shield, this is your ass. Morals are a total crock, Chasen. Now, let's shake your broad and get to the main event.'

'Easier said than done,' Chasen sighed. 'Kids leave home – ex-wives go on for ever.'

Rizzo was smooth losing Chasen's guns in his jacket.

'Your torch, your problem,' he said. 'Let's go, partner.'

'Nothing happens to her. You got that? Nothing.'

'Relax. I don't hand out freebie hits,' Rizzo drawled.

Chasen stepped out into gloom with Rizzo close behind him. Hannah recognized Rizzo, and her Spanish shirt was a bright orange target Rizzo could not miss if he felt threatened.

'About time,' she scolded, strolled closer.

Chasen half-turned to shield Hannah as he showed Rizzo where his Mustang was parked. Hannah kept walking, and she was pressed up against Chasen before he realized what was happening. He saw Rizzo lose his billed cap as his head jerked back with an O for a mouth. The sound of Hannah's knee knifing into Rizzo's crotch was a dull thud on a slack drum. Rizzo gobbled and went down on his knees. Hannah's boot took him in the side, shaking spittle from his mouth.

'Enough,' Chasen croaked, trying to lift Hannah away.

She eluded him and stamped on Rizzo's forearm, making him drop the Cobra he'd drawn. Her second kick slammed Rizzo on to his back, and she was relieving him of weaponry whilst Chasen stood there feeling about as useful as a wet dream in a convent. Hannah hauled Rizzo to his feet and laid him over the hood of the green tourer.

'You pair of fucks,' Rizzo moaned.

'You have the right to remain emasculated,' Hannah told him. 'Cuff him, Chasen, he's too cute by half.'

'Yes, dear,' Chasen sighed.

'Now you get to be a useful citizen,' Hannah said into Rizzo's ear.

Chasen's stomach fluttered when he entered the downtown offices of White, Hall & Marks. A rake of a woman in severe hornrims had him body-searched by guards with faces as flat as yesterday's beer, and escorted him down plush corridors to a panelled office as traditional as English tea served promptly at four. Joe Camponella's chair was rosewood and tooled leather. His desk was big enough to land light aircraft on, and his light-sensitive Pilkington windows turned the yellow sky to the acid green of antique bronze. The Dufy, the Fragonard and the Picasso were originals, and an accurate Portuguese map of California was dated 1574. The Chinese carpet had an identical twin in the Forbidden City, and the chair Chasen perched on had been crafted in the decade before tumbrils and aristocratic heads rolled in revolutionary France.

Camponella wore his urbane mask, and Chasen beamed across the pristine desk at him.

'Well?' Camponella said.

'You ain't bothered about my health, so I'll assume you want to know why I'm bothering a busy man like yourself. I'd kill your tape machine if I was you.'

'I think not, Agent Chasen. It is standard procedure when one is dealing with government officials whose verbatim version of any such meeting could well be at variance with the true event.'

'Take my word, Joe. This is for your ears only.'

'I remain unconvinced.'

'A smart man like you? The rising star in the Sicilian firmament? The Man Who Would Be King?'

'Have you been smoking something other than tobacco?'

Chasen rolled a small cigar in his knuckles.

'Only these stinkers, Joe. I came in to commiserate, seeing as how you lost one of your best soldiers down in Mexico. When *did* you last see Rizzo or Englese, by the bye?'

Camponella didn't shift in his chair or change expression.

'Some four days ago, I believe.'

Chasen lit his cigar and blew foul smoke.

'One of them bought the farm down there. You'll

315

miss whoever it was, won't you? You three being so close and all. Barney, Joe and Bobby, regular musketeers. I'll make you up a remembrance album from our photo-files to remind you of the good times now sadly gone the way of all things.'

'I remain quite ignorant of what you may be driving at. Is there a point to all this innuendo?'

'Sure is. Rizzo or Englese died when your cocaine transporter blew apart east of Tijuana. Doll Gardenia's gone. So has Shaggy Coltrane. Even that sadsack Jack Kurtz earned a round through the heart from a Mex cop named Ramirez. Is Sergeant Ramirez known to you, Joe?'

'Not at all, no.'

'Two negatives in a sentence is tautology. Double tut, Joe.'

Chasen's wink earned a flat stare.

'You should meet this Ramirez eyeball to squint, Joe.'

'To what possible end?'

'You ask "why?" when your ass is in the families' sling? Ramirez was there when it all went blooey, Joe. He survived the bang that crisped your merchandising to soot in five hot seconds. You got the call from Rizzo or Englese, remember? That call was real garbled, but we got the sense of it once we'd enhanced it electronically. Guess you did the same, huh?'

'I remember no such call.'

Chasen admired Camponella's composure as he splashed the rich carpet with cheap ash.

'The call that came through on your secure phone. Y'know, it's taken us months to breach that damned piece of circuitry, but we've by God done it, and now you're linked to one of the biggest drug busts in history. That makes our people glow with pride, but

316

you have to carry the can with the five families. My condolences, Joe.'

Camponella sat back with laced fingers.

'The call you allege I received,' he said. 'Let me understand you correctly, Agent Chasen. You have described some sort of criminal enterprise that went badly wrong. Not here in the continental United States, but across the border in a neighbouring sovereign territory over which your agency has no jurisdiction. Indeed, your charter expressly forbids agents of the Federal Bureau of Investigation operating outside the USA. You allege the involvement in this alleged conspiracy to import illegal substances across the international border of two men who are known associates of mine. You also imply that one of these men has died violently. You mention the demise of Mr Gardenia, which I understand may have been a tragic accident. You also spoke of a Jack Kurtz being shot to death by a Mexican law enforcement officer you identified as a Sergeant Ramirez. Am I correct so far?'

'On the button, Joe, baby.'

'Then I have to tell you, Agent Chasen, not only is this scenario a patchwork of unreliable and uncorroborated fiction that is totally reliant on innuendo rather than honest fact, it has also been baldly couched in the most crass of cartoon language. I suggest you take your tale of Old Mexico and peddle it elsewhere.'

Chasen hated Camponella with a wide and sunny smile.

'But I've got Ramirez, Joe. I've got him when it's *you* who needs him, if only to shut his damned fool mouth. And I do mean permanently. You let Ramirez talk inna wrong ears, you're chopped liver. The only reason that bothers me is, who do I deal

317

with when you're a floater in the East River?'

'You're clearly deranged, Chasen, so I'll humour you until the straitjacket arrives. What deal are you talking about?'

'Ramirez had four million dollars when he crossed the border. It had to have come from the crash site, but there ain't a scorch mark on any of the four packs. That surely means the rest of the laundered money has to be out there somewhere, huh, Joe? Like some smarty had gotten it away from the 'copter before it blew.'

Camponella pointed a steady finger.

'The bottom line. No frills.'

'I give you Ramirez to lose. We split the four million between us. We go get the rest of it and split that. Let Casey Pollard take the flak for screwing up. Let the five families figure the whole thing went blooey. You take care of Rizzo or Englese if either of them surface, and we go our separate ways.'

Camponella's laugh was dry and scathing, and his voice dripped with acid.

'Fifty-fifty? Are you sure you're being entirely fair to yourself? Why not take it all? Why share when there is no need? You allege you know where these fabulous riches are, go get them. Gather them up and carry them off to distant parts. Chasen, you moron, leave me out of your juvenile tales of buried treasure, your fantasy of wealth.'

Chasen allowed his face to sag. His mouth to part with a pop.

'You're saying "no"?'

'Resoundingly, you cretin.'

'You turn me down, you're in shit street. With me. With the five families. You really think I'll let you smell of violets without I get my end? We need each other, Joe. Together we both get out from under. We get to live the good life. Get to grow old and grey in dignity without eyes inna back of our heads.'

Camponella's calm was glacial.

'Keep your four million dollars, Chasen. It is a great deal more than you could possibly expect as a finder's fee for returning the entire capital sum to its rightful owners.'

Chasen snorted at that. Said, 'A bullet in the head ain't my idea of a finder's fee. There's no way of getting that money back to the mob without they ask questions that'll get someone dead, and you know it. This is the Twilight Zone, not the legit business world.'

'You have an insoluble problem.'

'You and me both, Joe.'

Camponella's lip twitched with distaste.

'And what am I to expect as retribution if I rashly continue to refuse your offer of an illegal partnership?' he sneered.

Chasen leaked smoke through an angry grin.

'Washington gets Ramirez and the four mill. You get Washington, and I get you. We'll swarm your operation, Joe. You won't get to make buck one for the mob. Your scowling face will be on TV from breakfast to midnight. The mob's shyster on prime time. Tut, Joe, you'll really piss them off. Remember what happened when Jimmy Hoffa of the Teamsters took Kennedy on in public? Hoffa disappeared, but I know the man who wears Hoffa's wristwatch. You know him too, Joe, and you know he's got another wrist.'

Camponella was hissing. He suffered face-slip as if shedding an outer skin, allowing Chasen a glimpse of the thing he really was. An evil. An inhuman darkness with nothing but contempt for human frailty. An abyss as empty as smoke. Feeding on life to survive, just as the dark mouths of night ate the sun of courage and left midnight nothing to despair in.

Chasen forced a laugh. Almost made it sound natural.

'Plan away, Joe. You're still a dead man walking. Put a hit out on me, why don't you? Or does somebody get to feed my heart to the carp in Japanese Gardens?'

'One should always plan for the unexpected, Chasen. The actuarial tables used by insurance companies prove that.' Camponella lifted his phone to his face, composed and urbane once more. Listened as a familiar voice spoke with ragged speed.

'I'm back across the border Joe,' Barney Rizzo said.

'Yes?'

'Cut loose and meet me at the old bonded warehouse. In two hours.'

'Why not come here?' Camponella hedged.

'When you're holding hands with the Feds? Your office security has more holes than a tuna net. Ask the Fed if he's cracked your phone codes, why don't you?'

'That has been mooted.'

'They've got that Mex mother Ramirez. He'll be spilling your beans right now.'

'You're well informed,' Camponella looked across at Chasen without seeing him. 'I don't know that I can meet that arbitrary deadline. I have an adherent of my own.'

'Shake the mother. Be there in two hours, or I talk direct to Chi. And Joe, leave your ten dollar words behind. Nobody's inna mood.'

The phone clucked like roosting hens and went dead. Camponella started to dial the bait shop in Santa Monica before his mind caught up with his

320

fingers. He laid the phone in its cradle and realized how smart and dangerous Barney Rizzo still was. The old bonded warehouse was the ideal place to meet, and the landward security fences would stop a small army.

Chasen jolted him back to full awareness with, 'Run outta threats, Joe?'

'Are you still here?'

'I'm waiting to shake on our deal.'

'No threats. No deal. Just leave my office.'

'Guess we're both dead men walking then, huh?' Camponella's sneer was chilling.

'You have my guarantee that your longevity is in jeopardy.'

Chasen backed away from the desire to slap Camponella hard. He ground his cigar to shreds on a rare Delpht tile instead. A self-closer stopped him slamming the soundproofed door, and the secretary in hornrims was there to show him into the elevator that took him down to street level. The security men let him out on to the sidewalk with no show of recognition, and ignored Chasen's comic bow of farewell.

He crossed the intersection at the old fire station and used store windows to satisfy himself he was not being followed.

Joe Camponella stared at the spot where Chasen had been seated. At the crushed cigar butt still wisping bitter smoke. At his own hands laced together on his blotting pad. Realizing he had no choice in the matter, he dialled the bait shop and gave the specialist there the location of the old bonded warehouse. It was to be hoped that he could deal with Rizzo and leave before the specialist took care of business. He mulled over his future options until it was time for him to leave, and when his limousine pulled away, two unmarked FBI vehicles fell in behind.

Charlie Dance was the first customer in the bookstore across from the offices of White, Hall & Marks, and he sweetened the girl running the place by paying $300 cash for a doorstep book on Chinese ceramics. The girl made him coffee as he browsed her window shelves for more treasures, and she was pleased to have him use her phone to alert Hannah when Chasen left the law offices. Learning about Rizzo, Charlie remembered an urgent appointment, and left the expensive book behind.

Walking rapidly in the opposite direction to Chasen, Charlie flagged the cab he had kept cruising the block for two hours, and had the driver pull in behind two limousines parked outside a trendy megastore whilst he went inside to buy a selection of garish beachwear at inflated prices. To assure his parking spot he had his purchase slip validated at the cash-out, and sat in the cab smoking one of his driver's Camels like a bored husband waiting for a shopping wife. He stubbed his long butt when the FBI vehicles nosed into traffic without indicating like regular citizens, and had his driver follow suit. There was a confusion of brakes and horns, then the simple task of following the three cars ahead to the Santa Ana freeway.

'Looks like we're headed for the bay area,' the driver said.

'Fine,' Charlie slid Hannah's magnum into the store bag between shirts and shorts. 'Don't lose them.'

'And kiss off a grand?' the cabbie laughed. 'You *must* be from outta town.'

'Like most everybody else in LA,' Charlie said with closed eyes. Dozing, he listened to the rushing sound of freeway surfaces change to the softer purl of tarmac. Some hard turns jolted his eyes open to find himself being carried along unmade dirt roads. The cab ran beside storm fencing and rows of garbage dumpers, and there were no other cars in sight.

'What happened?'

'Nothing, boss. Thought I'd detour. Keep some high ground 'tween them and us. Ain't no cover on that approach road, and I figured you want to get real close without being spotted.'

'Do it right, there's another five hundred in it for you.'

'Boss, you sure make a man salivate.'

Charlie grunted. Watched the regular highway appear to his left. Camponella's limousine had the road to itself. To Charlie's right, the waterfront came and went behind storage units and high cranes. Smog rolled off the sea as saffron smoke, and brisk waves washed through the jetties. Ships on the deep water moorings were flat frets in the yellow veil of overcast. A cormorant dried his spread wings perched on the boss of a flagmast, and the usual colony of pelicans had disappeared seaward. A Coast Guard cutter flashed morse ashore as a training exercise for local sea scouts, and a distant klaxon mourned the echoes it made.

Camponella's limousine went into the storage complex through wire gates, crossed a dry concrete moat by a swing bridge, and slowed to a halt outside a brown steel building. The FBI vehicles were nowhere to be seen, and Charlie spotted a small figure he recognized walking back along the dirt perimeter road. When Charlie had the cab halt beside her,

Hannah was hot, dirty and very angry indeed.

'That thorough bastard Chasen,' Hannah kicked a tyre. 'He and that mother Rizzo made some signal I didn't see. Next thing, I'm bundled out of the car. Me. He's trusting the wrong people again, Charlie.'

Charlie let Hannah in beside him and told the cabbie to take them back to a small marina they had passed. The bleached wooden pier was as grey as a seal, the office and the small chandlery were hard closed, and there were FOR SALE signs on the vessels beached on the narrow hard. Small boats bobbed in rows beside a tidal pontoon, and a yacht rolled its masts in the swell coming off the point.

'Perfect.'

Charlie hauled tourist junk out of his bag like flags of all nations. Told Hannah to find some things that fitted. Changed clothes himself, and paid the driver off.

'Ain't saying I ain't curious, boss. Guess I'll just have to be satisfied with the money, huh?'

'Damned if you're not wrong.' Charlie grinned, bizarre in hot clashing colours and a pea-green hat.

'What are we supposed to be doing?'

Hannah's cerise top left her midriff bare. Her veridian pants had pink patches, and she knotted a violat bandana around her throat with an angry flourish.

Charlie topped her out with another pea-green hat.

'Confusing witnesses,' he said, helping her down into a wooden tender and rowing her out to the small yacht with short, smooth strokes.

Agents Parrot and Blackwell followed Camponella's limousine without attaching any importance to the taxi trailing them. When they were sure of his destination they took a parallel route and let the surveillance helicopter from the LASD cover his progress down the main highway. In position on undeveloped land across from the storage complex when Camponella crossed the swing-bridge, they watched through powerful monoculars as he and his bodyguards entered blind-sided building. Tuning their headsets to the sound-actuated bugs inside the old bonded warehouse, they waited for a reason to call in the helicopter gunship on standby at Malibu Station.

They heard steel doors wind open and closed on electric rollers. Men strode across a paved area cracking out echoes like arthritic knuckles. A freight elevator sank to the lower jetty level with a prolonged whine, chuffed to a halt, and opened its screen door with a slam. Feet clumped on a boarded floor, another door opened and closed, and the footsteps faded into background nothing.

'What the hell?' Parrot said.

Blackwell removed his headset and looked like a mourner at his own funeral. 'They've gone straight through the building and out the other side. They're out on the jetty, I guess. And there's no way we can bug them out there.'

'Somebody should've thought that one out. Whadda we do, go round by sea?'

'You happen to have a speedboat in that sack of a suit?'

'The gunship has directional listening aids.'

'You think they won't notice that thing circling them?'

'Shit, you're calling it,' Parrot grumbled, saving his own sweet-smelling buttercups if things should go wrong.

325

'Leading from the rear again, huh?' Blackwell was convinced Parrot should change his name to Chicken. 'Saul Chasen ain't here to lean on. Just you and me, and this time we go in side by side. Nothing else works, right?'

'Call the 'copter,' Parrot said. Sweating ball-bearings.

'Together, right?' Blackwell insisted.

'What else is there?' Parrot asked the low yellow sky.

'Early retirement,' Blackwell said, calling Malibu.

The *Yahoo Queen* was flighty at the bow and dragged her stern like an overweight dowager mugged by flab and valium. Her marine diesel plodded out four knots of forward power as it thudded like a hangover. She responded to her helm with a crabbing yaw that staggered her across the bay as if the light slop and spray of wind against tide was a China Seas typhoon. Anybody watching the yacht's progress would have taken Charlie for a clod reading tacking manoeuvres from a manual over a jigger of dry martinis. Hannah and he had become Ethel and Clyde Bagdorf on vacation in sunny California from good old Charlottesville, Va.

Noon glare found holes in the dun murk and splashed the sea with pennies of shimmer as Charlie coaxed the *Yahoo Queen* into the mothballed commercial harbour awaiting redevelopment. The long concrete jetties stood on pilings crusted with barnacles, a boom lay across the mouth of the restricted Customs bay, and the main docking booth stared seaward, its blind and dusty windows looking for lost fleets. A solitary coaster with a freshly-painted superstructure was moored alongside the old bonded warehouse, its boarding ladder lowered.

Angling in on the stern, Charlie worked throttle and feed to assimilate a blocked fuel line. Gave himself enough power for a short burst of reverse screw, and brought the yacht in against the dock with hard side-rudder before killing the engine by starving it of fuel. Hannah got the stern line through a ring bolt, and Charlie went forward to secure the bow line.

No machinery cranked, no voices shouted orders or questions. No cranes dipped into holds for luxury imports. The hawsers holding the coaster in place creaked, a solitary gull screamed in passing, and water motion patterned about the pilings like slaps on soft skin.

'Guess we made it, Mrs Bagdorf,' Charlie slurred.

'No thanks to you,' Hannah shouted forward. 'And you said you knew about boats. Ha!'

'Hell and gone, Ethel. Allus putting a good man down for doing his darnedest.'

'Foul language won't make you competent, Clyde.'

'Don't thump your Bible at me, girl.'

'Will you watch your feet?'

Charlie used a boat hook to snag the stanchion beside the lower platform of the boarding ladder. Swayed clumsily and stepped into space. Kept his grip on the boat hook as he hit the water, and went under with a yelp. Came up spitting and choking, and after several attempts, hauled himself on to the ladder to stand there dripping with his silly green hat sagging over his face. Hannah's laughter was genuine if harsh, and the casul observer would have believed them to be a couple whose marriage had degenerated into mutual disregard, sharply illuminated by shafts of unkind wit.

'Clyde Bagdorf the drowning dentist,' Hannah crowed. 'King Neptune you ain't.'

'Listen to the real *Yahoo Queen*,' Charlie snarled. 'This tub must've been named for you. Or your mother's mouth.'

'Keep your bad mouth off my mother.'

'I've fixed her teeth. Gratis. Was like working in a man-eating swamp. That's a *real* bad mouth.'

'And you don't have terminal halitosis?'

'Real unfunny, Ethel. I should cut you and this tub loose right now.'

'Along with the house and half your income, Clyde honey.'

'In your lawyer's ear,' Charlie bawled. 'Keep your threats to yourself.'

'Promises, baby,' Hannah purred sweetly, seeing two uniformed men looking down at them from the dockside. 'And you're attracting attention to yourself.'

'Damned right. We need a mechanic to get us outta here. Hey! You guys gotta phone we can use?'

'This is a restricted area,' one of the guards called down.

'And I'm a wet dentist,' Charlie yelled back. 'What the hell's the matter with people these days?'

'Stand aside so I can squeeze past. I'll talk to them, Clyde.'

'You'll point your buns at them, more like.'

'That,' Hannah said, jumping lightly on to the boarding ladder, 'will not be necessary with these gentlemen.'

'Ha!' Charlie wrung water from his sopping shirt and let Hannah get several steps ahead of him. Then, his head down, he squelched after her mumbling to himself.

Hannah's cerise top had developed a lot of plump cleavage for the guards to enjoy as she climbed towards them, and the elder of the two took off dark glasses to show that his spit-grey eyes were all the way open.. The young thin-faced one glanced at Charlie a couple of times before losing interest in everything but the nimble and nubile lady bouncing all that creamy bosom at him.

'You'll send those boys blind,' Charlie growled, swaying like a careful drunk on the ladder. Stumbling to the top he leaned on the top rail to watch Hannah work the guards and to check on the immediate area.

The old bonded warehouse was brown and had a yellow trim. Had CAMCO INC C→ printed in bold white capitals on the blind side wall, and sported tall hangar doors at either end. Camponella's limousine shared the vast parking lot with a flatbed truck bearing the logo of a local security firm, and wind toyed with a CAMCO flag on a high pole over the gate for the inner chain-link fence. A generator on the stern deck of the coaster fed power to the main saloon. The drapes were drawn at the windows, but light showed through the porthole in the door. The elder guard offered to take a look at the *Yahoo Queen*'s fuel lines himself. If he proved unsuccessful, then the younger guard would drive Hannah and Charlie three miles down the coast to the nearest working marina.

'Hell,' Charlie said. 'I just need a phone. Ain't my bitching bathtub. Only took the thing out to see if she was worth buying. She ain't. Let the owner lighten his pocket book. Have somebody else oil himself up on that bitch.'

'You're the one who's oiled,' Hannah said sharply.

'Come on, guys, there has to be a phone,' Charlie said as if Hannah was a hole in the air.

'That how you want it, lady?' the elder guard asked Hannah.

'That's how Clyde wants it,' Hannah sighed, looking pitiful.

The elder guard eyed Charlie, nothing showing in his oddly ancient face. 'Then I guess there's a phone inside the warehouse. Just make it quick. Your problems ain't worth our jobs.'

'How long does it take to drop a dime,' Charlie said, stifling a monumental sneeze.

'Clyde,' Hannah warned. 'Stay civil, you hear me?'

'I'd hear you in Alaska,' Charlie said, trailing after Hannah and the guards.

There was an inset door in the gable end of the warehouse. The elder guard produced keys on a chain to let Hannah and the younger guard in ahead of him. When Charlie stepped through into interior dusk the door was closed and locked behind him. Weaving between crates and piles of folded cardboard outers, the guards took Charlie and Hannah up a floor by freight elevator, and let them into a caged area full of shrouded office equipment.

Bringing up the rear, Charlie heard Hannah's intake of breath, and swayed aside to see what had startled her. A man lay prone on the floor, his wrists and elbows tied with plastic cord. It was Saul Chasen, and the bruise on his jaw was as blue as a jay. Hannah went down on her knees to feel for a pulse in his neck, and Charlie's chest grew a spot of red light. He stood straight and still, shedding drunkenness as he stared at the silenced revolvers fitted with lazer sights bearing on him. The young guard turned his gun on Hannah to give her a glowing red earring.

'She's first,' he said. Matter of fact.

The elder guard helped himself to the Magnum in Charlie's waistband. 'You make a pretty poor dentist, Mr Dance,' he said.

'He's alive,' Hannah said, turning her face so that the red light was a bright Hindu marriage spot between her eyes. 'Did you have to hit him so damned hard?'

'Not our work, Mrs Chasen. Barney Rizzo decided he didn't want a witness when he settled his differences with Camponella,' the young guard told her as if he read totals from a register.

Charlie studied the elder guard and knew he was seeing a clever face mask of theatrical latex. The other man had transformed himself in a similar way.

'And did he?' Charlie asked.

'He would have if we hadn't intervened, Mr Dance. Let us say that both men will make redress for their mistakes in the only way our clients will find satisfactory. There is no leeway for crudity here.'

'Four minutes,' the younger guard said.

'They're both aboard the coaster?' Charlie knew he was right without a nod of confirmation. He visualized Rizzo and Camponella tied to chairs with taped mouths watching the seconds tick away.

'And you all get to join them if you don't co-operate fully.'

'Call it,' Charlie said. Tasting ashes and bile.

'Eighty million dollars of missing revenue, Mr Dance. I surely cannot make myself clearer, can I? It has to be returned, then you are free to leave the country within twenty-four hours.'

Charlie came to terms with his situation. Professionals as good as he ever was had him cold, and his options were all swept away save one. 'And them?' he asked.

'Mr and Mrs Chasen's lives are in your hands, Mr Dance.'

'That gets it said,' Charlie wanted a cigarette to taint his sour mouth. 'I made certain Chicago and

New York knew about the deal I struck with Camponella, you can check that out very easily.'

'We have that intelligence,' said the elder guard. 'And?'

'The FBI has four million and Sergeant Ramirez. I have six million more, the balance that was owed me. The other seventy million is buried at a *pollo* graveyard in Deadman's Gulch. The exact coordinates and a map are in the manager's safe at the Hot Melon Motel. You people need to go down there to collect Rizzo's and Englese's luggage, right?'

'Consider it done, Mr Dance. Can we rely on your permanent retirement from field work after this?'

'So long as I get to tie up a couple of things in London.'

Charlie steeled himself for a bullet that didn't come, making his own countdown as the younger guard checked his watch.

'That will serve the purposes of our clients very well,' the elder guard said. 'It's a pleasure dealing with an intelligent man, Mr Dance. You will take the Chasen's out to the flatbed truck in the parking lot. Drive south to the Waterside tourist area. Once there, have the truck valet parked outside the Mermaid Inn and leave immediately. Then you are on your own.'

'Suits me.' Charlie got Chasen over his shoulder and followed Hannah outside. The keys were in the truck's ignition, and with Saul settled between them, Charlie and Hannah left through magically opened gates to cross the swing bridge.

'Who were they?' Hannah asked, her teeth chattering.

'Specialists from Santa Monica.'

'They were so . . . cold. So detached.'

'And we owe our lives to that,' Charlie said.

He turned south at the main gate and stopped to check the underside of the vehicle for plastique and a timer. Found nothing, and followed a dirt track to the highway turn where he glanced in the rearview mirror. The bonded warehouse looked dull and solid, and the coaster lay calmly at anchor. Then the mirror shivered in its housing. The superstructure of the coaster threw window glass out and lost itself in an uproar of smoke and flame. Blast hurled dust clouds across the parking lot. Outlined the warehouse in a wild wall of heat, and lifted the flatbed truck on a punch of expanding air.

Charlie fought the steering and braked to let his ears hear again. To focus through a manageable blur induced by shock. Checked on Saul and Hannah, and saw the FBI helicopter bank in from seaward to be buffeted by rising violence. Saw it climb vertically as alarms rang all over the complex. Fires burned around Camponella's overturned limousine, and debris chunked down in the parking lot, bouncing and burning. The topmast of the *Yahoo Queen* had disappeared, and columns of seawater rose and fell as wet scatters on the quayside.

Hannah wept and stroked Saul's hair as if he were her lost child. Charlie found himself driving south past capped wells with a Camel burning between his clenched teeth. Found himself wanting the hottest and sudsiest of baths. The tallest and coldest of drinks. The driest of gins, the tartest of limes. A huge bed to sprawl on. A colour TV tuned to brainless fare that laughed at itself. The honest oblivion enough alcohol would bring.

Lucky Charlie Dance was alive. The five families had removed a couple of local cancers, and it would be business as usual by the weekend. Hannah and

333

Saul had survived, and it was time for celebration, wasn't it?

Wasn't it?

Not just yet, Charlie. Drive.

CHAPTER TWENTY

Charlie accepted a complimentary Irish from a stewardess with a Mayfair accent as the British Airways 747 turned for the pole, flying away from the sun into Arctic night. The first class section was full of Arabs and minor personalities jetting to London for some gala occasion, and a spoiled prince of the desert sulked when he was barred from smoking a foot-long cigar. Fighting bugeyed sleeplessness, Charlie dozed behind a magazine and let Hannah return to him in cool nakedness to make her final farewells. The stewardess plumped pillows and got blankets whilst Charlie and Hannah shared champagne and motel darkness without regrets or forward thinking. There were giggles as spilled bubbles fizzed on Charlie's chest, some tears after the first happy tumble, then a mouth-to-mouth struggle that came out as a damp and flaccid draw neither of them had wanted to win.

In the morning Hannah was gone, and her note had several false starts crossed out. What was left meant she planned to take care of Chasen's concussion until he was released from hospital. Then she would see where the winds would take her. Crumpling the note, Charlie found himself yawning until his jaw creaked. Two solid drinks put him out until he awoke for the landing at Heathrow.

There was rain all the way into the city, and the Savoy was awash with people impressed by their own lavishness. After a bath and a nap Charlie shopped in Burlington Arcade and Savile Row, in Bond Street and Piccadilly. A barber shaved him close at Simpsons, and he had afternoon tea at the Ritz. The efficient Savoy valet service had his clothes laid out and ready to wear within an hour, and he strolled up into Soho through a drizzling dusk.

Benny Shoesmith fogged up his Poland Street office with Woodbine smoke, and his pregnant secretary wore a fat smile and an engagement ring. Benny and Marigold were getting married at Caxton Hall and planned to honeymoon in foreign parts. Charlie offered dry congratulations, let them drone on about their future together, then got Benny out of there for the short walk to Brewer Street.

'You don't approve, do you, Chas?'

'Of the future Mrs Shoesmith?'

'There was nobody else for her to turn to.'

'Then you're her white knight. Old, but sexy.'

'Hey, I shouldn't have an heir? A wife? I should die alone?'

'We all do that, Benny. Just a matter of when.'

'You *don't* like her.'

Charlie stopped in Foubert's Place. Cupped Benny's crumple of a face in lamplight. Said, 'She'll squander your millions and spoil her kid at your expense. If you're lucky, she'll learn to play snap with you. She'll have headaches and ladies' problems every month as regular as a copper's tread. She'll nag you rotten to stop smoking in the house. Make you sleep in the spare room when you snore, and Benny, you'll love it, old son.'

Benny smiled his porcelain smile.

'Thanks, Chas.'

'Now you're happy, let's get to business.'

'I take your money, so let me advise you, right? We should let George Muscat stew for another six weeks. At least. The man is financially overextended, but you need him gaffed and hooked before you try reeling him in.'

'No need, Benny.'

'Hey, advising you is how I earn a crust. It had to be said.'

'You said it. Forget it.'

'You won't get him selling himself short. He's got some kind of hefty American backing, y'know. You'll find yourself talking partnerships with that pimp. *And* maybe doubling your money just to stay in the game. You can't ask me to stand by and watch you take a beating, Chas. Give it more time.'

'None left.'

'But, Chas . . .'

'But nothing. Can you get hurt whatever I do?'

'On my commissions? No in spades.'

'Then think of profits. You do have all the papers we need in that converted sofa you call a briefcase?'

'Yes, Chas.'

'Then let's get out of this weather.'

The skies opened as they crossed Golden Square and ran for the glittering canopy of The Minx Ranch. Hostesses. Sex Acts. Shows every hour. Members Only. Charlie ignored the doorman when he was asked for entrance fees, went down a flight of stairs into stuttering neon and amplified music, and ordered watered drinks from a butch waitress who went off to find the owner for him. Coloured spots spun over the stage where a fleshy girl shed skimpy undies. She was about as erotic as a kitchen table, and her female bride worked a fruit machine as if she pumped iron. Some Lebanese business men paid champagne money for carbonated fizz and fed it to hostesses they would never get into bed. A group of Croydon motor traders drank lager on empty

337

stomachs, and Brick Donovan chewed a stub of pencil over a crossword puzzle at the end of the bar. It took him a while to notice Benny had Charlie with him, then he eeled off his stool and went through a batwing door. When he came back with the waitress he said Mr Muscat could spare a few minutes if Charlie and Benny were quick about it, and led them down a dark passage lit by pinlight bulbs.

George Muscat's office was a nightmare of black glass walls flecked with gold, wall lamps with green glass shades, and imitation Chinese furniture in red lacquer. The framed prints were nasty Hong Kong copies of traditional Pillow Book originals, the bar looked like a cockeyed Shinto shrine with bottles and optics, and Muscat himself was a heavy old man buttoned into what should have been a good suit. There was too much belly behind his waistcoat, his swollen neck hung over his collar, and his lips were scummed with the residue of the antacid tablets he chewed between meals. There were pinch marks on the bridge of his nose where the glasses he wore in private usually sat, and he had the look of a man who had eaten too much too quickly. He waved Charlie and Benny into ladderback chairs, told Donovan to fix drinks and make himself scarce, then said:

'Only a matter of time before everybody comes to Uncle George. You it took a little longer than most, Charlie.'

'You can't rush destiny, George, and you got fat without me.'

Muscat touched tender fingers to his waistcoat.

'Slow metabolism. My temper's faster than my pulse rate, and you didn't come here to fight me. That would be expensive.'

Charlie allowed himself to smile. Said, 'Just

338

proves it all comes down to two things in the end: money and lumps. Let's you and I talk money first.'

Muscat banged his desk with a soft fist.

'Still hardnosing like you own Soho, eh, Dance? You don't. I do. The old days are long gone, and you're yesterday's man. You've had that old fart Shoesmith there making himself busy on my turf, and there wasn't a move he made I didn't know about before he'd finished coughing over his first Woodbine of the day. You came up with a nice little scheme, but it's a non-starter without me. I've got you right here in the palms of both hands.'

'You'll have to prove that,' Charlie said. He let his hand shake slightly when he took one of Benny's cigarettes. Drew smoke deep into his lungs and let it out with a sigh.

'With pleasure,' Muscat crowed. 'All those years of you looking down your long nose at me gets paid for. Right now. I control eighty per cent of the properties and freeholds you need to get Phase One of your project off the ground. How do you think that will go down in the City when you crawl back to them for their backing? A concrete balloon ain't in it. Without me you're a joke.'

'Name your price,' Charlie said.

'There ain't enough money in the world.'

'Eighty million says you're wrong.'

Benny looked sideways at Charlie, a nicotined finger probing an itch under his glossy toupee. Started to say something, then shut his mouth with a porcelain snap.

Muscat clapped his hands, his laugh a wheeze of delight.

'I've got eighty clicks already. You wanna see the cable? And just to nail your coffin closed, an American associate of mine will be here any moment to close the deal. Your scheme and your hide belong to me now, and there ain't a damn you can do about it.'

'Don't count your capital until it's banked, Muscat.'

'Don't you get it? It's over. All that's left is just how generous I'm gonna be buying up the few options you managed to get your hands on. With luck, you might have enough to buy yourself a ticket out of here. Maybe a lemonade at the airport.'

Charlie flicked ash somewhere. Sipped fine Irish whiskey and looked through a veil of smoke at the ceiling.

'A wise old man once taught me a valuable lesson, George. When you've got a man in a corner, always leave him somewhere to run. You don't, he'll maybe get desperate enough to come back at you. A man who's lost everything has nothing else to lose. That makes him dangerous.'

'Charlie, Charlie,' Benny Shoesmith mourned.

'Yes, Charlie,' Muscat said. 'You I'll pay what you laid out, just to be rid of you. You sign all your options over to me here and now. You declare that you assign me as the new negotiator with the two banking and investment houses you've been dealing with in the City. You get out of London, and you stay out. You want somewhere to run? Stick a pin in the atlas.'

'No other way of handling this, huh?' Charlie asked.

'You want to grovel? Go ahead,' Muscat said.

Charlie shook his head.

'I think you've had enough pleasure for one evening. Too much could give you a coronary. Tell the man how much it's gonna cost him, Benny. Straight figures.'

'Three million six,' Benny said as if his lungs had turned solid. 'Add another thirty thou for my unpaid commissions.' He opened his briefcase and began passing Charlie papers for his signature. A bump and grind number filtered through the walls to counterpoint the scratch of Charlie's Parker, Muscat wrote out a cheque on a Linen Bank with a desk pen, and Benny's stomach turned acid as he watched ice melt in his untouched gin and tonic. Brick Donovan put his head around the door to say the Yank had arrived, and Charlie said he'd like to finish the business before he was admitted.

'No problem,' Muscat said with a show of false generosity. 'A pleasure shared is a pleasure halved.' He scanned the papers Benny passed him without hurry, and when he was satisfied he handed the cheque to Benny with a flourish and, 'Don't spend it all in one place. OK, Brick, show the man in.'

'Turning the screw, George?' Charlie said, standing slowly.

'Wouldn't you?' Muscat asked, sitting back like a flaccid Buddah content with his lot. 'Didn't you for years and years?'

Charlie hooked his thumbs into his pockets and rocked on his heels, disgust in his face. 'A rich pimp is still a pimp, George. And that's what you'll always be. All the money in the world won't change that.'

Muscat rode that with a hating smile. Leaned forward to point a plump finger.

'You're still bought and paid for, Charlie Dance. Ain't nothing can change *that*.'

Donovan showed a man in and went away. Charlie watched the American cross the office to shake Muscat's hand, his bulk hiding the Maltese until he turned around to look for a free chair to sit in. When he saw Charlie his smile was warm and weary.

'Hullo, Kid,' he said. 'That's a hell of a flight on no sleep.'

'You two know each other?' Muscat couldn't believe it.

Larry Moffat's chuckle was as deep as a Kafka novel.

'Slightly. Jesus, Muscat, this is the guy you're screwing over this property deal?'

'Screwed,' Muscat corrected. 'He's out of it now.'

'Just as well,' Moffat grunted. 'For him, that is.'

Muscat looked bewildered. Held his gut and looked from face to face for enlightenment.

Moffat helped himself to a bourbon at the bar and took it down as a solid shot. Sat in the chair Charlie had warmed for him and gave Muscat his full attention. 'Guess you didn't wait for confirmation before proceeding here, Mr Muscat,' he said. 'As of yesterday, your consortium is liquidated. Your association with our people is terminated. Casey Pollard's body was exhumed from a dirt grave in Mexico, and with Doll Gardenia dead, you're out on your own. You can't expect dollar one from New York or Chicago for this real estate scam.'

Muscat was trying to rise from his chair, his face an unhealthy yellow. 'You tell that to Joseph Camponella, you overgrown messenger boy. He showed solid interest, and he knows this is no scam. This is legitimate business. The kind of thing the five families need.'

'They think not, Muscat,' Moffat said. 'And your insulting language isn't helping here. You think you can convince Joe Camponella, fine. Buy yourself a Ouija board.'

'This isn't happening,' Muscat sank back into his chair. 'I've got everything and more sunk into this scheme.'

Moffat stood next to Charlie, his face grim.

'Then you'd better make it work. On your own. You going my way, Charlie?'

'Why not?' Charlie said.

Muscat opened and closed desk drawers as though he looked for answers. Scattered papers and lifted the phone as if it were the ultimate weapon. Waved it at Larry Moffat and raved through strings of spittle.

'Your people can't do this to me, Moffat. Not to George Muscat. I'm family, you nothing. Family. They can't deny blood and marriage ties without they pay for it. I go, they go with me. All of them.'

Moffat moved quickly for his size. He slapped Muscat hard. Lifted him from his chair and slammed him back. Loomed over the frightened Maltese to stare deep into the wet, darting eyes.

'If I pass that message on, you're buried, Muscat,' he said with quiet force. 'And don't expect anything from your people in Sicily. They blew everything they touched. And you get sole credit for that, Georgie boy. Now, when they figure that out for themselves, who d'you figure they'll come looking for? Just you think about that long and hard. Then find some place in this shrinking world that isn't all bugs and jungle where you can hide. It's over, you dolt.'

Muscat gained a decade as he sagged in his chair. Moffat left him there and opened the door for Benny and Charlie. Brick Donovan fell in, his dull brain trying to understand what was happening.

'Whadda I do, Mr Dance?' he asked.

Benny Shoesmith poked a nicotine finger into his face.

'Get yourself a pregnancy test,' he said. 'You and your boss just got fucked.'

Out on the street the rain had lessened to a fine

343

mist that pearled on the hurrying umbrellas. Garish bulbs and tubes bled colour across the wet paving in wavering streaks, and all the passing cabs had their flags down. Standing in the foyer of The Minx Ranch, Charlie felt nothing for the man he had just helped to destroy. Had no sense of victory or elation. Just the weary knowledge that it was finally over. Larry Moffat's arrival should have been a calculation rather than a total surprise. Charlie knew that operating off the cuff in San Diego had been far too easy, even with Saul Chasen's help, and now it was clear that his act of charity in rough seas all those years ago had now been repaid in spades with interest.

The rain bounced up off the street in a wild and wet dance. Moffat yawned out at the downpour and gave in to exhaustion now that a bothersome debt had been discharged to the full. A bear of a man in heavy winter clothes who could not wait to get back to dry heat and linen suits. Benny Shoemaker grinned as he smoked, a very old man with a very young wife who saw a future where none had existed before.

'Charles Shoemaker,' he said. 'Good name for a son.'

'You what?' Charlie came out of his brown study to hear that and the single shot from below. It came through the ceiling duct as a metal cork blown from a steel bottle, as a muffled slap from the carpeted stairwell.

'More champers for the desert rats,' the door-keeper smiled.

A taxi turned in from Regent Street. Charlie flagged it down and ushered Benny and Moffat inside, told the driver to head for Euston Station and accepted a Woodbine to hold.

344

'Bloody weather's enough to make a man shoot himself,' the cockney driver said.

'Oh blimey yeah,' Charlie grunted, his mood as dark as the rainswept night.

Hot African winds swept Luqa Airport when Charlie crossed the tarmac to the Arrivals Hall where two constables escorted him to a small interview room. Inspector Ellul and Advocate Charlotte Bujega were already there, and had been exchanging conflicting views. When he had been cautioned Charlie sat on a hard chair and took off his coat and tie.

'The bad penny returns,' Ellul said. 'You surprise me, Mr Dance. I had not expected to see you back in Malta.'

'You need make no reply,' Charlotte counselled.

Charlie smiled at her and slowly shook his head. She had grown more beautiful in his absence, and he ached to touch her. 'Yes I do, my lovely advocate,' he said. 'I owe our friend the Inspector an apology and a full explanation.'

Ellul looked wary. 'Oh?'

Charlie asked for a cigarette and was given one by a constable. Ellul lit it for him, and Charlie took smoke down as he unbuttoned his waistcoat. Blew smoke up at the ceiling fan and watched the blades chop it into curling strands. Said, 'The Cunninghams returned to the island yesterday, and you will have read their sworn affidavits, I think. They were abducted and held to ransom by extortionists who used them to pressure me into parting with a substantial amount of money. This meant I had to leave Malta any way I could in order to negotiate with these people.'

'I fail to see why,' Ellul said.

'Do you, my clever friend? My funds are in another

country, a fact you will have checked out. To have attempted to deal at long distance with those monkeys would have caused delays that might have put the Cunninghams at even greater risk. Human life is more important than money, and your surveillance made it impossible for me to handle things my way, Inspector.'

'And was enough excuse for you to flout the law.'

'They're alive, aren't they? That's reason enough for me. If you wish to bring charges, I'm here to answer them.'

'What purpose would that serve?' Ellul sighed. 'I'd be cast as the officious policeman hounding a man who broke the law to save his friends. Charles Dance. Humanitarian. My God!'

'When was the law ever confused with justice, Inspector?' Charlie asked, his tone bitter. 'The Cunninghams are alive, but nobody could save my Margot, could they? You can't even give me the comfort of knowing her last resting place, can you? Let's face it, Ellul, we've both lost something. And I know my loss is the greater.'

Ellul closed his eyes and sighed his tension away. Sat still for several ticks of the wall clock, then, his eyes still closed said, 'Take your client away, Advocate. He is no longer relevant to my enquiries.'

'I can expect that confirmed in writing?' Charlotte said.

'Yes, yes. Anything for the quiet life,' Ellul said.

Charlotte bundled Charlie out into the concourse to get his passport stamped and collect his valise. 'Where to?' she asked behind the wheel of her Mercedes. 'Home?'

'I'll never go back there,' Charlie said. 'I want you to sell the place for me. Give the money to any charity. I don't want a penny of it.'

346

'Where then?'

'Paradise Bay.'

'But there's only a tourist hotel up there.'

'And the sea, pretty one. I need to swim. To get clean again. Inside and out.'

Charlotte checked the tumble of questions she knew she must ask. Took the road that wound out past the medieval city of Mdina and the ugly modern hotel squatting in its shadow. Turned through terraced fields and raw hills to the coast. There was a great stillness to the day, and prickly pears stood sentinel behind sandstone walls on either side of the tarred track as it rose to the bald headland above the bay. Charlotte parked beside the old watchtower that had watched for Suleiman the Magnificent's invasion fleet, and wandered away to look out over the sea whilst Charlie stripped and climbed into his swimming shorts. Ghargur Rock seemed closer than usual, and Charlotte visualized sharks cruising there in an endless search for food. The Mediterranean was rippled glass she felt she could stir into a maelstrom with a forefinger, and a light breeze brushed her long skirt against her calves.

Charlie squeezed her hand as he passed, padding on naked feet to the sheer cliff edge. There were fresh bruises on his hard lateral muscles, and she caught a glimpse of a healing cut in the hair above his left temple before he fell into a clean dive. Something snatched at her heart as he disappeared. It was as if he had dived off the edge of the world, leaving Charlotte and all the hurt behind.

She walked quickly to the end of the spur and saw the widening ring he had left on the surface wash itself to nothing. There was just her and the empty sea moving against itself, and she was never more alone than at that moment. She sat on a rock and kicked off her shoes. Broke off a dead stalk of grass to chew, tasting summer in its brittle dryness. Half-closing her eyes, she merged sea and sky into a huge and seamless oneness. Felt swamped by its uncaring infinity, and knew there had been other women during the time Charlie had been away from her. Wondered if he was washing them away in order to come back to her ritually cleansed of the immediate past. Or had he returned to Malta merely to tidy her away like any other loose end?

Charlotte opened her eyes in panic to sear her eyes with sunlight. She dropped the blade of dried grass and it fell away to the rocks far below her. There was no sign of Charlie in the great blue sprawl of water, and she thought of him drowned like his lost Margot. She realized she had no idea how long she had been sitting there. Five minutes? Ten? How long did it take a man to drown anyway? Fear came as a cold knife as she cast about, looking for a bobbing head or scissoring legs. Nothing.

Then Charlie was there shaking water out of his eyes and down into her upturned face. She laughed, tasting brine on her lips, and hugged his wet legs. Drew him down beside her to laugh into his face. To run fingers through his matted hair and laugh some more.

'And all this for a man who hasn't so much as kissed me,' she said, touching the new scar on Charlie's pectoral. 'Do you think you're man enough to handle such a task, Mr Dance?'

'Only if you'll become Mrs Dance.'

'Kisses first,' Charlotte said, pulling him to her.

THE END

THE SMOKE
by Tom Barling

When a Maltese assassin buries Archie Ogle, London's 'Godfather,' under a collapsed building, thirty years of peace are swept away as the old gangland loyalties end in a bitter struggle for supremacy.

Now everybody wants a piece of the action. Eyetie Antoni dreams of a Mafia empire in the West End. The Troys from Bethnal Green want Archie's Mayfair casinos while the Harolds want to destroy the Troys' control of the East End. The Tonnas from Toronto want Archie's international money laundry, the Triads see London as the drugs capital of Europe, and a shadowy City financier plans to forge his own organisation from the shambles.

Only one man – Charlie Dance, professional villain and Archie's top gun – stands in the way of all of them. Divided by greed and the brutal lust for power, they are united in one common aim – KILL CHARLIE DANCE!

THE SMOKE sweeps from climax to climax: across the battle-scarred map of London, through the drug networks of Asia to a final explosive confrontation in the diamond fields of South Africa where Charlie Dance makes a last desperate stand.

0 552 12504 0

SMOKE DRAGON
by Tom Barling

Charlie Dance has big trouble. Micky Raven down in Fulham has ideas way above his station and one of those ideas is to move in on Charlie's Soho patch. To slap Micky down wouldn't be too difficult but Charlie is already caught up in a vicious Triad war for the control of London's drug trade.

The Dragon Brotherhood is determined to wipe out the Snakes and Charlie is standing right in their way. The blades are out and Charlie and his are going to get hurt. Unless they strike and strike hard at the Triads and at Micky Raven. And Charlie has the muscle and the brains to do just that.

From the tense alleys of Soho to the dangerous streets of Hong Kong, *Smoke Dragon* explodes with raw energy and brutal power all the way to the final devastating confrontation.

0 552 13253 5

CROW'S PARLIAMENT
by Jack Curtis

Simon Guerney plies a lonely trade. He specializes in the rescue of kidnap victims; his unrecognized skills the last resort of the rich and desperate.

At first the disappearance of David Paschini seems a straight-forward abduction case and Guerney joins the boy's mother in New York to play out the usual waiting game. Once there he begins to sense inconsistencies in the pattern of events — but is is not until the unknown kidnappers demand that he travel to London that Guerney realizes the game has turned and that suddenly he is the prey not the hunter . . .

Strikingly original in its combination of power politics, the growing menace of kidnapping and the disturbing but very real world of ESP, *Crows' Parliament* will take its place amongst such classics of the genre as *Rogue Male* and *The Third Man*.

0 552 13081 8

A SELECTED LIST OF FINE TITLES
AVAILABLE FROM CORGI BOOKS

THE PRICES SHOWN BELOW WERE CORRECT AT THE TIME OF GOING TO
PRESS. HOWEVER TRANSWORLD PUBLISHERS RESERVE THE RIGHT TO
SHOW NEW RETAIL PRICES ON COVERS WHICH MAY DIFFER FROM THOSE
PREVIOUSLY ADVERTISED IN THE TEXT OR ELSEWHERE.

☐	12504 0	**THE SMOKE**	*Tom Barling*	£3.99
☐	13253 5	**SMOKE DRAGON**	*Tom Barling*	£3.99
☐	13081 8	**CROW'S PARLIAMENT**	*Jack Cutris*	£2.95
☐	13082 6	**GLORY**	*Jack Curtis*	£3.99
☐	12550 4	**LIE DOWN WITH LIONS**	*Ken Follett*	£3.99
☐	12610 1	**ON WINGS OF EAGLES**	*Ken Follett*	£4.50
☐	12180 0	**THE MAN FROM ST. PETERSBURG**	*Ken Follett*	£3.99
☐	11810 9	**THE KEY TO REBECCA**	*Ken Follett*	£3.50
☐	09121 9	**THE DAY OF THE JACKAL**	*Frederick Forsyth*	£3.99
☐	11500 2	**THE DEVIL'S ALTERNATIVE**	*Frederick Forsyth*	£4.99
☐	10050 1	**THE DOGS OF WAR**	*Frederick Forsyth*	£3.99
☐	12569 5	**THE FOURTH PROTOCOL**	*Frederick Forsyth*	£4.99
☐	13475 9	**THE NEGOTIATOR**	*Frederick Forsyth*	£4.99
☐	12140 1	**NO COMEBACKS**	*Frederick Forsyth*	£3.99
☐	09436 6	**THE ODESSA FILE**	*Frederick Forsyth*	£3.99
☐	10244 X	**THE SHEPHERD**	*Frederick Forsyth*	£2.99
☐	12541 5	**DAI-SHO**	*Marc Olden*	£2.99
☐	12662 4	**GAIJIN**	*Marc Olden*	£2.99
☐	12357 9	**GIRI**	*Marc Olden*	£3.99
☐	12800 7	**ONI**	*Marc Olden*	£3.50
☐	13214 4	**TE**	*Marc Olden*	£3.99
☐	13385 X	**MUSASHI: BOOK ONE: THE WAY OF THE SAMURAI**	*Eiji Yoshikawa*	£2.99
☐	13386 8	**MUSASHI: BOOK TWO: THE ART OF WAR**	*Eiji Yoshikawa*	£3.50
☐	13387 6	**MUSASHI: BOOK THREE: THE WAY OF THE SWORD**	*Eiji Yoshikawa*	£3.99
☐	13388 4	**MUSASHI: BOOK FOUR: THE BUSHDY CODE**	*Eiji Yoshikawa*	£3.99
☐	13389 2	**MUSASHI: BOOK FIVE: THE WAY OF LIFE AND DEATH**	*Eiji Yoshikawa*	£3.99

All Corgi/Bantam Books are available at your bookshop or newsagent, or can be ordered
from the following address:
Corgi/Bantam Books,
Cash Sales Department,
P.O. Box 11, Falmouth, Cornwall TR10 9EN

Please send a cheque or postal order (no currency) and allow 80p for postage and packing
for the first book plus 20p for each additional book ordered up to a maximum charge of
£2.00 in UK.

B.F.P.O. customers please allow 80p for the first book and 20p for each additional book.

Overseas customers, including Eire, please allow £1.50 for postage and packing for the
first book, £1.00 for the second book, and 30p for each subsequent title ordered.

NAME (Block Letters) ....

ADDRESS ....